MAGI APPRENTICE

DAN HENDRICKSON

ISBN : 979-8-9854425-5-7 (paperback)
         979-8-9854425-7-1 (hardcover)

Interior design by Booknook.biz

Dedication

This one goes out to my longtime friend Vern Edwards.

Vern, you have supported my writing from the beginning,

and I especially appreciate your love and prayers for this one.

Content

Foreword

One of the great joys of producing a piece of historical fiction based on an account out of the Bible is the time and effort one must spend in studying that section of scripture, biblical studies that others have done on it, and related recorded history of that period. My interest in the "Wise Men" of Matthew 2 had uniquely piqued when I first read Dr. Victor Paul Wierwille's book, ***Jesus Christ Our Promised Seed***, back in 1984. Although the astronomical constellations and configurations section of the book took me a while to ascertain, I eventually started to see the truth that God had His plan for man's redemption recorded in the stars and illustrated through the names and meanings of the stars that are apparent to the naked eye, and that He has revealed to His people from antiquity.

Reading that groundbreaking piece of biblical research inspired me to look deeper into the whole phenomenon of Jesus Christ being the "Promised Seed of The Woman" as recorded in Genesis 3:15. Most biblical scholars agree that this is the first biblical prophecy recorded announcing the coming of the Messiah. What Wierwille and others have documented is that this first prophecy profoundly ties into astronomical declarations of the coming of a champion, savior, king, and messiah. Scholars like Ernest L. Martin; *The Birth of Christ Recalculated*, and The Star That *Astonished the World*; E.W. Bullinger, *The Witness of the Stars;* and Joseph A. Seiss, *The Gospel in the Stars;* give compelling and convincing evidence that the true interpretation of the zodiac is that it declares the coming of a great one who would save the world and redeem mankind from his fallen state. All the aforementioned scholars agree that the zodiac has a definite beginning and end to its story and that in Genesis 3:15 the Creator promised "the seed of the women" would destroy the evil one. By this we see that the beginning of the story is the woman who will receive the seed from the Creator and then raise that offspring. The constellation that clearly represents this is Virgo. Then at the end when His work is done this seed would reign as king forever, which is clearly the constellation Leo. In my story this truth is a vital part of the narrative that shows the scholars of that day's point of division with part holding to the ancient scriptural base interpretation of the meaning of the zodiac and the others who held the mystical interpretation perpetuated by the influence of Greek and Western culture after the conquest of Persia by Alexander the Great.

Over the centuries there has been much speculation as to the date of Jesus's birth. The most popular today is the 7 BC theory that attests to a series of conjunctions that appeared in the constellation of Pices. Though compelling, they do not line up with what is known about the timing of the death of Herod the Great, which the gospel of Matthew shows to have happened a few months after the Wise Men (Magi) visited the child Jesus in Bethlehem. Also, Josephus's book *Antiquity of the Jews* cites a lunar eclipse around the time of Herod's death. The only eclipse that would have worked to fit in with all the biblical records happened in April of 1 BC. A more workable series of six conjunctions that occurred in the constellation of Leo can be found in the time between August of 3 BC and June of 2 BC. Both Wierwille and Martin agree that this is the period that Jesus was born. Other astronomical realities of that time cause both men to concur that Jesus's real birthdate happened September 11 3 BC. When looking at what is recorded in Matthew there is nothing that has the Wise Men with the Shepherds together the night of Jesus's birth. The word used for child in Matthew is a Greek word used for toddlers (between one and two years old) and not infants. This makes a lot more sense when considering that these Magi from the east would have to see the configuration in the stars, note their importance, and then worked out a way that they could journey from their homeland to Jerusalem then on to Bethlehem. This, too, is a vital part of my story.

It was back in the middle part of the 1990s that I became very interested in Herod the Great and his sons and grandsons. It fascinated me that such a vicious man existed and wielded so much influence in that part of the Roman Empire. Herod had many enemies, not the least of which was the Parthian Empire and Phraates IV, whom he threw out of Judea at the beginning of his reign. In fact, it was that victory over the second biggest empire in the world that won him the favor of Rome and subsequently made him ruler of a client kingdom.

So, the questions that kept bugging me were that if Rome and Parthia were at loggerheads, so to speak, over the country of Judea, how could an entourage of Parthian and Eastern Magi show up to Jerusalem and get his help in finding where the Messiah was born? How did they even gain safe passage into Herod's domain, and why did he help them? These questions intrigued me, and I started to look deeper into the history and culture of Judea, Galilee, Parthia, Rome, and Medea of that time.

As in any political climate, alliances, treaties, trade, and prejudices were constantly developing and changing. Within a fifty-year period before the birth of Jesus Christ, Rome went from a republic ruled by a senate to a dictatorship ruled by an emperor. During that time, you had the slave rebellion of Spartacus that was put down by Pompey and Marcus Crassus. Julius Caesar also played a part in that war; albeit smaller than the other two. The result was that those three formed the First Triumvirate of Rome where they split the rulership three ways.

Pompey had earlier gained notoriety for annexing Judea and Galilee, defeating and routing the pirates of Cilicia, and putting down rebellion in Pontus (Northern Turkey). Marcus Crassus, the wealthiest of the three whom history reveals did most of the work of putting down Spartacus's slave rebellion, felt he needed to shore up his reputation and took an army to Alexandria of Egypt (a Roman-controlled port), where he marched them eastward and endeavored to take land from the Parthian Empire at Carrhae. Crassus met his doom at the hands of a brilliant Parthian general by the name of Surena, who lured him into a trap where he employed his archers, light calvary, and cataphracts (heavily armored calvary) to annihilate the Roman army that was four times their size (79,000 to 20,000).

In my story, I capitalize on this extraordinary event and use Surena's legacy to boost the main character in the narrative. Yet it was the lesser and least known of this triumvirate, Julius Caesar, who came out on top and was installed as Rome's first dictator for life in 44 BC but one month later he was assassinated. It was his nephew Augustus who became Rome's first true emperor and probably the most successful. What is noteworthy about Augustus to my story was that when he was born in 63 BC, the astronomers of his time observed a star configuration that the astrologers in Rome had determined showed the coming of a new Roman king. So, incensed by this, the senate approved a slaughter of young boys in the area who were the children of Roman aristocracy that could lay claim to the long-deposed monarchy of Rome.

Because of the similarity between this and Matthew 2, it has been speculated that Herod the Great knew about this and capitalized on it when he ordered the death of all the males two years old and under. What we rarely consider when thinking about that atrocity is that Herod would have had to give an account to Roman authorities for such an act. His reporting that an entourage of respected Eastern Magi had informed him that constellation conjunctions occurred that marked the birth of one destined to rule the entire world would have been one of the few things he could have reported to them that could have gained their approval for his actions. Another thing to consider is that Herod the Great was falling out of favor with Augustus because of how much he incensed his own people in Judea for previous atrocities that he had committed.

There are so many other historical details and occurrences in the fifty years before the birth of Christ. The rise and fall of Cleopatra and Mark Antony, both of whom strongly opposed Herod and his claim to Judea. The expanded growth and influence of the Kingdom of Medea, which was situated due west of Judea. Medea comprised several Arabic tribes that banded together and formed a trading coalition that helped them expand into a sovereign state that both Rome and Parthia respected and had economic-dealings with. They actually served as an economic and diplomatic liaison between the two empires. The tribes that made up Medea could trace a lot of their ancestry back to the biblical patriarchs. Abraham's son, Ishmael, and Isaac's son, Esau, were the founders of two of these tribes that later became Medea. Herod the Great was the son of a Median princess.

Before the Parthian Empire formed, Alexander the Great from Greece had invaded Persia and brought about the Hellenistic era of influence to Asia. Much of the culture in that part of the world was changed forever, not the least of which was the influence of Greek mythology and astrology. This influx of western thinking into the Asian world had a profound effect on culture and religion and would later cause great conflict in the Parthian Empire.

Amid all this turmoil was a group of men who could trace their philosophical roots back to the Babylonian Empire of Nebuchadnezzar and his order of Wise Men or Magi. By far the most famous of those men in history was the Judean, Daniel, who was brought there to be a slave in the emperor's court. After he distinguished himself as someone who Nebuchadnezzar could trust above all other Magi, he was promoted to Master of the Magi. Having that kind of influence and authority, it is reasonable to conclude that Daniel would have instructed their ranks in the biblical principles of life and religion, which would include the biblical perspective behind the meaning of the astronomical constellations and planets.

Somehow in the six hundred years between Daniel and the birth of Jesus Christ, some of these men held true to Daniel's teachings and were able to determine that a series of noteworthy astronomical configurations and conjunctions that occurred between August of 3 BC and June of 2 BC heralded the birth of the long-awaited Messiah who was to be born of a Judean maid of the line of King David, and who was destined to rule the world. My rendition of Historical Fiction is an attempt to show how these remarkable scientists and astronomers could have been able to take this knowledge and act on it in a way where they could go see for themselves this great purpose of the ages, the birth of the long-awaited Messiah, the champion of the Creator, who would redeem humankind and be the savior of the world—Jesus of Nazareth.

Acknowledgements

There are so many that have helped me put this work together. Foremost, I am thankful for God almighty and His inspiration. Second, to my wife Cheryl for her tireless dedication in assisting me in any way she could. Tom Mullins and Teresa Jackson for their help in editing, and Carla Phillips for her beautiful artwork. Tom Hyman, who is my literary mentor and editor, for all his efforts. Hitch and the crew at BookNook.biz for putting the final pieces together for printing and publishing. This was a great team effort.

1

False Start

March 6, 6 BC.

Two gray-haired men in the sunset years of their lives stand in the middle of a large room that has deep blue tapestries as tall and wide as houses hanging from the ceiling three stories in height. In the center of the ceiling there is a domed window twenty feet wide and ten feet high, which allows the sunlight to ignite the sparkling silver-and-gold specks intricately woven into the tapestries depicting the twelve heavenly signs of the zodiac. It is the ornate halls of the Astronomical Sect of the Magi Temple of Babylon, once the mighty capital of the empire by that same name and now a major city of the Parthian Empire. Two masters of that sect continue their debate on a bold action one of them has decided to undertake.

One, more than a decade junior to the other, has his hands out, waving in an appeasing manner as he begs the elder to heed him. "Headmaster Farnah, please, you cannot just leave like this. The emperor has not granted us safe passage. You will not have his protection on your journey!"

The elder steps forward and puts an affectionate hand on his most trusted colleague and answers with a fatherly tone. "That is why you will not be accompanying me this time, Master Daraya-Vous.

Though I am sure the signs' meanings are clear, Cetus is wily, and until the seed of the woman fulfills his mission, this world is dominated by that serpent's evil. I will not risk the life of the only other man in our order who understands the signs of the zodiac as well as I. If I am wrong and he tricks me in some subtle way, responsibility then falls to you to continue the watch and look for the coming of the promised one."

Master Daraya-Vous sighs. His shoulders drop and he stares into his mentor's soft, brown eyes. Like his own, the eyes of Master Vinda-Farnah, headmaster of the Magi Astronomical Sect, do not easily adjust to the daylight shining through the projection dome. Both men have spent most of their adult lives taking their waking hours during the night, where they have devoted themselves to the study of the tapestry of the stars in the sky, in pursuit of understanding their meaning and their Creator's message to man. He shakes his head. "It's just that I do not interpret their meaning the way you do, Master. Jupiter is the king's planet, and surely that is the promised one to come.[1] But why would the Creator announce his birth by putting it in conjunction with Saturn, which represents the evil one?"[2]

Vinda smiles. "We have been over this many times, Daraya. They are in conjunction inside Pisces, which is the sign of the pouring out of the Creator's blessings on all mankind because His seed has vanquished the enemy and fulfilled his mission. This happened three times in a six-month period. The Creator is declaring His champion's victory at his very beginning. That is all."[3]

"Yes, Headmaster, I see the reasoning. But we are talking about the birth of a child. The promised seed of the woman. Would any father want to bring up all the conflict his son will go through, including horrific torture and death, while announcing such a joyous occasion? Would you announce your own child's birth by associating it with his archenemy and all that he will do to him?"

Master Vinda-Farnah pauses a moment to reflect on his most accomplished student's words. He smiles warmly. "Oh Daraya, you attribute too much human sentimentality to the Creator of the universe. I, too, was cautious and thought as you do now. But several days ago, we both saw it! The massing of Jupiter, Mars, and Saturn in Pisces. It is too much to ignore."[4] He sighs, shakes his head solemnly, and puts his hand on Daraya's shoulder again. "I cannot be swayed from this path, my dear friend. I am an old man, older than even you. Very few ever reach my years in this world. If I don't seize this opportunity, I feel I will have missed my life's very purpose. I leave tomorrow at first light. When I get to Jerusalem, I will inquire from their scholars where their sacred scriptures say the promised one will be born, and I will go see for myself the Creator's promised champion. When I find him, I will send for you."

Master Daraya objects, but Vinda stays him with a raised hand, turns and walks toward the exit, but stops and looks up to the dome. "Master Daraya-Vous, please have the first-year Magi apprentices clean the dome today. There are smudges obscuring the sun's rays on the tapestry's depiction of the zodiac. It will cause them to misread the signs and hinder them when they graduate to the night watch."

Daraya looks to his mentor. "It will be done, Headmaster Vinda-Farnah."

March 18, 6 BC, Tusbun, Capital City of the Parthian Empire

Two young men practice their sword skills, one on the other, in the palace courtyard of His Royal Highness, Emperor Phraates IV, ruler of the second largest empire in the world. One is dressed simply as a senior cadet in the royal officers' corps, but the other wears the distinguished princely apparel and a jeweled kufiya, marking him as the heir apparent to the Parthian throne. The prince, though a skilled swordsman, knows that the cadet, a very gifted fighter, is doing his best not to overwhelm him.

Prince Phraates V arcs his thrust in and down after having just blocked an overhead strike from his friend. The thrust almost makes a touch as the cadet blocks it at the ricasso and rain-guard just above the hand. "You are going too easy on me again, Rassan!" says the prince as he jolts back, barely missing a counter thrust after the block.

Rassan steps back and holds his sword up to his face and bows in the traditional manner. "Not so, My Prince! You almost had me on that one. It would have been a tie for this match."

Prince Phraates manages a frustrated smirk, takes his sword and imitates the cadet's gesture and sheaths it. He places an arm around his shoulder and ruffles his hair. "Always the modest one, eh Rassan?" He shakes his head, and they walk to the entrance of the palace. "If I had ten thousand like you, I could push the Romans right back into the sea. Then my father's empire would exceed that of Alexander the Great's."

"But then you would have to rule that vast empire someday, My Prince. Remember how hard it was for Alexander's generals to control all these lands after his death? Haven't you told me before that there is a point where more is too much, and too much can ruin even the wisest ruler?"

"I should take heed of what I say around you, Rassan. You never forget a word, do you?"

Before Rassan can answer, a tall, slender man wearing the robes of a Master Magi of the Magician Sect steps out from behind a pillar just inside the entrance. Rassan notices him first and immediately stops, steps back one pace, and bows his head in recognition of the emperor's chief advisor. His features have always reminded Rassan of a dark raven, like one would see in the deep deserts of Arabia. He has a pointed chin and nose accentuated by hawkish, dark eyes and thick eyebrows that contrast with his graying facial hair.

He first looks to Rassan. "His Eminence Phraates IV has ordered your company to intercept a rogue Magi astronomer attempting to enter the Roman Empire without his permission. You are to leave at once."

Rassan nods stiffly and turns to leave, but the prince holds up his hand. "Hold, Rassan." Then he turns to the Magi Magician. "Master Dvandas, I know you counsel my father and have certain authorities granted by him in his court. But I was not aware that those extended to interrupting my time with my personal sparring partner, who is also eighty-seventh in line for royal succession! Need I remind you that next to my father I have supreme authority in our empire and when in my presence you must ask me before issuing orders to any-one?!"

Master Dvandas cringes at the rebuke, but with a pristine courtly manner gained by years of climbing up the political staircase of the Parthian Empire, he smiles and bows his head. "Forgive my forth-rightness, My Prince. I mean no disrespect. It is just that this is a sensitive and urgent matter that must be attended to with all haste."

"Sensitive and urgent? Nonsense! The Astronomical Sect of the Magi frequently sends representatives to the Roman Empire to gather learning from other parts of the world to aid in their studies. What makes this so special?"

Master Dvandas holds up a hand in an appealing gesture. "My Prince, it is not the *what* but the *who* that is going and the *where* that makes this a sensitive matter. The *who* is Master Vinda-Farnah, head-master of the Magi astronomers, and the *where* in the Roman Empire is Jerusalem. He quests to find this promised seed of the Creator that they all prat about, whom he believes has just been born. I do not have to emphasize to Your Highness that a man of his stature in your father's empire should not be running amok around our greatest potential enemy. Especially by stirring up men like King Herod of Israel about the birth of a new king destined to rule the world!"

Prince Phraates breathes in deeply. "Rassan, do as Master Dvan-das has instructed. I will find out from my father what the meaning of all this is."

Rassan bows his head to the prince and then to the Magi Master and leaves.

As Rassan leaves, Prince Phraates turns toward the entrance to his father's court and makes his way toward the door when Master Dvandas steps up beside him. "A moment, My Prince?"

Phraates stops, clearly annoyed. "If you are going to warn me like you have before about entering my father's court unbidden, I will remind you once again that since he married my mother, a Roman slave who is now your queen, he has done away with that ridiculous tradition that holds a threat of executing even those of his own family who enter unbidden." He holds the magician's gaze with his own, not intimidated by the man's hawkish eyes, and continues. "Plus, there is the fact that Phraates IV, ruler of the Parthian Empire, has recently named me heir apparent to his throne, which makes it my court as well!"

Dvandas reels from this second rebuff from the prince. He now wonders if the prince knows that only a month prior, he strongly recommended to the emperor that he name his eldest son from his previous wife to be his heir. The thought tempts him to panic, but he quickly gathers his wits. "My Prince, I would never presume to counsel you twice on a matter that you and your father have already made crystal clear. My desire is only to inquire about your sparring partner of late, the cadet who just left to join his company upon your father's orders."

The prince stares back at the Master Magi. "And just what is your interest in Rassan?" He leans into the man's face. "Take care, for he is not only a distant cousin to the royal court, but I also count him as a friend and confidant. Someday he may well command in my army and may even hold a higher place of counsel in court than you do now."

Master Dvandas holds his hands up in an appeasing gesture. "Please, My Prince, I have no guile in my heart toward your ambitions for Rassan. On the contrary, I merely wanted to let Your Majesty know that I have heard many good things about him from his instructors at the officers' academy. They say he has an aptitude for study in religion and history. I thought he might benefit from an apprenticeship with us for a time. Having a well-rounded experience in all stratums of our society can only aid him in his future services to you."

Exasperated, Prince Phraates shakes his head. "What would you teach him, Dvandas? How to turn a staff into a snake, or mesmerize a weak-minded fool with a mystical gaze? Your sect of the Magi Order has always concerned me. Artapan, grand master of the Magi Order and follower of the prophet Zoroaster, barely tolerates your sect's practices of mysticism. And then only because my grandfather, and sometimes my father, have been intrigued by the apparent power you seem to wield. I much prefer Grand Master Artapan's staunch commitment to the moral and ethical conducts taught by Zoroaster, and the commitment to the scientific study of the Creator's message to all men in the tapestry of the stars adhered to by Master Vinda-Farnah and his students."

Master Dvandas does all he can to hold back the volcano of rage he feels pressing against his chest and his desire to rebuke this pup of a prince in a way he so richly deserves. "Again, My Prince, I mean no disrespect. I hope to only ensure that your father's heir has qualified counselors surrounding him when he rules."

"Or rather, that the counselors of my court are those you and your sect can control, eh, Master Dvandas?" Prince Phraates turns and heads toward his father's court. He grabs the latch to open the door and says over his shoulder, "You are not needed in court right now, Master Dvandas. Please see to your other responsibilities while I confer with my father about Master Vinda-Farnah's quest."

Dvandas bows his head. "By your leave, My Prince."

Master Dvandas watches the door close and considers that to enter the court could mean his own life would be in danger. He has obtained favor from Phraates IV, but to go against the heir apparent and the son of Queen Musa could bring dire consequences. He turns in the direction of his offices. He muses that the prince can forbid him from approaching Rassan about apprenticing with his sect all he wants, but his rashness has now cost the boy his life.

Entering the Magician Magi Sect offices in the royal palace, he sees his chief administrator, a short, bald-headed man with pale green eyes and even paler skin, coming toward him. The man steps up to him with a devious gleam in his eyes and an almost imperceptible smile cracking the corners of his tight-lipped mouth. He leans in close as his eyes dart from side to side, assuring himself that no one is within eye or earshot of them. "Headmaster Dvandas, I have confirmation that those we sent to intercept Headmaster Vinda-Farnah will overtake his caravan before the emperor's garrison can reach them. Our man will ensure that Vinda-Farnah will not survive, and I have instructed him to bring the sacred star charts directly to you."

After his humiliation with Prince Phraates, the news from his assistant is quite welcome. He takes Mihri's hand and shakes the man's shoulder. "This is welcome news, Mihri. The company from the royal garrison is being dispatched as we speak. When they find Master Farnah's party on the highway, bandits will be the blame for his untimely demise. He will not be alive to plead his case before the emperor as we feared. Between the ones we sent and our man in the garrison company, we will surely see all our goals achieved before this day's end."

"No chance of our recruiting the prince's sparring partner to our ranks, then?"

"None. I am afraid that Rassan will meet his end by the same hand that will take Master Farnah's," Master Dvandas says with a wicked sneer.

Forty Miles West of the Capital City

Master Vinda-Farnah, headmaster of the Astronomical Sect of the Magi Order of the Parthian Empire, lies amid his now-destroyed caravan. He reaches for his abdomen, where the masked man had just impaled him. The assailants came out of nowhere and descended on his caravan before they could even attempt to flee. His two body-guards fought valiantly to protect him and the others but were over-whelmed. But now Master Vinda-Farnah looks off to the road and can only feel sorrow as the realization that his quest has ended hits him. The words of the man who still holds the blade that impaled him burn like acid in his mind as the man pulls the sword free.

"You will never find what you are looking for, Magi."

Before the masked man can stab him a second time, a loud whis-tle pierces the air. A man standing lookout at the edge of the hill yells, "Royal Cavalry coming! We must leave now!"

The man looks down at Farnah, then sheaths his sword and reaches down to search for something. The lookout runs up to him and grabs his elbow. "All the gold in the Parthian Empire will not suffice me or my men if we die. Leave the man or we'll all be slaugh-tered."

The masked man yanks his arm away, runs to his horse, mounts, and leaves with his companions.

A tear runs down Master Vinda-Farnah's cheek as he considers the man's words. He reaches over to a crate lying on the ground next to him and grabs a long canister and clutches it to his breast. The pain in his body does not come close to the pain he feels in his heart as he considers the words that the man had spoken.

"He is wrong, you know. You have been called to sit at the same table that Abraham, Isaac, and Jacob will sit at. It is there where you will be welcomed by the one you have sought your whole life. In that day, all you seek will be revealed."

The words are spoken by a voice so pure and gentle it has the clarity of a mountain spring in the early morning. Master Vinda-Far-nah lifts his eyes and a man in the brightest white apparel he has ever seen stands before him, with the radiance of the noon sun in his eyes.

"Who are you?" Master Farnah asks, astonished.

"I am a messenger of the Almighty God, the Creator of the universe. He who wrote His plan in the stars of heaven, which you have so faithfully studied and declared. I am here to tell you, Vinda-Farnah, master of the Astronomical Sect of the Magi Order, that your sojourn in this world comes to its end, but fear not. The champion you seek will call you from the sleep that is now embracing you, and you will join him in his kingdom, for which there will be no end."[5]

Master Vinda-Farnah can find no words to respond. He simply clings to his canister of star charts that is never far from his touch, as another tear slides down his face.

The heavenly messenger kneels and touches the canister. He says:

"Take courage, faithful Magi, though the time has not yet come for God's destined champion to grace this world. The Almighty sends to you another who will carry on your quest; one who will faithfully watch for that blessed day as you have. His name is Rassan. Share with him the blessing of the Almighty that has been given to you and instruct him to bring these star charts back to Master Daraya-Vous. Tell him that they must look to the Lion of the Tribe of Judah. The answers you all have sought will be revealed to them there."

Vinda-Farnah looks up. "Your words will be obeyed," and the man then disappears before his eyes. He opens the canister and pulls out one chart and stares at it in wonder. Though he can feel that his life is slowly slipping from his ancient body, joy now fills his heart as he utters the word "Leo!"

On the Road, a Few Miles East

A company of twenty-five cavalry soldiers, led by their commander and his assistant officer-in-training, Rassan, makes their way west on the main road that eventually leads to the border crossing into the Roman Empire. Rassan lightly taps his heels into his mount's ribs and reins the beast toward his commander. He eases alongside the man and scans the road ahead. At first, all he sees is a hazy blur caused by the noon sun burning off the sands, rocks, and roads ahead. Then a thin cloud of white and gray smoke eases over the next hill in the road.

"Commander Dareh, something burns just over that hill!" Rassan says as he cups his hand over his brow and stands in his stirrups to increase his line of sight.

Commander Dareh stares in the same direction for a moment, then sits back in his saddle and shakes his head. "I swear, boy, you have the eyes of an eagle. Call the men to arms and lead the way. Make haste! We cannot afford any mistakes!"

Rassan canters his horse forward with sword drawn. All the men follow, keeping their heads down in case they are met with an enemy using a spear or bow. As they ease over the hill, they come upon two large, overturned wagons, one set on fire by a burning arrow. As they approach the scene they see two soldiers lying on the ground, their faces in the dirt and their mounts fallen beside them.

An icy chill goes up Rassan's spine as he ascertains the slaughter that took place here. He makes his way through the debris and comes upon an old man wearing the robes of a Magi Master. He is partially propped up against what is left of a huge storage chest that must have fallen off one of the wagons. Commander Dareh is checking the rest of the caravan for evidence or signs of life when he hears Rassan yell. "Commander, I've got a Magi Master over here!"

"Find out if it is Master Vinda-Farnah! I'll be there in a moment," Commander Dareh yells back. He then pulls another man in Magi robes from a burning carriage overturned on the side of the road.

Rassan dismounts and walks over to the man and kneels to see if he can find anything that might identify him. He searches his garments and tries to pull a large, tubular canister from his grasp. The effort causes the man to open his eyes. Startled, Rassan jumps to his feet and steps back.

Still clinging to the canister, the man whispers, "I am Master Vinda-Farnah of the Astronomical Sect of the Magi Order. Are you Rassan?"

"Yes, I am Rassan, of the emperor's garrison. How do you know my name?"

Master Farnah holds up an unsteady hand to motion the young man closer. "Please, Rassan, sit with me. My time in this world is almost at an end, and I have much to tell you and little time to do it. But first, tell me this—do you believe in the one all-powerful Creator of all things, and that He will someday send His promised champion to free all mankind from the evil that dominates this world?"

Stunned by the question but feeling sorrow for the old man, Rassan sits down and answers. "I come from a military family. My education in the ways of religion has been sporadic. My father served in Emperor Phraates III's calvary, and then commanded in Phraates IV's. Tomorrow, I will graduate from the royal officer's academy. But to answer your question, yes, I do. What my father taught me showed me to respect the prophet Zoroaster's teachings and that of Belteshazzar, the great Judean prophet who served three emperors. The one God, Creator of all things, is the only God I regard, and His promised savior is my heart's desire."

Master Farnah exhales with relief. "He said you would carry on in my stead. He even told me your name."

Rassan looks back and forth over the area, then back at Farnah. "Who are you talking about, Master Farnah? Who told you my name?"

With a shallow chuckle and brief smile in his old and dying eyes, he looks up and says, "He was the messenger of the Almighty God in heaven, a holy angel sent to comfort and guide a dying old Magi in his final moments." With all the strength he has left, he holds out the canister and places it in Rassan's hand, then closes his eyes and prays. "May the grace of the Almighty strengthen you and may His spirit guide you into His light and promise." He then opens his eyes and says, "You must get this to Master Daraya-Vous at the Magi Astronomical Temple in Babylon. Tell him that your quest will be realized in the constellation of Leo. It is there you both must look for the announcement of the coming of the promised seed of the woman, the champion who will save all mankind and vanquish the evil one once and for all."

Rassan clasps the canister in his right hand and leans in close. "Why do you say *we*, Master? I am not a Magi and I know almost nothing of the meanings of the stars in the sky."

Master Farnah leans back and closes his eyes, and with his last breath he says, "Of course not. First you must become a Magi Apprentice."

Master Farnah slumps to the ground and Rassan folds his arms across his chest. For a moment, he stares at his lifeless form, then at the canister he now holds in his hands. He notices the lid is not screwed on and he removes it. As he does, a single chart protrudes from the many rolled up inside. Seeing that it must have just been replaced, he reaches in and pulls it out and looks at the label: *Constellation Leo.* Rassan looks at the chart. As he scans it, his eyes catch an inscription close to the star Regulus, noted as the brightest in that constellation. Then he sees it—a notation written in ancient Northern Aramaic: "The Lion of the Tribe of Judah depicts the Messiah as the King of Kings. He will inherit the throne of his father, David, and his kingdom will never end. Noted by Belteshazzar, Master of the Magi."

"Belteshazzar! The Judean prophet my father told me about." He remembers his father telling him of the great Babylonian King Nebuchadnezzar promoting this prophet to master of all the wise men and magicians in his empire, which included the entire Magi order. It was the stories of that man being taken from his homeland as a slave and rising to be the most powerful man in the empire under the emperor himself that convinced Rassan that he would honor no other God but the one Belteshazzar called *Jehovah*. He later learned that Zoroaster called that same God, *Ahura*[6]. Both taught that He is the one and only creator of the universe.

"Rassan, is that Headmaster Vinda-Farnah?"

Rassan looks up and sees Commander Dareh standing over him with a quizzical look on his face. "Yes, Commander, this *was* Headmaster Vinda-Farnah, headmaster of the Astronomical Sect of the Magi Order. He died a few moments ago."

Commander Dareh kneels and places his hand on the dead Magi's throat. After a few moments of finding no pulse, he looks up. "Did he say anything about who attacked him or why?"

Rassan stands and straightens his uniform. "No, Commander. His only concern was for these star charts." He holds out the canister containing the charts. "He asked that I see that they be returned to Master Daraya-Vous at the Magi Astronomical Temple in Babylon as soon as possible."

Commander Dareh stands up and reaches for the charts. "Give them to me. This is Magi business. I will hand them over to Master Dvandas when we get back. He is the highest-ranking Magi in the palace. He will know what to do with them. It's nothing we need to concern ourselves with."

Military habit instinctively has Rassan handing them to his commander, but before the man can grasp the canister, Rassan pulls it back and embraces it to his chest. An overwhelming sense of protective concern erupts from his core and he looks the man in the eye with a steely gaze. "Master Vinda-Farnah's last words to me were that I place this canister into the hands of the now headmaster of the Astronomical Sect of the Magi Order, Master Daraya-Vous. I invoke my right as a member of the first hundred in legal succession to the Emperor Phraates IV to request of him alone permission to do so."

Commander Dareh stares at Rassan, astonished at the brashness of the boy and enraged at the out-and-out usurping of his authority. He grinds his teeth and walks to his horse and mounts it. He looks down at Rassan. "I have served the emperor for my whole life. A good deal of that time was under your father before he died. Never once did I see or hear of him invoking the right you just did. You have embarrassed me before my own men, Rassan. This insult will be remembered, and someday returned in kind, boy!" He then digs his heels into his mount and canters back toward the royal palace.

Rassan stands there, bewildered by his own actions, but even more bewildered because he knows that what he did was right. He just does not know why. With Commander Dareh gone, Rassan feels obligated to see that the cleanup and salvage of Master Farnah's caravan is taken care of. He scans the scene and sees that the men have put out the fires that threatened to consume the wagons. He looks to an older man who is the highest nonofficer rank and says, "Jaban, get the bodies in the wagons and use four of our cavalry horses to draw them back to the capital. I will take two men with me and follow Commander Dareh back to the palace. When you get there, report directly to garrison command. I will be at the palace to make my petition to the emperor."

The man nods and issues the orders, then walks up to Rassan's mount, leans in, and in a hushed tone says, "Commander Dareh was a coward to send you out front when we first arrived. I never liked the man. He is no soldier. He served your father all right—as a messenger, secretary, and scribe. It is known among the men that he seeks the favor of Master Dvandas. Be wary of him, Rassan. You showed steel today. Your father would be proud."

With that, the man orders two soldiers to accompany Rassan and then returns to the men and organizes the cleanup and retrieval of the dead.

2

A New Path

Royal Court of Phraates IV

Phraates V stands next to his father's throne and listens to Commander Dareh's report on the mission to intercept Master Farnah's caravan.

"And so, Your Eminence, by the time we arrived, Master Farnah had been mortally wounded and his entire caravan wiped out. We searched everything and could find no clues regarding who it was that attacked them. I tried to procure the ancient Magi star charts to give them to Master Dvandas, but Cadet Rassan invoked his right to petition you to take them back to Babylon, claiming that it was Master Farnah's last wish."

Before his father can respond, Phraates V steps from his father's side and moves so close to the commander that his nose is but inches from his face. "Your men arrived a few moments before you entered court, Commander. Your sergeant sent me his report. You ordered Rassan to lead your men into the ambush site while you trailed behind. Care to elaborate on that decision, Commander?"

Dareh nervously looks to the emperor and sees the look of confusion on his lord's face, then he looks back at the prince, swallows, and replies. "The boy is to commission tomorrow into His Highness's royal garrison. I thought the experience of leading seasoned warriors would bolster that occasion for him."

The prince disdainfully waves his hand at the man, walks back to his father's side and puts his hand on the backrest of the emperor's throne, and stares at the commander. "You also stormed off, leaving your company after Rassan invoked his right of petition concerning the star charts. You knew that outside of your presence a cadet had no authority to command. It was fortuitous that he had Sergeant Jaban take over in your absence and then followed you back. Why did you find it so necessary to get back to the palace so quickly, Commander?"

Beads of cold sweat now cover the commander's face and neck as he looks to the emperor and the prince for a trifle of compassion. "Forgive my impetuousness, but I only sought to bring news of the day's events to His Eminence as quickly as possible. I was told that the matter of Master Vinda-Farnah's unsanctioned journey was a delicate issue and of great concern to you both. I only wished to satisfy your need of pertinent news."

Thinking that if he just presses a little more, he can expose Commander Dareh's hypocrisies and curb any wrath that may fall on Rassan, the prince steps forward to continue. But a hand reaches up and clasps his arm. Emperor Phraates IV looks to his son and then to Commander Dareh. "Phraates, that is enough. Commander Dareh did not act outside his bounds, and neither did Rassan. Dareh here served under Rassan's father for many years. I cannot imagine that he could hold any ill will toward the boy, although the boy has inherited his father's proclivity for theatrics." The emperor chuckles and then shakes his head. "To invoke such privilege is rare indeed. He must be quite determined to satisfy Master Vinda-Farnah's dying wish." The emperor smiles at Dareh. "Commander, you are dismissed."

Commander Dareh bows his head and quickly exits the throne room. The emperor looks at his son. "Now, let us see how Rassan handles his first visit to court. You did coach him properly?"

"As best as time would allow, Father," Prince Phraates replies.

"Good. Now let Rassan in. I've been looking forward to this."

Rassan stands nervously outside the throne room as the doors open and Commander Dareh quickly exits. The man is in such a hurry that Rassan swears he did not even notice him standing there. He steps back as one guard grabs the door that Dareh just exited through and holds it open as the voice of the emperor booms through.

"Cadet Rassan, you may enter our presence!"

Rassan's eyes scour the hall, and he sees the emperor and his son at the other end of the room on a raised platform. He rehearses what the prince told him about entering the court and then steps forward, comes to attention, bows his head, and extends his right hand in the formal court greeting. "Your Eminence, may I step forward to make my petition?"

Emperor Phraates IV holds the young cadet in the formal bow for a few seconds longer than normal. Then he lowers his scepter. "You may step forward and make your petition, Rassan. We, the ruler of the Parthian Empire, recognize our cousin and son of one of our most beloved generals."

Rassan steps up to the throne, kneels on one knee, and touches the scepter with his right hand. "Your Eminence, light of the world and protector of the realm, I come to you on behalf of Headmaster Vinda-Farnah of the Magi Astronomical Sect."

The emperor's smile drains from his face. "It grieves us greatly that Master Farnah attempted a pilgrimage to Jerusalem without our leave or protection. But nothing justifies his murder at the hand of bandits on the road not forty miles from the palace. As impetuous as his attempted journey may have been, it was not deserving of his death. What is your petition, Rassan?"

Rassan reaches inside his cloak and retrieves the canister of star charts that Master Farnah gave him and holds it out.

"What is this, Rassan?"

"They are the sacred star charts of the Magi Order. Master Farnah had them with him on the road. It was his dying wish that I bring them back to Babylon and hand them to Master Daraya-Vous, the next headmaster of the Astronomical Sect of the Magi Order."

Emperor Phraates IV reaches out and takes the canister and rolls it around in his hands a few times, then opens it and pulls out some charts. "Yes, I remember these. My father would talk about them from time to time. He said some of them date back to the time of Nebuchadnezzar himself; and that the Hebrew Prophet Daniel, who served in his court, worked on these with the Magi of that time. A veritable treasure indeed."

He hands them to his son and then looks at Rassan. "When I was a boy, my father Phraates III entrusted these to the grand master of the Magi Order at that time. That was a royal decree written in the law of the Medes and Persians and cannot be overturned. These must be sent back immediately to Master Daraya-Vous, who then must seek counsel from Grand Master Artapan on whom he wishes to steward them. I see no need for you to take on this task, Rassan. I will dispatch this with my royal mail delivery under my personal seal. No one will dare interfere with it then."

At first, Rassan is relieved to be free of the burden. But then the same overwhelming desire to protect them wells up and he asks, "If it pleases Your Eminence, the prince has been pressing me of late to choose what path I will take after my graduation. I have decided to seek out Master Daraya-Vous in the Magi Astronomical Temple of Babylon and apprentice with that order for a time. If this request is granted, may I also have the honor of carrying the charts there and putting them into Master Daraya-Vous's hands?"

The emperor leans back against his throne and places his hand to his chin, then shakes his head and starts to say, "No…"

But his son steps up to him with the star charts still in his hand and a devious gleam in his eye as he remembers his conversation with Master Dvandas that morning. "Father, this is interesting because Master Dvandas approached me earlier and shared some insight about

Rassan that might help you make your decision about this matter. The headmaster of our Magician's Order of the Magi feels that Rassan has shown incredible aptitude in the study of religion and history while attending the royal military academy. He requested of me that Rassan be granted a time to apprentice with the Magi to further develop these long suits. It was his learned opinion that time with the Magi would only increase Rassan's value as a future leader and counselor in my court."

The emperor raises an eyebrow. "Master Dvandas said this, did he?"

"Just this morning, after Rassan left with Commander Dareh to seek Master Farnah's caravan."

The emperor looks back at Rassan and laughs. "Well, Rassan, I don't think you fully appreciate what you're trying to get yourself into. But the Astronomical Sect of the Magi Order is the most demanding of its apprentices. Intellectually, you will be challenged beyond anything our military academy has put you through." He holds out the star charts to Rassan, who receives them gratefully. "Tomorrow you will be a full officer in the emperor's garrison and, as your first assignment, I charge you with delivering those sacred charts to Master Daraya-Vous in Babylon with all haste. We also grant you leave to apprentice under his authority until he deems it fit to release you back to our service."

Phraates IV looks to the side and motions to one of his ministers to give Rassan something. The man immediately reaches into a golden chalice on a table and pulls out a coin about the size of a drachma then walks over and hands it to Rassan.

"That is the symbol of my personal commission to you, Rassan. It empowers you to have our full leave and protection in accomplishing all that we have commanded you to accomplish. When your work is done and you are released, you must return it to our court so that our scribes can record it. This coin holds the most prestigious of commissions in my empire, Rassan. Steward it and the mission it empowers you to fulfill with your whole heart."

Rassan receives the coin from the emperor's minister, then formally bows and salutes. "I will give my life in service to see your wish is carried out, Emperor." Rassan then gracefully exits the royal court. The emperor looks over at his son and laughs. "If Rassan is anything like the rest of our officers who've chosen to get a taste of studying with the Magi, I fear Master Daraya-Vous will send him packing back to us in a year at the very most. Which, incidentally, should give you time to find him a suitable wife. His time of betrothal is long overdue, and we promised his father on his deathbed that we would take care of this matter."

Phraates V shakes his head and laughs. "I know, Father. I will attend to it during that time. As for his apprenticeship with the Astronomical Sect, I think he may surprise us both. Rassan has always marched to the beat of a different drummer."

Outside the royal court chamber, Rassan clutches the star charts canister to his chest. He can't get out of his mind his encounter with Master Magi Farnah. Ever since the man placed his hands on him and charged him with his dying words, his eyes have somehow been opened to newer and higher things. He always felt that the Creator would make known what He wanted him to do with his life. But he never in his wildest dreams thought it would be to learn how to read the stars and see the divine message in them. But as the prospect crosses his conscience, a thrill erupts in his core that he can hardly contain.

He steps toward the door that leads to the courtyard where he and the prince were sparring earlier. As his hand reaches for the latch, the door swings open and on the other side is his friend Sasheen. The man is half a head taller than Rassan and wears the uniform of an officer of the royal garrison. He grabs Rassan by the shoulders and shakes him. "Rassan, did you truly do what I heard?" He then steps aside to let the cadet through. "Well?"

Rassan's shoulders sag a little and he lifts his right hand to rub his tense brow. "If you mean, did I invoke my birthright to petition the emperor to carry out the last wishes of Master Vinda-Farnah of the Magi Order, then yes, I did."

Sasheen stares at his young academy friend for a few moments, then chuckles. "You were always impetuous, Rassan. When I was your platoon leader in the academy, I thought for sure you would be the death of me before I graduated." He shakes his right index finger in front of Rassan's nose. "Not because I was afraid of that sword hand of yours either, but you have a knack for getting into trouble by pushing your luck." He leans in closer. "Tell me, what was the emperor's response to your request?"

Rassan holds up the star charts canister. "I am, by royal decree, to take these to Babylon and place them in the hands of Master Daraya-Vous, now head of the Astronomical Sect of the Magi Order. I am also to present myself to him as apprentice to his order for my post academy education."

Sasheen stares at the canister, shakes his head, and puts both hands on Rassan's shoulders. "Have you utterly lost your mind? Accepting a royal decree from the emperor himself is an honor any cadet dreams of, but to willingly put yourself through the torment of studying with those stargazers in Babylon is a torture no soldier should ever have to go through. You should have come to me. I would have gotten you in with Master Dvandas. His order is much more interesting, and the fringe benefits! Ah, my friend, you don't know what you are denying yourself!"

Rassan smiles and shakes his head. "You know my family would be very upset with me if they heard I had taken part in some of those magician rituals you told me about. Besides, the decision is already made, and I go under the emperor's authority. I could not change my mind now, even if I wanted to."

Rassan grasps his friend's arms and squeezes them, then turns and makes his way back to the cadet barracks.

Late that Evening, Offices of Master Dvandas

Commander Dareh steps into the darkened offices of the royal court's counselor, Magi Master Dvandas. The hairs on the back of his neck stand on end as he spots the one he seeks, reclining on a chaise lounge chair, gazing up at the ceiling at some kind of astrological depiction made up of different size hanging balls. A voice from the darker part of the room behind Master Dvandas speaks. "As you can see, I've duplicated the shadow that fell across the quarter moon two nights ago."

Commander Dareh pauses in the shadows and looks to the metal ball representing the moon and sees that a light is being focused on it from a box with a lensed cap that has a candle inside it that's sitting on the table. One side of the ball is completely illuminated, save for a small corner. The ball representing the moon has lines engraved into it that cut it in relatively small rectangular sections, with some form of writing in each.

"You divined this to mean that Farnah would fall, and from the report sent to Emperor Phraates IV from garrison command, that fact has been verified. We only need to wait for Commander Dareh's report to us to find out if he retrieved what you asked of him."

"Yes, Mihri, I know, and where is the good commander? It has been many hours since he returned to the palace."

Commander Dareh takes a deep breath and steps forward. "I am right here, Headmaster Dvandas. Pardon my tardiness, but circum-stances prevented me from joining you sooner."

Mihri also steps from the shadows and up to Commander Dareh. "Pray tell us the meaning of your prolonged absence, Dareh. And do you have the charts that Master Farnah was carrying?"

He sucks in a heavy breath. "I would have what you want if that impetuous cadet Rassan did not invoke his birthright to beseech the emperor to fulfill Master Farnah's dying wishes."

Mihri steps up to Commander Dareh. "What were Master Farnah's last wishes that Rassan thought were so important as to beseech the emperor?"

Dareh swallows and turns to meet Master Dvandas's icy stare. "To take the star charts back to someone named Master Daraya-Vous in Babylon."

Headmaster Dvandas's face contorts in rage. He lunges from his seat and points a finger at Commander Dareh. "Prince Phraates IV forbade me to enter court today. This is the first time I have heard this ghastly report. After talking with Mihri earlier, I secluded myself in my private chambers so that I might divine what to do next. This Master Daraya-Vous you speak of will now be the headmaster of the Astronomical Sect of the Magi Order. He must never get his hands on those charts. They are the most ancient of their kind in the empire." He turns and walks over directly under the ball representing the moon, then looks up at the area that is shadowed and waves his hand in the air. "Farnah greedily held on to them his entire time as headmaster. If they make it to Babylon with the emperor's blessing, Grand Master Artapan will once again award them to their sect and I will never see them. This is unacceptable news. How could this have happened?"

Dareh feels the electricity ignited by Master Dvandas's wrath prickle across his body. "Like I just told you, Master Dvandas, the boy invoked his right to beseech the emperor on Master Farnah's—"

Dvandas waves him off and turns toward Mihri. "I was talking to you! I thought our agent would deal with the boy. Where was he?"

Mihri steps forward, casts a menacing look at Commander Dareh, then turns back to Dvandas. "The men we hired for the operation were spooked by the size of the garrison's squad. They did not want to engage them and they fled."

Dvandas stares at his aide for a few moments, then lets out an exasperated breath. "Curse those damn mercenaries and curse that bunch of astronomers. We are the true prognosticators of the hidden will of the gods in the celestial movements of the heavens. Yet these astronomers repeatedly seem to gain favor in the most peculiar of ways." He looks over at Darch. "You sent Rassan in the lead, as we discussed?"

"Of course. He was the first one there. Your man should have had plenty of time to kill him and escape. I even prolonged joining him when he was with Master Farnah, thinking your man was hiding someplace to ambush the boy. I waited as long as I could before my men got too suspicious."

Mihri steps forward. "Master Dvandas, our man tried to retrieve the charts, and the captain of the mercenaries threatened to kill him for that. He had no opportunity to stay and kill the boy."

Dvandas grinds his teeth and walks over to his desk where the light projector is still illuminating the brass ball depicting the moon. He reaches down and opens the lid and blows out the candle inside. "If not for the fact that Farnah is dead, I would have you both killed. Strange how that for all our prognosticating and planning, we have only seen one third of those predictions come to fruition. Farnah is dead, true, but the prince's favorite would–be confidant still lives, and he now has the charts that by all the gods should be mine!"

3

Friends for Life

Next Day, Palace Stables

Rassan could hardly sleep the night after making his petition to Emperor Phraates IV. Before the first rays of the sun kiss the palace domes, he races through the palace courtyard with his belongings to the stables where his journey to Babylon will begin. The graduating class of officer cadets will assemble in the royal courtyard in one hour, but he cannot wait until after the ceremony to get his things in order for the journey. As he approaches the area where his caravan is being assembled, he spots a scruffy-haired stable boy lounging in an empty stall. "You there, come here and help me with my things." The boy looks at first like he is going to ignore Rassan, but when he realizes Rassan is from the garrison, he jumps up and runs over.

Rassan sees the eagerness in the boy and surmises he probably came here from the city and has had no luck getting anyone who would pay him to help. He looks at the stable, then at the boy. "You were hiding in there so that one of the caravan bosses did not make you work for free, eh?" The boy nods and gives Rassan a sly look. "But garrison officers always pay nicely for help with their mounts," Rassan says as he gives the boy a grin, sets his things down, and places a drachma in the boy's hand. "Tell the stable boss that you are serving the emperor's emissary to Babylon, and that you are charged with preparing my mount and stowing my belongings in a carriage. Show him this." Rassan reaches inside his jacket and pulls out a small coin with the depiction of Phraates IV on the front and a number on the back that shows to all that the one charged with the coin is acting under the direction and decree of the emperor.

The boy nervously gazes at the coin for a moment, then reverently back at Rassan. He knows that to steal the coin or falsely use its authority in the Parthian Empire comes with penalty of death. As the boy stares, Rassan inquires, "Do you know what that is?"

The boy slowly nods his head. "You are on a mission for the emperor. That coin gives you great power to carry out your mission."

Rassan inwardly feels he can trust this boy and tosses the coin to him. "Good. Now, where is the officer in charge of the caravan?"

The boy eagerly catches the coin and stares at it for a moment longer, and then places it inside his clothing, smiles, and points to a large carriage at the other end of the stable area. As the boy reaches for some of Rassan's things, Rassan notices that the boy has some type of tattoo on his right shoulder. It has a six-pointed star inside a circle that is interlined with the shape of a hexagon. "What is the meaning of that symbol on your arm? I have never seen it before."

The boy sheepishly smiles. "I do not know, Master. It has been there since I can remember. My parents died when I was very young, and I was orphaned in the city since then. No one has ever told me what it means."

Rassan just nods and then makes his way in the direction the boy had pointed. The coin is safe with the boy. The Parthian Empire had a penalty of death for abusing the coin. He turns around and looks at the boy and shouts, "What is your name, boy?"

"Arsam!" the boy yells back.

"Well, Arsam, there will be another full drachma for your purse when I return if all I have asked is accomplished."

"Thank you, Master. I will not disappoint! What is your name?"

"Rassan."

Rassan continues on and passes three other carriages and at least fifty mounts being prepared for the journey. He realizes this caravan is of significant size and will have to be led by an officer of at least a commander's rank. He closes his eyes and prays that it will not be Commander Dareh. When he gets closer to the large carriage in the front, he hears a familiar voice shouting orders to people around him. He smiles broadly when he sees that his friend Sasheen is the one giving the orders. Sasheen turns in Rassan's direction and returns the smile. Immediately, Rassan recognizes the commander's rank insignia on his uniform and comes to attention and throws a smart salute to his newly promoted friend.

Sasheen returns the salute and steps forward. "Relax, Cadet. In less than an hour you will be a full officer and won't have to be so formal with me. After I left you last night, I went to the barracks and finished my nightly duties and was about to turn in when I received a summons to the palace by the emperor. When I arrived, it was late into the night and Master Dvandas was there with the emperor, discussing your mission to Babylon. They informed me that I was being promoted and would take charge of this caravan as I headed to Babylon with you to assume my new post as second-in-command to the Babylonian garrison commander. I am betrothed to General Barach's daughter, and he will retire soon and want me to be his replacement."

Forgetting his military discipline, Rassan rushes up to his friend and grabs his hand and shakes it. "This is fantastic news, Sasheen! It will be like when you were my platoon leader all over again. For the next few months, I will be one of your officers. It will be perfect."

Sasheen yanks his hand away. "You forget your place, Rassan. Your time in this caravan will be spent as the emissary of the emperor, and until you hand the sacred Magi star charts to Daraya-Vous in Babylon, I am charged with protecting you and your mission with my life."

Rassan steps back as the impact of his friend's reproof blows through him. "Forgive me, Sash… uh, Commander. I will keep my place in your command."

"Good. Now you should join your fellow cadets in the courtyard. The emperor and his son will attend the ceremony. It would not be wise to be late!"

One Hour Later, Palace Courtyard

Twenty-three cadets stand at attention in formation in the courtyard in front of the palace steps, where Emperor Phraates IV and his son, Phraates V, are joined by Garrison Commander General Tubok, Commander Dareh, and Master Dvandas. The general is finishing his commissioning of the new cadets into the officer's corps of the Parthian Calvary as Commander Dareh and several of his aides step down to pin each cadet with their officer's insignia. Phraates V sees that Commander Dareh has one of his lower-ranking subordinates assigned to pin Rassan's insignia on, and he steps away from his father into the courtyard. The action of the prince is noticed by all, and the proceedings come to a halt as he steps up to Rassan and smiles at the officer who was about to pin him. "If you don't mind, I wish to handle this one," Phraates V says.

The man's eyes dart nervously from Commander Dareh to Headmaster Dvandas, who both, though perturbed about the break in the routine, have no recourse but to accept the actions of the heir apparent. He holds out the insignia. "Of course, My Prince."

Phraates V takes the pin and turns to Rassan. The prince's face is red and he almost bursts out with laughter, but he suppresses it and gives the new officer a subtle wink as he pins the insignia on his lapel and salutes him. "Well done, and welcome to the officers' corps of the Parthian Empire."

A Few Moments Later

"So, Rassan, your first assignment is being the emperor's personal emissary to Babylon. Nice. When will you be back?"

Rassan turns around to be greeted by several of his fellow newly commissioned officers. Spending years drilling and training with the same group invokes an almost familial familiarity with these men and Rassan counts them as brothers. He steps up to the one who just spoke. "I am also to report for postgraduation studies with the Astronomical Sect of the Magi Order once I've handed some star charts off to Master Daraya-Vous. The emperor said that how long I stay is completely up to the Magi headmaster."

Rassan's friends stare at him for a few moments in silence as his news sinks in, then he bursts laughing. Then, others join him in his mirth. The man reaches up and scruffs Rassan's head and replies, "They are the strictest of the Magi sects and it sometimes takes apprentices over ten years of study before they can move on. You will be an old man the next time we see you, Rassan!"

Rassan holds up his hand to stave off their continuing banter when a familiar voice booms out, grabbing all the newly commissioned officers' attention, and then has each man bowing in the presence of Emperor Phraates IV. "I do not think it amusing that Rassan is about to carry out his emperor's orders. That we are having him continue his postcommissioning studies with the Magi Order in Babylon is upon the wise counsel and recommendations of our most loyal and trusted advisor, Headmaster Dvandas. Why, he told my son just yesterday morning that Rassan should consider an apprenticeship with the Magi Order—that his aptitudes in the study of religion and history show that he is well suited for more extreme academic endeavors."

Standing next to the emperor, Master Dvandas is the one who is now doing everything in his power to suppress his astonishment. He scans the courtyard until he focuses on another group of officers where the prince is now engaged in a lively conversation. While holding him in his gaze, he says to the emperor, "Your Eminence, I was not aware that His Highness the Prince shared with you our conversation in the courtyard about Rassan and his future studies. When I made my suggestion, I had referred to his staying here at the capital and apprenticing in my sect of the Magi Order."

As the words leave his mouth, the prince turns to meet Dvandas's gaze with a mischievous grin and nods his head at the Magi master, making it clear he is not to be toyed with. Dvandas sucks the air through his teeth and his heart races with anger. He turns to the emperor. "If His Majesty will pardon me, I have pressing court business I must see to. May I have your leave?"

Phraates IV waves his hand at Dvandas without looking his way. "Of course, my old friend. The ceremony is completed. Go on, I will see you in court shortly."

Dvandas bows his head and quickly exits the courtyard, keeping his eyes down so as not to make eye contact with the prince, who is taking no small pleasure in his silent victory over the manipulative Magi.

Rassan steps up to the prince and clears his throat to make his presence known. "Pardon me, Your Highness. I just wanted to say goodbye before I join the caravan."

A bright smile crosses the prince's face as he turns to greet his companion. He grabs his arms in the traditional warrior grip. He looks Rassan in the eyes. "I will miss our sparring sessions, Officer Rassan. Few can educate me in sword-play as you do! To think that I am sending away probably my finest swordsman to go study in the strictest sect of the Magi Order. Are you sure you want to do this? Remember, you are before one of the few people in the world who can get you out of this torture you have insisted on putting yourself through. Once you leave my presence, your destiny is set!"

Rassan sighs. "I cannot explain it, but this is something I have to do, My Prince."

Prince Phraates steps back and waves his hand. "Remember your duty to your emperor to give full diligence to the task he has assigned to you, then come back to us when you are released to do so by Master Daraya-Vous of the Magi Order in Babylon."

Rassan bows his head. "By your leave, My Prince."

May 7, 6 BC, Eight Weeks Later; Halfway Between the Parthian Capital City and the City of Babylon

The cool of the desert night breeze blows through the tent door flaps as they sway in its embrace. It is a welcome sensation for Arsam after traveling in the scorching desert sun all day. His master sent him to get the star charts, and he has found them. He holds the treasure in his hand under the watchful eye of the guard assigned to the royal emissary tent. He glances sideways and smiles at the ever-present Parthian sentinel, who has never said a word to the young stable boy since their departure from the capital. Through his time growing up on the streets of the capital, he has felt that same disdainful gaze from many of the city constables and important merchants who look at his like as little more than a smelly annoyance, useful for only the lowliest of tasks like washing feet, mucking out stables, and disposing of toilet pots. He feels like the man does not want him to touch the charts that are the reason the whole caravan was commissioned. But he knows he will do or say nothing because the emperor's emissary has granted him with the keeping of Rassan's commissioning coin, and that makes him as untouchable as Rassan himself. He takes the canister and tucks it under his arm and rushes past the man to meet Rassan at his small private fire outside his tent.

Rassan sees Arsam making his way to the campfire with the star charts under his arm. His eyes go skyward, where the evening sky has just become dark enough to see the sparkle of the stars protruding through the dark-blue backdrop of the heavens above him. A thrill goes through his heart as he turns back to his servant, eagerly anticipating their time looking at the charts and comparing them to their heavenly counterparts.

Arsam takes his seat next to Rassan and hands him the canister. He, too, has become enamored with their nightly meetings of late as he and his master work together to understand the meaning of the ancient charts.

Rassan opens the top of the canister, pulls out the charts and lays them on a rug placed in a position where the desert wind is blowing the small campfire embers away from its precious contents. The material that the star charts are made of has a reflective quality to it so that the images on the charts stand out in lower light settings like campfire, moonlight, and starlight.

Rassan is careful not to mix up the order by which the charts are stored in the canister as he lays them out so that the edge of each chart can be seen on the left side of the stack before the next chart begins. His hands go to the last chart and he places his finger on the depiction of the star Regulus, ponders it for a moment, then turns to Arsam. "This is the first chart that I looked at after receiving the canister from Master Vinda-Farnah. I pulled it out because the way it was hastily put back into the canister made it seem like this was the last one he looked at before he died."

Arsam stares at the chart for a moment, then says, "Why do you think he was so interested in this chart, Master?"

"His last words to me were that I was to tell Master Daraya-Vous that we would find our answers in 'The Lion of the Tribe of Judah.' This chart shows the constellation Leo."

"So, do you think there is a connection between the constellation Leo and the Judean legend?"

"I think Master Vinda-Farnah thought so, and this backs up that claim." Rassan thumps the place where Regulus is depicted with his index finger. "Look at the notation just under this star."

Arsam puts his face a few inches from the area Rassan is pointing to and endeavors to read the inscription. He sounds out the words that the symbols represent, which Rassan has recently taught him. "Theee Li-o-nn oo—f t-hee..."

"Sorry, Arsam, I keep forgetting that you're just learning how to read." Rassan looks at the inscription and reads it aloud. *'The Lion of the Tribe of Judah depicts the Messiah as the King of Kings. He will inherit the throne of his father David, and his kingdom will never end. Noted by Belteshazzar, Master of the Magi.'"*

Arsam's heart skips a beat. He jumps to his feet and studies the stars in the sky, trying to find the constellation Leo. Then he points and says, "Master, does that mean that the promised seed will come to us from Leo out of the sky?"

"I don't think so, Arsam. Belteshazzar said that he will inherit the throne of his father David. To call David his father means that the promised one will be a descendant of David, and therefore, must be born here on earth. Besides, remember that we found out last night that the signs of the zodiac are in order. Leo is the last, and Virgo is the first. In Virgo, we learned a virgin would give birth to the promised seed."[7]

"How can a virgin give birth, Master? If she is a virgin, then how can he be a son of David when he has no father? That is impossible."

Rassan leans back and looks up at the stars. "You are asking a question that I have no answers for, Arsam. Perhaps when we reach Babylon, Master Daraya-Vous will tell us both."

"I wonder what Master Daraya-Vous will say when he hears that you have been pulling out the Magi's sacred charts every night of this journey and looking at them under the light of an open fire."

Before Rassan can turn and respond, the night breeze shifts and embers from the fire drift to the rug where the charts are laid out. He and Arsam frantically gather them up and put them back in the canister. When they turn, they see Commander Sasheen standing next to Rassan's tent, eyeing both of them with a tense, disapproving gaze.

"Officer Rassan, I know that as the emperor's emissary to Babylon, those charts are your personal responsibility until you place them in Master Daraya-Vous's hand," Commander Sasheen says as he steps up to the pair, pointing at the canister in Rassan's hand. "But this caravan was formed for bringing you to Babylon to do so. If something were to happen to them on the way there, it would mean both our heads."

Rassan gulps and tries to calm his racing heart. His eyes dart to Arsam and then back to the commander. "I am sorry, Commander. It's just that I thought since I will study at the Magi Observatory in Babylon after I deliver the charts, I should try to get some understanding of what I have gotten myself into."

Commander Sasheen stares at Rassan for a few moments, then the corners of his mouth curl into a smile. He walks up to his friend and puts his arm around his shoulders and walks him back to his tent. "Rassan, you have always been the most annoying and impetuous person. Just what makes you think you can understand anything about those charts on your own?"

"Well, Commander, since you asked, we have found that they reveal a starting and ending point to the signs of the zodiac. The order of the charts is that they begin with the sign of Virgo and end with the sign of Leo. And though it seems like a circle that our world goes through each year as these different signs manifest themselves in the stars, the charts' order dictates that there is a definite beginning and end to their meaning."

Commander Sasheen stops in his stride and releases Rassan and turns to face him, a look of profound disapproval in his eyes. "Rassan, that is the most ridiculous thing I have ever heard in my life. You forget that I have done some of my postacademy studies under Master Dvandas in the capital. He is the head of one of the three branches of the Magi Order, and he taught us that the zodiac signs are a perfect, mystical circle that mark the world's path through the heavens in a year's time. They have no beginning and no end and, therefore, have an infinite amount of knowledge to give. That is why everyone's personal destiny can be discovered if they are studied by one gifted with the abilities to interpret their meanings."

Before Rassan can respond, Arsam blurts out, "But Master, did we not just see a note in the charts written by the Hebrew prophet Belteshazzar and former headmaster of all the Magi that stated the signs of the zodiac show the story of man's downfall to the serpent and of the coming of the Creator's champion, who will rescue us all from his rule forever?"

Sasheen smirks at the boy, then looks at Rassan and sighs. "You see, this is why you don't share ancient treasures like the sacred Magi star charts with an uneducated stable boy, Rassan. Master Dvandas warned us against the teachings of the one the boy refers to. The key word there is 'HEBREW'! In Judea, he is known as Daniel and is credited with the writing of a large scroll that makes up part of their own sacred scriptures. Dvandas taught us that it was this Daniel who truly corrupted the Magi Order and caused it to split into factions after his death." Sasheen shakes his head and laughs. "He was just a slave, Rassan. The emperor of that time took a fancy to him and promoted him way above his station. Then the ungrateful lout used his new position to push his own Hebrew theology upon the greatest empire in the world. History has since proved to us that it was simply a ploy to get the emperor to free his people and send them home. Which, if you recall your history, the Persian Emperor Artaxerxes did. Master Dvandas told us that this Hebrew prophet Daniel is the reason that the gods do not look as favorably on our lands as they once did, and that is why we are plagued with these Romans who keep expanding into our lands."

Rassan stands there perplexed by his friend's words. He cannot deny that the Judean people are among the most despised and looked down upon in the empire. When the Romans annexed their lands over a hundred years ago, some saw it as a blessing from the gods that the empire would no longer have to tolerate their constant bickering and complaining. Even his own great-grandfather, who was an officer in the imperial calvary, said that the Roman invaders just cut their own throats by taking on that lot of xenophobic religious zealots. But then he thinks about his father, who rose to the highest rank of anyone in their family line. He had a much more sympathetic view of the Judean people. He taught Rassan that with a few exceptions like their most famous of kings, David, the great holy men and prophets of their faith mostly rose from the ranks of the common men in that society. That they were more times than not at odds with the religious and political leaders of their times.

He sighs and shakes his head. "Commander, you are entitled to your opinion, and I respect your right to say it, but it does not mean that what you say is the absolute truth. My father taught me to respect the prophet Daniel and what he accomplished in Babylon during his life there. No one can deny that Nebuchadnezzar was the greatest of the old emperors, and he held Daniel in the highest of regard. Truly there has to be some grand design for his decisions to do so."

Sasheen reels back when Rassan mentions his father. Everyone in the Parthian military knows who General Surena was and how much the emperors Phraates III and IV loved him as a man and a general. It was him and his battalion of archers at the Battle of Carrhae that turned back the Roman General Marcus Licinius Crassus's invasion of the Parthian Empire of 53 BC. To appear to sully the words of such a man, especially to his son, could bring great disgrace to an officer like himself. "Rassan, I am not a philosopher, and neither are you. We are both soldiers in His Majesty's royal calvary. Our place is to defend the empire at all costs. Neither of us is qualified to debate these points." He places his hand on the star charts canister and continues, "You have been entrusted to safely deliver these charts to Master Daraya-Vous of the Magi Order in Babylon. I have been entrusted to make sure that nothing hinders you in that mission. Therefore, I must insist that you do not pull these charts out near an open flame ever again. If you must look at them, let it be in the daylight."

Later, Two Hours Before Dawn

Rassan finds it hard to sleep after Commander Sasheen rebuked him so sharply. Sasheen was always one of his closest friends going through the academy. When he entered the academy, Sasheen was the upperclassman. He feels especially bad because it was Sasheen who took a special liking to him from the beginning and started mentoring him in the ways of an officer-in-training in the Parthian military. He glances over to the bedding next to his and sees that Arsam is sound asleep.

Rassan sits up and decides to take a stroll around the camp to see if Commander Sasheen is awake so that he can apologize. As his feet touch the sandy desert floor in his tent, he feels a sudden rush of panic. He instinctively reaches for the sword next to his bedding, straps the scabbard to his hip and makes his way to the entrance. Outside he hears the muffled sounds of men struggling. Arsam is now awake and sitting up, looking at him. He holds his finger to his lips in a hushing manner and points to the canister of star charts between their beddings and then to a spear propped up against the tent behind him.

"Protect them with your life!" he whispers.

Rassan then checks the side of the tent door. Even though the light from the flames of the main campfires can be seen dancing against the canvas, there is no silhouette of the guard who has stood at the spot every night since they had left the capital. He pulls back the tent flap with his left hand, ready with his drawn sword in his right. He peers out and sees two figures. One is behind the other, with one hand wrapped around the other's mouth and his other hand trying to impale his victim with a sword. The man being attacked is Rassan's guard.

Rassan lets out an ear-piercing scream and launches into the duo. The attacker, shocked at the sudden noise, pushes away from his victim to meet Rassan's assault. Instead of helping Rassan fight the attacker, the guard grabs his midsection, falls to his knees, and lets out a groan. He looks up at Rassan. "He stabbed me. I can't help you! Cry for the guards! You and the star charts are all that matter!"

Rassan barely acknowledges the man's words before he encounters the attacker. He hears Arsam yell at the top of his lungs from inside the tent, "Guards! We're under attack!"

Steel meets steel as Rassan brings his sword to bear in a side-armed parry, deflecting a forward thrust from the attacker. For the first time, he gets a look at his opponent. The man is dressed in black, his face covered with a black scarf. He is wielding a gladius sword, which is standard Roman military issue. The blade is double-edged and is considered a magnificent weapon when used in close combat, especially when surrounded by fellow soldiers wielding the same style sword. But this man is alone and Rassan is wielding his Parthian Military Sassanian blade, which is four inches longer and single-edged. He hops back, avoiding another attack as his opponent arcs his blade upward, using the momentum from Rassan's parry to catapult his blade up to the left as he slices it right, missing his throat by inches.

Rassan is not one to use standard military swordsmanship unless it suits his purposes, but he recognizes this man's style of combat and anticipates his next move. The attacker brings his blade hand up from the ground and twists it to the sky, trying to slice across Rassan's throat once again. This time Rassan widens his stance, parries the man's blade with an upward arch block that catches his opponent's sword handle in the cross-guard of his own sword, then twists the blade, breaking the man's grip on his blade. He grabs the blade with his left hand and sidekicks the man in the stomach, knocking the breath out of him and making him stumble backward. Now armed with both blades, Rassan steps in and holds him at bay with them and yells, "Someone call Commander Sasheen! I've been attacked by a bandit. He looks to be a Roman soldier deserter!"

The would-be bandit stares at Rassan through his mask and lets out a guttural roar of frustration. Then he reaches down and grabs a handful of dirt and rocks and hurls them into Rassan's face. The man barrels into him, knocks him to the ground, and retrieves his sword.

Though blinded by the attack, Rassan gets his own blade up in a defensive maneuver as his attacker steps closer, intending to finish him off. And then a rock hits the man's sword hand. Soldiers come rushing up the path to the tent. The attacker shakes his head, furious at the turn of events, and steals off into the night.

Rassan bolts to his feet, wipes his eyes and starts to give chase when he hears one of the soldiers yelling out an order. "You four, protect the emperor's emissary! The rest of you, after the bandit!"

Rassan looks back toward the entrance of the tent and sees the boy, Arsam, who had just thrown the rock, standing there with the charts in one hand and a spear in the other. "Give me the charts and go find Commander Sasheen and bring him here!" he yells.

"That won't be necessary, Sergeant."

All eyes turn toward the voice and they see Commander Sasheen running in their direction from the wilderness beyond the camp. He comes up the path, surveys the scene, then immediately goes to Rassan and puts both hands on his shoulders and shakes him. "Are you all right? Where are the star charts?"

Before Rassan can answer, Arsam runs up to him with the canister in his hand and says, "They are still safe, Master. I would have protected them with my life, but there was no need. The way you fought that man, it was incredible. Even though he was much bigger than you, he did not stand a chance." He hands the charts to Rassan, beaming from ear to ear.

Rassan takes the charts from his servant and as soon as he feels them in his hand, a deep sense of relief goes through his whole being. He shakes his head and reaches out to ruffle the boy's hair. "A good soldier should be ready for anything, Arsam. If not for the sergeant here and the rest of the guard coming when they did, I don't know if I would have survived the night."

"But Master, you held your guard up and staved him off. Plus, after I threw the rock, I grabbed your spear and readied myself. He would have been dead before his blade could reach you, even if he was able!"

Commander Sasheen steps between the two and stares incredulously at Arsam for a moment, then turns back to Rassan. "Maybe this boy has more to him than I gave him credit for, my friend. Be that as it may, you will no longer be allowed to pitch your tent at the edge of the camp."

"But Commander, it is hard to make out all the stars at night with the large campfire blazing. It will be very difficult to continue my studies!" Rassan replies, exasperation in his voice.

Commander Sasheen holds up both his hands to stay Rassan's objection when he hears his men returning. He immediately steps out to meet them.

"Commander, we circled the entire camp looking for the bandit and found nothing, but one of my men caught a glimpse of a man on a horse galloping away to the west. Should we pursue?"

"No. I will send a man to the nearest Parthian outpost and tell them an attempt was made on the life of the emperor's emissary by a deserter of the Roman army. There cannot be that many of them this far east. With the blessings of the gods, they should be able to track down such a person."

Rassan is startled by his friend's words. "How did you know it was a Roman deserter? I have not told you that yet."

Commander Sasheen shakes his head and laughs. "Rassan, you forget that you have a very loud yelling voice when you want to use it. I heard your call for help, saying you thought he was Roman, when I was all the way on the other side of the camp. That's why I came through the shortcut in the trees over there."

Rassan looks at the trees and then to where the bandit ran off and points his sword straight out to the desert. "Too bad you just did not continue straight out. That way you would have run right into the bandit and caught him."

June 30, 6 BC, Three Nights Later, a Day's Journey from the City of Babylon

Rassan and Arsam are bedded down for the night inside their tent. It's late and the only people appearing to be awake are the four guards now surrounding Rassan's tent. Two nights ago, the guard that was assigned to this post died of the wounds he received from the mysterious Roman bandit who attacked Rassan. There is a breeze stirring the desert that foretells of a fierce storm brewing.

About half a mile east of the camp and behind a hill, two men talk under the cover of darkness, one on a horse and one standing next to it. The man on horseback leans down and says, "Master Dvandas will not like my report. How many times are you going to fail to kill that boy and get him his prize?"

"It's not my fault. That guard proved to be more of an obstacle than they told me he would be. Then when Rassan woke up he attacked before I was ready for it."

"Ha! You mean you are sorry the boy woke up at all? The whole of the emperor's garrison knows of his skill with a blade. That's why Phraates V practiced with him."

The man grinds his teeth and snarls. "I had him. If his servant hadn't thrown that rock and the guards were not so close, he would be dead now."

"So would you be, my friend. His servant would have killed you with that spear. Then everything would have been lost! Once they discovered who you are, it would be easy to trace everything back to Master Dvandas, and then he and all concerned, including me, would have paid with our lives!" He shakes his head. "Well, at least you were able to get your bandit outfit and sword back to me in time and return to camp before anyone noticed your absence." He sits straight up and nudges his horse. "Make no aggressive moves against the boy until you hear from us. I will send word to Master Dvandas. Now we must petition those charts at Grand Master Artapan's court and keep them from being entrusted to Master Daraya-Vous."

4

Headmaster

Eight Weeks Later, Magi Astronomical Temple, Babylon

Rassan, Commander Sasheen, and Arsam enter through the main doorway into the observatory section of the Magi Astronomical Temple. A deep sense of excitement goes through Rassan's whole being as he considers that his promise of returning the sacred star charts for Master Vinda-Farnah is almost complete. His heart is filled with total wonder as he sees the twelve huge tapestries hanging from the ceiling, surrounding the huge dome-shaped window in the center. He and Arsam immediately recognize that they are much larger versions of the charts that Rassan now clings to his chest. He knows that word was sent to the Temple that he had arrived in Babylon that morning and was headed there directly, but there appears to be no one to greet them. Rassan steps ahead of his companions, searching for someone to talk to.

"Why did you come here, Rassan? Those charts are Grand Master Artapan's responsibility. He is the one to decide what sect of the Magi will have them, not you!" Commander Sasheen grumbles.

Rassan turns and pulls out the coin given to him at Emperor Phraates IV's court over three months ago, shows it to his friend, and replies, "My commission is to bring these charts to Babylon and place them in the hands of Master Daraya-Vous, head of the Astronomical Sect of the Magi Order. To do otherwise would be disobedience to our sovereign and a death penalty for all of us!"

"I am afraid that we have a slight problem, then. I have not officially been named headmaster of the Astronomical Sect of the Magi yet," a voice says behind Rassan. He turns to see the source of the voice and is greeted by a man who is clearly of advanced years but whose demeanor and presence radiate the power and vigor of one much younger. His hair is gray and his deep blue eyes stare at Rassan with a disarming, almost mirthful flavor.

Rassan immediately feels a positive connection with this man. He walks up to him and says, "That is for others to decide, Master Daraya-Vous, but my commission from Emperor Phraates IV is to place these in your hands." He then extends the canister for Daraya-Vous to receive.

The Magi takes the canister from him. "What did Headmaster Vinda-Farnah say to you before he died?" he asks.

"First, that I place those charts in your hands. Then he told me to tell you to look to the Lion of the Tribe of Judah for the answers you seek, and that I should continue this watch with you by reporting to begin my training as a Magi apprentice."

While clutching the charts to his chest with his left hand, Daraya-Vous reaches out with his right, grabs Rassan's shoulder and shakes it. He looks deeply into the boy's eyes and says, "Leo!"

Three Days Later, July 21, 6 BC, City of Babylon, Grand Master of the Magi Order's Court

The court of Grand Master Artapan of the Magi Order is larger but plain compared to those of the Astronomical or Magician Sects. He oversees the part of the order that adheres to the teaching of the Persian prophet Zoroaster. Humility and discretion are their disciplines. Today he sits in his chair of judgment as he listens to Master

Dvandas's assistant, Mihri, closing out his official plea to be given the sacred star charts.

"So, you see, Grand Master Artapan, it would only be fair and in the best interest of the *entire* order of Magi for the sacred star charts of the Magi Order to be entrusted to Master Dvandas's care. The Astronomical Sect has had them for over six centuries, and it is past time to let others in the order steward them and gain more insights from their study."

Artapan gazes solemnly at Mihri for a moment, then he looks over to Master Daraya-Vous. "Do you find it strange that Master Dvandas would send his assistant to make this plea, and yet when it was time for him to be recognized as the head of the mystical sect of Magi, he insisted I make a personal journey to the capital?"

Master Daraya-Vous tries to answer but Mihri interjects. "Grand Master Artapan, this entire court must realize that Master Dvandas is Emperor Phraates IV's most trusted advisor and is not at liberty to leave his presence for any length of time. When he begged your presence at the capital, it was because that is what the emperor wanted."

"Funny, I was in the capital, having been sent by Grand Master Artapan to escort Master Dvandas here for his recognition ceremony. As I recall, he made several petitions to the emperor to send for the Grand Master to come so that he could be recognized and installed in Phraates IV's court instead of here," Master Daraya-Vous says with a hint of sarcasm in his voice.

Mihri glares at Daraya-Vous with barely veiled indignation, then directs his voice to Artapan. "Grand Master, I am an official representative of the head of the Magician Sect of the Magi and therefore am allowed by our laws to petition in this court. Master Daraya-Vous is only an officer in the Astronomical Sect of Magi and can only speak when he is addressed by someone in here who has authority to speak, which at this moment only includes you and me!"

Grand Master Artapan gazes at Mihri, astonished at his insolence. He sighs deeply. "Of a truth, those are our laws, Mihri, and by their letter you are correct. But if you recall, I did direct my question to Master Daraya-Vous, at which time you interjected your opinions. However, you bring up an essential element of our laws in that you pointed out that headmasters of each sect or their official representative need to be present at all important decisions that impact the entire order. So, now that you are done with your petition to receive the sacred star charts, we can proceed with the rest of the day's agenda." He smiles and looks over to Master Daraya-Vous and says, "Please step forward and kneel, Master."

Daraya-Vous steps forward, goes down on both knees and closes his eyes as he folds his hands in front of him in a prayer gesture. Grand Master Artapan then places both hands on his shoulders, turns his eyes upward, and says, "Great and Almighty God, Creator of all things, we ask that You accept this man, Your humble servant, to continue the watch as headmaster of the Astronomical Sect of the Magi. Help him lead his brothers to be diligent in studying and proclaiming Your sacred truth written in the tapestry of the twelve signs of the zodiac. Bless his efforts so that they bring joy and enlightenment to us all."

Artapan then steps back and looks out to the room that has a small representation from the Magician Sect but is primarily filled with members of the Astronomical and the Zoroastrian sects of the Magi. "It is my pleasure to present to everyone, Headmaster of the Astronomical Sect of the Magi, Daraya-Vous!"

Mihri stands to the side and nods slightly as the rest of the room, save for his comrades, erupts in thunderous applause, welcoming the new ruler as the head counsel of the Magi Order. Once the applause dies down, Grand Master Artapan turns to the table behind him and retrieves the canister that holds the sacred star charts and says, "Headmaster Daraya-Vous and Mihri, representative of Headmaster Dvandas, please present yourselves."

Mihri rushes to place himself as close as he can to the charts in the grand master's hands. His eyes greedily devour them as his hands itch to grab the canister. It is all he can do to keep himself from yanking it out of the grand master's hands. Headmaster Daraya-Vous gently turns to face Artapan and wait for the decision regarding who will receive the charts.

Artapan looks out over the crowd and then to the two before him. "These sacred charts were made under the care of Belteshazzar, Grand Master of the Magi Order, six centuries ago. It was his instruction that there should always be a body within our order that devoted themselves to deepening our understanding of the Creator's written declarations in the ancient meanings of the stars. The Astronomical Sect of the Magi founded by him is that group. When the charts were completed, he entrusted these charts to them." He then focuses on Mihri and says, "Please inform Headmaster Dvandas that his petition is denied." Then he smiles and looks out and continues. "It is to the Astronomical Sect of the Magi that we entrust these sacred charts, under the supervision and stewardship of Headmaster Daraya-Vous." Artapan then reaches out and places the canister in Daraya-Vous's hands.

Mihri finds it hard to keep from trembling with rage as this travesty transpires before his eyes. He glares over in Daraya-Vous's direction, then looks back at Grand Master Artapan and says, "Those charts are foremost the property of the Parthian Empire and, therefore, it is the emperor himself who has the final say about who should steward them. I will take my leave to inform Headmaster Dvandas of your decision. I am sure he will want to speak to the emperor about it." He then turns and walks out of the room.

Grand Master Artapan's reply is loud enough for everyone to hear, "I dispatched a messenger to the capital with letters detailing my acknowledgment of Daraya-Vous as headmaster and entrusting him with the star charts the moment the emperor's emissary arrived four days ago. They are traveling light and fast and should be there in two months. At best speed, you will be back one week after my message reaches the emperor. Goodbye, Mihri!"

The impact of the Grand Master's words slams into Mihri's ears, and he cringes as he approaches the exit to the Temple. Pride and arrogance do not allow him to show how daunted he is by their meaning, and he quickly leaves. Standing outside the entrance are Rassan and Commander Sasheen. Both are eager to hear what has transpired within. Mihri stops and looks at the commander with a sneer. "As expected, Artapan has awarded the charts to the care of Daraya-Vous. I also learned that a dispatch was sent to the capital with this news the day you arrived, Commander. Seeing that Master Dvandas used his influence to gain you this post as second-in-command of the city's garrison, I wonder why you did not tell me of this right away? Unlike your friend here"—he waves his hand at Rassan—"you are apprenticed to our order for your postacademy studies. Your loyalties in matters of religion should be with us."

Commander Sasheen swallows nervously. "I only learned of the dispatch this morning, Mihri. You were already in your private meeting with the Magi Council. My superior, General Barach, has had me looking into taking control of my responsibilities to prepare for succeeding him. A roster of dispatches to different parts of the empire, including the capital, was only given to me this morning to review. As soon as I saw the record of a dispatch to the capital by Grand Master Artapan, I rushed over here to tell you."

Mihri glares at Commander Sasheen for a few moments, thinking to rebuke his carelessness, but remembers Rassan, and then a delicious idea enters his mind. He smiles and turns to the boy, who has been silent through this whole discourse. "Tell me, Rassan, have you begun your apprenticeship under Daraya-Vous yet?"

Rassan gulps, glances briefly at his friend, Commander Sasheen, then turns back to Mihri. "No, he told me that my apprenticeship would begin after he was officially recognized as the headmaster of the Astronomical Sect. So, I guess that I will start today."

Mihri steps closer to the young officer, his demeanor changing from that of a bitter rival to a concerned and eager mentor. "I believe that you still have not weighed all your options in the furtherance of your education. The opportunity for you to study under the Magician Sect of the Magi is still available to you right here in the city of Babylon. Your commission from the emperor was to report to Daraya-Vous with the star charts and place them in his hands, which you have achieved splendidly to the satisfaction of the entire Magi Order. Though you are committed to study with that sect, there is nothing hindering you from seeking other avenues of learning in your free time."

He turns and places a hand on Commander Sasheen's shoulder. "I have already introduced your superior here to those of the Magician Sect here in Babylon and would do the same for you. A broader spectrum of understanding of the mystical signs in the zodiac and their personal impact on your own life could only be both profitable and fascinating to an astute student."

Before he can answer, the door opens behind them and Headmaster Daraya-Vous steps out and waves to Rassan. "It is time, Rassan. Grand Master Artapan would like to meet you and acknowledge the emperor's commissioning of your apprenticeship under my supervision."

Rassan acknowledges the summons and looks back at Mihri. "Thank you for the offer, sir." Then he turns and rushes to the door. Daraya-Vous stands aside and lets him through.

Mihri glares at the entrance for a moment, then locks eyes with Commander Sasheen. "We must have that boy under our control. Entice him to learn from the Magician Sect, perhaps by showing him the great delights and pleasures we offer a young man like him. Try to find out everything he learns from those charts. If we cannot own them, perhaps through his eyes we can at least gain more insight into their secrets."

Back inside Grand Master Artapan's halls, Rassan smiles at Daraya-Vous, drawn to his fatherly demeanor and gentle nature.

"What did Mihri talk to you and the commander about just now?" Daraya-Vous asks him.

"He wants me to consider studying with the Magician Sect of the Magi in my spare time while here in Babylon. Before I left the capital, Prince Phraates V said that Headmaster Dvandas wanted me to do an internship with him." He looks down and shakes his head. "Before giving his life in service to the emperor, my father forbade me to have anything to do with the Magician Sect of the Magi. I don't think I will take any of their offers."

Daraya-Vous puts his hand on Rassan's shoulder. "Though I doubt you would have the energy to pursue any other curriculum while here, if you keep up with your obligations to us, you are free to seek any other learning you like. We have found that only the students who freely choose to dedicate themselves to our disciplines without compulsion may truly excel in our form of study. Now come, the grand master is waiting."

Rassan bows his head and smiles as he acknowledges Master Daraya-Vous's words. A thought crosses his mind. "Master, I moved my things into the room you designated for me at the Temple and there is not enough room for my servant, Arsam. Where will he stay?"

"Rassan, Magi apprentices may not have servants. But I had someone speak with Arsam yesterday and he has agreed to be part of my staff at the Temple. He will stay with the other children at the Magi orphanage and earn his keep by taking care of the Temple with the other servants. I am told by some of the other Magi who have spoken with him that they are impressed by how much he learned from the star charts with you on your trip. But, at present, he is too young to be a Magi apprentice. Perhaps in a few years, if his interests and aptitudes continue, I would be glad to accept him as thus."

A deep well of gratitude fill Rassan's heart at hearing these words. "That would be a marvelous thing, Headmaster. I think you will be quite pleased with this arrangement."

Master Daraya-Vous puts a hand on Rassan's shoulder and motions him to the main cathedral entrance. "I agree. Now come, the grand master has waited long enough."

5

Apprenticeship

Three Days Later, Sunrise in the Main Hall of the Magi Astronomical Temple

Arsam stands before the tapestry that depicts Leo in the observation hall. He was told to meet the master of the Temple cleaning crew here one hour after dawn, but he wanted to come early to see this great wonder he had heard about from his early childhood. Tales of the three-story-high tapestries depicting the twelve signs of the zodiac at the Astronomical Temple in Babylon were told all over the empire. He cannot help but go to the one that depicts the same constellation that he and Rassan studied so many times on their three-month journey from the capital. He points to the top left side of the constellation where the star Denebola is represented at the tip of the lion's tail and traces it forward until his finger is pointing toward the star Regulus at the right shoulder. "There it is!"

"There what is, might I ask?"

Startled, Arsam turns and is greeted by the kind smile and twin-kling eyes of Master Daraya-Vous, who is looking back and forth between Arsam and the tapestry. Arsam sucks air between his teeth to calm his racing heart. Though he has seen the headmaster of the Temple from afar, this is the first time that he has met him. "Uh, the star Regulus, Master Daraya-Vous."

Daraya-Vous steps beside Arsam and points to the star. "Why is that one of such interest to you, young man?"

"Forgive me, Headmaster, my name is…"

"I know who you are, Arsam. Now tell me. What is so important to you about Regulus?"

Arsam becomes even more nervous because now he feels that what he is about to reveal will get him and Rassan in trouble with the headmaster. But he has no choice. "I am sorry, Headmaster, but my master Rassan and I spent our evenings studying the charts in that canister." He points to the canister that is now fastened with a rope at both ends and hangs from the shoulder of Master Daraya-Vous. "Rassan showed me the notation by the great Hebrew prophet Daniel, known to us as Belteshazzar, just under the star Regulus in those charts. It said, *'The Lion of the Tribe of Judah depicts the Messiah as the King of Kings. He will inherit the throne of his father, David, and his kingdom will never end. Noted by Belteshazzar, Master of the Magi.*"

An intense flutter goes through Daraya-Vous's stomach as the boy flawlessly recites the notation. Over the decades, Headmaster Vinda-Farnah and he had seen that notation many times, but since Rassan has returned and shared with him the last words of his friend and mentor about what the angel told him, he has renewed his interest in the constellation and the chart. He laughs and pats the boy on the back. "Don't be concerned. Neither Rassan nor you did anything wrong. Master Vinda-Farnah himself entrusted these sacred charts to Rassan's keeping, and he proved quite faithful in that task." He then points to the star Regulus on the tapestry. "That star has a meaning of royalty to it. It is one that holds great truths concerning the coming reign of the Creator's champion, who will someday take the place of the bright and morning star and rule the universe forever."

Arsam looks up with wonder in his eyes at Regulus's representation on the tapestry and in a barely audible voice mouths, "King of Kings!"

Headmaster Daraya-Vous smiles at the boy. "I pass through here every morning after having concluded my shift of a night study of the stars. If you care to be here before your work begins, I would enjoy continuing these little chats."

"That would be fantastic, Headmaster! I will be here whenever I am allowed."

Two Hours Later, Main Lecture Hall, Magi Temple

All eyes in the room look up to see Headmaster Daraya-Vous walk into the hall where Rassan and four others are awaiting their first official meeting with him. Rassan finds it hard to breathe as he anticipates beginning this path that Master Vinda-Farnah set him on over three months ago. Though convinced that this is the path that the Creator has called him to, there is also the nagging concern that he will somehow not measure up.

When he was shown his quarters a few days ago, he also met the others he now sits with, and he got to know a little of their backgrounds. The tall, slender boy seated next to him is Rita-Raina and comes from the city of Babylon. His name means protector of truth. The one next to him is Hymayeak, which means gifted with good faculties, and he is from Persia. Seated directly behind him is his cousin, and he also comes from Persia. His name is Whama, and that means turning his mind to good. Behind Rassan is Kaufa, and he is from the far western part of the empire, a province called Abia Bein, and his name simply means born in the mountain.

The first three come from Magi families that have for generations had members come to dedicate themselves to the study of the signs of the zodiac under the Astronomical Sect of the Magi. The last one, Kaufa, comes from a military family like Rassan's, but he found that the calling of his heart was to study the Creator's message in the stars. And, like Rassan, he journeyed to Babylon to make that a reality. Kaufa was in Rassan's caravan and journeyed with them as one of Commander Sasheen's soldiers, though Rassan rarely saw him because his unit was part of the rear guard and journeyed behind the main caravan.

Because three of the five in the group were basically raised to be Magi, and he and Kaufa were not, he found himself drawn to the boy and wanted to be friends. But Kaufa only engaged in brief conversations with Rassan over the last couple of days and would not say much about his background.

Rassan looks around at the others and feels a nagging sense of inferiority. Three of them have spent their lives preparing for this day, and he only decided on this path less than half a year ago. He is not used to feeling any sense of inferiority in academics. While at the military academy in the capital, he was always the head of his class and many times more advanced in his studies than his senior classmen. But by the time most showed up to be trained as officers in the emperor's army, they had little interest in study outside of military matters. Rassan loved to read as a child and his father encouraged it, saying that a good military leader must be well versed in all aspects of life and culture to understand for what and why he is fighting. But, save for Kaufa, the boys he is seated with are basically intellectuals of the most elite families of that cultural caste, and only for extraordinary reasons does he find himself numbered among them. Now the five of them sit in the lecture hall, waiting for the headmaster to begin his talk.

Master Daraya-Vous clears his throat and points to the rear of the room to an engraving on a wall that is illuminated by torches on either side. The engraving is comprised of a large circle with depictions of constellations all around and in it so that the line of the circle goes through each. In each constellation, there are pictures drawn that represent the name of that constellation. "Who can tell me what this is?"

Before anyone raises a hand to answer, Rassan blurts out, "That is the planisphere of the twelve signs of the zodiac that we see from our world in one year's time."

"Very good, Rassan. Why does it take one full year to see these constellations?"

"Because the message from the Creator is vast, and it takes that long for all of those signs to appear in our sky."

Master Daraya-Vous smiles and nods his head. "Good. Now, someone else, please tell me in what constellation of the zodiac does the Creator's message begin, and then in which one does it end?"

Hymayeak raises his hand and Daraya-Vous acknowledges him with a nod. "There has been much speculation over that point throughout the years, Headmaster. But the consensus throughout the empire is that since the zodiac is a circle, there is no beginning and no end. That each of the constellations is equal in importance."

"So, Hymayeak, are you saying that if something comes first, it is the most important, and that which is last is the least?"

"No, Headmaster, but the circle has long represented the meaning of reality and the truth behind eternity. That it has no beginning and no ending is its mystical and mysterious representation of time."

Daraya-Vous sighs as he recalls that Hymayeak comes from a family that is heavily influenced by the Magician Sect of the Magi. He was surprised to see that a representative of them opted to study with the astronomers and now realizes that there is a lot of work ahead for him and the new apprentice in helping him see the true meaning of the Creator's message in the stars. "Hymayeak, you are going to find that our sect of the Magi is more scientific in our approach to studying the heavens. We don't look at them for the infinite possibilities they hold in predicting the future or in describing the nature of any one human, but for the meanings the Creator had the ancients ascribe to them, considering His plan to rescue man back from the evil that now rules this world. When you find the time in your studies, I suggest you look into the studies we have on the Egyptian monument in Giza by the Nile River, known as the Sphinx. It is in that study that you will find the answer to my question."

Before Hymayeak can answer, Kaufa interjects. "In the first part of the first book written by the Hebrew prophet Moses, it says one purpose is that the stars were set in the heavens to mark the great one who is to come."[8]

As all the young men in the room turn to look at Kaufa, a gleefully astonished look manifests itself on Master Daraya-Vous's face. "I was not aware that you have knowledge of the Hebrew Scriptures, Kaufa. They are forbidden in the empire except in designated Jewish settlements where there is a sanctioned synagogue."

Without expression or emotion, Kaufa answers. "My mother is from a Jewish settlement near the border of Armenia. Her father is a rabbi of such a synagogue. She married my father when he was in the Parthian army. Because he was away so much, she was allowed to stay in her ancestral village with my grandparents. During those times, I went through some of the training that Jewish boys did. But because I was of mixed blood, I could not attend the formal school, so my grandfather conducted my education personally."

Daraya-Vous rubs his hands together in an enthusiastic gesture. "Wonderful. That is precious information to have, Kaufa. Grand Master Artapan gave myself and Headmaster Vinda-Farnah leave to travel to the nearest Jewish settlement and ask questions of the local rabbis concerning the prophecies of their Messiah, seeking enlightenment on how it relates to our search in the heavens concerning the Creator's coming champion. But it has been some time since we had someone here who is trained and knowledgeable in the Hebrew scrolls. This will prove quite enlightening, Kaufa. I am pleased to know this about you."

For the first time since meeting him, Rassan can see that Kaufa seems a bit rattled and self-conscious because of the headmaster's words. He makes a mental note to speak with him after the orientation is over to see if he can help him.

Headmaster Daraya-Vous continues. "Well, let's proceed. We of the Astronomical Sect of the Magi were founded by the first Grand Master of the Magi, Belteshazzar, almost six centuries ago. Since that time, we have dedicated ourselves to seeing the Creator's plan that is revealed in the twelve signs of the zodiac. Though not a popular notion today, Belteshazzar was of Jewish descent and was very knowledgeable of their sacred scrolls. He even contributed to them, and his writings, along with the rest of the scrolls, are read in Jewish synagogues around the world. So, you can understand my excitement at the revelation of Kaufa's education in those scrolls. It was Belteshazzar who showed the Magi back then that the Hebrew prophecies of a coming Messiah parallel that of the promise in the stars of the Creator's champion who will someday free all mankind from evil."

Daraya-Vous reaches under the table near him and pulls out a single piece of parchment that has recently been written on. He holds it up for all to see. "Who can tell me what this is?"

Rassan's hand goes up immediately and Daraya-Vous nods in his direction. Rassan then says, "That is a sketch of last night's stars in the southern hemisphere."

"How can you tell, Rassan?"

Rassan stands up and walks to where the headmaster is holding the sketch and points to the lower left. "For starters, that is the very tip of the constellation Pisces Australis, which has something to do with the southern fish receiving the waters of blessing from the urn bearer in the constellation of Aquarius." Then he traces his finger to the right and comes to a depiction of a brighter star. "This is Antares, which is the tip of the head of the scorpion that is endeavoring to sting the foot of the Creator's champion as he wrestles with the serpent trying to steal his crown. These were all visible last night."

The headmaster can barely hide his astonishment at Rassan's already emerging prowess in identifying constellations and remembering their meanings. The rest of the boys in the room are simply shocked to the core. Once they'd found out that Rassan and Kaufa were from military families, they wrote them off as those who might stay at the Temple for a year. But first seeing the headmaster's reaction to the revelation of Kaufa's knowledge of the Jewish scrolls and now Rassan's understanding of the constellations has them a bit shook.

Daraya-Vous sees the developing situation and decides to relieve some of their anxieties. He smiles at Rassan and points to his seat, gesturing for him to take it, then he looks over the group. "You all are aware that Headmaster Vinda-Farnah was killed by bandits while caravanning to Jerusalem for Magi business. Rassan's regiment was dispatched from the capital to find and aid him, but when they arrived, it was too late. Upon finding the headmaster, he charged Rassan with his dying breath to return the sacred star charts to my hands as quickly as possible. To do that, Rassan had to petition the emperor himself for leave, and then make the journey to Babylon to return the charts to our order. In granting that petition, Emperor Phraates IV not only commissioned Rassan to be his personal emissary and hand-deliver the charts, but to also stay in Babylon after doing so and be put under my charge as a Magi apprentice."

He reaches down and grabs the canister containing the charts that hangs under his right arm and holds it up. "So, for three months, Rassan enjoyed a privilege that even a headmaster rarely gets. Every night of his journey, he would study the star charts that were originally drawn by Belteshazzar himself and compare them to the constellations in the heavens."

Sounds of astonishment and grunts of dissatisfaction are voiced by some apprentices, but Daraya-Vous raises waves a finger dismissively. "Remember, this privilege was granted to him by the emperor himself. According to the very protocols of the royal decree, only Rassan had authority over the charts until they were returned to us. So, he did nothing wrong."

He holds up the sketch again and points to it. "Now, back to the briefing. Every night when the elliptical is at its highest, four groups of Magi take positions on the roof of the Temple and study the constellations that present themselves, each group taking one quadrant of the sky. We break them down into the North, South, East, and West. Each group is to make a sketch of their quadrant as it appears that night and follow the stars' courses until dawn. When our shift is done, they hand the sketches to me, and I bring them to the observation area of the Temple, where I give them to your instructors. The first- and second-year apprentices will then be shown those sketches as their lessons for the day. Behind the Tapestry Observatory is a library that contains the total knowledge of what our order has accumulated over the last centuries concerning the meaning behind the names attributed to each constellation in the twelve zodiac signs.

"After a brief lecture on the night's sketches from one of your instructors, you will then proceed to that library where you will learn everything you can about the meaning behind the constellations depicted in the four sketches. You will also have time to study and compare the sketches to the tapestries in the observatory. This acclimates you to your eventual graduation into the night watch, where you will someday join the rest of us in observing the stars every night. As Rassan pointed out earlier, it takes an entire year for the full spectrum of the zodiac to appear in our sky. This shows the Creator's wisdom in allowing all of us time to study His message and be accurate in our findings. Thus, our curriculum is divinely set, and that is how a Magi of the Astronomical Sect is trained."

Rita-Raina, who has been mostly silent, raises his hand and Daraya-Vous motions for him to speak. "Headmaster, since one of our peers has had the unfair advantage of studying what can only be described as this sect of the Magi's most precious treasure for an unprecedented three months, will it be available for the rest of us to look at them from time to time?"

Daraya-Vous is not shocked by the young man's request. Rita-Raina is the son of one who had held great promise in the Astronomical Sect of the Magi long ago but left to pursue studies with the Magician Sect at the capital. The boy was left here in Babylon to be raised by his mother. Though his father has visited him on rare occasions outside of his father's current rank at the capital and his family legacy as Magi, the son hardly knows him. He solemnly sighs. "Rita-Raina, you come from one of the oldest families in the Magi Order. I know that your education to this point has been the very finest in the empire; and because of your father's status in the capital, you have been afforded many privileges and given access to many treasures of knowledge from all sects of the Magi. But, to answer your question, no, you will not be given access to the sacred charts unless I am using them to instruct you and your fellow acolytes."

Rita-Raina's eyes take on a cold hue. He turns to Rassan and fixes his gaze upon him. "Interesting that you brought up my supposed privilege because of my father, Headmaster. It might be advantageous for all to be aware of Rassan's family and the privileges he enjoys because of his father."

Astonishment crosses Rassan's face. "You know of my father?"

"Who doesn't know about the famous General Surena, who defeated the Roman General Marcus Licinius Crassus at Carrhae? You, being his only child and heir, are you not in the first hundred of royal succession to the Parthian throne?"

Astonished and confused, Rassan sits numbly, unable to respond.

Daraya-Vous's voice takes on a harsh tone. "Rita-Raina, you entice an interesting political discussion. On the one hand, we have the son of a national Parthian hero and a member of the royal family. On the other, we have the son of one of the three highest-ranking members in the Magi Order and the personal court counselor to Emperor Phraates IV. Now, if this were the Magician Sect of the Magi, these would be important considerations in how either of you would be treated. But this is the Astronomical Sect of the Magi, and we care nothing for these matters in the inner workings of our order. I believe that is the very reason your father left us while still apprenticing here and went on to the Magician Sect. Yet you have apprenticed with us. If you find our mind in these matters unacceptable, I suggest you renounce your apprenticeship here and seek education elsewhere."

Daraya-Vous holds up the sketches and hands them to another Magi that has been off to the side. "Please follow Master Artesan into the Tapestry Observatory and he will begin your first lessons. Oh, and Rita-Raina, if you have anything you would like to discuss with me, please make an appointment with my aides on your free time. Thank you!"

He smiles at all the new apprentices and leaves the room.

Rassan sits in his chair while the apprentices and Magi instructors file out. He can't help but feel that what was said in this meeting is going to haunt him throughout his time here. He stands, ready to follow the others, when he feels a hand on his shoulder and turns to see Kaufa with a curious look on his face. "My grandfather served under your father against the Romans at Carrhae. You are no older than I am. He must have been ancient when you were born."

Rassan shrugs. "My mother was his second wife. His first died childless a few years after he wed her. He was sixty-five years old when I was born. My mother was very young, having been given to him by the emperor when she was of marriageable age. He died when I was sixteen, just two years after I entered the academy in the capital. My mother died of a sickness shortly after my father died."

Kaufa shakes his head. "When I heard you were said to be the son of General Surena coming here to study at the Astronomical Sect of the Magi, I thought it was a joke. The few times I saw you in the caravan, I almost thought you were an imposter or simply adopted into Surena's family. But after hearing what the headmaster just said, I have decided that you are simply out of your mind. No one of your stature comes here!"

Rassan grabs his things, laughs, shrugs, and points to the door. "We should hurry." While walking together through the door, he says, "You know, before I met Headmaster Vinda-Farnah, I would have totally agreed with you. But what he said to me and the blessing he put on me opened my eyes and changed me somehow. There is no other path that my heart sees for me to take."

Kaufa looks at him intensely, examining his eyes for falsehood or pretense. He then relaxes and says, "I believe you."

Fifteen minutes later, the group finds itself in the center of the Tapestry Observatory, seated on the floor in a semicircle around Magi Artesan as he points to one of the four sketches of last night's stars and continues his instruction. "As you can see from these sketches, the most notable of the constellations that are visible in this section are Ophiuchus, Serpens, and Scorpio. If you will look to the tapestry where these constellations are depicted with the ancient symbolisms drawn into the constellations, you will take note that the champion is wrestling with the serpent to prevent him from keeping the crown of rulership depicted by the star configuration Corona Borealis, while at the same time he is in danger of being stung in the foot by Scorpio. Now, this depiction in the zodiac carries a great deal of meaning and truth that we can glean to enlighten us to the heavenly struggles that go on for the control of creation. It would appear that the champion is about to be ambushed blindly as he struggles, but look to your right. Can anyone tell me what is counterbalancing this attack?"

Rassan raises his hand. "That is the constellation Sagittarius, and his bow is trained on the scorpion. The arrow is aimed directly at the stinger of the scorpion, which will make its attack on the champion null and void."

"That is quite perceptive, Rassan. The enemy will always attack from several vantage points, but the Creator will also have multiple counterattacks in place to aid His champion when needed."

"Let's not forget that Rassan is the son of General Surena, who defeated a Roman army four times the size of his own forces by using the bow and killing the enemy from afar," Rita-Raina blurts out. "His military mind would naturally notice anything that would bring attention to the weapon that brought his father such notoriety!"

Everyone laughs. Rassan's cheeks flush at the jab and he finds himself once again without words to rebuff the rudeness of his fellow apprentice.

Magi Artesan glares at Rita-Raina. "I will tolerate no childish mocking in my instruction time, Magi Apprentice Rita-Raina. We are here to study the Creator's messages in the heavens, not to partake of senseless boyish rivalries and useless criticisms. Rassan was correct in his analysis of the constellations and their relative meanings. Nothing else matters."

Rita-Raina nods his heads. "Forgive me, Magi Artesan. It will not happen again." Then he slyly gazes at Rassan and mouths, "You don't belong here."

The lecture continues for another half hour as Magi Artesan goes over the other sketches and the constellations depicted in them, then takes the apprentices to the library behind the Tapestry Observatory and teaches them how the scrolls, books, and charts there are organized. When he is done, the apprentices are left with the Magi who takes care of the library, where they are given access to any resource they feel is helpful in the study of the sketches. Rassan and Kaufa choose to pair up, and so do Hymayeak and Whama. Rita-Raina pursues his studies alone.

6

Allies From Afar

October 15, 6 BC, Three Months Later, Royal Court of Emperor Phraates IV

Having done the entire trip to Babylon on horseback at a much faster pace than Rassan's caravan, Mihri stands in front of the royal throne of the Parthian Empire only three months later. He faces the emperor, his son, and Headmaster Dvandas as he makes his report concerning his recent trip to Babylon. Dvandas spent the previous evening going over every detail with him about what transpired in Babylon and the decision about the star charts by Grand Master Artapan. He was furious when the grand master's messenger showed up two weeks prior and informed the emperor of Grand Master Artapan's decision, and then received his blessing to take back to the grand master. He was sure that if Mihri would have made it back first, he would have been able to persuade the emperor to consider granting him steward-ship of the charts. But as it stands now, the charts will remain with the Astronomical Sect until the death of Headmaster Daraya-Vous, at which time they will once again be eligible for another party to steward them for the empire.

Mihri considers the fact that his master has little use for the charts as a source of knowledge, but he seeks to suppress their influence from spreading any farther than they have. Especially since the charts were the original work of an Israeli slave who lived six hundred years ago, and who was bent on propounding the foolish doctrine of a Messiah coming from that insignificant and annoying little nation. He knows Dvandas has done everything in his power to keep this tale of a promised king who will rise out of Israel and rule all nations someday from taking any root in and gaining any curiosity in the court of Phraates IV. Mihri thinks Dvandas is too narrow-visioned about the value of the charts to the Magician Sect of the Magi, and, therefore he did not inform his master of his instruction to Commander Sasheen to get any information he could from Rassan about those charts.

When Phraates IV dismisses him, he moves to the side to leave the inner court. As he passes through the door of the inner court, he hears the introduction of the Nabataean ambassador, who has come to discuss state business with the emperor and his son. A crooked smile crosses Mihri's face. Next to the Astronomical Sect of the Magi, there is no other influential power in the East that his master is leerier of than the Nabataeans. Once made up of the disjointed and often warring tribes of Arabia, in the last century they have somehow banded together to form a most impressive network involving the trade and distribution of precious commodities like myrrh, gold, and frankincense. They have yet to distinguish themselves as a military force to be reckoned with, but that hardly matters. Their unique and lucrative trade abilities afford them access to and gratitude from the Parthian and Roman Empires.

This would hardly worry Master Dvandas, but the heads of the tribes that now rule the Nabataeans claim a lineage back to Esau, the brother of the Israelite's patriarch, Jacob. King Herod of Israel is the son of the princess Cypros from that patriarchy. Though the Nabataeans claim to be a polytheistic culture and have patronages to many gods and goddesses, there is a growing sect in their ranks that propounds a very similar doctrine to the Judeans of Israel, the Zoroastrians, and the Astronomical Sect in the Parthian Empire. Thus, this sect had adopted the label of Magi and has had some written communication with the Astronomical Sect in Babylon. Also, their affinity for and support of Israel have proven to be of notable concern to one such as Mihri's master, considering Herod the Great's family ties with their own monarch and their developing religious views.

The thought of trying to stay and aid Master Dvandas in the next moments as the Nabataean ambassador makes his petition briefly crosses Mihri's mind, but seeing the prince standing next to his father on the throne quickly banishes that thought. Unlike his master, he has no stomach for making Phraates V an enemy.

The Nabataean ambassador is a man of middle age and medium height. His beard is full and black but showing highlights of gray at the edges. He has dark brown eyes that illustrate his robust and jovial nature. As he makes his way to the Parthian throne, his steps are light and vigorous, exemplifying a man who is always on the move and has important business to attend to but finds great joy in doing so.

In a rare gesture of respect, Phraates IV stands and waves his hand in welcoming the ambassador to his throne. "Ambassador Samekh, it is good to see you, my friend. I trust your liege, our friend and ally Aretas IV Philopatris, is well and truly prospering in his domain?"

A smile crosses the man's face as he bows and throws a similar gesture with his hand. "He is, Your Grace, and he also sends his greetings to you and your son."

Phraates IV looks to his son, and nods for him to answer. Phraates V steps forward and says, "It is always good to see you, Samekh! We received the latest shipment of gold for our minting smiths two weeks ago, and the first of the new coin with my father's image has already been delivered to the palace. The smiths tell me that the Nabataean gold is always the finest they work with. Please tell your king that there will be many more orders for it soon."

"This is splendid news, Prince Phraates. My liege will be very pleased when I tell him your words. Our trading services are always open to the great Parthian Empire, and we look forward to much more profitable and mutual commerce with you."

"I am told that a shipment twice the size of what we ordered of your gold was sent by Carthage merchant ships to Rome just three weeks ago. Care to explain this sign of your sovereign's apparent proclivities, Ambassador Samekh?"

The emperor and his son turn their eyes to Master Dvandas as the man steps forward.

Prince Phraates bolts out of his seat, barely suppressing his anger at the Magi. He points his hand at him. "Dvandas, neither I nor my father asked for your opinion or counsel to be shared, you—"

Ambassador Samekh chuckles and waves his hand nonchalantly at the prince. "It is a valid question, Your Grace. Two-thirds of the gold we sent to Rome was in payment for their extraordinarily expensive levies and taxes that they impose on us when using their roads and shipping lanes. A burden that we are always extremely grateful is not laid upon us by our Parthian brothers. Your dealings with us are always considerably less expensive than those incurred from Rome."

Phraates IV stares back at Master Dvandas. "My son was correct," he replies in a cold voice. "No one, not even you, may speak in this court without having my or my son's leave to do so. You will remain silent and let us continue our dealings with the ambassador uninterrupted!"

Dvandas nods in silence and steps back to his place against the wall behind the emperor, grinding his teeth in frustration.

The emperor then turns back to Ambassador Samekh. "Forgive the tenacity of my counselor, Ambassador. He only has our best interest at heart, but his zealousness in doing so can prove irritating. So, what is the nature of the Nabataean ambassador's petition to the Parthian throne this day?"

Samekh brushes off Dvandas's interruption with a dismissive wave. "No offense taken, Your Grace. Ours is a small petition to bring to you. As you already know, I am the head of the Magi Order in the Nabataean court. It has been made plain to us in the last few decades that our religious pursuits coincide with those of the Astronomical Sect of the Magi Order in your court. We have had some rather lengthy and robust correspondence with them over the years and would like to enhance that relationship by sending a delegation of our Magi to Babylon, led by me. We would like to meet with the new headmaster of the Astronomical Sect, Magi Master Daraya-Vous. This would give us the opportunity to compare our findings and learn from each other."

As the ambassador finishes his petition, Phraates V cannot help but lean back in his seat and notice how the petition has caused Dvandas's countenance to contort and disfigure in the most delightful way. He stands and moves closer to the ambassador with a huge grin and declares, "What an excellent idea, and the timing could not be more perfect. Master Dvandas's assistant, Mihri, was here before you giving his report to the emperor that he was just in Babylon and could give Master Dvandas's blessing and acknowledgement to Daraya-Vous's installment as headmaster of the Astronomical Sect. My father, having already received a dispatch from Grand Master Artapan a few weeks ago, had sent his blessings and acknowledgement of this installation. So, this would be a grand opportunity for us to show our gratitude to the Nabataeans and all their benefits of a commercial partnership with this throne."

He then turns to his father and smiles brightly at him and Master Dvandas, who, though still silent, is so enraged that he looks to explode. "Father, I suggest that we not only grant this petition of safe conduct to Babylon for Ambassador Samekh and his companions, but that we provide a detachment of our own royal cavalry as protection for them."

Dvandas steps up and touches the emperor's hand. "Your Grace, perhaps we should take some time—"

"I told you to remain silent, Dvandas! Speak again and I will have you removed from this court." The emperor throws off Dvandas's hand and motions him back against the wall. Then he turns his eyes on Ambassador Samekh. "Your petition is granted. My son will work out the logistics with you, and he has our permission to assign a full regiment of cavalry to escort you to Babylon and back." He then stands. "I will take my leave. Dvandas!"

"Yes, Your Grace?"

"Come to my private office in two hours. We need to discuss your role as counselor, and what you may and may not do in my court."

"Yes, Your Grace, I will be there." Dvandas bows deeply, moves to the side exit, and leaves the court.

7

Seeds of Treason

One Hour Later, Dvandas's Private Study

As Mihri steps toward the entrance of his master's private study, he sees the silhouette of a veiled woman, who he believes is Queen Musa, slip out the door and dash down the hall in the opposite direction he just came from.

"You wished to see me, Master?"

Dvandas looks up from his desk and sees Mihri standing in the doorway to his study and waves him in. "Yes, Mihri, come in. We have little time to talk because the emperor is expecting me in one hour, but I want to discuss a delicate matter with you."

"Of course, Master. What is it?"

Dvandas raises his head from the papers he has been working on. Dvandas's hawkish dark eyes bore into Mihri's for a moment, and then he says, "It is time for the line of Phraates to cease once and for all."

Mihri's eyes dart back and forth, scanning the area for unwanted ears, then he moves in closer to the headmaster. "Master, such words if heard by anyone but me could spell instant death to us all."

"Don't think me such a fool, Mihri. I had all the Magician Magi sections of the palace evacuated before you came. They are all outside preparing for the stargazing and soothsaying ceremony tonight in the main courtyard. It is just you and me here now."

Having entered Dvandas's study from a secret entrance known only to him and the headmaster, Mihri was not aware that the area was vacated. He straightens his posture and takes a deep breath. "This is because of the Nabataean ambassador's request. You never wanted his faction of the Astronomical Sect of Magi to have close ties with their counterparts in Babylon. The emperor's granting of Samekh's petition ruins that and gives their collaborations royal sanction."

Dvandas shakes his head in frustration and pounds both fists on his desk. "It is one thing to deal with the constant demoralizing and circumventing of my influence by that little half-breed son of the emperor's. But now I have to deal with the Nabataean Astronomical Sect of Magi developing close ties with Daraya-Vous and his lot in Babylon! We know that the wealth the Nabataeans bring to the empire, plus their equally lucrative connection to the Romans, will do nothing but cause Phraates IV to give more and more credence to the Astronomical Sect, which will spell the demise of our own."

Mihri knows that when the headmaster gets this enraged, he can do little but agree and try to give a word of wisdom on how to solve the problem. "Master, what is done in court is not easily overturned. The assassination of an emperor and his son is one way for sure, but also the most dangerous. At one time, the whole of the Magi Order had the authority to remove one emperor and set up another, but that is a day that no longer exists. We simply do not have the powerful families we once did. True power in the East has rested with those who control the religious beliefs of its people. But when the Greeks conquered our lands, that system was diminished. Now, with the Romans ruling half the world, we contend more with ideas of racial purity and cultural cleansing. The way of Persia and Babylon is more and more a forgotten ideal. Somehow, we must—"

"Use it to our advantage, Mihri!"

Startled, Mihri looks up to see a devious gleam in his master's eyes. "What do you mean, Master?"

Dvandas rubs both hands together and exclaims, "This is why you are my second, Mihri! The broadness of your perceptions always aids me to see deeper into the actual solution that the gods are revealing to me. Don't you see it? It isn't a war between us and the Astronomical Sect that we want to propagate. No, we want to start a cultural revolution that will purge the Parthian Empire of any outside influence and return us to the ways of our ancestors." He then raises both hands. "Which would mean that no boy whose mother was a Roman slave gifted to our Phraates IV by Octavian of Rome for mere pleasure should sit on the Parthian throne!"

Mihri raises his hands in a cautioning fashion. "Please, Master, you do not want to be heard."

Dvandas's eyes dart from side to side. "There are many in the empire who, though reluctant to speak these things, believe them furiously. Some are powerful families. We must reach out to them and promise them our support and counsel should they decide to act, which we will move them to do when the time is right."

Mihri puts his hand to his chin, considering his master's words. He raises his right index finger and waves it back and forth. "Half of the royal garrison is loyal to the Magician Sect of the Magi Order. Our outreach efforts of inviting and including them in our more erotic pleasure ceremonies have proved quite fruitful. We will need the military's support when your plan comes to fruition. I suggest we double our outreach efforts with that class."

"An excellent idea. By the way, do you believe that our newly promoted Commander Sasheen in Babylon will recruit that boy Rassan to our sect?"

"That remains to be seen, Master. There is a slight chance, but remember, he is the son of General Surena, and you know what the general thought about our sect."

"Yes, that arrogant ass's legacy still lives strong in the empire. All the more reason to win his son over to our side. His family will have a strong say in anything that has to do with the emperor. We must be circumspect."

Private Study of Emperor Phraates IV

The emperor is not as angry with Master Dvandas as he let on in the royal court. But to see that his son and the Nabataean ambassador, Samekh, were shown proper respect, he felt that a slight public humiliation was in order. Phraates V will be emperor someday and he will tolerate no disrespect to his son, not even by Dvandas. The Nabataean ambassador is just too important to the economic stability of the empire to allow any schism to develop in the Parthian court with him or his sovereign. That the Nabataeans have not developed a military strength beyond that of defense with the purpose of developing a strong trade relationship with the Parthians and Rome is a brilliant tactical move. It forces both empires to unwittingly act as protectors of that kingdom, so he wants to clarify that Parthia is the greater of the two, especially in the eyes of King Aretas IV Philopatris.

"Headmaster Dvandas to see you, My Liege."

The emperor looks up and sees his advisor standing in the doorway next to the royal guard, and he motions the man in and points to the seat in front of his desk. Careful not to show any emotion, Dvandas steps forward and takes his seat. "Your Grace, I wish to apologize for my behavior earlier. I—"

The emperor raises his hand. "Master Dvandas, I have always found you to be a sensible and forthright counselor in all matters, save for those that concern the inner squabbling that goes on in the Magi Order."

"Your Grace, I do not intend to—"

"Dvandas, please, do not provoke me. I am trying to show you some mercy here. The Nabataean kingdom is too important to the welfare of the empire for us to not accommodate them for any reasonable request. Allowing their sect of Magi to send a delegation to Babylon to confer with the Astronomical Sect is not an unreasonable request, agreed?"

Dvandas can see that Phraates IV will tolerate only one answer to this question, and he solemnly bows his head. "As you wish, Your Grace."

The emperor smiles and holds both hands out in a jovial gesture. "But in the interest of fairness, I believe that a representative of the Magician Sect of the Magi should be in Samekh's caravan. This should ensure that your interests may be represented in this historic collaboration of religious scholarship between our two realms."

Dvandas sits there, stunned by the generosity of the emperor in extending such an opportunity. But the wheels of his mind quickly change gears, and he stands and bows deeply. "Your Grace, wisdom is, indeed, one of your most notable qualities. I thank you for this gesture of kindness to our sect. I have just the man I would like to send." As he waits for the emperor to speak, another idea crosses his mind. "Your Grace, I believe this caravan should be commanded by one of our most capable men."

"I agree, Dvandas. Who do you have in mind?"

"Commander Dareh, of course. He is by far the most seasoned of our military commanders that we could spare from the capital."

"Acceptable, and who do you intend to send as your representative to Babylon?"

"I do not think it befitting that I should go. My first allegiance is to you, Your Grace."

"This I also agree with. So, whom?"

"It is an historic event. Your Grace has given permission for this to happen, so I believe that none other than my second-in-command, Mihri, should go."

"This also is acceptable. Please draw up the proper documents and I will sign them in the morning. And Dvandas..."

"Yes, Your Grace?"

"Should my son ask, tell him you got a harsh tongue-lashing from me and that you promised to keep your place in court henceforth."

"Of course, Your Grace. I will return in the morning with those documents ready for you to sign after you have taken your breakfast."

Later that Evening in the Royal Courtyard

Headmaster Dvandas and Mihri sit together with the rest of the Magi across the courtyard from the emperor and his son. Three of the Magician Magi are in the center in front of everyone, giving a lecture on the meaning of the stars depicted that night and how they proclaim great prosperity and health for the Parthian Empire, and especially for that of the emperor and his son. Without taking his eyes off the presentation, Mihri quietly asks, "Considering the emperor's gesture of kindness to you today, do we still intend to go ahead with your plans from earlier?"

"Of course, Mihri. The emperor's gesture only enforces my conviction that the gods have set us on this path. Not only will you be able to disrupt the Astronomical Sect's collaboration with the Nabataeans, but you can also oversee Rassan's recruitment to our order. With Commander Dareh's presence and the imminent succession of Commander Sasheen as general over the Babylonian garrison, your efforts will go completely unhindered."

May 1, 5 BC, Babylonian Garrison Courtyard

Rassan and Commander Sasheen circle each other with sparring swords in their hands. Though Rassan has had little time for anything but his studies at the Magi Astronomical Temple, Sasheen insisted that he devote at least one morning a week to maintaining his military disciplines. At first, Master Daraya-Vous objected to the order, but a dispatch was sent to the capital and the reply from the emperor's palace was that Rassan was an officer in the imperial cavalry and should always maintain his disciplines in that. The order came from Master Dvandas because he was the first one to see the dispatch, and he used his position as chief advisor to act in the emperor's stead to issue the reply, thinking that it would give Sasheen more opportunity to entice Rassan into their order of the Magi.

Though in an intense training duel with the swords, the pair is simultaneously in a heated debate concerning the meaning of the twelve signs of the zodiac. "Rassan, how can you be so naïve? The universe is there to declare our destinies. Each person is born under different signs of the zodiac and those stars guide and foretell that individual's life. They are the gods' ways of telling us how they have ordered our lives," Sasheen says as he presses his attack with a high thrust.

Rassan meets the thrust with a right parry and skips to his left while slashing with a backhanded maneuver that scores a slicing touch across the chest. Commander Sasheen stops and looks down at the chest guard he wears for sparring and sees the slice. He holds his sword up in front of his face and bows to Rassan for his victory point. Rassan mimics the gesture and sheaths his sword. He then smiles and says, "The Creator wrote His plan to save all mankind from the wicked one in the twelve signs of the zodiac. Each sign gives special knowledge and hope to man to look forward to the day when He will send His champion to save us all. That is the true meaning of the zodiacal signs, Commander."

Commander Sasheen glares at him for a moment. "So, since you won the match, I am just supposed to accept this nonsense that the entire universe tells the story about just one man?"

"I never said that it was only about one man, Commander. But it emphasizes and illustrates the Creator's champion as its dominant theme throughout, the one who will come to redeem mankind from the rulership of the wicked one and free us to serve and know the Creator."

"Ha, there you go again, prating about this mysterious, wicked one that tricked mankind into bondage. Who is this mysterious entity, and why doesn't he have a name?"

"He has many names, Commander. But one constellation that represents his nature is Cetus. Though the largest constellation in the sky, it is also the most elusive. It has no pattern of when it will appear in the southern hemisphere. He is the great sea monster who subtly hides, stalking his prey and taking them unawares. Though he cannot be bound by an ordinary man, the promised seed of the woman, the champion whom the Creator will send, will not only bound him, but will trodden him underfoot."[9]

Sasheen stares at Rassan. It was just a few years ago that Master Dvandas himself declared that Cetus, also named *Ninmah* by the Chaldees, who is the great birth giver to the first gods, showed him favor. Dvandas showed him this by explaining to him that since Cetus's brightest star, *Menkar*, lined up perfectly with the brightest star, *Al Debran*, in his birth constellation of Taurus on his birthday, he was highly favored. Dvandas interpreted that to mean that Sasheen would conquer Cetus's enemies as the offspring of the bull.[10] He sneers at Rassan. "How can the mother of all the gods be defeated by a boy?! That is the most nonsensical thing you have ever said, Rassan."

Rassan gives his commander the customary military salute. "I must take my leave and be back at the Temple within the hour. They are not my words, though. The Creator wrote His plan in the stars. I simply try to understand and declare them to the best of my ability. I am sorry if you are offended." He raises a finger in the air and waves it mirthfully. "Perhaps you should take your objections up with Him. He wrote them, not me." Before Commander Sasheen can respond, Rassan exits the courtyard, leaving him with his thoughts. Commander Sasheen stands there for a few moments, grinding his teeth, fuming that Rassan's ability to best him with the sword is second only to his infuriating adeptness at debate.

"He is the son of General Surena, possibly the greatest tactician the Parthian Empire has ever had, a quality he seems to have inherited from him. You will never win him to us by theological debate."

The words cause Sasheen to turn around. He sees Mihri coming through a doorway from the garrison kitchens. Mihri arrived in Babylon a month ago, having spent less than a month at the capital before he was sent back with the Nabatean Magi delegation. It was Mihri who brought back the response from the capital, ordering Rassan to report to Commander Sasheen once a week for military training. He had felt relief when he saw that Mihri and Commander Dareh were with that party and was elated to discover that Mihri would stay indefinitely.

General Barach ignored all matters relating to religion and tolerated his officer's' indulgences in any of those matters only to a degree. Unlike the capital, where the Magician Sect of the Magi maintained an aggressive recruitment of the military, Barach's command was much less tolerant of such practices. Early on, he warned Sasheen about being too aggressive in inviting his officers to the erotic ceremonies that were so popular in the Magician Sect. He cited that overindulgence in such activities caused men to be less reliable. He told Sasheen that if he was too aggressive, he would send him back to the capital, cut all ties with him, including his betrothal to the general's daughter, and ask for another replacement to assume his command upon his retirement. But now that Mihri and Commander Dareh were in Babylon, the recruitment of the military in Babylon will be much more aggressive, and General Barach will have no say in the matter because both men are here upon special assignment from the emperor regarding matters of religion and are, therefore, not under Barach's jurisdiction.

Sasheen waits until Mihri is close and then looks from side to side for unwanted ears and eyes. In a hushed tone, he answers. "I have tried everything, including trying to persuade him to come to a ceremony with me. He is always too busy to go or do anything but train with me once a week."

Mihri considers the commander's words. "Tell me, Commander, when is the last time you enjoyed the company of a woman in indulgence of your sensual appetites?"

Commander Sasheen stares at the Magi for a moment, then answers. "You know perfectly well when that was. You yourself presided over the Spring Festival of Akitu for the Magician Sect two days ago. The priestesses of the Temple of Zarpanuta, consort of Marduk and goddess of fertility, were brought in and we all partook."

"Yes, and a marvelous ceremony it was! And yet here you are, betrothed to marry General Barach's daughter."

Commander Sasheen's face turns red with indignation. "One has nothing to do with the other, Mihri. It is my right as a faithful follower of the Magician Sect of the Magi to freely take part in all the religious ceremonies honoring the gods, now and when I am married. What is your point?"

Mihri steps closer to the shaken commander and puts a calming hand on his shoulder. "My point is that you and Rassan are almost the same age, and yet he is not even betrothed to marry anyone, and my sources say that he has not yet known the pleasures of the flesh."

"I told you I have invited him to all our ceremonies, but he refuses."

Mihri thinks on the matter. "Because both his parents died while he was still attending the academy, our boy has not yet been betrothed to a young maid. Perhaps it is time that his family found a suitable wife for him."

"Mihri, I don't see why that has anything to do with him joining our order."

"Rassan will be head of his family someday, but not until he is wed. The emperor appointed a nephew of General Surena's to lead the family until he is ready. It was done as a matter of formality, because everyone expected the boy to stay in the capital to be near

Phraates V as part of his court when he assumes the throne. If it were to happen that he had not married already, the emperor would choose a wife for him. But now he is here and being trained to be a Magi, and his sect rarely avails themselves to high court positions. As I recall, the nephew is much younger than Surena was and lives near Babylon. His name is Bozan, and he rules a village just south of here. As far as I know, he has not yet visited Rassan."

Commander Sasheen throws up his hands. "Where are you going with this reasoning? Do you propose for this Bozan to force Rassan to take a wife? What about when Rassan becomes the head of his family? This Bozan could lose everything he has if he angers Rassan! And how, pray tell, will that bring Rassan over to our sect?"

Mihri nods. "Because, Commander Sasheen, the maid that he will be betrothed to is going to be one of our own! A priestess from the Temple of Zarpanuta, whom we will insert into Rassan's life to seduce and manipulate him. When the time is right, we will perpetuate a scandal implicating the young officer and the girl, at which point this Bozan will have no choice as head of the family but to step in and force them to marry."

Commander Sasheen thinks back to his experiences with the priestesses of that Temple and knows that if anyone could pull off this kind of manipulation, they could. He laughs. "Of course! Then she would be the one to subtly convince Rassan that his true calling lies with the Magician Sect of the Magi, thus bringing him over to our order."

Mihri holds up his finger and waves it in the air. "Then when his apprenticeship is finished here, he and his wife go back to the capital, where he will assume his duty as head of his family and be totally under our control."

"Then we will have another Magician Sect's counselor close to the new emperor," Commander Sasheen says as he thinks through the logic of Mihri's plan.

Recalling Headmaster Dvandas's secret plan to depose Phraates IV, Mihri smiles and simply nods his head as he walks away to his offices, telling Sasheen over his shoulder: "I will make the arrangements with the high priestess of the Temple in choosing the perfect girl for our plan. For the time being, just continue your training sessions with Rassan and try to provoke him as much as you can to argue his points of theology with you. Any frustrations this causes him to have with you will give our girl an opportunity to assuage and manipulate him into her web of control."

"You have done this type of thing before, haven't you?" Commander Sasheen says.

"Subtlety and manipulation are the very core of our power as a sect, Commander. How do you think we won you over to us?"

"I came to the Magician Sect because I saw that it is the true path of the gods."

"No doubt, Commander, and it was the gods themselves who used that palace chambermaid's enchantments to bring you to us! That little indulgence almost cost you your betrothal to General Barach's daughter. If it were not for Master Dvandas stepping in and saving your position, one could only imagine what a sorry state of affairs you would be in now, would they?"

Commander Sasheen thinks back to the debacle that almost cost him his commission. Even now, his position and marriage to his superior's daughter is precariously teetering between success and failure, depending on how he can meet the old man's expectations. Anger swells up from his belly. "Wait, it was you and Master Dvandas that set that whole thing up to force me to join your sect?!"

Mihri offers a guttural chuckle with his reply. "We are simply the hands and the feet of the gods. Let their will be done, always!"

Before Commander Sasheen can reply, Mihri walks around the corner of the courtyard and out of sight. Sasheen stands there for a few moments as it dawns on him that their pursuit to entice and then enslave Rassan is something he has been a victim of himself. He shakes his head, knowing that for good or ill he is trapped and can only proceed on this path that is set before him.

8

Mentors and Manipulators

Next Morning, Magi Astronomical Temple Observatory

Rassan and Arsam stand under the tapestry depicting the constellation of Cetus discussing how the constellation in the southern hemisphere has been seen creeping over the horizon a few times in the last couple of months. A few months ago, Arsam told his former master that Headmaster Daraya-Vous had been meeting him here every morning to chat with him about his interests in the star charts. The Magi always walks through the area at the same time on his way to prepare for the morning lecture and discussion with the apprentices about the previous night's findings.

Upon learning of the chats, Rassan has sought to join them. Arsam points to the head of the sea monster's depiction drawn in the constellation. "That is *Menkar*, the star that was barely visible on the horizon one week ago."

Rassan sees the star and remembers the lecture on the constellation given by Magi Artesan a few days ago, discussing the subtlety of the enemy. "He is elusive and always seeks to attack when least expected. The only one who will defeat him is the seed of the woman, the great champion who will crush him under foot."

A familiar, cheerful voice speaks from behind them. "Yet the Creator of all things shows us we can resist and overcome his attacks."

Rassan and Arsam turn to be greeted by Headmaster Daraya-Vous's warm smile.

Arsam is the first to speak. "Headmaster, we did not notice you joining us. We were just discussing the subtleties of the enemy."

"I know. A fascinating and enticing subject, the enemy. He can certainly cause us to want to follow his every move and learn everything we can about him."

Rassan remembers the rest of the lecture about Cetus and how Magi Artesan warned the apprentices not to get too overwhelmed in their study of the enemy. Their focus should always be on the principal theme of the zodiac, and that is the promised seed. "It is just an interest that Arsam had, Headmaster. I was just trying to elaborate a little on its meaning."

The headmaster walks up to the chart and points to a configuration of stars that Cetus has his paws draped over part of and asks, "Rassan, do you remember what the meaning of this action is that Cetus is taking?"

Rassan studies the area for a moment. "That is the depiction of Cetus trying to stay the flow of the river Eridanus, which represents the last judgment of the Creator on the sea monster and his eventual annihilation."

A fourth man joins their group and points to the star tapestry next to Cetus and says, "Here we have Orion with his foot standing in the same river, represented by the star, *Saiph Rigal*, ready to deliver the damning blow to the head of the monster."

The three look over and acknowledge Ambassador Samekh, head of the Nabataean Magi delegation. Daraya-Vous walks over to him and places his right hand on the man's shoulder. "So true, my friend. It is always important to note that no matter how formidable and sly the enemy appears, the Creator always has him surrounded with greater might than his own and a constant reminder of his imminent defeat. A truth our apprentice and cleaning servant here should keep in the foremost of their thinking."

Ambassador Samekh smiles broadly and looks to Rassan and nods. "Apprentice."

Rassan immediately bows his head. "Ambassador Samekh, greetings."

Samekh then focuses on Arsam and grins as he takes a deep breath, turns to Daraya-Vous, and points in the boy's direction. "This is the one you told me about?"

"Yes, Ambassador Samekh, this is Arsam. He came to us with Rassan. As an officer of our emperor's royal cavalry and his personal emissary to bring back to us the sacred star charts he enlisted Arsam as his personal valet."

Ambassador Samekh steps up to the boy and places both hands on his shoulders. "I have been the Master of the Nabataean Magi for half my life, and until a few weeks ago have never laid eyes on the sacred star charts of Belteshazzar. Headmaster Daraya-Vous has told me you and Apprentice Rassan studied them for three months, every night."

Arsam nervously gazes at Rassan, who only offers a blank expression, then looks to Headmaster Daraya-Vous for guidance. The headmaster chuckles and walks over to Arsam, puts an affectionate hand on the boy's head, and ruffles his hair. "Come, Arsam, it has already been declared by Grand Master Artapan that neither of you did anything wrong."

He winks at Rassan and continues. "Ambassador Samekh, I don't think I told you this, but when Arsam became our apprentice's servant, he lacked the ability to read or write. It was during their time together that Rassan instructed the boy on both. And a very fine job he did too. Arsam has continued to learn, and since he spoke both languages before learning, I can attest that he is competent in reading and writing Parthian and Aramaic, therefore enabling him to study our tapestries here and use our libraries. In my judgment, if it were not for his age, he could competently join with Rassan's class as a second-year Magi apprentice."

Arsam's heart flutters with nervous disbelief as Master Daraya-Vous's words sink in. He can hardly fathom that he is hearing them.

Ambassador Samekh steps up to him. "How well do you remember the details of those star charts you and Rassan studied while on your journey here from the Parthian capital?"

Arsam gulps, trying to calm his nerves as he answers. "Before Rassan taught me to read and write, I had to memorize things in pictures in my mind. Now that I understand the languages inscribed on them, I often visualize the notes when I stare at the tapestries in this chamber. I believe I can recall most, if not all, on the twelve charts."

Samekh walks up to the tapestry depiction of Virgo and points to the branch in the woman's hand. "Headmaster Daraya-Vous showed me the chart of this constellation last night. Next to the branch in the woman's hand there is a note written by Belteshazzar himself. What does it say?"

Arsam walks over to where the ambassador is standing and studies the chart for a moment while he searches his mind for the answer. A few moments pass and he lets out a sigh of relief. "This branch in the hand of the woman represents the promised seed that she will give birth to and raise. This is depicted by the smaller constellation to her left known as Coma, where she is shown raising him from a baby, and that he would be the desire of all nations."[11]

Headmaster Daraya-Vous brings his hands together in applause. "A flawless quote, Arsam. Nicely done indeed!"

The ambassador nods to the boy and turns back to Daraya-Vous. "Remarkable! He is everything you said he would be. He could copy from memory most, if not all, of the star charts. I wonder, though. There seems to be a tight bond between these young men. Will they be able to separate?"

Rassan steps forward hastily and asks, "Headmaster, what is the ambassador talking about? Why would we need to be separated? Arsam cannot copy the charts. That would be disastrous!"

Daraya-Vous sighs. "Rassan, you know that the Nabataean delegation of Magi coming to Babylon is an unprecedented event. Until now, our only communication with them has been through written correspondence. Phraates IV opened a wonderful opportunity for our two groups to finally meet in person and share knowledge."

"But, Headmaster, Arsam is a subject of the Parthian Empire. If he were to do this, it would brand him as an outlaw with a death sentence on his head," Rassan blurts out.

Ambassador Samekh looks over to Daraya-Vous. "Allow me to explain to the boy. True, if he were a Parthian." Ambassador Samekh walks over to Arsam and pulls the boy's sleeve up on the right side and points to the tattooed depiction on his shoulder that Rassan had noticed at their first meeting almost two years ago. "This shows that Arsam is the child of a Nabaeatean tribe that manned many of our trade caravans. I surmise that he must have been orphaned in a raid while enroute to your capital, and he simply grew up there out of necessity." He then turns to Rassan. "Magi Apprentice Rassan, why do you call me Ambassador Samekh, and not simply Headmaster Samekh, as is my place in the Nabataean Order of Magi?"

Rassan sighs deeply. "In the Parthian Empire, the only religious authority that is recognized are those that are sanctioned by the emperor. Here you are referred to as Ambassador Samekh because your order of the Magi has not officially been recognized by the empire. However, your status as the Nabataean ambassador has."

"That is correct, Rassan. This brings us to the availability of the star charts. You know that, outside of the brief time they were in your care, only the appointed headmaster of a Magi sect in your empire has ever been allowed to handle them, and only he may show them to others. Even the duplicating of them as stated by the headmaster is forbidden to any Parthian subject. But Arsam is not a Parthian subject. He is simply a refugee and native of Nabataea."

He then turns back to Arsam and holds out his hand in an appeasing gesture and continues. "As the official ambassador from the Nabataean Court, it is my privilege to offer you passage to and sanctuary in your homeland. You see, in the Parthian Order of the Magi, an apprentice cannot be accepted into the order under eighteen years of age; but in my kingdom, we accept apprentices as early as thirteen."

Rassan's eyes fix on Arsam's face, and he can see a glow of excitement. He remembered that he judged Arsam's age to be about fourteen when they left the capital, and that would make him barely sixteen now. He smiles and nods his head at Arsam. "It is totally up to you. I gave up my rights as your master when I became an apprentice."

Master Daraya-Vous steps forward and places a hand on Rassan's and Arsam's shoulders. "If Arsam agrees to apprentice with Ambassador Samekh's Order of the Magi, he will have no obligation to me or our order and is free to draw anything he likes under Ambassador Samekh's authority. I knew this would not be easy for you two to consider. Ambassador Samekh and I have talked about this at length for several days."

He holds up the canister containing the sacred star charts. "These charts were originally drawn for all Magi of the Astronomical Sect who have committed themselves to preserving the meaning of the Creator's message in the stars. In the six centuries that have passed since Belteshazzar made them, they have passed through one empire to another. Now, under Parthian law, they are to stay inside the empire, and no one may make copies. Like the Hebrew Scriptures, they have been suppressed, and, therefore, extremely difficult to share with others."

He points to the star tapestries. "The notes written on them are not even copied on our own tapestries. Ambassador Samekh, head of the Nabataean Magi loyal to the Astronomical Sect, may not even look at them outside of my presence. We have long shared as much knowledge as we were allowed to with him and his predecessors, but no duplication may be made or shared by any headmaster. But you and Arsam brought a whole extra dimension to this predicament. By your acceptance of Master Vinda-Farnah's request to carry these charts back to us and under the protection of the emperor, having received his royal commission as his emissary, you did what no one outside of a headmaster has done in centuries. Studying the charts and inviting Arsam to join you has opened a fantastic door for us to finally bless our Nabataean brothers with this most special and precious gift."

He takes a deep breath and fixes Arsam in his gaze. "Arsam, you have a remarkable ability in the memorization of complex things. You could give to Ambassador Samekh and our brothers what I am forbidden to do."

Arsam fixes his eyes on Rassan. "Are you sure you don't mind?"

"Of course not, my friend. This is a great opportunity for you."

Arsam then turns to Ambassador Samekh. "It would be my honor to return to Nabataea with you and apprentice under your authority. I promise I will give you everything I remember about the star charts."

Ambassador Samekh claps his hands with glee, wraps an arm around Arsam's shoulders, and leads him to the library where they can talk more about the apprenticeship.

Rassan stands there considering that after Ambassador Samekh's delegation leaves Babylon, he might never see the person he just now realizes is his closest friend.

Daraya-Vous sees the concern on his apprentice's face. "We have all grown quite fond of Arsam. The Creator brought the two of you to us for a grand purpose. I believe Arsam has just realized part of that purpose in bringing the Nabataean Magi a remarkable gift that will bring our two groups much closer together in study and fellowship." He taps the sacred star charts canister under his arm and continues. "This knowledge that Belteshazzar committed to the Astronomical Sect of the Magi was never meant to be hoarded and kept secret. Ambassador Samekh is a master at the astronomical sciences, and with Arsam's aid will take all of us much farther in our learning of the Creator's plan to send His champion to save mankind from the wicked one, as foretold in the stars."

Rassan's shoulders relax. "I understand, Headmaster. It's just that this has shown me how dear Arsam has become to me. I am happy for him, though. Ambassador Samekh will introduce him to his people and culture, and he gets to be a Magi apprentice to boot. But when he leaves, I will miss him."

Daraya-Vous motions for Rassan to walk over to the two tapestries representing Virgo and Leo, holds up both hands, and points to each. "Rassan, it has been over a year now since your group has joined our ranks, and there is still much debate in your class about the Astronomical Sect's belief that the ecliptic cycle begins with Virgo and ends with Leo. You and Kaufa are the only ones who have told me that you believe it to be true. Hymayeak and Whama are adamantly opposed, and Rita-Raina is skeptically affirmative."

Rassan chuckles. "Yes, Headmaster, it has been a topic of much heated discourse among us since our first day here with you. There were times I felt Rita-Raina and Kaufa were going to come to blows."

"What made Rita-Raina see our point of view on the subject?"

"When he took the advice that you gave Hymayeak and researched the Egyptian Sphinx in the library. When he came back that night, all he could say was that the translations of the ancient hieroglyphics would need to be double-checked, but that establishing the beginning and the ending of the ecliptic seems to be the meaning of the monument."

"Yes, Hymayeak took my advice also, and after his research he grudgingly acknowledged that the Egyptians who wrote the hieroglyphics explaining the Sphinx affirmed that the zodiac starts with Virgo and ends with Leo. But then he pointed out that this interpretation was recorded around the same time that Joseph the son of

Israel was governor over Egypt, concluding that Pharaoh would have let his priests and scholars be influenced by the Hebrew."

He pauses for a moment, considering the situation. He then points to the two tapestries. "Fundamental disagreements like whether these two represent the beginning and end of the zodiac has driven a wedge in our order and given the Magician Sect ammunition to discredit us in the empire. This is an example of what you and Arsam were discussing earlier about Cetus and his subtleties. In most opinions, this is an insignificant matter. But if the zodiac truly is the Creator's way of showing us His plan for mankind, then all of it must be understood according to His original intent and not by any Magi's whimsical attempts at speculation."

Rassan stares at the tapestries for a few moments then turns to Daraya-Vous. "When Headmaster Vinda-Farnah handed me the sacred star charts, he said that the heavenly messenger told him to have us look at the Lion of the Tribe of Judah, and it would be there that we would find our answers concerning the coming of the promised seed of the woman." He points to the Leo tapestry. "Leo is the Lion of the Tribe of Judah." And then he points to Virgo's. "And Virgo is the woman. This is not an insignificant matter, Headmaster."

Daraya-Vous considers the last words of his former master that the boy shared with him when he arrived. *He said you would carry on in my stead. He even told me your name.* "I have initiated a formal debate over the matter that will be done between members in your class. I fear this disagreement is not limited to the apprentices. I suspect that some of the Magi here at the Temple are not yet fully convinced. You, Kaufa, and perhaps Rita-Raina, will work on a presentation to convince the panel on the merits of Virgo and Leo being the beginning and end of the zodiac. Hymayeak and Whama will argue against. Both sides will be free to seek the counsel and aid of any Magi of our sect here that is not part of the panel."

"Headmaster, do you know who disagrees with this belief among the other Magi?"

"I have my suspicions. But remember, Rassan, ours is a scientific study of the zodiac and, therefore, we try not to discourage debate. However, we all need to be convinced and unified on this matter."

Rassan gets so caught up in the debate's matter that he almost forgets about Arsam and Ambassador Samekh in the library. "Headmaster, how long before Ambassador Samekh and Arsam must leave?"

"The ambassador told me they must leave within the month," he answers.

"When do you want us to have this debate before our sect, Headmaster?"

"I was hoping to have it take place within the next three weeks, if you and your fellow apprentices can be ready by that time."

Rassan turns his gaze to the library. "Headmaster, I know that Ambassador Samekh is not officially recognized as part of our sect; and Arsam, now being an apprentice of his order, has no standing here either. But would seeking their counsel in this matter be acceptable?"

"Rassan, you and any Magi apprentice have been granted complete access to our library and its full contents. Ambassador Samekh is our guest by special permission of the emperor himself. That alone gives him and any of his colleagues the same access. Once in there, you are all a part of our accumulated knowledge and are free to discuss and share insights with one another."

"Then, Headmaster, with your leave, I will begin my preparations for the debate you have assigned me to partake in."

"You have my leave, Rassan, and I saw Whama, Hymayeak, and Rita-Raina go in there earlier. I have not yet seen Kaufa this morning. Could you tell the ones who are there about the debate and tell them to see me if they have questions?"

"Of course, Headmaster."

A Few Hours Later, the City of Babylon by the River Euphrates, Near the Ruins of Nebuchadnezzar's Hanging Gardens

Kaufa makes his way to the waterfront, where in the message he received from the garrison earlier that morning informed him to meet with his former commander. As soon as he heard that the man had arrived in Babylon with Mihri, he knew this summons would come. He never cared for the man; Commander Dareh was more of a high-ranking clerk than a soldier. Being under his command was more about protecting the man's image and status and less about being a soldier in the empire's service. Kaufa much preferred the leadership style of Commander Sasheen, whose command he was under during the journey to Babylon. Though newly promoted and young, his command was much more like what any soldier preferred—disciplined, focused, and battle ready.

He arrives at the dock designated by the message and leans against a large wooden pole as he looks at the area where the famed hanging gardens were said to have been before the great earthquake two hundred years earlier reportedly destroyed them.

He detects movement to his left, but makes no move to acknowledge the approach of his contact. A familiar voice greets his ears. "Corporal Kaufa, it has been a long time since we have seen each other. Has a year of studying with the Magi Astronomical Sect retarded your military disciplines? I am still your superior officer and expect you to come to attention in my presence."

"Pardon me, Commander, but it is Magi Apprentice Kaufa now. My enlistment in the royal garrison was ended the moment I reported to Master Daraya-Vous one year ago. This transition was approved by the royal court and had the imperial seal on it."

Commander Dareh starts to rebuke Kaufa when he hears another voice behind him. "Commander, he is correct. Magi Apprentice Kaufa has no obligation to you or the military. But he owes me much, because it was I who helped him receive that approval and seal, providing permission to apprentice here."

Mihri walks up and places a hand on Kaufa's shoulder. "Kaufa, it is good to see you. Your reports of your experiences here under Daraya-Vous have been fascinating. I must admit that there were times I doubted your ability to prove to him that you are a worthy apprentice. But everything I have heard would show that you have done just that."

Kaufa lets out a sigh of relief seeing Mihri come to his aid. He bows his head. "Thank you, Master Mihri. I will always be indebted to you for the opportunities you have provided me to serve in the empire."

Mihri looks to Commander Dareh. "You see, Commander, there was no need for harshness with our friend here. He knows where his loyalties lie."

The commander waves his hand in a dismissive gesture. "You are right, of course, Mihri. Old habits and my familiarity with Kaufa's status as a soldier under my command obscured my judgment."

Mihri turns back to Kaufa. "So, tell me, is there anything interesting going on inside the Astronomical Sect with the Magi apprentices? Have you been monitoring young Rassan like I asked? There has been little in your monthly reports about him. Headmaster Dvandas would love to hear any news you have about his son, Rita-Raina."

Kaufa's eyes go wide at the revelation of Rita-Raina being Headmaster Dvandas's son. Mihri had instructed him to report on both him and Rassan in his monthly dispatches. But in Rita-Raina's case, Headmaster Daraya-Vous's words calling him the son of one of the most important men in the Magi Order never made sense to him until now.

Mihri sees the astonishment on the young man's face. "Headmaster Dvandas does not share this information openly. His son hardly knows him, and the boy holds some disdain for his father. When he began his Magi apprenticeship with the Astronomical Sect, his father was furious. But then came the incident with Rassan getting the emperor's seal to come to Babylon with the star charts and apprentice in that same order; and with your availability to be here as well, we thought it must be foreordained of the gods to aid the Magician Sect in increasing its influence in the empire."

"What is it you need from me, Mihri?"

"The Nabataeans have caused our sect some distress, with Ambassador Samekh gaining the emperor's leave to officially visit the Astronomical Sect in Babylon. Nabataea brings great wealth to Parthia, and Phraates IV and his son are eager to accommodate them. We want you to find a way to discredit anything Samekh is doing here without hurting our emperor's relationship with the Nabataean king."

Kaufa shakes his head in exasperation. "I am only an apprentice in the Astronomical Sect, and Ambassador Samekh is the special guest of Headmaster Daraya-Vous. Also, Grand Master Artapan has visited our Temple over the last few weeks to spend time with Samekh as well. What could I possibly do that could disgrace such a man?"

Mihri steps in closer to Kaufa, and his voice takes on a menacing tone. "The Magi Order has many protocols and traditions that must be adhered to. Surely, being half Judean, you realize this. The Hebrew Scriptures are forbidden throughout the empire except in sanctioned Jewish synagogues. If a Magi wants to look at them, he must petition Grand Master Artapan to visit such a place. The sacred star charts that Headmaster Daraya-Vous now stewards for the empire are not to be looked at except in his presence. Surely you could observe some break in a protocol that might help us."

"Suppose I do observe some break in our protocols by the man and then report it? Then what? If Master Daraya-Vous does not expel me, I will at the very least never have his trust again. How will that aid you and your purposes?"

"This would never be a permanent assignment for you, Kaufa. You belong to Headmaster Dvandas, and he will have other work for you after this task is complete."

Kaufa stands there and watches as the two men leave, reeling from their arrogance. True, he owes Mihri much for all he's done, but for him to order him to openly shame a man like Samekh goes against Mihri's assurances that all he needed to do in Babylon was to observe and report the workings of the Astronomical Sect from an apprentice's perspective. Now he must expose himself and betray those he was beginning to count as friends.

What bothers him the most is that just before he came to this meeting, Rassan found him and informed him of the upcoming debate that he, Rassan, and Rita-Raina would work together on. He told him the whole story about Arsam and Ambassador Samekh and how the headmaster exposed a loophole in the protocols concerning Samekh's counsel in the upcoming debate. It was simply brilliant, because all they had to do was meet him in the library; and since the ambassador's visit was approved by the emperor himself, Samekh is allowed to discuss theology and astronomy with anyone who is there. Kaufa knows there is no way he can humiliate the man with that, but it does provide an opportunity for him to study him. He turns and makes his way back to the Astronomical Temple.

9

Someone New

Same Time, Central Market in the Main Square of Babylon

Rassan makes his way across the courtyard in the main square of Babylon to the merchant's tent, where the headmaster sends him once a week to purchase fresh papyrus and writing ink for Temple use. He loves these weekly walks because they give him time to meditate on all he is learning as a Magi apprentice. The more he thinks about the upcoming debate to prove that the zodiac's beginning and end are represented by Virgo and Leo, the more excited he gets. To do it with Kaufa and even Rita-Raina will be exhilarating. The way the headmaster figured out how they could seek Ambassador Samekh's help and involve Arsam really has his confidence at a peak that the Creator's hand is very much involved in all of this.

He approaches the main commerce section of the courtyard and hears some obnoxiously loud merchants and customers trying to negotiate. This makes it hard for him to focus. There are so many people, horses, carts, and livestock in the area that it is hard to see very far ahead. But as a camel and his owner move across the path in front of him, he finally sees his destination. He reflects that Headmaster Daraya-Vous has only one merchant he will deal with for papyrus and ink for Temple use, and his place of business is now just a few paces beyond where the camel has just stepped away. He hurries to the area inside the large tent where the merchant has his main table. On either side are makeshift shelves containing hundreds of rolls of fresh papyrus, and on the center table directly in front there are dozens of small bottles of the black ink. Each apprentice is allowed one roll of papyrus and a small alabaster bottle of ink every week with which to make notes from their studies at the Temple. As he approaches the table, he calls out "Baazar!" while scanning the area for the merchant.

"May I help you?" comes a sultry female voice from behind him. He turns and immediately steps back. His eyes are greeted by a very attractive young woman in her late teens or early twenties. He has still not gotten used to the fact that women in Babylon go about with their faces unveiled. In the capital, this is unheard of, but his father once told him that other parts of the empire allow for this. She has brown hair that is pulled tight at the sides and in a bun on the back. The hair is wrapped around a single white rod approximately four inches long, which is the only ornament in her hair. Rassan finds it refreshing, as most of the women in this part of the empire pack their hair with all kinds of gold and silver embroideries.

Her gown is simple but elegant, full length and draping over each shoulder, with the sleeves coming down to the top of the arms on each side. It is dark gray with white trim and the front is left open, revealing an underdress embroidered with purple, tan, and green designs. This is held together by a single gold ring at her breastbone. Her face is beautifully bronzed, and her eyes are the most piercing brown he has ever seen. She is a natural beauty.

He inhales deeply. "I, uh, I am here from the Magi Astronomical Temple to pick up our weekly order. Is Baazar here?" She steps to his side and grazes her shoulder against his as she makes her way behind the central table. The touch, though innocent and unavoidable because of the tight surroundings, makes Rassan's heart beat faster.

Once around the table, she holds Rassan in her gaze for a moment, then replies. "My uncle Baazar is not feeling well today and is seeing a physician. My name is Varaz, and I am his niece. As for the Magi Astronomical Temple order, let me see." She pinches her chin with her thumb and index finger, and then scrunches her face in a contemplative fashion as she scans the immediate area for the items. Rassan finds the gesture makes her even more attractive. Her eyes fall on the wooden crate behind her table and she says, "Here it is." She picks up a piece of parchment and reads, "Magi Astronomical Temple order, ten rolls of parchment, five small bottles of writing ink, and some writing feathers. Already paid for. Will be picked up by a Magi apprentice." She looks up from the note. "You must be Rassan, correct?"

Realizing that his dark gray robe and black Kufi with a half-moon and star embroidered on the front distinguishes him as being from the Magi Astronomical Temple, he is not surprised that she knows he is an apprentice, but knowing his name startles him. He swallows nervously. "How do you know my name?"

She picks up the order and hands it to him over the table and replies with a giggle: "I asked my uncle the name of the apprentice who would come for the order, and he told me."

Rassan swallows down the embarrassment. "Oh, that makes sense."

As he reaches across the table to take the order, he sees a small tattoo under her right ear. "Are you a member of the priestess order for the goddess Zarpanuta?"

Her hand reflexively goes to her neck and she repositions her clothing to cover the tattoo. Then she brings her hand to her mouth. "My father sold me to the order when I was very young. I grew up in the Temple and was going to be a priestess, but after my father died, my family decided they wanted me to come home and wait for them to find a suitable betrothal for me. All of us were given the tattoo at a very early age."

Rassan breathes a sigh of relief. Headmaster Daraya-Vous warned all the apprentices about the Zarpanuta priestesses and how they would aggressively pursue enticing any young men, but especially those from good families, to take part in their erotic rituals. His friend Commander Sasheen is constantly badgering him about going with him to experience the pleasures of those rituals. The only sect of Magi that will have anything to do with them is the Magician Sect. The headmaster would never forbid apprentices from partaking in any religious experience sanctioned by the empire. But he warned them that those from the Astronomical Sect who accepted an invitation from the priestesses would almost always drop themselves from continuing their apprenticeships.

He takes the order, sets it in front of him and sighs. "It must have been awful for you to endure being raised like that. Your family must be congratulated for rescuing you from such a fate."

A brief flash of disdain crosses Varaz's face, but she does her best to project an expression of hurt and humiliation. "I am aware of what your order thinks of the priestesses, but being raised in the Temple of Zarpanuta has little difference to being recruited to the emperor's own harem of concubines."

Rassan's cheeks flush again as he realizes her words carry the truth. Being a member of the first hundred in royal succession, he has seen the outside of the emperor's harem in the capital and can attest to the truth that it is just as big and lavish as the goddess's Temple here in Babylon. "I apologize if I have caused offense, miss." He holds out both hands and gestures pleadingly as he points out, "You are not a member of the priestess's order. Your dress and demeanor declare you to be an honorable young maiden. I only wanted to imply that you must have gone through a lot in your transition, and I respect that."

She smiles brightly. "Apology accepted, Magi Apprentice Rassan." She looks at the order. "This is double what you usually pick up. Is there anything special going on at the Temple?"

"Well, yes. My class of apprentices is preparing for a debate over the structure of the zodiac."

Intrigued, she puts her hand to her chin. "What aspect of its structure, may I ask?"

"Which constellation marks the beginning and which is its ending," Rassan replies.

"Interesting. I have heard that the Astronomical Sect says that the zodiac, though depicted in a circle, believes it has a linear interpretation. Is it also true that you do not believe that the gods show each of our personal destinies in a study of the stars?"

"That question has both a *yes* and *no* answer to it. You see, the destiny of all mankind written in the Creator's plan depicted in the zodiac is to redeem us from the evil that now rules this world. In the very beginning of man's existence in this world, he corrupted himself and gave himself into slavery to the Creator's worst enemy. The stars proclaim that someday the Creator will send His champion to defeat the evil one and put man back in a state better than before his fall. So yes, we believe the stars proclaim all our destinies. But to pretend that the stars of the constellations visible during the time we were born somehow hold the key to understanding personal destinies in our brief lives here on earth is something we do not believe they show."

"So, Rassan, you say that the zodiac simply proclaims a divine, grand plan for all of mankind and that it does not matter what sign any of us are born under? Then what is the purpose of this debate over the zodiac's beginning and end? Why is it so important to your order?"

Rassan scans the area, and his eyes fall on a small sitting stool in the corner, and he asks if he may use it. Varaz motions for him to take it, and he brings it back to the table and sits. "First," he says, "the purpose of each sign being visible predominantly for one month out of the year is to give man ample time to study it and glean its many truths that the Creator had written there. And second, the beginning and the end of the zodiac give us a definite timeline and explanation of how our rescue by the champion of the Creator will come to pass."

"Then, what is the beginning and the end of the zodiac, according to the Astronomical Sect?" she asks, surprising herself that she is becoming genuinely curious.

"Headmaster Daraya-Vous and former Headmaster Vinda-Farnah agree it must start with the constellation Virgo and end with that of Leo. A key element in this debate is the existence of the Egyptian monument of the Sphinx. It has the head of a woman and the body of a lion. Literature we have in copies of hieroglyphics concerning that monument supports that the ancients had it erected to signify the beginning and ending constellations of the zodiac. Incidentally, most headmasters of our sect have believed this to be true, and it has been widely accepted in our order for centuries. But it has never been officially adopted, and that is the purpose of the debate."

"But if this is so important to your order, why have apprentices do the debate? You would think that the most experienced and wisest of your order would be the ones to partake."

"They will partake, but as counselors and mentors to those of us who are debating. The Astronomical Sect believes that if something cannot be taught well enough for a student to gain a firm grasp of the concept and then adequately communicate it, then it needs further study and more development."

Surprise and shock cross Varaz's face as Rassan's words sink in. She mumbles, "At the Temple of Zarpanuta we were given sheets of doctrine to memorize, and then were made to pledge our lives to its writing. If we disagreed or sulked, we were beaten for our insolence. All that mattered was that we could repeat it back and obey it without question." She then looks up and realizes that she said that out loud and covers her mouth. She darts her eyes back and forth, scanning for anyone else who might have heard.

Rassan's eyes dart back and forth as well, and then he looks at her. "There is only you and I here, and your words are safe with me.

Besides, you are no longer a member of that order, and I am sure that your family would protect you from anyone who might seek your harm. If they couldn't, then I would. My family still holds influence in the empire, and I am a friend of the crown prince Phraates V. I assure you that you are perfectly safe."

"You know the crown prince! How is that possible?" she asks, barely able to suppress her astonishment.

Rassan clears his throat and suppresses a groan as he realizes this conversation has gotten to the place that he has put himself in a position to appear to be trying to impress this girl. Master Daraya-Vous frowns on any Magi or apprentice using their family connections to sway anyone's opinion of them. That is why talk of one's background inside the Temple is only tolerated to a limited degree. He stands and grabs the order again. "I am the only son of the late General Surena. I really must be leaving." He turns but can't stop the impulse and blurts out, "I will be back here next week. Perhaps we may talk again." Then he quickly turns and walks away.

Varaz watches the Magi apprentice leave. When he is completely out of sight, she says, "He is gone now. You can come out."

Commander Sasheen emerges from behind a tall stack of unbound papyrus in the far corner of the tent. He steps briskly up to Varaz and examines her from head to foot with a smirk on his face. He presses his lips together. "It's hard to believe you are the same girl from the Temple. At the spring festival that Mihri conducted two weeks ago, I fancied you as the incarnation of the Greek goddess Athena."

She swallows to stifle the panic trying to rise in her chest. She is terrified that the Magi apprentice's revealing of his relationship with the emperor's son could cause her to fear for her life someday. "No one told me how important this Rassan is. Are you trying to get me killed?"

Sasheen holds her in his gaze for a moment, reveling in her panic and the power it seems to give him. "Rassan's father was the great General Surena, and he is his only heir. But Rassan is also at a crossroads and is on the verge of denouncing his claim to be the head of that family. Should he move on to become a Magi in the Astronomical Sect, his influence with them may diminish and the lordship of that family could go to another." He reaches out and places his hand on her shoulder to appear to console her.

She immediately brushes his hand aside. "Careful, Commander Sasheen. You forget that you are betrothed to the daughter of General Barach, and we are not in the Temple, and you have no religious privileges with me here."

He reels from the rebuke and stifles the impulse to strike her across the cheek. He steps back a pace. "But your purpose is to entice him away from that order and show him that his true calling is to become a member of the Magician Sect. With us, he would not need to renounce his titles or influence and you could share in all of them as his wife. If you consider this, you will see that no matter the outcome, you are safe from retribution. If he stays in the Astronomical Sect, he will have no influence to harm you. And if he leaves, it will be that he is so taken by you that you will be his reason for drawing breath." He smiles and shakes his head. "I am personally most confident of the latter—that you can entice him with your many gifts. It was fascinating watching you reel him in like you did, pretending to be abused by the Temple of Zarpanuta when you heard what free thinkers Astronomical Sect apprentices may be. He felt genuine concern for you and your well-being. I cannot wait to see how you will finally trap my old friend, Rassan."

She gazes at him with veiled contempt. "Who says I was pretending?"

He shrugs his shoulders. "When learning anything worthwhile, discipline and training can sometimes be harsh companions. Well, I need to go now. Mihri has made sure that Baazar will not get in your way here and will back up your story of leaving the order." He then turns and hastens away.

Her eyes follow Sasheen to the edge of the courtyard. She thinks how unlucky she was that he chose her as a companion at the festival. If not for that chance and unsatisfactory encounter, it would be another here in her place, trying to ruin that nice young Magi apprentice's life. She thinks back to the fascinating conversation she had with Rassan about the zodiac and the meaning of the Sphinx. She then remembers her own journey to that far-off exotic land of Egypt when she was just a ten-year-old and first-year acolyte of the Temple. Her mistress was commissioned by the priestesses of Zarpanuta to go to the magnificent library in Alexandria and research that very monument to see its relationship to their patron goddess. On the way, they stopped in Giza to look at it for a few days before proceeding to the coast. She remembers how exotically beautiful it was, and that it never impressed her as an idol to some goddess, but as something different. She also remembers that her mistress had not been thrilled with evidence she found at the library concerning the Sphinx, and though she brought many texts and an ancient stone hieroglyphic back with her to Babylon, nothing more was said about the trip. She makes a mental note to find those things and discover what they revealed about the Sphinx that was so disappointing.

As Rassan makes his way back to the Magi Astronomical Temple, he finds it hard to breathe as he thinks about his encounter with Varaz. After losing both of his parents before they could negotiate a suitable betrothal for him, the stewardship of his family was temporarily put on his cousin, Bozan. Technically, it would be up to him to find Rassan a future wife. But his friend, Prince Phraates V, told him that once he is ready, he should tell him, and he and the emperor would see to the matter, like the emperor did with his father's second marriage. Having just met the girl, he knows it is preposterous, but he toys with the idea of sending a dispatch back to the capital asking the prince to consider negotiating having Varaz betrothed to him.

He pushes the impulse down for the moment and thinks through how he, Kaufa, and Rita-Raina are going to prepare for the debate. But Varaz continues to invade his thoughts.

The next day, Rassan shows up unexpectedly at Baazar's tent, claiming that he did not buy enough ink the previous day, and he stays a full hour, talking to Varaz about more of the upcoming debate. Every day after that, he somehow convinces himself to find an excuse to visit her and talk. Soon, people notice his visits and conversations swirl about a Magi apprentice from the Astronomical Sect who is seen talking in the market with the niece of Baazar, the papyrus merchant.

10

The Matter of Debate

One Week Later, Astronomical Sect's Library

Seated at a long table in the back of the study area are Rassan, Rita-Raina, and Kaufa, with several parchments comprising of star charts, drawings of the Sphinx, notes, and scrolls. Rassan and Kaufa are fully engaged in taking notes and cross-referencing facts. Rita-Raina sits with his eyes darting from them to where Hymayeak and Whama are seated across the room at a similar table studying documents and conversing with two of the senior Magi of the Temple.

Rita-Raina cannot believe that he finds himself aligned with the two apprentices that have no Magi background in their families. He muses that even if they could solidly prove to the entire Astronomical Sect that the purpose of the Egyptian Sphinx was to set the beginning and the end of the zodiac, it would still have a minimal chance of winning the majority vote.

Headmaster Daraya-Vous would vote for them, of course, but his vote would only be used if there were a tie. Then he looks up and sees the other reason he feels that they have no chance of winning. Ambassador Samekh and Arsam come into the library from a side entrance that opens from the headmaster's chambers. He is completely perplexed about why the headmaster would offer the counsel of a foreigner and a servant boy to the apprentices who are representing his own stance in the debate. When his father finds out what side he represented and who he is now forced to work with, he will be very upset with him. That thought only deepens his conviction to continue down this path. Aggravating his father was something that rested well in his being.

Although Samekh is not recognized as a Magi in the Parthian Empire, he is still the official ambassador from the Nabataean kingdom and is here by permission of the emperor himself. Everyone in the library rises when he enters and gives him the customary bow of respect, which he happily returns as he and Arsam make their way to Rassan's table. When he gets there, Rassan beams. "Ambassador, Kaufa just told me that the subject of the Lion and its relation to the Tribe of Judah is referenced from the first book of the Hebrew scrolls, referring to when Israel was blessing his son, Judah. That it is him foretelling that their Messiah would come out of Judah's line."[12]

Samekh motions for everyone to have a seat. He nods to Rassan and then looks at the documents on the table and finds a copy of the star chart with the constellation Leo in it and holds it up. "Headmaster Daraya-Vous told me of Rassan's encounter with Vinda-Farnah outside of the capital. He told you that the answers they sought were in the Lion of the Tribe of Judah, which we know from the sacred star charts of Belteshazzar refers to this constellation here."

Before Rassan can respond, Rita-Raina points at Kaufa and says, "Ambassador, I understand that the Hebrew scrolls attest that the savior of the world is to come from the Judean people and that Kaufa has knowledge of those writings. But we are preparing for a debate to take place before the Astronomical Sect of the Parthian Empire's Magi. Those scrolls are forbidden throughout Parthia except in sanctioned Judean settlements. Using them as a reference to build our case as to the beginning and ending of the zodiac could prove disastrous!"

Kaufa's cheeks flush and he looks like he wants to attack Rita-Raina, but Ambassador Samekh holds up his hand and stays him from saying anything. "Magi Apprentice Rita-Raina, you have a point in that the Hebrew Scriptures are not something that we can solely base your debate before the Magi Council on. But remember, I am an ambassador of the Nabataean kingdom and have had much experience with negotiating treaties, discussing economic trade, and many other matters with not only the Parthian Empire but also the Roman as well. Though those two great powers pretend to ignore that anything could be of importance coming from the small country of Israel, they have more times than not had to acknowledge that the Hebrews and their scrolls have had much influence over the world for thousands of years. Therefore, it would be a fallacy of the grossest extreme to ignore their influence in our present debate. But your point is well taken, and I believe you should be the one to lead us in finding non-Judean documentation to back up our debate points."

Rita-Raina looks back at the ambassador with a sense of bewilderment. "Wait a minute, it was only a few weeks ago that I was totally convinced that the zodiac had no beginning or ending. If not for what I found in this library about the meaning of the Sphinx, I'd be sitting over there." He points to the table across the room where the others are seated, preparing for their part of the debate.

Samekh looks sternly at the apprentice. "Good. Now, retrieve those Egyptian parchments for us. While you are at it, see what else you can dig up. We'll stay here and continue our discussion of the Hebrew contribution to our debate."

Rita-Raina, now completely exasperated with the ambassador, darts his eyes between Rassan and Kaufa and sees right through their weak attempts to hide the pure delight they both are having at his being told what to do by a foreigner. He stands and pulls together what dignity he can muster and says, "I think a comparison of the Greek and Egyptian interpretations of the zodiac would be a good place to start. After I get those documents for you, Ambassador Samekh, that is where I will focus my attention."

"Good choice, Rita-Raina. I suggest you investigate the Chaldean and Persian manuscripts that predate the times of Alexander the Great and the Hellenistic Empire. A good place to start would be the Chaldean astronomer, Naburimannu, who was a contemporary of Belteshazzar six hundred years ago; the Persian astronomer, Al-Khwarizmi, who lived eight hundred years ago; and another Persian astronomer, Khayyam, who lived over a thousand years ago. These parchments should still be in the librarian's holder for refiling, seeing that Headmaster Daraya-Vous and I spent the greater part of last night going over their writings and charts that you have here."

Rita-Raina's cheeks are now flushed with embarrassment at finding out how knowledgeable of a foreign Magi Ambassador Samekh truly is. He nods and makes his way to the librarian's section to find the parchments.

Once he is out of earshot, Samekh winks at Rassan, Arsam, and Kaufa and chuckles. "He really is a remarkable boy. It will be interesting to see what he comes up with. The Greek's version of the meaning of the zodiac is really our greatest rival. They have taken the ancient meanings of the stars and completely hidden their true nature. The Magician Sect of the Magi is the one that has really embraced most of their interpretations. Rita-Raina's father, Headmaster Dvandas, is adamant about following their train of thought. I've met him several times and a more arrogant man in Parthia there is not. Our stance in this debate goes against the very core beliefs of the Magician Sect of the Magi in Parthia. Once he hears that his own son is debating on our side, he will be livid. The boy has courage."

He folds his hands together and rubs them vigorously as he scans the parchments and sees what he is looking for. He grabs it and holds it up to the young men sitting at the table. "Here, we have the constellation of Virgo. We are going to endeavor to prove to the Magi Council that this is the beginning of the zodiac, and thus the starting point of the Creator's message to mankind. How do you men suggest we do that?"

Arsam and Rassan both look like they are about to say something, but Kaufa interjects. "I told the headmaster once that the first scroll of the Hebrew Scriptures says that the Creator put enmity between the seed of the woman and the serpent, and that the serpent would bruise the seed of the woman's heel, and that the seed of the woman would bruise his head. That section of the scroll is the very first prophecy given for the coming of the Messiah, or the Creator's champion.[13] Literally, that means that the Creator's champion would be the offspring of the woman, represented by the constellation Virgo."[14]

Rassan and Arsam lean forward and both point to the right hand of the depiction of the woman and the brightest star in the center of her hand. Rassan says, "That is the star *Al Zimach*, and it represents the branch in her hand, which foretells the coming of the promised one."

Ambassador Samekh smiles. "Very good, Rassan. How does a branch foretell the coming of the Creator's champion?"

Arsam nods his head and before Rassan can answer, he says, "In the notes written on the sacred star charts, Belteshazzar states that the branch stands for the seed of the woman and is, therefore, her offspring, and that he would have many aspects to his nature; but some of the most notable are of him being the son of man and the son of the Creator, a servant to his fellow man, and a king." [15]

Rassan laughs. "Thank you for answering for me, Arsam. I was just about to say the same thing."

Arsam's eyes go wide as a chill of embarrassment goes through his stomach. "Sorry, Rassan, it's just so exciting getting to be a part of all this with you and Ambassador Samekh. I forgot about my place. It won't happen again."

Rassan chuckles and pats his young friend on the back. "Nonsense, you are here at the special invitation of Headmaster Daraya-Vous, and your place is as the assistant to Ambassador Samekh. You have just as much of a right to speak your mind as any of us."

Samekh looks approvingly at both young men and then points to the constellation of Coma, which is depicted on the same chart to the left of Virgo. "This chart depicts the Creator's champion as 'the Desire of all Nations' and shows him being nurtured by his mother, Abu Masher, the virgin.[16] This also ties the constellations of Virgo and Leo together, Virgo being the mother of the king and the one who raises him, and Leo being the king she raised him to be. Most Persian, Chaldean, and Egyptian astronomers who predate the Greek Empire agree that this is the meaning of the two constellations. Kaufa, how do the Hebrew scrolls complement these concepts?"

Kaufa stares at him for a moment, trying to think, then says, "I don't have the entire collection of Hebrew scrolls memorized, Ambassador, but I think that there is a passage in the Prophet Haggai's scroll that uses the phrase 'the Desire of all Nations ...'"

"No one expects you to know it all, Kaufa. But any insight you have from that perspective will be very helpful."

Rita-Raina spends the rest of the day looking into all the things he was asked to, and then finds a secluded area of the library to merge what he has found. As he spreads the scrolls and star charts out on the table, Hymayeak and Whama step out from behind the closest shelves, holding some parchments, and sit down across from him. They are far enough away from Ambassador Samekh's group and behind several shelves, so they will not be noticed. Hymayeak is the first to speak. "So, are you really serious about taking the side of the headmaster in this debate, Rita-Raina?"

"Unlike the two of you, I do not ignore facts," Rita-Raina answers. He points to the copies of hieroglyphics about the Sphinx. "There is no ambiguity about what these say. The purpose of the Sphinx is to show that the zodiac begins with the constellation Virgo and ends with Leo."

Whama takes the scroll and looks at it for a moment, and then he looks back at Rita-Raina. "A copy, indeed, and not the original. How do we know it was copied and translated properly? This also shows that the copies of these hieroglyphics come from the same period that the Hebrew slave Joseph was made the head steward in Pharaoh's house. So, even if it is authentic, it could still only show that the Hebrew could have had its meaning altered to back up his own beliefs. As Pharaoh's main steward, he would have had this power."

Rita-Raina shakes his head with annoyance and points to the bottom of the parchments. "This is the seal of the headmaster of the Astronomical Sect." Then he lowers his finger to just below the seal and points to another stamp that has a quarter-moon figure and a star just to the right of it. "And this is the mark of the reigning grand master of the entire Magi Order, authenticating it. Challenging this document's authenticity would be to insult both. Not an intelligent maneuver to undertake in a debate governed by Magi."

Hymayeak and Whama stare incredulously at the marks, momentarily surprised, but then they recover and focus back on Rita-Raina. Hymayeak answers, "Rita-Raina, we would never pretend to insult our elders, but this debate is long overdue. The Astronomical Sect needs to catch up with the rest of the world on this matter. The whole cosmos contains everything about each of our lives. It's a genuine mystery. Your own father knows this to be true, and even the grand master has not ruled on this matter yet."

Rita-Raina sucks air through his teeth at the mention of his father. "Leave my father out of this! He never cared to be involved with me or my mother. Why should I be persuaded by any opinion of his? As for Grand Master Artapan, everyone knows he will rule on this from the counsel he gets from the Astronomical Sect. He barely tolerates the Magician Sect as Magi and only because of their constant meddling with matters of politics within the empire."

"This is true, but the grand master is old. Some say that your father will be chosen as his successor. The influence he holds at court will be taken seriously when the new election is held upon the Grand Master's death," Whama says with a little more timidity in his voice after Rita-Raina's outburst.

Rita-Raina leans back in his chair. "Headmaster Dvandas holds a high level of influence with Phraates IV and revels in letting everyone know about it any chance he gets. But the emperor's son, Phraates V, cannot stand the man and has, upon many occasions, embarrassed him publicly at court before the emperor. What do you propose will happen once he sits on the Parthian throne? Perhaps you amuse yourselves with thoughts of Grand Master Artapan dying before Phraates IV? Even if he does, what do you think the prince will do when he hears that my father is trying to take over the whole Magi Order?"

At that, Whama and Hymayeak both stand and dart their eyes back and forth, looking for anyone who may have noticed Rita-Raina's outburst. The prospect of others discovering that they are trying to turn him to their side is not something they want known.

"No one lives forever," Whama replies. "Not emperors, headmasters, or even a prince." He and Hymayeak then slink away.

Rita-Raina watches his fellow apprentices move to the other side of the library and take their seats with the rest of the Magi who are working with them. He sits there in shock at the subtle hint of treason against the emperor, his son, and the grand master. He muses that he knew his father's ambitions have no limit, but to hear from his fellow apprentices' hints of plans that could already be in place to move on these powerful men shakes him to his core. Frankly, he really did not believe that the issue they were debating could cause that much interest in the Magi Order. Even if the grand master were to legitimize Headmaster Daraya-Vous's stance on the zodiac, the Magician Sect would do as they have done from the beginning—ignore it and proceed with their own interpretations, unless they were going to use this debate to somehow discredit the Astronomical Sect in the eyes of the empire and capitalize on the momentum to proceed against any who sided with them.

He realizes that he could end up on the wrong end of all this. But then an enticing thought crosses his mind. If he could somehow help win the debate and then get the grand master to sanction their stand, then all this could easily blow up in his father's face, at which time the treason could be exposed, and Headmaster Dvandas would finally get what's coming to him. A very enticing thought indeed. This would require considerable thought, weighing all his options before deciding which path to take. He returns the parchments to their proper place in the library, then gathers his things and makes his way back to the table where Ambassador Samekh, Rassan, and the others are still working. He steps up to the ambassador and says, "I need to go to the observatory to check on some things, then I will retire to my quarters. I'll tell you what I found in the morning."

"Did you check on those astronomers I suggested?" Samekh asks.

Rita-Raina's left eyebrow lifts slightly. "I did. Your suggestions were quite enlightening. It would seem that before the Greek Empire took over the Persian Empire, the predominant consensus among Eastern astronomers was, indeed, that the zodiac had a beginning and an end, and that it started with Virgo and ended with Leo."

"Very good, Rita-Raina. I look forward to hearing your insight on these matters after your research is completed." Ambassador Samekh holds up both hands to each of the Magi apprentices. "In the upcoming debate, each apprentice from this table will be tasked with presenting a different aspect of our argument to the council. It is my belief that Rita-Raina is most suited to present the history of the interpretations to the meaning of the zodiac. By that, I mean he should show where the differences of opinions originated and what cultural influences they were developed from."

Rassan turns to Kaufa, and they both nod their heads in unison. Rassan looks back at Ambassador Samekh and replies. "Agreed. Rita-Raina has already proved that his education and prowess in history and culture far exceed our own. He is the most suited to handle this aspect of the presentation." He then looks at his friend Arsam and sadly smiles. "It is unfortunate that Arsam cannot be a part of the presentation. His memory of the sacred star charts and the notes from former headmasters, especially those of Belteshazzar, would prove invaluable."

"Indeed, you are correct in that reasoning, Rassan. Not to worry. We have plenty of time to prepare, and you two have already developed such good corroboration in your study of those charts that you will be quite suited to handle the presentation from that perspective admirably." He then looks to Kaufa and says, "There is a Judean synagogue south of Babylon, in a settlement that the Nabataean caravans frequent. I have kingdom business there next week. Since you are the grandson of a notable rabbi, you would have access to the Hebrew scrolls in that synagogue. I want you to accompany me to that place, where you can prepare your presentation about the Hebrew belief of a coming Messiah and how he will rise out of the tribe of Judah, which is represented by the constellation Leo."

Kaufa, though taken aback by the suggestion, is exhilarated at the prospect. He nods his head. "The headmaster must approve…"

Ambassador Samekh holds up his hand. "Approval already given, Kaufa."

Rassan shakes his head. "Ambassador Samekh, you already knew which aspects of the debate each of us should handle, didn't you?"

The ambassador stands, stretches, and picks up his things. "Of course, Rassan. What do you think Daraya-Vous and I have been discussing for the last several evenings? Now, Arsam, we must be off to see the headmaster and give our report. Good day, Apprentices."

Same Time, Royal Palace at the Capital

Dvandas is livid about the revelation of the last report he received from Babylon. He expected that a debate would have to happen over the true meaning of the zodiac and fostered its coming to fruition by sowing discord in the Astronomical Sect for years. But to think that Rita-Raina would choose to represent a stance that is in direct opposition to his own has him unbalanced with anger. "My son must be out of his mind!" he mumbles under his breath as he prepares to enter the royal court. Aware that showing the emperor any emotion that has nothing to do with the day's business could bring harsh consequences, especially if his son, Phraates V, were to show up. He takes a deep breath and lets it out slowly as he steps forward to stand by the emperor's right side and listen to the day's business.

It is not a pleasant sight to see that the first order of business has to do with a delegation sent from the Nabataean's court. He comforts himself with the thought that at least he does not have to deal with Ambassador Samekh. The man is just the Nabataean's counterpart to Headmaster Daraya-Vous, and anything he would have to say or do in his court's behalf would be represented from an Astronomical Sect's perspective. It disturbs him that the emperor gave Samekh leave to visit the Astronomical Sect in Babylon, and he cannot help but think that the delegation has something to do with their chief ambassador's visit. The man that is on one knee before the emperor's court is not someone Dvandas recognizes, but he concludes that he is one of Samekh's men, and he will not allow the man to have any undue influence in the court today.

"We, Emperor of the Parthian Empire, recognize Ambassador Temal of the Nabataean Court," the emperor proclaims as the man rises and makes his way to the proper place before the throne. Once there, he gives the proper bow and gestures of respect, then says, "Emperor Phraates IV, I bring greetings and gestures of respect from my liege, King Aretis Philopatris."

He raises his hand and six men in pairs come in, carrying large wooden crates. When they get close to the ambassador, they put the crates down and open the lids. The first crate is full of freshly minted gold coins with the emperor's image on them. The second is full of the finest processed frankincense in the world. The third is full of the best Nabataean myrrh. As the lids are lifted, the sparkle from the coins reflects on the ceiling of the palace, and the exquisite aroma from the other two fills the room.

The emperor's eyes go wide with glee. He stands and goes directly to the crate of gold coins, grabs one, and lifts it to his eyes to study it.

"This is an unexpected but delightful surprise. Did King Aretis have these made in his own mints for our pleasure?"

"That he did, Your Majesty. He heard your mints are taking longer than you wanted them to in producing your new coins, and he asked me to have this chest of samples made and presented to you as a gift. And to tell you that, if it serves your needs, he would be happy to offer the services of the Nabataean mints to help expedite the production of your new coins."

Phraates IV nods approvingly, takes the coin and walks back up to his throne. He smiles at Dvandas, who immediately reaches out to receive the coin. But instead of handing it to him, the emperor looks over at his son and hands him the coin. "What do you think of the craftmanship?" he asks.

Phraates holds the coin up to the light and turns it over twice. "Exquisite craftmanship, Father!" He then hands it to Dvandas. "Don't you agree, Dvandas?"

Everyone in the court knows that Dvandas was handed the responsibility of having the coins ready for the emperor for his upcoming visit to the eastern part of the empire in four months. What no one knows is that he purposely slowed down the process because of his plans to unseat Phraates IV and his son. He is furious at the thought that if the Nabataeans can take up the slack and fulfill the emperor's desire, it will hinder many of those plans. He receives the coin and mimics the emperor and his son's actions, holding it up to the light and turning it around in his hands a couple of times, studying the detail. "It appears to be exactly like our own, Your Majesty." He looks at the ambassador. "Is the gold at the proper level of purity for a coin that carries the Parthian emperor's image on it?"

Ambassador Temal reels from the not-so-subtle insult from Dvandas. "Have it melted down and check the purity yourselves. The test will show that the gold has gone through at least seven cycles of purification."

The emperor gives Dvandas an irritated glance, then turns to the Nabataean ambassador. "We would never assume to doubt the integrity of the Nabataean court, Ambassador. We are delighted with your offer to help in the minting of our new coin and are delighted to receive the gifts. After you leave our presence, please make an appointment with my son and Dvandas to discuss terms for the gaining of the minted coins from your liege. Would there be any other matters you would like to discuss with us?"

"There is one other matter, Your Majesty. Ambassador Samekh seeks your permission to remain in Babylon to fellowship with the Astronomical Sect of Magi for a few more months."

Before Dvandas can say anything, Phraates V places a hand on his father's forearm and says, "Ambassador Samekh has been a true liaison for us and the Nabatean court, which continues to prove a most profitable relationship for us, Father. I counsel granting this request."

"Your counsel is wise, my son. But I would need to know the details for that extension, Ambassador."

"Of course, Your Majesty. The Astronomical Sect of the Magi has announced that a debate will take place concerning the true meaning of the zodiac. As is their custom, the debate will be conducted by Magi apprentices who are counseled by senior members of the Magi in their sect. Though he is not a Parthian Magi, Headmaster Daraya-Vous has asked Ambassador Samekh to counsel the group of apprentices that represents his stance on this matter. As Your Majesty is aware, Ambassador Samekh is Nabataean's chief astronomer and head of our Magi."

Phraates IV looks over at his son. "Did you know about this upcoming debate?"

"I did, Father. Only because the last letter I received from Rassan told me about it, and that he would be one of the debaters representing Headmaster Daraya-Vous's stance."

The emperor looks back at Ambassador Temal. "This is wonderful news, Ambassador. Though we are only mildly interested in the substance of this debate, to hear that our kinsman, Rassan, will have access to receive counsel and tutelage from a person of Ambassador Samekh's caliber does our soul good. Your request is granted. My son will see that the proper orders will be sent to Babylon immediately."

Dvandas is doing all he can to contain his anger. A devious idea crosses his mind and gives him inspiration to speak. "Your Majesty, it just occurred to me that you and I will be in Babylon in four months while you visit the eastern parts of your realm. Perhaps it would be advantageous for you to be there to hear the debate yourself. Since your kinsman will be involved, it will be the perfect opportunity to see for yourself how he is doing while on this adventure you sent him on almost two years ago. Also, this debate is of such a nature that Grand Master Artapan will oversee its proceedings and, though not required, it would be profitable for myself to attend, being the head of the Magician Sect of the Parthian Magi. After all, once the debate is over and the grand master has tallied the votes and ratified the decision, it still needs to come to you for empirical acknowledgement. If done while you are there, this can all be handled quickly and efficiently."

Temal is taken aback by Dvandas's suggestion. "Your Majesty, the debate is scheduled to happen in less than two months."

Dvandas knew this but is undaunted. "True, Ambassador," he replies, "but these things are fluid and can be adjusted to suit the emperor's timetable." He then turns to the emperor and says, "Your Majesty, allow me to handle this internally with the grand master and Headmaster Daraya-Vous. I am sure that once they know when both of us can be there, they will accommodate."

The emperor puts his hand to his chin and thinks for a moment, then looks to Dvandas. "You know I dislike interfering with Magi business, especially when someone as capable and loyal as Artapan is overseeing things. But if you can make this all work, then go ahead. If not, I will simply acknowledge it when we get there. As for Rassan, we do plan to summon him when we are there to see how he is doing."

Dvandas takes a quick glance in the prince's direction to see if any objections are coming and then focuses on the emperor. "It will be my pleasure to handle these matters. Your Majesty, it was never decided if your son will join us for this trip. Have you decided? I think it would be an excellent education for him to see some more of the empire."

The emperor holds up his hand to stay Dvandas's question and focuses on Ambassador Temal. "Please send our thanks to King Aretis for his kind gifts and his offer to help us in our minting. You are free to leave our court, Ambassador."

He lets the man exit, then turns to Dvandas. "I am glad you asked your question here in our court, Dvandas, because I want it recorded that Phraates V will remain in the capital and handle daily matters in my stead while we are away. We spoke about this last night and agreed it would be the best solution all the way around. Though he does lament giving up a chance to see his companion, Rassan, he knows that his duty to the throne and the needs of the empire come first. So, next month when you and I depart, he will stay here and rule in my name."

After the court adjourns, Dvandas makes his way back to the Magician Sect's section of the palace. He is unhappy that the emperor and his son will not both be on the trip to Babylon. His hope was to arrange for their demise on the return trip. The day was not a total loss, though, because with the emperor present to see the Magi Astronomical Sect humiliated in the upcoming debate, he can use that to strengthen his chances of succeeding Grand Master Artapan and someday completely wiping out the Astronomical Sect once and for all. When he gets to his office, he drafts a letter telling Headmaster Daraya-Vous to postpone the debate until the emperor arrives. He then drafts a similar letter to Grand Master Artapan, leaving out the demand about the debate but informing him that he and the emperor will be arriving in four months.

11

Hidden Truths

Next Day, Temple of the Goddess Zarpanuta

Varaz has been very careful to maintain her persona as a former priestess's acolyte, now merchant assistant, so she no longer dons her own priestess robes, even while in her Temple. She knows that to fall out of character in any way could ruin her chances of enticing Rassan to ask his family to seek a betrothal with her. She is very aware that any lie worth its salt must have some truth in it or it will be easily exposed. She is Baazar the papyrus merchant's niece, and she has worked for him in the past. But that was before she took her vows as a priestess of Zarpanuta. She has always been one of the more physically alluring in her order, and, therefore, much sought after during the erotic ceremonies held at the Temple.

But now that she is on a special assignment negotiated by the Magician Magi, Mihri, with her own high priestess, she does not want to draw any undue attention to herself, especially after her encounter with that pig Parthian commander, Sasheen, at her uncle's stand the other day. She had half a mind to report his stupidity to Mihri after he vagrantly spoke about their encounter at the spring festival. Then a strange but warm feeling of hope goes through her when she contemplates that the successful outcome of her mission will be marriage to an honorable man like Rassan. In that outcome, she would no longer have to partake in the festivals and could devote herself to him and his family's responsibilities. She finds the prospect of devoting herself to one such as Rassan not unappealing at all.

Lost in thought, she fails to notice the entrance of the high priestess into the waiting chamber.

"Varaz, is there something you need, dear? I thought we agreed that you were not to come here until your mission is complete and your betrothal to the Astronomical Sect apprentice has been formed."

Varaz clears her thoughts and immediately goes to one knee, taking the high priestess's right hand in hers and kissing her insignia ring. "Forgive me, Madam. I was lost in strategies concerning my mission and did not hear you enter."

Once a priestess ascends to the high priestess's office, her name is never used. She must always be referred to as either Madam or High Priestess. Because Varaz was her personal acolyte before her ascension, she knows her true name but will never speak it again. When she lifts her head, her eyes meet the hard blue eyes belonging to the beautiful but stern face of her superior.

The high priestess lifts her hand and Varaz immediately stands. She places her palm on Varaz's cheek. "You were one of my most brilliant acolytes and could have been my successor someday, Varaz. It pains me to think that the devil, Mihri, and his master, Dvandas, are taking you away from me to serve their own political aspirations. A betrothal to the future head of the family of one of Parthia's most famous generals is barely a suitable alternative to my intentions toward you, but Dvandas has grown powerful in the Parthian court, and to not accommodate his wishes is neither wise nor safe. Tell me, what brings you here?"

Varaz bows her head. "Only to further my mission's success and do your bidding, Madam. There is a debate brewing within the Magi ranks that Rassan has been called on to partake in."

"You speak of their conflict over the true meaning and purpose of the zodiac?"

"Yes, Madam, but the stance of the headmaster of the Astronomical Sect is that it has a beginning and an end that is depicted by the constellations, starting at Virgo and ending with Leo."

Varaz's words bring up an unpleasant memory that she knows Varaz has some knowledge of. "You know that subject is one of my least favorite to discuss!"

"I do, Madam, and I have no ambition to remind you of painful memories, but I believe that the existence of the evidence we have here in the Temple of Zarpanuta is pertinent and could be used to our advantage if handled delicately."

The high priestess takes a step closer to Varaz, suddenly angry. "How can my greatest failure that nearly cost me the high priestess chair ever be of any use to us?"

Varaz keeps her composure. "Because, Madam, you hold the proof that the Astronomical Sect's stance on this matter is corroborated by the most ancient of astronomers. Something that would ruin Dvandas's and Mihri's plans to sabotage the upcoming debate. That means you have leverage over the Magician Sect of the Magi. Something I know you have wanted for as long as I can remember."

The high priestess's eyes bore into Varaz's soul for a few moments as her words sink in. She smiles, places both of her hands on the young priestess's shoulders and shakes her. "You have always been my favorite, Varaz. Only you could take one of my biggest mistakes and turn it into something that could benefit me." She embraces her for a moment and then turns toward the door. "Come, let us go find that thing and have a good look at it. I swear I have not seen it in a decade."

They make their way to the archives chamber at the other side of the Temple, where Varaz dismisses the chamber steward and then helps her superior find the item they seek. Minutes turn into hours as they uncover enormous stone and wooden boxes, looking for the item. Just as the high priestess's patience is about to give out, Varaz exclaims from across the room, "Here it is!"

The high priestess looks up and sighs. "Finally. I put it in here thinking I'd never look for it again." She walks over to Varaz and investigates the stone box and sees several rolls of papyrus lying on a piece of a hieroglyphics stone tablet. Varaz removes the papyrus, and the high priestess reaches in and pulls the tablet out. "I thought this would be a crowning jewel to our order's emergence in dominating religion in the empire. I was so sure that our little trip to Egypt would provide me with the historical documentation that the Sphinx of Giza is the astronomical monument that proves once and for all that Zarpanuta is the Supreme Goddess in the heavens, and that even Marduk himself was her subject."

She holds the tablet out to Varaz and exclaims, "I've taught you to read hieroglyphics. What does this say about the Sphinx?"

Varaz steps closer to the tablet in her superior's hand and translates the symbols. "Be it known to all that gaze upon this monument that the heavens declare the Creator's plan. A woman will give birth to a champion, and he will turn men away from darkness and to the light. The woman is Virgo and her seed is the Lion, Leo. This marks the beginning and end of the divine zodiac, which shows the seed's path and man's redemption." She looks up at her superior and says, "But has it been said that the papyruses we have that were copied from this date back to the Pharaoh Zoser, while a Hebrew named Joseph was his chief steward?"

The high priestess smiles sadly. "Yes, that is true. All the copies we have are dated back to that time. It was probably the Hebrew, Joseph, who had them made. But look at the inscription on the back of the tablet."

Varaz turns the tablet over in her hands, blows off some dust, and again starts the translation. "Inscribed by Assoxed, chief counselor and chief astronomer to King Kufa Cheops, Pharaoh of Egypt." When she finishes reading the inscription, she lifts her head. "Kufa of Egypt reigned over a thousand years before Zoser. This tablet was made about the same time that the Sphinx was built."

The high priestess solemnly nods. "Yes, and this is the oldest artifact known in existence that gives the ancients' purpose in constructing the Sphinx of Giza. When I got to the library in Alexandria of Egypt, it was in the possession of the priests of On. They were quite enthusiastic about bargaining a high price for its purchase. I know now that they were just eager to get it out of Egypt because it contradicts so many of their beliefs. They told me that On forbade them to translate it to anyone and that I would have to seek its decipherment from another source."

"That is why you brought the Egyptian scholar on our return trip. You had me sit with you as he taught you hieroglyphics. But you never had this out when I was present," Varaz says as she holds up the tablet.

"No, I wanted to be the only one who knew its meaning until I could publicly reveal it to the high priestess at that time. But once I translated it, I was so upset I almost dashed it against a stone and burned the papyruses that came with it."

"How did you handle the high priestess when we returned?"

"Well, I had to give an account for the expense. So, I told her that the hieroglyphics were of a nature that translations will take much longer than I expected. She was always more interested in our next festival and soon forgot about the matter." She gazes at the tablet for a moment. "To think that this will bring me some of the power and influence I sought when I originally went after it. Headmaster Dvandas will now be a bit more accommodating to my needs. Summon Mihri, my dear. Tell him it is important, and that we must speak at once."

She hands the tablet to Varaz and walks out of the chamber. Once at the door, she looks over her shoulder. "Have that tablet and the papyruses stored in my personal vault and tell no one where they are." A thought hits her mind. "Varaz, take off that dreary costume and put on your priestess attire. Once I talk with Mihri, the terms of your betrothal to that Magi apprentice are going to be much more in our favor and not his."

"I will, High Priestess," Varaz says, bowing her head.

Once the high priestess is gone, Varaz gazes at the tablet and the papyruses. Her mind goes back to the last couple of days and how she was so amused and flattered by how Rassan found excuses to come back to the central market and talk with her. She admits to herself that the passion with which he would recount all the unique elements of the upcoming debate he was preparing for intrigued and excited her. Having entertained many soldiers at her order's festivals, she could see by his mannerisms that he was part of that caste but is intrigued by how much more there is to his character. She must admit to herself that she is drawn to Rassan. It then hits her that she holds in her hand the key to turning the debate in Rassan's favor before the Magi Council. She shakes that thought vigorously from her mind as she calls the chamber steward to help her move the things to the other side of the Temple. Once there, she dismisses him and puts them in the vault herself.

Later That Evening, High Priestess's Private Chambers

The guards at the entrance to the high priestess of Zarpanuta's private chambers immediately recognize Magician Magi Mihri and open the doors to let him through. When he steps in, his eyes are greeted by the exquisite presence of the high priestess herself. He has always been infatuated by the woman's beauty and sensual presence. He loves the power and influence his master Dvandas has over her and her order. A few weeks ago, at the ritual for the spring harvest, being the highest-ranking member in his order afforded him the privilege of choosing her as a partner. His throat goes dry at the memory. Staring at her makes his hairless head perspire.

He moves closer and asks, "High Priestess, to what do I owe the honor of this late-night summons?"

"Magi Mihri, thank you for heeding my call. I have a matter of profound interest to you and your master that I wish to speak to you about. Please have a seat while I fix you some refreshment." She points to a reclining chaise lounge. Mihri smiles and has a seat while the high priestess walks over to an ornate marble table with several vases filled with different wines and ales. She already knows his preference and pours him some Arabian ale in a goblet and hands it to him. He brings the goblet to his mouth and swallows half of the ale in one gulp.

To his disappointment, the high priestess ignores the space next to him and sits down across from him on a small stool. She demurely smiles at him, reveling in his disappointment, and says, "I have called you here because I have knowledge of your plans concerning the son of General Surena and your intended demise of the Astronomical Sect of the Magi."

Mihri puts his drink to the side and lets out a short, irritated huff. "High Priestess, you are an extremely intelligent woman. Headmaster Dvandas and I suspected that you would eventually realize some of our plans. Be warned, we will not tolerate any interference by you or your order. The consequences would be dire."

Under normal circumstances, Mihri talking to her like that would have been cause for great concern. But that was before she had something that could really hurt his master's plans. She stands up and walks over to the marble table and pours herself some sweet Babylonian honey wine and takes a delicate sip.

"My dear Mihri, Headmaster Dvandas's plans are safe. I only wish to talk with you about the upcoming debate that will take place in the Astronomical Sect of the Magi."

Mihri immediately stands. "What do you know of such things?"

"Only that it is one reason you contracted my order to have one of our priestesses entice the son of General Surena to want to seek a betrothal to her, and then have her seduce him out of the Astronomical Sect of the Magi."

"I think that besides the debate, these points are part of our original deal. I ask again what this is all about?"

Now, having Mihri a little unhinged, she knows it is time to put her key card on the table. "I know that the debate is to decide the age-old question in the Magi Order concerning the true meaning of the zodiac. And that whoever wins that debate before the Magi Council will have their findings ratified by the grand master himself. If the findings favor the stance held by the Magician Sect, it will give Master Dvandas the clout he needs to be voted in as the next grand master of the Magi Order, at which point he can dissolve the Astronomical Sect and take over the rest of the Magi. Which he wants to accomplish before the death of Phraates IV and the succession of his son, whom everyone knows cannot stand the Magician Sect and would not allow Dvandas to accomplish his goals."

He is astonished that this harlot of a high priestess has figured this much out about their plans, but he still cannot understand why she thinks she can benefit from it. "Even though your words are true, what makes you think that anything you have could give you any more than what we have already promised you?"

"Because, my dear Magi friend, I have proof that the Astronomical Sect of the Magi is completely accurate in their belief that the ancient Egyptian Sphinx proclaims that the nature of the zodiac is the Creator's story of how He will send His champion to save mankind. That the zodiac begins with the constellation Virgo, the mother of the champion, and ends with the constellation Leo, which represents his ascension as king to his rightful throne as the Son of the Creator."

A cold chill goes down Mihri's spine at the impact of the high priestess's words. He inhales deeply. He pushes his face up close to hers, his attitude suddenly full of menace. "What could you possibly have that could prove such a thing?"

She takes a step back, lifts the goblet to her mouth, takes a sip of her wine then laughs. "The dedication plaque of the Sphinx written by the chief astronomer to Pharaoh Kufa Cleops, with the seal of both and the date on the back."

Despite himself, Mihri has to sit down and catch his breath. He already knows that Kufa lived hundreds of years before the Hebrew slave Joseph and that any artifact from his court could hold much sway in a debate among the Magi today. He looks around and finds a cloth to wipe his brow and then he looks over to the high priestess. "How is that even possible? Anything of that nature would be in the archives of the priests of On. They would die before releasing anything of that nature to the outside world."

The high priestess takes her seat across from Mihri and laughs again. "True, Mihri, but you fail to consider that after the demise of Cleopatra, their order was sent into chaos. Egypt cannot function without someone to sit in Pharaoh's place. When I visited them twelve years ago, they had begged Augustus Caesar to name himself Pharaoh so that their oligarchy could continue as before. But they also knew that as Pharaoh, the Roman emperor would have full access to all their secrets. Having the true purpose of the Sphinx fall into Roman hands was more than they could bear. So, they sold it to me. At the time I purchased it, I thought it would proclaim Zarpanuta as chief among the gods and thus exalt my order. But when I deciphered its true meaning, I had it hidden…until now."

"When can I see this plaque, High Priestess?"

She laughs. "Oh, Mihri, if this negotiation goes as planned, neither you nor Dvandas will ever see it. The only time I will allow it to appear in public is if you force me to present it to Grand Master Artapan. I don't think that you or your master will ever want that to happen."

"What do you want, High Priestess?"

"Well, at first, I was going to demand that you release Varaz from her mission to marry the Magi apprentice, Rassan. But after looking into the matter, I found that he is highly favored by Prince Phraates

V and could find himself as influential in his court as Dvandas is in his father's. That being the case, it is in my best interest to let this little ruse of yours continue. But once they are married and he is under the control of the Magician Sect of the Magi, I want full access to them both and a say in whatever counsel he gives to the emperor."

Mihri grinds his teeth. He sees she holds the best cards in this little game and does not want to rock the boat for Master Dvandas's other plans. "I will send a coded dispatch to Dvandas immediately detailing your conditions for keeping the existence of the plaque silent. Be warned, High Priestess, Dvandas does not like to be blackmailed and his wrath can be fierce when pushed. As for now, we will continue on the same path together. Agreed?"

"Of course, Mihri. As I said, it is now a mutually beneficial plan and I want it to succeed as much as you."

With that, Mihri hurriedly exits her chambers. The high priestess enjoys another glass of her honey wine and calls for her chamberlains to come and entertain her.

12

A Matter for Family

Two Weeks Later, A Small Settlement Thirty Miles South of Babylon

Commander Sasheen reins his horse in as he holds up his hand for the two cavalrymen who accompanied him to do the same. He does not know the name of the settlement that he just rode into, but he does know that the man he seeks has a large farm on the outskirts of it. He looks around the tiny central market and sees a woman and young maiden selling produce in the shade by a well. He dismounts his horse, hands his reins to one of his men, and walks in their direction. He guesses the woman is in her late forties or early fifties, and that the girl with her must either be her granddaughter or a maid, because she cannot be over twelve years old. As he approaches her, she dismisses the young girl and stands up for his arrival. "How may I be of service to an officer of the emperor's calvary?" she asks.

He smiles. "I am Commander Sasheen and I seek Bozan, the cousin and steward of the house of the late General Surena."

"Then you seek my husband, and he is in the fields today and will not be back at the farm until this evening." She looks behind to where she sent the girl and calls, "Mahre, come here."

"Yes, Grandmother."

"Mahre, this is Commander Sasheen of the emperor's calvary. He has official business with your grandfather and will come home with us. Start cleaning up the stand and loading the wagon." She turns back to Sasheen. "If you and your men will be patient, we should be ready to leave within the hour. There is a tavern across the courtyard where you can refresh yourselves while my granddaughter and I make ready to escort you back to the farm."

At first impulse, he is tempted to rebuff her and insist that she make ready faster, but his throat is dry, and the horses could use watering and a rest. "That is acceptable, Madam…uh, I did not get your name."

"Mahre, the same as my granddaughter."

"Well then, Mahre, wife of Bozan, steward of the household of General Surena, my men and I will be back within the hour to follow you to your farm."

Four hours later, Commander Sasheen and his men, while following Mahre and her granddaughter's cart, come to the crest of a hill and see a house made of stone and a barn at the base of the hill with a few dozen sheep grazing in the pasture just outside. Beyond are acres of wheat and barley fields. The farmhouse has a well just to the side of it, and a watering trough for animals. Though not lavish in construction, like houses in the capital or Babylon, the farm exudes a flavor of elegance and abundance. Though trees are scarce in this area, there are a couple of fig trees close to the house that provide some shade from the blistering summer sun. He puts his hand to his mouth to amplify his voice as he calls ahead, "Mahre, wife of Bozan, is this your husband's farm?"

"Yes, it is, Commander Sasheen. You may use the trough to refresh your horses and then come in and I will have my servants see to your needs. My husband should be back shortly. Once my granddaughter and I have secured our cart and horse and put our things away, we will prepare for the evening meal and accommodations for you and your men."

As they approach the gate, a small caravan of men leading oxen and carts appear at the edge of a wheat field. One of them, an older man, lifts his arm and waves his hand as he shouts, "Mahre, I see you are back early, and you bring guests. What is happening?"

Before she can respond to her husband's call, Commander Sasheen prods his horse and canters it toward the party ahead. He holds up his hand to stop his men from following. When close enough to speak, he reins his horse and says, "Bozan, steward of the house of General Surena, I am Commander Sasheen of the emperor's royal calvary, and I am here on official business and must speak privately with you at once."

The man who Sasheen just addressed holds the younger man's gaze for a few moments as the words sink in. Then his steel-gray eyes take on a sharp expression. "I am still General Bozan of the emperor's royal calvary, and though I am no longer actively serving I will hold that rank until my death. Now, get off that horse and greet me in the proper military fashion!"

Commander Sasheen realizes that he has made a huge mistake. He jumps from his horse and, while still holding the reins with his left hand, takes his right and places his fist across his chest, bows his head, and salutes the man in proper military fashion. "Forgive me, General. I was not aware of your rank in the emperor's forces."

Bozan holds Sasheen in his salute for a few moments and then returns it. "Perhaps before you ride out from Babylon to talk to someone about official business, you should find out exactly who they are, Commander!" He steps closer to a now trembling Sasheen. "Didn't General Barach tell you my rank when he sent you to talk to me?"

Commander Sasheen gulps and replies, "General Barach did not send me. Mihri, assistant to the emperor's first counselor, Headmaster Dvandas of the Magician Sect of the Magi, did."

The general's eyes bore into him with an unreadable expression.

Beads of sweat drip from Sasheen's face. He realizes that he did not give the general's wife the respect her stature would have required of him. He gulps and tries to add, "General Bozan, again, I was not aware of your rank in the emperor's army…"

Before he can finish, Bozan throws his head back and bursts out laughing. He steps forward and places a meaty hand on Sasheen's shoulder and roughly shakes it. "You are one of those silly capital officers that grope after the Magician Sect of the Magi to partake in all their erotic festivals. General Barach told me about the recruitment efforts from that group going throughout the royal cavalry. When I served under my uncle in the war against Marcus Crassus of Rome, he ordered all of those black-hooded whore brokers out of our camp. He told me we could not have the men being bedazzled by all their alluring intoxications of wine and women."

He pauses and looks at Sasheen like one would look at a naughty, disappointing child, then shakes his head and continues. "The only reason that sorcerer Mihri would send you to me is to gain influence over my uncle's son, Rassan. Be warned, Commander, I made a vow to General Surena that his only son would be the head of our family someday. The emperor gave me stewardship of that seat because he knew I would never seek to keep it. Though I do not agree with Rassan becoming apprenticed to the Astronomical Sect of the Magi, it is still a profoundly better choice than the sect you have followed. Out of respect for his father, I have kept myself out of his business and I will not interfere unless he absolutely needs me."

"But there is a genuine need, General. Rassan has—"

General Bozan holds up his hand. "We will talk after you and your men are settled and fed." He looks back at his wife and grand-daughter, smiles and waves, then focuses back on Commander Sasheen. "Since you have cut short my dealings in the village to sell my produce, you and your men can take the carts that my wife came back with and help with the unloading and storing of the goods, along with the care of the beasts. My servants will direct you where needed. Once you are done, I will have food sent from the house to the stables, where you will be housed for the night. After your meal, I will visit you and we will discuss your business here."

Later that evening, Commander Sasheen and his men finish their meal and begin to set up their bed rolls on the dirt floor of the general's barn. He cannot believe that Mihri did not warn him that Bozan was a general in the army. He is obviously retired, but in the Parthian military, one keeps his rank for life in case his is ever needed.

When he is finally settled down from the general's strong rebuke, he realizes that it all made perfect sense. Who else would the emperor trust to steward a military house as prestigious as Rassan's then its highest-ranking military member? While putting the produce away and caring for the animals, he forms a strategy on how he can talk to General Bozan to enlist his help with Rassan's betrothal.

Out of the corner of his eye, he sees movement coming from the house and recognizes that it is the general. He looks to his men and calls them to attention as the general enters the barn, and in unison they give him the proper salute and respect his rank demands.

He returns the salute and says, "At ease, men. Commander Sasheen."

"Yes, General!"

"Follow me."

"Yes, sir." Sasheen takes off after the general, who has already left the barn and is waiting in the house's courtyard. There is a small firepit with a pot of something brewing over the fire, hanging from a pole constructed above it. The general takes a single cup and pours some hot liquid in it and looks to Sasheen. "There is a cup over there. If you want some, this tea is very good once it is hot."

Sasheen is tempted, but seeing how the general did not offer to pour him one himself, he knows that the man is not in the most hospitable of moods regarding him or his men. He surmises that his next words will make or break his intended outcome. He knows that humility and apologies are the only course left to him.

"General Bozan, my actions since I arrived at the village have been inexcusable. First, making your wife break early and leave, and then not helping her. Then arriving here and demanding your attention without the proper protocols employed are an insult to you and those who trained me. Please forgive my rashness and allow me to explain why I am here."

General Bozan walks over to the extra cups, grabs one and fills it with some hot tea and hands it to him. "Finally, you sound like an officer of the emperor's royal calvary. You now have my attention, Commander. Proceed."

"Sir, I would first like you to know that I did not seek General Barach's leave to come here, but I used my connection with Mihri to get authority because I did not think the general would have agreed with my reasoning and would think that it was none of my business."

General Bozan lifts his cup to his lips, takes a sip, then chuckles. "You seem to have a talent for digging a hole deeper and deeper with your words, Commander."

"I know, General. It sounds bad, but let me finish." He nods and Sasheen continues. "You see, sir, Rassan is a good friend. I was his drill instructor in the academy, and a finer swordsman and smarter cadet I have never known."

"He gets those traits from his father. Proceed, Commander."

"Thank you, General. You see, when he petitioned the emperor to bring the Magi star charts back from the capital to Babylon, I wanted to be with him, so I asked Headmaster Dvandas if he could use his influence to get me in that caravan so that I could watch over him. That is how I was promoted to the rank of commander and put in charge of the caravan. The headmaster already knew of my betrothal to General Barach's daughter and thought it would be simple to get the emperor's approval for this because I was scheduled to come to Babylon within the year, anyway."

He pauses for a moment to find out if the general is buying his twisting of the truth.

The general responds. "I knew that Barach's future son-in-law was coming to Babylon to train to succeed him. But that and your friendship with Rassan still does not explain why you are here, Commander."

Commander Sasheen swallows. He knows he must handle this next part just right. He can't just coerce this man whom he thought was just a low-level aristocrat that he could bully or entice into taking his desired action. Now he knows he must win him to his cause. "Sir, I came out here to get your help in saving Rassan from being publicly disgraced, and then punished by the emperor!"

The general puts his cup down. "What are you talking about, Commander?"

"Rassan has been seen by many people in the central market fraternizing with a young maid who is a member of the priestesses of Zarpanuta."

"Rassan would have nothing to do with those whores! His father and I never let our men publicly fraternize with any of them, and we strongly recommended that they not partake in any of their festivals!"

Commander Sasheen forces himself to take a calming breath. "General, I don't know why, but she is working in the central market at her uncle's papyrus stand. She does not wear her priestess clothes, and the only way you can tell that she is a member of that order is by the tattoo on her neck. Perhaps her family has taken her back. I know that her father, who sold her to the high priestess when she was very young, is now dead. Perhaps her uncle has bought her back and now intends to betroth her to someone. Not common, but not unheard of. In some circles, a wife with her training would be very sought after and could fetch a considerable dowry."

General Bozan glares at Sasheen for a few moments, then calls for his wife. "Mahre, could you join us in the courtyard? I need your counsel."

"What is it, husband?" Both men turn and see Mahre coming from the stables.

"Commander Sasheen here has brought disturbing news about Rassan to my attention."

"Rassan? Oh my, I trust it is not too serious!" She steps next to her husband and gazes at Commander Sasheen with obvious worry in her eyes.

The general takes her hand in his own, and strokes it soothingly, attempting to allay her worries. "Rassan has found a female infatuation in the central market. He has been seen talking with her by many."

She sighs, relieved that it is just that. "We have talked about this upon occasion, Husband. The time of his betrothal is long overdue." The general is about to speak, but she holds up her hand and continues. "I know that Prince Phraates V said that he would handle this in time, but I fear that the affairs of state have caused him to not act as quickly as he should. Rassan is a young man, and it is not wise to hold him this long from having a proper betrothal to a future wife."

"But there is more. The girl that Rassan has been talking to seems to be, or at least has been, a priestess of the Temple of Zarpanuta. Commander Sasheen believes she was bought back from the Temple by her uncle, and he seeks a betrothal for her. How would you perceive her as a potential mate for my uncle's only child?"

She stares at Commander Sasheen. "Your impertinence and rashness is now understood, Commander. This is a very delicate matter. If not handled properly, Rassan could find himself disgraced before the emperor and shamed in front of his family. But it is not unheard of for a maiden to leave the priestesses of Zarpanuta and marry. Our laws and traditions guarantee that since her service in the Temple was practiced under the empire's sanction for religious duties, her status as a marriageable maiden does not diminish when and if she leaves the order."

The general sighs with palpable relief and begins to speak, but his wife then says, "There is, however, the problem to deal with that Rassan has been seen talking to her many times in public. This might hurt him if you do not act quickly, Husband."

He holds up both hands and exclaims, "What do you suggest I do? I am only a temporary leader of my uncle's family, and the emperor's son did publicly say that he would find Rassan a wife."

Mahre, now totally in her element, continues. "Two things, my Husband—leave with Commander Sasheen tomorrow and investigate this matter personally to see if she could be a good match for Rassan; and, if so, inquire about a negotiation with her family regarding their betrothal, and then send an official report to the emperor detailing the full matter and your desire as temporary head of the house of Surena to arrange the betrothal. With your permission, I will also go with you to Babylon and give you my counsel and aid throughout this delicate process."

As husband and wife are speaking, Commander Sasheen stands with bewilderment on his face, astonished that this woman, who he met a day ago, must be much more than he first judged her to be.

General Bozan sees his confusion. "Mahre's father was twenty-seventh in the royal line of succession when I was betrothed to her. She grew up in the royal palace in the capital. My uncle, General Surena, negotiated our betrothal. She understands matters of state and protocols much better than I. She has, on many occasions, kept me from embarrassing myself. We would all be wise to follow her lead in this matter."

Sasheen is speechless as he contemplates the damage he almost brought to himself and his career by how he has handled these two since his arrival. If they ever discover his true intentions here, he fears that not even Dvandas could save him from the consequences.

Two Days Later, Astronomical Temple

Rassan found it difficult to sleep last night as he anticipated his visit to the market in Babylon this morning. It has been hard for him to think of anything but Varaz as of late, and he knows others are noticing his distraction. Even Rita-Raina has appeared to make more progress in his studies preparing for the debate than he has. Both Kaufa and Arsam have said that he needs to focus more on his responsibility to the headmaster in representing his stance on the matter. He knows they are correct and fully intends to give his all to fulfilling his duties and being prepared to represent his part of the debate. It's just that his conversations with Varaz have been so incredibly stimulating. He did not know that the priestesses of Zarpanuta were so versed in the study of the stars, although he has to admit that most of their knowledge comes from the stance of astrology. That discipline professes that the movement of celestial bodies can be interpreted to prophesy the future of any individual once it is surmised what zodiacal sign they were born under. That belief is what he will argue against in the upcoming debate. Still, her knowledge and passion for her subject is infectious, and he tells himself that their conversations are giving him profitable intel into what he will be up against in the debate.

Then the troubling thought crosses his mind that perhaps he should slow down his meetings with Varaz in the market. A memory flashes through his mind of the time he and Arsam were speaking in the Tapestry Observatory about the constellation Cetus and the headmaster and the ambassador joined them. They warned Rassan and Arsam about being too distracted by studying the intricacies of the enemy and not focusing on the vastness of the Creator's plans.

He asks himself, *Why do I revel in the time I spend with Varaz? What is it that motivates me to want to see and speak with her every day?* The answer is so obvious it only takes him a moment to admit it to himself. In his almost twenty years of life, he has never spoken to a woman, outside of his mother and her maids who helped watch over him, as much as he has with Varaz. After the death of his father while he was in the academy and with his mother dying shortly after that, there was no time or availability for him to associate with a female. The prince told him that when the time was right, he would find a suitable wife for him to marry.

Then came the encounter with Headmaster Vinda-Farnah outside the capital that set his life in a whole new direction. His father once told him that there is a hollow place in a man that can only be filled by a woman. But at the time he said this, Rassan was twelve years old, and the words were only lightly received. But now he feels their true meaning. All the boys from his class at the academy came in betrothed to a maid and are now living as married men upon graduation. Even his classmates at the Magi Astronomical Temple are married and have their spouses housed in Babylon. All the Magi are married. Everyone has a spouse except him. And Arsam, of course.

He now sees how he needs to proceed. He believes he might be falling in love with Varaz and that he should start acting in a way befitting of his station and seek permission to inquire about a betrothal with the maid. Word would have to be sent back to the prince for this to move in any direction. But before that happens, he must first talk to Headmaster Daraya-Vous.

Rassan, now determined about his course, makes his way from his chamber in the apprentice section of the Temple and turns the bend into the main hall that leads to the Tapestry Observatory when he sees Arsam running in his direction. The boy runs up to Rassan, red-faced and a little out of breath. "Rassan, the headmaster has summoned you to his chambers. You must hurry. It is very urgent!"

"What is it, Arsam? I was just about to seek an audience with him when you found me."

"I am not sure what is going on, but this morning Grand Master Artapan, Commander Sasheen, General Barach, and another high-ranking military man came to the Temple and went straight to the Headmaster's quarters and met with him for about an hour. When they were done, the headmaster found me and sent me to fetch you."

A flutter of panic goes through Rassan's chest. "Then I guess we better hurry."

By the time they reach the headmaster's office, Rassan can barely keep his rapidly beating heart under control. All he can think of is that maybe it has something to do with the prince as the porters open the door to allow him and Arsam into the chamber. When he steps in, he immediately bows to Grand Master Artapan and Headmaster Daraya-Vous, but he is momentarily stunned by the presence of his cousin, Bozan, and his wife, Mahre, with the group. He has not seen them since the death of his father, when the emperor named Bozan temporary head over the family. When he first arrived in Babylon, they sent him word that when he had some time, he could come visit them or they would come to the city and see him, but that has not yet happened.

He is even more taken aback that Bozan is dressed in his general's uniform. He fears that some great war has broken out and they are all being called back to service. Protocols and discipline soon take over and he comes to attention and salutes the generals, along with Commander Sasheen. The grand master then brings the meeting to order. "Rassan, thank you for joining us. And thank you, Arsam, for fetching him for us."

The grand master of the Magi has always been the empirical head of all things religious in the empire and everyone in the room acknowledges his authority. He looks directly at Rassan. "Magi Apprentice Rassan, please come here. The rest of you may have a seat."

The rest of the people in the room take seats, forming a semicircle around them, while Rassan stands in the middle of the room, in front of the Grand Master.

"Rassan."

"Yes, Grand Master?"

"You have been summoned upon request of General Bozan, who is the temporary head of your family until you can assume that role yourself."

Rassan finds his cousin on his right and briefly makes eye contact with the man. Immediately, he perceives that something is bothering him. "What might the purpose of the summons be, Grand Master?"

Artapan looks to General Bozan, then to the others. "Since Rassan's status in the empire is both as an officer in the royal calvary and a Magi apprentice, I felt it necessary for both of his superiors to be a part of this meeting. As for explaining why you are here, I think the matter should be detailed by your kinsman, General Bozan." He holds out his hand to Bozan and says, "General, if you would?"

Bozan smiles and stands. "Yes, Grand Master, thank you." He then walks over to Rassan and puts a gentle hand on his shoulder. He holds Rassan in his gaze for a moment, then glances at Commander Sasheen. "Your friend came to my home a few days ago and brought me some concerning news. You have been seen almost every day in the market, engaged in long conversations with a young maid at a papyrus stand where your Magi Order purchases supplies. He told me that, to some, it would look like you are courting the girl openly."

Astonished, Rassan simply gazes at Bozan as his words sink in. The revealing of this meeting's purpose stuns him. He was just about to come and talk to the headmaster about this very thing, and now he finds that he has been called out in front of all his superiors to answer for it. He knows Bozan would only have his best interests at heart. His father once told him that there was no other man he trusted more. He holds his cousin's gaze with his eyes as he collects his thoughts. "I was on my way to talk with the headmaster about this situation when Arsam found me. My status as a Magi apprentice and an officer in the royal calvary are at risk by this matter. Therefore, I would like to pursue receiving permission to seek a betrothal with the girl from her family. I know I cannot do this myself. That is why I wanted to talk to the headmaster first."

Everyone in the room sighs in relief at Rassan's words, and Bozan steps up to him and places an affectionate hand on his shoulder. He then turns to the grand master, Headmaster Daraya-Vous, and General Barach. "Considering this, I would like to offer my support as trustee of the family of Surena in aiding his son in this matter. With your permission, I will draft a letter to Prince Phraates V detailing the circumstances and petitioning his blessings to proceed, and then I will make preliminary inquiries with the maid's family about negotiations of betrothal."

Grand Master Artapan holds Rassan and Bozan in his gaze for a few moments, then looks to one side at General Barach, who gives an approving nod, and then to the other at Headmaster Daraya-Vous, who does likewise. Then he looks back at the pair in front of him. "General Bozan, you may proceed in this matter."

"Thank you, Grand Master."

Grand Master Artapan then excuses everyone in the room and motions to Daraya-Vous. "Headmaster, we need to discuss the upcoming debate. I have just received word that Headmaster Dvandas wants to attend. The dispatch from the capital informed me that the emperor is coming to Babylon in four months and Dvandas demands that we postpone until then."

That the Grand Master's demeanor is radiating with irritation at having to deal with this news is apparent to Daraya-Vous. "Grand Master, I understand you are as anxious as I to see this matter concluded. But considering the present circumstance, perhaps this news is fortuitous."

"How so, Headmaster?"

"As is our way, each side of the debate will be conducted by apprentices that are tutored by either faction. Rassan is the lead apprentice of the faction representing my stance. This extra time will give him the opportunity to settle his personal matters regarding the betrothal negotiations and still be fully ready to carry out his part in the discourse."

The grand master considers Daraya-Vous's words. Then the corners of his ancient lips curl into a smile. "Headmaster Daraya-Vous, Vinda-Farnah was wise to choose you as his successor. He often told me that your trust in the Creator's providence and help is the finest he has ever known. You know Dvandas seeks my seat and will use anything, including your humiliation before the emperor, to shame me and guide him to replace me before I even die."

"Yes, Grand Master, we both know that has always been one of Dvandas's evil intents. But I am convinced that the Creator wants this debate to take place so that unity can prevail in my order. After Headmaster Vinda-Farnah went on his rogue trip to Jerusalem, there has been unrest and even doubt among some in the Astronomical Sect that we are on the right path. The astronomical conjunctions that he based his trip on were compelling and fell in line with what Belteshazzar instructed us to look for, but they did not hold the correct emphasis and, therefore, could not be the proper sign of the coming of the Creator's champion that we are looking for."

"How then does the emperor's presence and Dvandas's ill intent help you bring that unity in your order, Headmaster?"

"With the Creator, there are no coincidences, Grand Master. Should the debate go in my favor, and by all that I hold as holy I believe it will, you as Grand Master will give it your seal of legitimacy. But, having the emperor personally here in Babylon, he can immediately acknowledge it with an empirical seal and have it recorded where none can change it."

Grand Master Artapan places an affectionate hand on Daraya-Vous's shoulder. "Though I believe the Grand Master's seat of the Magi should always be held by Magi who follow the Prophet Zoroaster, I must admit that you, Daraya-Vous, would make a superb grand master someday."

Outside the headmaster's offices, Rassan looks for his cousin and sees him walking with Commander Sasheen toward the Tapestry Observatory. "Bozan!" he calls out as he hurries in their direction. Once Rassan gets to them, they stop. He first looks to Sasheen, sighs, and says, "Though I wish you would have voiced your concerns to me first, I am grateful that you could get my kinsman involved."

Sasheen is surprised that this is coming together as planned and that no one has seen through his deception. "All of us, including the prince, should have thought about this before you left the capital. The only reason I am not married yet is that my family was in negotiations with General Barach throughout my whole academy training. Then I had to wait until I was transferred here because he wanted the man that was to marry his daughter living in Babylon and training to be his successor. But at least I knew that matters of matrimony were settled for me. Until now, you, my friend, have lived in a state of limbo in this matter."

General Bozan chuckles. "You should be grateful that you have friends like Commander Sasheen here, Rassan. If not for him, I would have been oblivious to your dilemma and possible humiliation. Not to worry, though. The son of my former superior and kinsman will now have the full support of his family in settling this matter. My wife, Mahre, whom you know is very adept at this sort of thing, is here with me in the city to guide both you and me through all the intricate details in the betrothal negotiations."

"This is welcome news, Cousin. I am sorry that I have not been out to visit you since arriving. The Astronomical Sect has a more rigorous academic curriculum than anything I have ever taken part in, and that includes my time at the royal academy. But now, being presented with the opportunity to spend time with you and the girl is a very pleasant thing to look forward to."

Sasheen can't help but to get in a jibe at Rassan's comment about his studies. "I warned you about this path, Rassan. You should have heeded me when I offered you a chance to apprentice with the Magician Sect. At least with them you could have taken part in some of their more interesting festivals and not had all this tension build up inside you so that you would seek an inappropriate relationship with a young maid."

General Bozan spins around. "Commander Sasheen! Rassan is the son of General Surena. His father taught him to never partake in any of those disgusting festivals of which you speak. True, a disservice has been done to him by those of us who should have known better and sought a wife for him. But, despite that, he has conducted himself admirably even though he was talking openly with a young maid in the market. I appreciate your help in this matter, but now I will ask that you leave me and my kinsman alone so that we may speak of family matters."

Humbled, startled, and reproved by the general, Commander Sasheen gives a quick salute and hurries out the closest exit. Once he is out of earshot, the general turns back to Rassan. "How well do you know this man? I cannot make up my mind about him. First, he makes me feel like he is your closest ally, and then he says stupid things like he just did."

"He is a fine officer, Bozan. I think he just got caught up with the Magician Sect at the capital, and that is what you are sensing. General Barach does not allow the Magician Sect to be so aggressive with their recruitment in Babylon as they are with military officers in the capital. He has tried to persuade me on many occasions to check out many religious activities with them since our academy days. As you stated, my father held that sect in much disdain, and I could never bring myself to accommodate."

Bozan wraps his arm around Rassan's shoulders. "You honor your father, my boy. Now, let's go to my wife, Mahre, and have her help us write the letter to the prince and see to getting you betrothed."

13

Betrothal Negotiations

Later That Afternoon, House of Baazar the Papyrus Merchant

Mihri is very glad for the news that his master will be in Babylon in three months. Especially since the emperor himself will be with him. He still finds it disconcerting that the high priestess of the Temple of Zarpanuta could have the gall to blackmail him into giving her more power in the religious circles of the empire. The possibility that she has some ancient artifact that could pull the rug out from underneath his feet and cause Daraya-Vous's people to win the upcoming debate has had him on edge since learning of it in her chambers.

He knows he must proceed as before and make sure that Rassan is fully enticed away from the Astronomical Sect before the debate takes place. So, he promised the high priestess everything she wanted if she would continue on the path of allowing Varaz to entice Rassan and lead him away by becoming betrothed to him. That is why he is now standing in the chambers of Baazar the papyrus merchant. Sasheen told him earlier in the day that General Bozan had just received permission from Grand Master Artapan, General Barach, and Headmaster Daraya-Vous to seek a betrothal between Rassan and Varaz; and he is here to make sure Baazar is ready when Bozan and his wife arrive later that evening to inform him of their intent and the letter that will be sent to the prince.

As he sits on the fine Roman-style sofa in the room sipping the chilled tea just served to him by a servant, a very nervous and sweaty Baazar comes running into the room. "Magi Mihri, welcome to my home. I came as fast as I could. I did not have my coach or driver, so I had to run here from the market."

Mihri points to a chair next to his and gestures for Baazar to sit. "That is quite all right, Baazar. I am here to inform you that our plans to have your niece betrothed to the Magi apprentice Rassan are being escalated by his kinsman and guardian, General Bozan. He and his wife Mahre will be here this evening to inform you of their intent to begin negotiations of betrothal, which will take place as soon as they hear from Prince Phraates V. Their letter to him was dispatched this morning and should reach the capital in a month's time. If all goes well, we should hear a response from him within two months."

Baazar takes a towel from the shelf behind him and nervously wipes his forehead. "I received a note from the high priestess of Zarpanuta that all of this was put on hold until further notice. I have no proper authority over my niece, seeing as how she really is a priestess of that order and, therefore, under their authority. Until the other day when you brought her to my tent in the market and informed me of your plans, I had not seen her since she was nine years old when her father sold her to that Temple. How can I negotiate when she is not mine to give? By all our laws, she belongs to them, and I have no authority in this matter."

Mihri stands up. "I have already spoken with the high priestess, and she has promised to go along with my plans. She obviously has not updated you yet, but that hardly matters. Dvandas and the emperor will be in Babylon in three months, and he wants this matter completely settled by that time. When General Bozan and his wife come here tonight to talk, you are to be overjoyed at the prospect of your niece being betrothed to the son of such a prestigious family as that of General Surena. You will inform them that you will patiently wait for the response from the capital and will not entertain any other offers of betrothal for Varaz. Is that clear, Baazar?"

"Of course, Mihri, I will do as you command. I did not know that the emperor and Headmaster Dvandas will be here in Babylon so soon. It is just that my vocation depends on the patronage of many of the Temples in Babylon. Next to the Astronomical Sect of the Magi, the Temple of Zarpanuta continues as a very lucrative account. I simply do not want to endanger that relationship."

Mihri knows that he now holds the man where his heart truly lives, and he takes his seat once again, confident that he can control him. "Baazar, I have already told you that once you have fulfilled our request and Headmaster Dvandas ascends to being Grand Master of the Magi Order, you will be the chief supplier of all religious institutions in Babylon with the possibilities of expanding your network throughout the empire. Within a few years, you could possibly become the richest papyrus merchant in the Parthian Empire."

Baazar stares at Mihri for a few moments as the words sink in. "I will do whatever you want me to do. Please let me know how to proceed."

Evening, Outside Baazar's Home

Rassan is so nervous as he, his cousin Bozan, and Bozan's wife, Mahre, make their way to the front of Baazar the papyrus merchant's house. In a normal betrothal negotiation this is quite common, because both prospective spouses will have most likely not seen each other before and would have been much younger than he and Varaz are. Introductions are traditionally heavily chaperoned and planned out in every detail. But he feels like he knows Varaz quite well…and maybe that is why he's so nervous. He wants her with all his heart, and the thought of having to negotiate with her uncle for her hand has really gotten him on edge. Then there is the aspect of having to get his friend the prince involved, which will drag out these negotiations for months. Rassan's anxiety goes unnoticed by Bozan, and it is Mahre who walks over and takes Rassan's hand and squeezes it. "Take a deep breath and calm yourself, Rassan. Remember, you don't have to do or say anything. Bozan and I will handle the introduction and negotiations," she says.

Rassan meets her eyes and takes a long, slow breath. "It's just that even if everything goes perfectly with Varaz's uncle, you still can't even begin negotiating until we hear from Phraates V. What if he disapproves? Varaz is a simple merchant's daughter and niece! I am the son of the great General Surena. Phraates V and his father, the emperor, promised Surena that they would find a wife for me. What if she is not good enough for them?"

Mahre looks to her husband, and he nods his head. "Rassan, by what we have heard, the prince holds you very dear to his heart and has noble plans for you. But he is also the heir to a mighty empire and must look to the future of his throne. Your family line affords you the privilege of being in the top one hundred in empirical succession. My father was an even closer relative to the Phraates family than yours and when he looked for a husband for me, he was told to seek a family that would put our offspring outside the top one hundred. Though Bozan is your cousin, his father was your father's younger brother and fell out of the hundred, thus eliminating our children from being in that as well. So, you see, Rassan, we believe the prince will have similar reasonings and look on this betrothal as a profitable one for all parties concerned."

Rassan grabs both Mahre's hands. "Politics is not my strongest area, Mahre. Your insight is refreshing, to say the least. I believe the Creator has blessed me with meeting Varaz, and I think He also knew I would need you." He lets go of her hands and turns to the door. "I am ready whenever the both of you are."

Bozan calls out his salutation and inquiry for Baazar the papyrus merchant and a servant opens the door, bows, and steps aside as Baazar comes forward and says, "General Bozan, Mahre your wife, and young kinsman Rassan, you are most welcome to my home. Please come in."

Rassan is now standing between Bozan and Mahre and, as custom dictates, he bows his head yet remains silent as Bozan guides their party into the house, following Baazar to the inner court. Once there, Rassan is shown a seat on one side of the room, where he has a direct view of Varaz. She is now wearing a veil over her face and has an intricate, white-laced shawl over her hair. Her dress is of the same material and design as the shawl and covers her completely from the middle of her neck down. Though the only thing that he can see of her are her hands and eyes, he can't stop his heart from beating so fast that it feels like it will burst from his chest. He swears she is the most beautiful creature he has ever laid eyes on, and it is taking all his self-control not to run over to her and tell her that. Bozan walks over and puts a calming hand on his shoulder and then looks to Baazar. "Thank you for meeting with us, Baazar."

"This pleasure is mine, General. My humble home is graced by you and your family's presence," Baazar says as he directs his servant to serve refreshments to his guests.

Bozan receives the drink handed to him and takes a sip. When he does, Rassan and Mahre follow suit. He then places his drink on a table and says, "As you know, we are here to open negotiations for the betrothal of Rassan to Varaz. Before we begin, you understand that Rassan is the son of the great General Surena and is thus responsible to Emperor Phraates IV and his son. Upon his father's death, Phraates V promised Surena that he would find Rassan a wife when it was time. Because of this, a dispatch has been sent to the prince asking for his blessings upon this negotiation. It will be about two months until word from him is received by us. So, all that we discuss today and going forward until we hear from the prince will be contingent upon what he says."

Upon hearing about the involvement of the emperor and his son in this negotiation, Baazar nervously wipes his forehead with a piece of linen. The only thing that is keeping him settled is the promise Mihri made to him earlier of the riches and honor he will get from aiding in this part of his master's plan.

"General, all of this has been quite surprising and unexpected," Baazar says with as much sincerity as he can muster. "We only received Varaz back into our home recently, and though I had planned to find her a suitable husband, I thought we would wait until she gets more accustomed to not being at the Temple of Zarpanuta. But she has informed me of her desire to be Rassan's betrothed and, therefore, has made it easier for me to proceed with these negotiations. I understand the gravity of your position and I assure you that my house will be very patient to hear from the prince in this matter."

Upon hearing Baazar's words, a thrill goes through Rassan's heart. He realizes she may want this as much as he does. His eyes longingly reach out to hers. She greets them with a twinkle in her own and a subtle nod to authenticate her uncle's words. Bozan and Baazar are totally focused on one another and do not take notice of this subtle exchange, but it is obvious to Mahre. She stands and moves to her husband's side. "I believe that you and Baazar should continue this discussion in private. I suggest you allow me to act as chaperone and bring Rassan and Varaz somewhere where they can talk. Seeing as how they are already well acquainted with one another, I don't think that the traditional betrothal introductions should be necessary. They could find much profit in just catching up on each other's lives. What say you, my husband?"

Bozan looks back to Baazar and asks, "If that is acceptable to you?"

"Of course. They can all meet out in the garden on the side of the house." He gestures with a hand. "My servants will show you the way."

Mahre nods to her husband and turns to Rassan and Varaz. "If you two would join me, we will follow the servants to the garden where you may talk freely with one another." Varaz stands and comes up next to Mahre and takes her arm. Rassan follows them to the garden. When they arrive, they find a small garden with a large olive tree nestled in the center. The tree is surrounded by a cobblestone path, and there is a small outdoor table with chairs. All three sit down.

Mahre gazes at both for a moment, then smiles. "Oh my, I thought I would collapse from sheer boredom in there! The two of you have not seen each other or spoken in almost a week. It must be driving you crazy. Please, just ignore me and catch up with each other." She looks back toward the doorway and chuckles, then turns back to the pair. "Varaz, please keep the veil on. I know Rassan has already seen you, but it is for the men's sake and their attempt to keep this as traditional as possible."

Rassan and Varaz look at Mahre for a moment, then turn to each other and giggle. Varaz is the first to speak. "Rassan, how goes the preparations for your debate?"

"Very well, thank you. Although we just heard that it is being postponed for three months because Emperor Phraates IV and his chief advisor, Magi Master Dvandas, are coming to Babylon and want to be present for it."

Though the high priestess has already told her these things, Varaz reacts with surprise and concern. "Oh my, Rassan, that must be very alarming to you, having to debate before the emperor himself?"

"It's not as bad as you think, Varaz. I grew up in the capital and attended the military academy at the palace. So I have had chances to be around the emperor, and I am also friends with his son, the prince. As for being officially before his throne, there was the time I petitioned to bring the sacred Magi star charts back to Babylon to give to Headmaster Daraya-Vous. That was probably the scariest thing I ever did. But the Creator saw me through that, and He will get me through the debate as well."

"Speaking of that, are you still stuck on proving before the whole

Magi Order that the grand purpose of the zodiac is to describe the Creator's plan to send His champion to save mankind from evil?"

Rassan settles back in his chair and collects his thoughts. This is common ground between him and Varaz, and frankly what he finds so attractive about the girl. She really knows how to challenge him, and sometimes she tempts him to look at the other side of the issue. So far, this has only strengthened his confidence that Headmaster Daraya-Vous is right, but she makes him think. "Of course, I am set on that path still, Varaz."

She raises an eyebrow. "So then tell me, Rassan, what new things have you learned since our last discussion that could convince me you are on the right path?"

Fascinated, Mahre gazes at the two as the conversation unfolds and Varaz continues to ask questions about Rassan's endeavors in the Magi Astronomical Sect, and he answers with eager enthusiasm. She wonders how they have developed such an intellectually stimulating relationship already. It took her and Bozan years after their wedding to know and understand each other enough to talk as they are. Then it dawns on her. Their relationship is not founded solely on physical attraction. Rassan is passionate about this girl's heart and mind and eagerly seeks her opinion about things most important to him. Varaz also seems quite comfortable sharing her thoughts and insights with him. Deciding that they could use a modicum of privacy, she gets up and says, "Pardon me, but this garden is so beautiful. I am going to take a stroll around it to inspect. I will be within earshot should you two require anything of me."

Once away from them, Mahre endeavors to stand behind the olive tree for a while and listen, but they continue to talk about astronomical things and that has always been a subject she has found little interest in. So, she strolls farther away to the other side of the garden, where she is delighted to find several fruit trees.

After a while she feels that the sun has moved to a point which indicates that at least an hour has passed, so she makes her way back to Rassan and Varaz. As she approaches, she can make out the latest point of discussion having to do with the constellation Taurus. Varaz is passionately stating her point of view.

"Rassan, it is the sign of the warrior class. I am not saying that every man born during Taurus's presence in the heavens is destined to be a warrior. But it has been proved over and over that men born under that sign have a more aggressive nature. Look at the history of Taurus! First, he was spared by the king but later became mad and could only be tamed by Herakles. That is the flavor of the sign, and when the constellation is studied and interpreted by real Magi much can be found out about an individual's life who is born under that sign."[17]

Rassan ponders the statement for a moment, then answers. "You are referring to the Greek interpretation of the meaning of the constellation Taurus. In the Astronomical Sect of the Magi, we have been seeking the more ancient meanings of the zodiac. When Alexander conquered the Persian Empire, his people brought all these new ideas to our lands. Much was lost of what our own astronomers have documented for us down through the centuries. For instance, the brightest star in the constellation of Taurus is in its eye and is the Aramaic word *Al Debaran,* which means the leader or governor. At the tip of the horn is the star *El Nath,* which means wounded, or slain in sacrifice.[18] These are names for those stars that came to us from the ancients long before the Greeks conquered our lands. As the savior of the Creator's people, the champion will give himself unreservedly to them to the point of sacrifice and death. As governor and leader, he will put down all enemies and rule over them. Taurus depicts his nature as that of a savior and conqueror who will stop at nothing until his mission is complete."

Varaz's eyes go wide with astonishment and frustration. She likes what she is hearing, but that does not help her in her mission to get Rassan away from the Astronomical Sect. Frankly, he is making her think that what she has been taught is wrong, not vice versa. She also realizes that these conversations are the most stimulating she has ever experienced, and she would be very content to continue them all day with Rassan.

As she is preparing to respond, an *UHM!* is heard and they both turn to see Mahre. "Have you two talked any about the ceremony, or where you will live after you are married? I know the Astronomical Sect provides housing for its Magi and their spouses, but Rassan is also a military officer and could take advantage of the Babylon officers' garrison housing as well. Bozan and I lived there for many years until he retired and took over his father's farm east of the city. The garrison really is quite nice, and we can make sure you both get the best quarters available. After your first child arrives, you are going to need all the room you can get."

Mahre stares at both, knowing she has left them speechless with her words. Though Varaz's face is almost completely covered, she can still tell that her cheeks are flushed, and her eyes are fighting back tears. Rassan is so stunned by the words that he grabs his drink of cooled tea and guzzles the whole thing, trying to stifle the volcano of emotions erupting in him. He shyly looks over at Varaz. "Uh, we haven't talked about the wedding yet. We were just catching up a little first."

Mahre chuckles and raises a hand. "We've been out here for over one hour and all you two have talked about are matters of religion and astronomy. I swear one would think you're a couple of ancient Magi discussing the deep, dark secrets of the universe, and not a potentially betrothed couple."

Rassan is now so embarrassed that he can hardly look Varaz in the eye. While staring at the table his words are barely audible as he says, "I am sorry, Varaz. I have done nothing like this before. Commander Sasheen heard reports of our conversations in the marketplace and went to see General Bozan for advice. I was on my way to talk to Headmaster Daraya-Vous about the possibility of seeking a betrothal with you when I was summoned before him, Grand Master Artapan, and General Barach, to answer for my behavior. When I told them what I wanted, the Grand Master asked Bozan and Mahre to handle the inquiry for betrothal. I really want to marry you, and I hope you want to marry me as well."

Varaz knows that this is what she and the high priestess planned for, but she can't squelch the rising butterflies in her stomach as she considers being Rassan's wife. "Rassan, my uncle talked to me about this when word came from your kinsman. Since I am only recently departed from the Temple's service, he thought it best that I was fully aware of and had a say in this negotiation. The answer is yes, I wish to proceed and be betrothed to you."

Rassan stands and reaches for Varaz's hand, but Mahre stops him in midmotion with her arm. "It is good that you two are talking about the matter at hand, but we are going to proceed with this betrothal as traditionally as possible, given the circumstances. Part of that is no physical contact until you are married."

Deeply disappointed but understanding his kinswoman's words, Rassan retakes his seat but can't help staring at Varaz's beautiful brown eyes. Varaz holds his gaze and, to break the tension of his disappointment, blurts out, "What about Cetus? Surely the great sea monster and servant to Poseidon has nothing to do with the coming of the Creator's champion!"

"Actually, Cetus is a servant to no one, Varaz. He is the great monster of the deep, representing the evil one who tricked mankind out of the rulership of this world that was granted to him by the Creator Himself. As to his relation to the champion, the brightest star in that constellation is *Menkar,* and its ancient meaning is that of being bound and subdued. The only one capable of such a feat is the Creator's champion, who will do that very thing someday."[19]

Mahre rolls her eyes and tries to think of a way to get them back on track when Bozan and Baazar come through the door from inside the house. "Mahre, I trust all is going well with the introduction part of the betrothal process?" Bozan says as he steps up to her and places an affectionate hand on her shoulder.

She reaches up to clasp her husband's hand in her own. "We will never have difficulties in getting these two to talk with each other, Husband. It would appear that their entire relationship will be built on theology and astronomy. There was only a moment since we were out here that I could direct them to consider matters of matrimony. But it revealed to me how serious they are about each other."

Bozan smiles and turns his gaze to Baazar and nods his head. "Then I count this first meeting a successful beginning to our betrothal negotiations. Baazar, I, my wife, and Rassan will take our leave. We will be back in one week to let the couple spend more time together, and we can work out some more details on how to proceed, contingent upon word from the prince." Baazar bows his head and waves his hand in front of him in a gesture of peace and respect. Bozan emulates the gesture and he and his family retreat through the closest exit from the garden to the street.

For the next month and a half, Bozan returns with Mahre and Rassan for the betrothal negotiations and to allow Rassan and Varaz to spend time together. During that time, Rassan pours all his resolve into preparing for the debate. His sessions with Varaz only prove to strengthen and sharpen his acuteness to articulate his case. She continues to challenge him in ways he would not expect, which forces him to dig deeper and study harder so that he can give her clear and concise answers that she has no recourse but to concede to their validity. Headmaster Daraya-Vous's optimism in their victory is elevated to new heights as Rassan's conviction grows day by day.

14

Bitter Enlightenment

One Day After the Seventh Betrothal Meeting, Temple of Zarpanuta

Varaz stands outside the high priestess's office, waiting to be received. She called for the meeting yesterday after her betrothal session with Rassan. They once again spent almost the entire time talking about the upcoming debate, which is to take place before the emperor and Grand Master Artapan in less than a month. Just a few days ago, word was received from Prince Phraates V giving his blessing on their union. She is very pleased with the positive response from the emperor's son but is also frustrated because she is nowhere nearer to enticing Rassan out of the Astronomical Sect of the Magi than when she started. If anything, she has lost ground and their conversations have only galvanized his resolve. The door opens and a menacing-looking, muscular Temple servant steps aside and allows her to enter. She makes her way in, and as she makes a turn at some ornately carved ivory columns that outline the entrance to the high priestess's private office, she is greeted by her superior.

Seated at her desk in her Temple festival robes, the high priestess looks especially seductive in the revealing apparel. The three-day fall festival has just culminated the night before, and she is still dressed for the occasion. She stands and holds out her hand, which is immediately grasped by Varaz, who then kisses it and takes a knee in worshipful respect.

"Arise, Priestess Varaz. To what do I owe the joy of seeing my favorite acolyte?"

Varaz releases her hand and stands. "Thank you for seeing me, High Priestess. My purpose is to seek counsel."

"What counsel are you in need of, Varaz?"

"I have come to a crossroads in my mission, Madam. Rassan is nowhere nearer to leaving the Astronomical Sect than when I started. Though our betrothal is sanctioned by Prince Phraates V himself and we are to be wed within the year, I have failed to convince Rassan to leave his station and join Headmaster Dvandas's sect. If anything, I seemed to have strengthened his conviction to the Astronomical Sect."

The high priestess considers Varaz's words. In a dangerously low tone, she asks, "How exactly did you accomplish this phenomenon?"

"I used everything I have ever learned in the Temple of Zarpanuta to show him the error of the Astronomical Sect's beliefs. We have debated for months, and nothing seems to work with the man. The more I bring up, the harder he studies and comes back at me with mind-boggling logic that I have no answers for."

"You seriously tried to debate the boy with logic and theology? Is that how I taught you to bend a man's will to get what you want?"

Varaz's cheeks flush. She knows what the high priestess is getting at, but the thought is so completely absurd to her. Exasperated, she answers. "I have been trained in the fine arts of seduction for my whole life but never for the circumstances this mission has put me in. Rassan has never seen me in anything considered even remotely provocative. All our meetings at my uncle's house are chaperoned, and I am covered from head to toe in clothing, with my face covered by a veil. The only thing that we may do is talk, and the only thing he wants to talk about is the upcoming debate."

The high priestess gets up and walks around her desk and reaches out to feel the material of her sleeve and collar. "I see your point, but physical allure is not all that I have taught you. A priestess of our order is also taught the fine arts of deception, deflection, and manipulation. There are subtle ways to get a man intoxicated with our presence, even if he cannot look upon the sweet fruits of our bodies. Our words and mannerisms should be as provocative as our figures. Bending men to make them think we are all they want and need is the very core of our discipline. You know this, don't you?"

"Of course, Madam. And, um, in the beginning, I diligently pursued this course by intriguing him with my understanding of the zodiac. His heart does truly lie along that path, and I successfully inserted myself into being a part of that passion with him. That is why he went to seek counsel from his headmaster to pursue our betrothal. I had him so enticed that he visited me in the marketplace almost every day to talk, even when he knew it could bring undo attention and even scandal to himself."

The high priestess raises an eyebrow as understanding jells in her. "You are falling in love with this Magi apprentice, aren't you?"

"I am going to marry him, High Priestess," she blurts out a little too fast and with more passion than she would have liked.

The high priestess laughs and walks around her desk and takes a seat. "Varaz, there is nothing wrong with our having affection for our pets. But we are never to forget who the master truly is in the relationship. I see that this young man has intrigued your academic sensibilities. You were always one of our best students in theology, and your ability with languages is unparalleled in our order." She gazes at Varaz a little and then comes up with an idea. "You know we just finished the fall harvest festival and you have not partaken in any of our events since you began this mission. We use our ceremonies and festivals to entice and control key men in our communities. But it is not just the erotic parts that serve our purpose. Social events where we simply interact with them can also prove quite advantageous to us."

Varaz nods uncomfortably. She finally says, "Madam, I can't be seen by anyone in the Magi Order at any of our events, whether social or ceremony. If Rassan ever found out that I have not left our order, he would break all ties with me!"

"Yes, I understand this, but tonight General Barach is having a social gathering at his house that is only available to his top officers in the area. I have been invited, and with that I am always allowed to bring an assistant. Tonight, that will be you."

Varaz gasps. "General Bozan is Rassan's kinsman and the one handling the betrothal negotiations with my uncle. If he recognizes me with you, all our plans will be ruined!"

"Has he ever seen your face, or even talked with you during those times?"

"Well, no. But he's been to my uncle's home eight times, and I was there every time," she answers with a little less trepidation.

"Don't worry, Varaz. I know about General Bozan. He and Rassan's father always despised our order. Men see what they want to see. You will be dressed in priestess clothing and sitting with me. He will do his best not to notice us at all. My presence might even keep him from attending."

With a nagging feeling of an impending catastrophe, Varaz nods her head in agreement.

Later That Afternoon, General Bozan's Temporary Apartment at the City Garrison

Rassan is now in his officer's uniform and sitting, talking to Mahre about the betrothal meetings. "I am so pleased the prince sent a reply so quickly, Rassan. You must be overjoyed that we can finally schedule your and Varaz's wedding."

Rassan reaches over and grasps the mug of cool iced tea and takes a long, slow drink. Beads of sweat run down his face as he has just finished his sparring session with Commander Sasheen before coming to General Bozan's and Mahre's apartment inside the garrison. He finds it funny, but whenever he puts his uniform on, it feels like it belongs to someone else. He has become so accustomed to his apprentice robes that nothing else seems comfortable. He finishes his drink and wipes his forehead with a cloth provided by Mahre and says, "It is truly a dream come true. I could not have seen this come to pass without Bozan's and your help. I will be forever grateful for your care and concern in this matter."

Mahre leans forward and puts her hand on Rassan's knee. "Oh please, Rassan. Do you have any idea how hard it is to get Bozan away from that farm these days? I swear, these last two months in the city have been like a holiday for me. You forget I was raised in the capital, and city life is truly my preference. Besides, our daughter and her husband are doing well managing Bozan's family estate; and little Mahre, my granddaughter, has been handling the market in our village satisfactorily. If I had my way, we would stay here indefinitely."

From behind them a voice booms. "You may have your way if Commander Sasheen doesn't start impressing me a lot more than he is."

Both turn to see Bozan standing in the doorway. Rassan stands immediately and gives Bozan a smart salute. Bozan returns the salute and smiles. "I cannot figure out your friend, Rassan. General Barach asked me to evaluate him as a replacement for him upon retirement. Sometimes, I think he is the perfect military officer, but there is just something about him that I don't like."

"Isn't Commander Sasheen betrothed to General Barach's only child, Husband?" Mahre asks.

He sighs. "Yes, he is. Sasheen's family negotiated the betrothal from the capital, but Barach did not want the marriage to take place until he was of sufficient rank to begin his training to take over the garrison in Babylon."

"I was overjoyed when you told me about his coming a few years ago. It kept you from assuming Barach's place and allowed us to retire from public life and enjoy our family."

Bozan chuckles. "Yet you still pine for city life, my wife. I swear, understanding your mind is harder than defeating a Roman legion."

Rassan, intrigued, asks, "You were to succeed General Barach as commander here, Bozan?"

"Not a job I wanted, but there are only two paths open for an old warrior in times of peace. Retire, or take on a political appointment. I chose the first. After serving most of my life under your father, becoming the commander of a city garrison was quite an intolerable thought. But I was second highest in rank to Barach and the obvious choice for the position when he would have stepped down."

"Now Commander Sasheen is in line for that position because of his betrothal to the general's daughter?"

"Yes and no. General Barach came to me when he heard I was back in the city on personal matters and asked me to help him evaluate Sasheen. It seems your friend has him concerned as well. I agreed, and because of that, my commission was temporarily reactivated. I will continue aiding the general in this and other matters until after the emperor's visit in three weeks."

"Why are you and General Barach concerned about Commander Sasheen? I believe him to be a fine officer with much ability as a military leader."

"That's just it, Rassan! A garrison command post is not what a young and capable military commander should look to do. We need excellent commanders in the field protecting our borders and keeping the peace. He should want to go somewhere where he could make a name for himself, not prematurely try to fill an old man's shoes. Think about it. Before you found the calling to pursue the life of a Magi, would you, as a young officer, want to be stuck commanding a garrison?"

"Absolutely not!" Rassan blurts out as the logic all comes together for him.

Bozan nods his head. "You see my dilemma then, don't you?" He then notices that Rassan is sweating profusely and walks over to a shelf and grabs a cloth and gives it to him. "You've just come from your weekly drill and sword practice with Commander Sasheen. Tell me how he is doing in maintaining your disciplines. Are his skills increasing?"

Rassan takes the cloth and wipes his head. "Well, to be honest, his sword play is not as good as it used to be. At the academy I would usually beat him, but he could manage a win here and there and our bouts were always close. Now, he can hardly keep up, and I find myself being the one to drill him."

Bozan shakes his head. "Your father once wrote to say that he fancied you to be the greatest swordsman in the empire. That was when he started training you at ten years of age. When I heard that Prince Phraates V picked you out of the senior class of the academy to be his sparring partner, I counted that prediction fulfilled. Tell me, do you decipher the stars in the heavens and all those ancient charts with the same tenacity and skill you do with that sword that hangs at your hip?"

Rassan is quick to answer. "Greater tenacity and love! It is my life's calling to study the Creator's message in the stars. I have never been more sure of anything in my life, Bozan."

"Then it is that calling you must be true to most no matter what, Rassan. I know that every step of your life has been ordered by others, especially your father. But if you feel the hand of the Creator on your heart, then the only sane course for you to take is the path He calls you to."

Mahre places a hand on Bozan's shoulder to get his attention. "Husband, remember General Barach's dinner. He sent word that you are expected to appear, at least for a moment."

Bozan grimaces and replies, "Must I?! Those women from the Temple of Zarpanuta will be there, and I hate fending off their attentions."

"I have it on good authority that only the high priestess herself was invited, and I think she has bigger fish to bait than you, Husband. Just give your greetings to the general, make a toast to him, and come home. You will be fine."

Bozan sighs and resigns himself to listen to his spouse, then turns his attention to Rassan. "You should accompany me. It would do General Barach good to see you in uniform, and I could use the support. Come, I will have my carriage take you to the Magi Temple when we are finished."

One Hour Later, Garrison Banquet Hall

Varaz's beauty and presence outshine even that of the high priestess as she sits next to her at a table close to the front, where General Barach and his top officers are seated. She can feel the eyes of almost every man in the room devouring her beauty. She and the high priestess purposely are wearing clothing that covers their exotic figures enough to be modestly social. But instead of stifling the men's desire for their attention, it only seems to heighten it. It has been months since she had taken part in occasions like this one and has to admit that it does not feel the same. Before, she used to revel in the power she could wield over men; but now, after knowing Rassan, this all seems so superficial and petty.

Just outside the garrison banquet hall, Mihri sees Commander Sasheen about ready to enter. He steps up to him. "I've heard that General Bozan has been ordered to make an appearance here tonight. Stay out here until he arrives and slow him down. I want to discuss something with General Barach, and I don't want him interrupting. I need to take a seat first and wait for the general's family to arrive before I can talk to him."

Commander Sasheen's face takes on a look of disappointment because he wanted to be there when his betrothed, the general's daughter, entered. But he knows better than to refuse Mihri's orders and simply nods his head and stands by the door as Mihri enters. Mihri quickly finds his table and takes a seat. Within moments, the general stands and his wife and daughter come into the banquet hall and take their seats.

Mihri waits a little, then gets up from his table in the room's corner and walks over to General Barach's table. Varaz takes notice. She marvels at how Mihri got himself invited. It probably had something to do with political maneuvering, because the emperor would be in the city in three weeks and his master, Dvandas, would be with him as his chief advisor. As he walks by, he directs a smug look of self-satisfaction at the high priestess and Varaz. Intent on showing them who the most important religious official in the city truly is, he makes his way to General Barach and starts a conversation without waiting to be invited to do so.

The high priestess has an evil gleam in her sharp, green eyes. She stands up and motions Varaz to follow. She puts her hand to her mouth as if to sigh nonchalantly and whispers to Varaz. "Watch me bend these imbeciles to my desire without offering them anything in return." She makes her way to the general's table and stands behind Mihri and clears her throat to get their attention. The general looks up and Mihri turns to see who would dare interrupt his conversation. Before he can say a word, she walks around him and flashes the general a sparkling smile. "I am glad you are together, because I have a request that concerns both of you."

Sitting next to the general are his wife and daughter. Neither wants to have to endure watching a conversation the general would have with any priestess of Zarpanuta. The general places a hand on his wife's shoulder and replies, "High Priestess, can't this wait until later?"

She smiles and moves in a little closer and answers. "No, it cannot, General. You see, the priestesses of Zarpanuta just put on the fall festival for the city of Babylon, and our members are taxed beyond their capabilities. Yet the garrison officers and the members of the

Magi Magician Sect continue to seek private religious services, but we need to conserve our efforts to be in full force for when the emperor shows up in three weeks. I am told that a full legion of men is with him, and the officers in that detachment will need our care when they arrive."

General Barach's jaw muscles clench and his cheeks redden as he feels the weight of his wife's and daughter's stares. He turns to Mihri and barks, "You are to prevent all Magi from visiting the Temple of Zarpanuta until after the emperor and his party depart from Babylon!" He then summons his attaché, who is standing next to his table. "Find Commander Sasheen and tell him I want two officers guarding the entrances to that Temple, and they are to arrest any Magi or garrison officer who tries to enter until after that time."

The man gives a quick salute and scampers off in search of Commander Sasheen. The high priestess smiles at how fast the general responded to her request and casts her eyes on Mihri, reveling in the poorly veiled look of rage in his expression.

Outside, Commander Sasheen sees General Bozan coming through the outer door, but it is pure panic that seizes him when he recognizes Rassan in his military uniform beside him. He knows that the high priestess showed up with Varaz earlier but did not think anyone here, including the general, would recognize her as the niece of Baazar the papyrus merchant. But Rassan is a completely different matter. He hurries in their direction, desperately trying to think of a way to keep Rassan from entering the banquet hall. As he runs up to them, a voice from behind him yells, "Commander Sasheen, I have orders from General Barach that you are to carry out immediately!"

Three sets of eyes turn to see the general's personal attaché standing in the entrance. Sasheen glances over to General Bozan first, while cold sweat drips down the side of his cheeks. "Sir, uh, Rassan and I have a matter to discuss from this morning's drills. May he and I have a word privately?"

Bozan rolls his eyes and huffs, "Commander, your superior officer and mine just sent his personal attaché to give you urgent orders. Whatever you need to talk to Rassan about can wait. Attend to your duty, Commander!"

Sasheen holds Bozan's glare for a millisecond before he caves, salutes him, and turns to the attaché. "What are the general's orders?"

"All garrison officers and Magi are not to visit the Temple of Zarpanuta until after the emperor leaves Babylon. You are to arrange for two officers to be there at the front of the Temple with orders to arrest any men from those two groups who try to enter. Can I tell the general you have received his orders and will carry them out immediately, Commander?"

Sasheen takes one more nervous look at Rassan then another at General Bozan and says to the attaché, "Yes, you may tell the general that I am carrying out his orders immediately. Uh, Rassan, please join me. I could use your help."

Bozan's eyes bore into Sasheen. "Commander, have you lost your senses? Rassan is acting as my personal aide today. Go find someone else to help you!"

"Oh, uh, of course, General. I merely thought that if he came with me, the other matter could be handled as well." Sasheen searches Bozan's face for a sign of relenting and finds none, then salutes and hurries off to carry out Barach's orders.

Bozan looks at Rassan and laughs. "Now that is the best news I've heard all day. After those disgusting rituals they have had there for the last week, it will be nice to see them all shut up in their Temple for a while and out of my hair, with all their distractions to men like Sasheen. I might just enjoy this dinner after all. Let's go in."

Rassan smiles and nods as he follows Bozan into the banquet room.

The attaché comes in and tells the general that Commander Sasheen was found and was given the orders. As they make their way back to their table, the high priestess looks at Varaz and smiles. "You see, men can be manipulated by a woman. We are not limited to our allure, only our imaginations."

Suddenly the doors to the banquet hall open and General Bozan steps through. But it is not the sight of him that sends a chill of terror up and down Varaz's spine. Behind him is Rassan. Though she has never seen him in uniform, it is undeniably him. When their eyes meet from across the banquet hall, he recognizes her. Immediately, her hand goes to her face in a feeble attempt to mask herself from his stare. A loud gasp leaves her lungs and the high priestess looks at her, then in the direction that she is trying to avoid with her eyes. The high priestess sees General Bozan with a young aide and does not understand Varaz's reaction. She puts her hand to her mouth and whispers, "Calm yourself, girl. There is no way the general will recognize you!"

Varaz steps closer to her superior and whispers back, "That aide is Rassan! He is in uniform today."

The high priestess feels immediate panic. She scrambles in her mind, trying to come up with something to avert this disaster. She looks to the corner of the room where Mihri is already standing, and from what she can see, he is having a similar panic attack. Before she can say anything, General Bozan steps past her to General Barach's table to make his greeting. He is oblivious to Rassan's predicament because he wants to get in and out of there as fast as possible. Having to walk right by the high priestess of the Temple of Zarpanuta only intensifies that desire. Meanwhile, behind him, Rassan slowly makes his way to Varaz, never letting go of her eyes with his own. When he gets to her, he just stops and remains quiet and motionless while staring at her. General Bozan gives General Barach a salute and says, "Greetings, General..."

General Barach, seeing what is going on behind Bozan, stands and stays him with an upraised hand, then points to the high priestess, Varaz, and Rassan, and says, "I believe you have a problem to deal with, General. Let's try to not make a scene here!"

As Bozan turns to see what the general is pointing at, he is immediately confused and concerned. He makes his way over to Rassan, nods his head to the high priestess and her companion, who is now in a locked stare with Rassan, and asks, "Rassan, do you know this priestess?" He steps a little closer and says under his breath, "You are making a bit of a scene in front of General Barach and his family."

Rassan inhales deeply and lets out a painful sigh, then releases his stare with Varaz and looks to Bozan. "General, you have met this priestess of the Temple of Zarpanuta many times. This is my betrothed, Varaz." He takes his right fist and wipes a tear from his cheek, takes another deep breath, then turns and leaves the garrison banquet hall.

Astonishment and anger grip Bozan's heart. He turns menacingly to the high priestess and steps close enough for only her to hear his words. "I don't know what game you are playing here, High Priestess. But Rassan is a beloved friend of the prince and known well by the emperor, who will be here in three weeks. He will not take kindly to anyone mistreating or manipulating one of his heir's favorite people."

The high priestess's throat is so dry she can barely respond. "General Bozan, please, this is all a huge misunderstanding. Varaz's membership in our order is almost over. These things take time, so in the interim, I just asked her to join me here out of a courtesy, because I had no one else to accompany me."

"High Priestess, please. At least you have admitted that. Anyone knows that the Temple of Zarpanuta would let no one wear its priestess's attire if they were not still part of the order."

All eyes turn to see General Barach, standing directly behind Varaz. "Take heed how you answer my question, young lady. For I carry the emperor's authority in all matters of security for the city of Babylon. Are you still a member of the priestess's order of Zarpanuta?"

Varaz is so stunned by Rassan walking out without saying a word to her that she barely has the strength to answer the general. She knows that lying could mean her life, so she simply nods her head, affirming that she is. The high priestess blurts out, "General, she is almost out of our order. She has not taken part in any of our rituals for almost a half year now, and—"

"Enough of your scheming, High Priestess. You and your aide must leave. I need to confer with General Bozan regarding how he wants to proceed in this matter."

Seeing that there is no relenting in the general's demeanor, the high priestess takes Varaz by the arm and quickly escorts her to the nearest door. They step out into the hall and find Mihri waiting for them. His eyes dart back and forth across the hall, looking for anyone who could hear them. "What is wrong with you? Your pride, High Priestess, has ruined months of careful planning and maneuvering. Headmaster Dvandas is going to be quite angry with you when he arrives with the emperor. In fact, once General Barach talks to the emperor, your order might need to look for your replacement."

Mihri's threats have the opposite effect on the high priestess. With hellish fire in her tone, she replies. "Don't assume that I don't know how important this upcoming debate in the Magi Order is to Dvandas. He thinks that it could propel him to the Grand Master's position if it goes his way. Remember, I have something that could ruin that for him. And now that General Barach has stationed his own men at my door until after the emperor leaves, you have no chance of ever getting your hands on it. Tell your master to use every influence he has to protect me and my order, or I swear by Zarpa-nuta, if I fall, he will fall with me!"

She then grabs Varaz's arm and quickly exits the garrison building.

Once they are outside, Varaz pleads with her. "High Priestess, the general caught me off guard! I feared for my life if I lied."

The high priestess stops and holds Varaz's shoulders. "Priestess Varaz, you did the right thing. If you had lied and been found out, both of us would have been in grave danger. This is all my fault. I should have never brought you with me to this banquet. Don't worry, we will survive this setback and move on. When we get back to the Temple, you must remain there until after the emperor and Dvandas leave Babylon."

"I understand, High Priestess."

Back Inside the Banquet Hall

Both generals have retreated to the back of the banquet hall so that they may speak in privacy. General Barach's demeanor is that of annoyance tempered with concern for his friend, Bozan. "For you, I will disregard Rassan's breaking of protocol and leaving without being dismissed, Bozan."

"Thank you, General Barach. He was completely unbalanced by this deception. So was I. You know that Rassan's betrothal arrangement is the only reason I returned to the city and agreed to my temporary reinstatement. Now, with your leave, I will find my wife and we will take care of Rassan."

"You also need to tell Headmaster Daraya-Vous about what just happened. It was the emperor himself who placed Rassan in his care, and we can do nothing without his consent."

"Of course, General, you are right. Mahre and I will seek him out first. Rassan probably needs time to reflect and gather his thoughts."

"Agreed. Please see that this does not adversely affect the emperor's visit. He does not get around the empire all that often, and when he does, changes seem to happen."

Bozan nods his head, gives his superior a salute, then turns and leaves.

15

Cetus Is Wyly

Later That Day, Magi Astronomical Temple

Though he spends most of his waking hours at night studying the stars, Daraya-Vous, headmaster of his order of the Magi, cannot sleep after he leaves his morning lecture to the apprentices. He knew Rassan would not be there this morning, but he could not quell the nagging feeling that somehow the lecture was exactly where the boy needed to be. He spends the rest of the morning and part of the afternoon in the Temple prayer area, lifting his thoughts and concerns to the Creator, anticipating some type of wisdom to help him deal with his anxiousness concerning Rassan. All of the Magi in his order maintain a solid discipline of praying three times a day, as Belteshazzar taught them in the beginning of their order's formation. He often noticed that Rassan was the most faithful in his class to this discipline, and he would find Rassan there in the afternoon when he awoke.

As he is leaving the prayer area, he sees Kaufa approach him. Kaufa had only recently returned from his trip to the Jewish settlement to study the Hebrew scrolls, hoping to discover what they had to teach about the Creator's message in the zodiac. He was fascinated with some things the boy had learned from the scrolls of Psalms and Job. Kaufa will be very prepared for his contribution to the debate, which brings him back to his concerns about Rassan. Rassan is his main debater and will use his understanding of the sacred star charts like no other apprentice could. Kaufa hurriedly steps up to Daraya-Vous. "Headmaster, General Bozan asks to speak with you. He and his wife have upsetting news about Rassan that they must share with you. They are in the Tapestry Observatory waiting for you."

"Thank you, Kaufa," he says, and immediately hurries in that direction.

As soon as he steps through the door, General Bozan confronts him with the bad news. "Headmaster, we have all been deceived. The maiden, Varaz, to whom Rassan has recently become officially betrothed, is still an active priestess in the Temple of Zarpanuta. We discovered this today when he accompanied me to a banquet held by General Barach. When Rassan and I arrived at the banquet hall, we found the general in a conversation with the high priestess. Rassan recognized that her aide was Varaz herself, dressed in the priestess's robe—which, as you know, is forbidden to anyone but an active priestess in that order."

Daraya-Vous is stunned by the revelation. "Where is Rassan?"

Bozan looks to his wife first, and she shakes her head. He then looks at the headmaster. "He left soon after he recognized Varaz. He said nothing to her directly, but he was very upset. I felt it best to leave him be until I could talk with you."

"We must find him immediately!" Daraya-Vous replies. "Darkness threatens to take him from the light. We must proceed with urgency."

Same Time, Babylon City Merchant's Courtyard

Commander Sasheen cannot believe how everything fell apart so quickly. He knows that he should have stopped Rassan from entering that banquet hall, but how could he, with General Bozan right there? As soon as he finishes setting up the officers to guard the Temple of Zarpanuta per General Barach's orders, he rushes back to the garrison to see if Mihri is still there to confer with him. When he arrives, Mihri is waiting for him at the entrance. He orders him to find Rassan and bring him to a certain Magician Magi's home in the city. Mihri tells him that Rassan is very vulnerable right now, and that the Magi's skills could be exactly what could now entice the boy to their side. Sasheen sets off immediately to find Rassan. He searches the entire garrison and even goes to his Temple and inquires at the gate whether Rassan has returned there. The only other places he can think to check are the central market and then Baazar the papyrus merchant's home to see if Rassan has headed to either of those places to confront Varaz's uncle.

He walks around the corner of one stand in the central market and sees Rassan still in uniform, standing in Baazar's tent, involved in a heated conversation with the merchant, his fingers on the hilt of his sword. Sasheen rushes to deescalate the situation. When he gets there, Rassan is yelling at Baazar. "Why did you deceive me? You had no authority to offer her in betrothal negotiations. She's the property of the Temple of Zarpanuta and not eligible to marry!"

With beads of sweat rolling down both cheeks, Baazar screeches back in terror. "I had no choice! They would have ruined me and perhaps even killed me if I did not comply."

Before Rassan can press more, Commander Sasheen fears Baazar will cave in, so he blurts out, "Who are 'they' if I might ask?"

Rassan whips around, his hand dangerously close to drawing his sword until he recognizes his friend. But he is hardly relieved by his presence. "You have no business here, Commander. I am perfectly within my rights to seek justice in this matter. I and my whole family have been insulted by this man."

Commander Sasheen frantically searches his thoughts to answer the incensed man before him. "Rassan, as a soldier you may challenge this man to a duel of honor, but as a Magi apprentice you are bound by the code of your order. How would Headmaster Daraya-Vous judge your actions should you pursue that course?"

Rassan stares blankly at his friend. Struck by the logic of his words, he falls to his knees and bows his head and weeps. Sasheen motions to Baazar to go away. But as the merchant leaves, Rassan looks up. "Wait, you said someone threatened you. Who was it?"

Again, desperation fills Baazar's eyes as he looks imploringly to Commander Sasheen. The commander nods his head and says, "Rassan, you understand that you are to be the head of a powerful family in the empire someday. Many would seek to control you. The high priestess of Zarpanuta is one such individual. Baazar is right to fear for his life in crossing her. In Babylon, her reach is far and tenacious. But he now has no need to worry, because General Barach has put her Temple on lockdown and will not allow anyone to come or go without being monitored. I am told that he is going to talk with Grand Master Artapan about limiting her order's influences in the city."

When he finishes, he waves his hand, telling Baazar to leave so that he and Rassan can talk more. Once the merchant is gone, Rassan again bows his head and weeps. "I never knew love for a woman until I knew Varaz. I feel my heart has been ripped from my chest. Help me, Sasheen!"

Sasheen can barely keep himself from laughing at the pathetic man before him. To think that Rassan is the son of Parthia's greatest general and one of the most skilled swordsmen in the empire brought to his knees by a mere woman! But he has his orders from Mihri and must continue to nurture this fool like he is his dearest friend in the world. "Rassan, you must not give up on finding a suitable wife. Varaz is only a woman that deceived you. Forget her and find one who is worthy of your station and rank."

"You don't understand, Sasheen. I may never marry after this affront to my soul. How could I ever give my heart to another?" Rassan stands and tightens his fists as he shakes them in the air. "Damn her! Despite this deception, she is everything I have ever wanted in a mate and more. I can't get over her."

Commander Sasheen steps up to Rassan and gently shakes his shoulder. "Rassan, she is a priestess of the Temple of Zarpanuta. She has studied the art of enticing men her whole life. You are simply an unprepared victim for such an attack. That is all. Your heart will mend and then you will move on."

"I don't know, Sasheen. Perhaps I will renounce my claim to being head of my father's house and leave it to Bozan permanently. Then no one would be interested in seducing me and I will live my life as a Magi who has no wife. It is rare, but not unheard of."

Sasheen feels the panic rising in his chest again. This is the last thing that Mihri or Headmaster Dvandas wants. Then he remembers the Magician Magi who Mihri wanted him to take Rassan to. "Rassan, we should go to a Magi counselor to discuss this. There is a very good one close to here who I believe could give you answers that will settle you."

Rassan looks up with a bit of hope in his expression, but with foreboding as well. "I don't want to seek a Magician Magi who will endeavor to read my stars and prognosticate my future, Sasheen. You know that is not the purpose of the stars."

Sasheen sees the caution and hope in Rassan's expression and says, "This is not a stargazer, Rassan. He is a Familiar."

Rassan has never heard that term before. "What is a Familiar?"

Sasheen knows he has to be careful, so he gives only a partial definition of that art. "It is a Magi who is spiritually attuned to the past and can ferret out a unique individual's family's desires in certain areas. He can tell you what your mother or father would have desired for you to do in this situation."

"How could they know what my dead father or mother would want?"

"What I have been told is that everyone leaves an impression on the spiritual realm that can be tapped into by those sensitive to it. Once they do, they can counsel an individual like the person who is gone would have."

Rassan still feels a sense of foreboding but he is also hurting, and the thought of hearing what his father would have said in this situation is exactly what he feels he needs right now. "OK, Sasheen, I will go only because you are my friend and I trust that you will not lead me astray."

Commander Sasheen sees that his deception has been successful. He points his hand in the direction of the house of the Magi that has a familiar spirit, and he and Rassan walk there.

Half an Hour Later, Same Spot

Headmaster Daraya-Vous, General Bozan, and his wife Mahre rush into the tent where Baazar has his papyrus stand, looking frantically for Rassan or the merchant. Neither one is there, but an attendant is there behind the table, ready to serve customers. Daraya-Vous steps up to the attendant. "Pardon me, I am Headmaster Daraya-Vous of the Astronomical Sect of the Magi Order. We are patrons of this papyrus stand. Where can I find your master, Baazar?"

"I am sorry, Headmaster, but Baazar is not here. Your representative from the Temple was here, but he was wearing an officer's uniform, and he and Baazar were arguing. It got a little heated and another officer from the garrison came in and stopped it from escalating. They left for the city about half an hour ago."

At the mention of the second officer, General Bozan asks, "Describe this second officer to me."

"He was a little taller than the one who usually shows up here in Magi robes, and he seemed to have an air of authority about him. He deescalated what I thought would end in violence. The Magi wearing the military uniform then fell to his knees and wept. The taller one then told him that there was a Magi in the city who could counsel him in the same way his father would."

Alarmed, Daraya-Vous steps forward and asks, "Did he say who or what kind of Magi he was referring to?"

"I don't know, Headmaster. He just said that the Magi was some kind of 'Familiar' and was sensitive to things like that."

Daraya-Vous turns to General Bozan and his wife. "I know what Magi he is referring to! He is a member of the Magician Sect and has a familiar spirit. It is necromancy and is pure evil. They impersonate the dead to deceive the living. I don't believe that Rassan would knowingly seek out such a person unless he is being lied to by the one taking him there. I know where this one lives. We must go there at once!"

Meanwhile, Rassan and Sasheen come to a large house on the corner of a neighborhood that houses the wealthier citizens of Babylon. It is even bigger than the one that Varaz's uncle, Baazar, lives in. Rassan cannot shake the feeling that this is all wrong, and a small voice inside his head tells him to leave there and get away from Commander Sasheen as fast as possible. Sasheen is about to call out to the owner of the house when Rassan puts up his hand and says, "I am sorry, Sasheen, but this feels very wrong. I think I need to go see the headmaster and—"

A loud voice booms from the now-opened door of the house. "Rassy, come in here. We need to speak!"

An icy chill runs up and down Rassan's spine as the familiar words touch his ears. There is only one person who has ever talked to him like that—his father! Rassan's face contorts in a fearful and astonished expression. He shakes almost uncontrollably but he can still hear that small voice telling him to leave. When he turns to do so, the iron grip of his friend's hand grabs his shoulder and spins him around and walks him toward the open door. "Rassan, don't be ridiculous. I told you that this man is sensitive to people's families and can tap into their wisdom and counsel. There is nothing to be afraid of. Just come and meet him. After that, if you want to leave, I won't stand in your way."

Rassan looks at his friend, then at the door. When he does, the voice comes again, "Rassy, come on. You need my help. I am here."

Still unsure, he allows Sasheen to escort him into the house. When they arrive, they are greeted by a large, baldheaded, muscular servant holding a candle in his hand. The house is made of stone and there are no windows in the section they are in, so once past the door, it becomes very dark. The servant motions for them to follow him, and Sasheen continues to guide Rassan to a little room off to the side that is even darker. Once inside and with the servant's candle illuminating the room, they are greeted by a middle-aged Magician Magi sitting cross-legged on the floor with his eyes closed and a pasty-gray hue to his face. There looks to be some sort of steam pouring from his nose and mouth and gathering next to him, taking on the shape of a man.

When Rassan sees that, he immediately jerks and tries to leave, but Sasheen tightens his grip. A voice from the other side of the room speaks. "He is almost ready to manifest himself. Give him a few more moments and all that you need to know will be revealed."

Rassan looks up and over and sees that the owner of the voice is Mihri, who has just stepped out of the shadows. Rassan has never liked Mihri or his master, Dvandas, and he quickly decides to leave, even if he has to draw his sword on his friend. Before he does, though, the same voice—the voice of his father—comes out of the man sitting on the floor. "Rassan, I know what has happened to you. You have been deceived by vain men who don't see the universe for what it is. That is why you're vulnerable to deception by those who would manipulate and control you to use my house for their ends."

He glares incredulously at the seated man who is speaking to him in his father's voice, and then he looks to the side and sees that the apparition that is forming is that of his father. Confused and panicked, he blurts out, "What in the name of the Creator is going on here?"

A powerfully authoritative voice booms from the door behind Rassan and Sasheen. "The Creator does not sanction this nor is He pleased with the abomination that is taking place here. He will not permit it to have his servant, Rassan. He commands these things to cease, NOW!"

The apparition that is forming immediately falls apart, and the man on the floor falls on his side and his body begins to convulse and shake. Bozan, who was standing next to Daraya-Vous as the headmaster declared his demand, now steps forward with another candle in his hand. He looks at the muscular servant with the candle and sees that he is contemplating attacking the headmaster and his party. He holds up his hand to the man. "I am General Bozan of the city's military garrison. If you show any aggression, I will be forced to subdue and arrest you. Be warned—attacking a Parthian military officer unprovoked carries a sentence of death."

He turns to Rassan, who is staring blankly at the man who was imitating his father. With more light in the room, it is apparent that the man is in some type of physical trauma and is gasping for air. A film of mucus covers his face and shoulders, and his countenance is even paler than before.

The servant stops and acknowledges the authority before him. Daraya-Vous steps over the man on the floor and up to Mihri and booms, "Leave my apprentice alone, evil one! The next time I find you meddling with people in my order, I will have you brought before Grand Master Artapan and charged with an insurrection!" He then looks to Rassan, and in a much gentler tone says, "Come, Rassan. I know you did not pursue counsel from these in a way that violates our beliefs. They have endeavored to deceive and manipulate you in your weakest hour. I heard you trying to leave as we approached. You are innocent and the Creator is pleased."

Rassan nods and walks over to the headmaster, and looks him in the eye. "All that I desire in my life is to continue the watch with you. My heart belongs to the Creator's message in the stars, and to that end will I give my all. Please take me home."

Daraya-Vous puts his arm around Rassan's shoulders and looks to Bozan for direction.

"You two go on and take Mahre with you," Bozan says. "I will finish up here and join you shortly."

Daraya-Vous nods and walks out of the house with Rassan and Mahre.

General Bozan waits until he is sure that they are gone and then turns to glare at Commander Sasheen, who has been standing in the back corner of the room, feebly attempting to hide himself. "Commander Sasheen!" he bellows.

"Yes, General," he says as he steps forward and gives a shaky salute.

"I am disgusted with what I see here. Your actions as a commanding officer in the emperor's army are reprehensible today." He puts his face so close that his hot breath burns Sasheen's eyes. "You think that your path to greatness and honor is so finely laid out for you here in Babylon? But consider this. General Barach wants to retire after the emperor's visit in another month. Whether or not you are to be his successor once you and his daughter have married, he has left to my choice. If I desire, he will let *me* assume his command, and then it will be left to me to evaluate you ever assuming command of this garrison or any other post. And there is nothing that this Magi"—he points to Mihri—"or his master can do about it. Do I make myself clear, Commander?!"

"Yes, General," Sasheen whispers.

"Good. Now get this man to a healer, and make it clear to your friend Mihri that neither General Barach nor I will tolerate his presence at the garrison. He can wait to see if someone from the emperor's party will invite him when they arrive. But until then, he's banished from there."

When Headmaster Daraya-Vous, Rassan, and Mahre made their way out of the house and to the street, Rassan is so shaken by what has transpired that he feels ashamed to speak. Mahre sees his discomfort and endeavors to console him. "Rassan, you have been deceived in horrible ways, as have we all. There is no need for shame. Be thankful that Headmaster Daraya-Vous and Bozan knew what to do and came to your aid."

"Thank you for your words, Mahre," Rassan replies. "All of you showing up when you did keep me from being a part of something I would have regretted for the rest of my life."

Mahre smiles brightly. "Don't worry, Rassan. Bozan and I will always be here for you. We will continue to look for a proper maid for you to wed."

"I have no interest or energy for that now, Mahre. My life belongs to the Astronomical Sect of the Magi Order, and to them will I give my full efforts. I no longer have a heart to pursue marriage and family. I think that Bozan and you should start thinking about permanently leading my father's house."

Taken aback by his words, Mahre places her hand to her mouth. "Rassan, that is neither my nor Bozan's wish. Your father was quite clear when he asked the emperor to have Bozan steward your responsibilities until you were ready. I don't think—"

Before she can finish, Daraya-Vous, who has been silently listening, interjects. "I do not believe you are in a proper state of mind to be making such a decision, Apprentice. Put your feelings of this matter in the silent part of your heart and incubate them for a while. The Creator called you to us, knowing exactly who you are and what you bring. Perhaps there is still more He has planned that neither of us now sees."

Mahre smiles at the headmaster and nods her head in approval. "The headmaster speaks with wisdom, Rassan. Heed his words."

Rassan's shoulders relax and he looks to the ground. "I will obey your words, Headmaster. Thank you."

Daraya-Vous smiles and pats Rassan on the back and points toward the Astronomical Temple. "Good, now let's go home. We have an important debate to prepare for, of which you are my principal speaker."

One Week Later, Temple of Zarpanuta

Varaz has been staying in her room for most of the time since leaving the garrison with the high priestess. She is not concerned so much with the presence of the garrison officers stationed outside of the Temple. She appreciates their presence. Her time away has opened her eyes to exactly what she has been a part of here, and she does not like what she now understands. The Temple has been less active since General Barach ordered that his military officers and any Magi refrain from any of their festivals and religious ceremonies. That left the patronage of local nobles and wealthy merchants to keep the Temple active, but even they are not as many. And she could not be happier about that, because after taking many months away from the Temple's activities, she acknowledges that what they do there—though religiously garbed—is nothing more than that of a high-priced brothel, which much to her surprise now sickens her to the core.

All she can think of is how awful Rassan must feel and how much he must despise her. The high priestess was right when she observed that Varaz was falling in love with the apprentice. He reached something deep in her that no one else has ever done. He woke up her mind and got her questioning everything she thought she believed. His pure-hearted quest to understand the Creator's great message in the stars put a hole in the heavily calloused barrier she had formed around her own heart, and now she feels so open and vulnerable. But instead of being afraid of her new vulnerability, she wants to embrace it and fill it with what she was learning from Rassan.

From a window on the third floor she looks down and sees that the officers guarding the Temple area have just changed and, to her delight, one of them is now Commander Sasheen. She despises the man and knows that he was never truly Rassan's friend but only stayed close to him because of the importance of his family and his connection with the prince. She realizes that Commander Sasheen is probably the most adversely affected officer in the garrison by General Barach's new orders. The man practically lived at the Temple of Zarpanuta when he was not serving in the garrison, taking every advantage of the religious festivals and ceremonies they offer in the name of worship. Now he has to guard and keep all garrison officers away, including himself. She decides to go down and give him a piece of her mind about what an awful, two-faced "friend" to Rassan he truly is, and then threaten to make known his duplicity to Rassan. She looks to her dresser, dons her most modest priestess robe, and proceeds to the entrance.

Commander Sasheen's ears are still burning from the tongue-lashing he received from General Barach after he heard about what transpired at the house of the Magi with the familiar spirit. General Barach's family is almost as important to the emperor as Rassan's family. Phraates IV would never be persuaded against the man with anything less than undeniable proof of pure treason. If such a charge were submitted then proved false, the accuser would surely be put to death. That is why he was so eager to marry into the general's family. Once there, he would no longer need to hang on the shirttails of one such as Rassan but could have his own legacy and path in this world that could one day outshine that Magi wannabe.

As he stands next to one of his junior officers, lost in his thoughts, he is suddenly startled by a female voice.

"Serves you right, you pathetic hypocrite! You call yourself a friend to Rassan. You don't know the meaning of the word."

Commander Sasheen spins around and finds Varaz standing behind him, looking on him with contempt. His hand reflexively reaches for his sword, but he catches the astonished look on his companion's face and thinks better of it. "What are you doing outside the Temple, Priestess? The general commanded all of you to stay inside unless you are scheduled to take care of the market or maintenance business."

Varaz laughs and walks around the men to face them with the sun to her back and says, "That is my purpose, Commander. I am here to tell you that there will be some women in the courtyard this morning doing some gardening."

Annoyed that Varaz is the one delivering the message and surmising that she is just using it as an excuse to taunt him, he orders, "Fine, now get back inside."

She stands there just long enough to make him want to do something about it and then starts for the door. "Your ambitions are collapsing all around you, aren't they, Commander? Word has it that General Barach is reconsidering your taking his daughter to wife and that he has asked General Bozan to take over after the visit of the emperor. Meanwhile, your master Dvandas's little weasel Mihri is banned from the garrison and will soon be humiliated when the Astronomical Sect of Magi debates their case before Grand Master Artapan and the emperor next month."

Enraged, Sasheen steps up to Varaz and sticks his nose in her face. "Don't be so sure of your facts, Priestess! More hinges on this debate with the Magi Order than you might think. When the headmaster of the Astronomical Sect loses the debate, Headmaster Dvandas will use the victory to discredit Daraya-Vous's order before the emperor and have it disbanded. Then where will your precious Rassan be, Priestess?!"

Varaz steps back, nauseated by the commander's closeness. "Why are you so sure they will lose?"

Commander Sasheen laughs. "Because everything they are basing their beliefs on is rooted in Hebrew doctrine and lore. Dvandas has been steadily poisoning the emperor's mind against those people ever since King Herod of Judea pushed us out of Jerusalem and gave the country to the Romans. When Daraya-Vous is shown to be trying to indoctrinate the empire with their beliefs, he won't stand for it and the Astronomical Sect will be no more."

Varaz glares at Commander Sasheen, dumbfounded by his words. She tries to recollect any references to the Hebrew Scripture Rassan might have made in all their conversations. She remembers him telling her that another apprentice, Kaufa, was to research that end of the debate, but never once got the idea that it was the main point of the discourse. But then it hits her. The sacred star charts that Rassan had the unprecedented opportunity to study while coming here were originally drawn by Belteshazzar, the Hebrew slave who served three emperors and controlled the whole Magi Order and founded the Astronomical Sect. She turns and walks back into the Temple.

"I won't let you get away with this!" she shouts and closes the door behind her.

16

Changing Times

November 15, 5 BC, Arrival of Phraates IV to Babylon

Grand Master Artapan stands next to the chief magistrate of Babylon, with General Barach on his other side. The occasion called for nothing less than the three highest-ranking officials in the city to be out front and center to greet the emperor and his caravan. He has met the emperor on several occasions, the most notable of which was when he officiated in the ascension of Phraates IV upon his father's death. He liked the man and found him to be logical and reasonable. Most of his choices were to be commended in having the best interests of the empire and its people at heart.

The only thing he does not approve of is that a self-seeking opportunist like Headmaster Dvandas has risen to the position of chief counselor to the emperor. Artapan did not ascend to the Grand Master's chair of the Magi Order by being a fool. He clearly sees the hand of Dvandas in the postponement of Daraya-Vous's debate over the true meaning of the zodiac.

In his heart, he knows that Daraya-Vous's stance is correct and falls in alignment with the teachings of the Prophet Zoroaster. But the political implications of this debate could be very much in Dvandas's favor should it go against the Astronomical Sect headmaster's stance. He cautioned Daraya-Vous about this, but the man was fervent in his belief that all this controversy must be decided so that his order could have unity and continue their faithful watch of the stars for the coming of the Creator's champion. The headmaster's stubbornness, though annoying, is also one of his qualities that continues to earn Artapan's respect and support. He looks up and sees that the caravan is entering the garrison courtyard.

Tens of thousands of Babylonians have swelled the city over the last few days in anticipation of the visit, and the air is filled with electricity. A full legion of Parthian calvary split in formation and take their mounts and line up on either side of the courtyard as the emperor's carriage rolls in. The chief magistrate waits until it comes to a full stop. Then he steps down from the stairs in front of the garrison's main building and, along with General Barach and Grand Master Artapan, proceeds to a predetermined spot about fifteen meters from the carriage.

All three take a knee, awaiting the emperor's emergence from his carriage. The coach attendants then open the ornately fashioned golden doors of the carriage and one of the men steps forward and gets down on all four limbs in front of the door and waits for the emperor to use him as a step. First to emerge, though, is Headmaster Dvandas and a general from the capital's garrison. Each man steps to opposite sides of the door and takes a knee as they bow their heads. Trumpets begin to sound from the surrounding walls of the garrison, where people are packed to see the emperor. A voice booms from the roof of the garrison. "People of Babylon, your Emperor, Phraates IV!"

The volume of cheers and applause is almost deafening as the emperor makes his way over to the chief magistrate and his companions. The capital's garrison general and Headmaster Dvandas fall in beside the emperor. He steps up and places his hand out to the magistrate, who takes it and kisses his ring while the other two stay kneeled with their heads bowed. "Arise, my trusted servants. Know that your emperor is pleased with the welcome he receives from this ancient and beautiful city."

The chief magistrate is the first to speak. "Emperor Phraates IV, Babylon is honored with the presence of her supreme ruler. The city awaits your pleasure, Sire."

"Thank you, Chief Magistrate. We appreciate your overtures on our behalf."

Before anyone else can speak, Dvandas steps forward. "The emperor must be escorted inside, Chief Magistrate. Please lead on."

As the man acknowledges the order from the chief counselor of the emperor, Phraates IV holds up a hand to stay him. "Nonsense, Dvandas, we will stay here a while and enjoy the hospitality of this city." He then turns to the crowds on the wall and raises his hand and shouts, "Your emperor is pleased with your welcome! You have our gratitude."

The crowd erupts with cheers and applause again as the emperor waves at each section of the wall. He then turns and looks to Grand Master Artapan and nods his head in respect and walks toward him. "It is good to see you again, my old friend. I trust the years have been kind to you?"

Artapan bows his head and gives the emperor a gesture of blessings with his hand and says, "We are honored by your presence, Sire."

The emperor turns to Dvandas and says, "Headmaster Dvandas, the grand master had sent word that he would need your presence in the Magi Council for a few days once we have arrived. I leave you to his care."

"Emperor, are you sure that is wise? You will need my counsel here at the garrison."

The emperor chuckles. "Not to worry, Dvandas. I have one of Parthia's wisest generals to stand in your stead while you fulfill your obligations to the Magi Order." He then holds up his hand to stay any further objections by Dvandas and walks over to General Barach. "Barach, my old friend. It is so good to see you. We have much to talk about. Tell me how Surena's boy is doing these days. My son tells me he is going to be married soon."

"There have been some upsets to those plans, Your Eminence. But I am told that Rassan has buried himself in his preparations for the upcoming debate in the Magi Order and is doing well."

"Upsets?! You will have to brief me, but not now. Let's go in."

"Of course, Emperor."

The emperor and the general make their way to the entrance as Dvandas hangs back with the grand master and chief magistrate, grinding his teeth in frustration. He has been waiting for a chance to explain the catastrophe of Rassan's betrothal gone wrong before anyone else could give their version. Mihri sent him a private communication via messenger to their caravan a few weeks ago and he has not broached the subject, fearing the emperor might make a hasty decision and have someone punished that Dvandas did not want. He steps forward, working up the courage to interrupt the emperor and General Barach's conversation, when the grand master says, "Let them be, Dvandas. Your and Mihri's meddling in Rassan's life has ended. For the next few days, you are under my domain. Now come, we have much to discuss."

Dvandas turns and glares at the grand master, ready to rebuke him for his insolence. But something in the old Magi's eyes tells him that the only one who would suffer from an outburst by him would be himself. "Of course, Grand Master. This is your domain."

The grand master proceeds into the garrison building, with Dvandas following. Once inside the hall, the grand master sees that the emperor, General Barach, and the chief magistrate have already found their way to the head table of the main banquet hall, and he proceeds to join them. Dvandas hurries up beside him and finds that when the grand master takes a seat, there are no more seats left. To the right of General Barach, he recognizes that the man taking up the last seat is someone who he knows but has not seen in over a decade—General Bozan, the former aide and nephew to General Surena. He looks to the grand master, who nods his head to the left, where he sees a table with Mihri and two other members of the Magician Sect of Magi seated with him. Then he notices that seated at the table on the right and directly in front of the head table are Headmaster Daraya-Vous, Rassan, Ambassador Samekh, and a boy he does not recognize.

Having spent the last fifteen years as the chief counselor to the emperor, he feels the slimy tentacles of jealousy and contempt for this slight against him. When he looks to the emperor, he sees that Phraates IV is obviously ignoring him. He walks over to his table and stands before Mihri and the others and waits for them to stand. The three are on their feet immediately and bow. Mihri steps around the table and gives a bow of obeisance as he says, "Headmaster Dvandas, it is good to see you after so long an absence. Please have a seat."

Much to his dismay, that place puts him close to Headmaster Daraya-Vous, who is sitting just a few meters over at the other table. When he sits, at first he does not look at the man, but protocol demands it and he knows the grand master is watching, so he turns and says, "Headmaster Daraya-Vous, greetings to you and your companions."

Daraya-Vous gives a courtly bow and welcoming gesture with his hand. "Greetings, Headmaster Dvandas, and welcome to Babylon. I trust your itinerary with the emperor has been both prosperous and profitable to the empire." He then adds, "It is unfortunate that the emperor did not plan this trip two years earlier. For then, you may have attended my installation as headmaster of the Astronomical Sect of Magi, as I and Headmaster Vinda-Farnah did yours at the capital."

Dvandas reels from the jibe and notices that both the emperor and Grand Master Artapan heard Daraya-Vous and are now watching the conversation. He reaches out with both hands and grasps Daraya-Vous's hand and with all the feigned sincerity he can muster exclaims, "Truly a tragic but unavoidable slight to you and your order, Headmaster! If not for pressing matters of state and the needs of the empire, I surely would have attended. I trust my most trusted assistant and confidant"—he points to Mihri—"sufficed in some small way."

Daraya-Vous looks over at Mihri. "Why yes, he was quite helpful in the matter of my order retaining the sacred star charts for another headmaster's term."

Dvandas stands there for a moment, his cheeks burning at the insult. He is about to say something when he hears the emperor clear his throat. When he looks in his direction, Phraates IV's eyes motion him to take a seat, and he does. The hall continues to fill with more dignitaries, military and political officials, and religious leaders as the servants set the meals out for the head table and the rest of the attendees.

One of the last tables to be filled is in the very back, where the high priestess of the Temple of Zarpanuta will be seated with two of her assistants. When she comes in, Bozan notices and leans over to General Barach and points her out. Barach leans over to the emperor and then points in her direction and says something in his ear. Phraates nods his head and raises his right hand and extends it to Daraya-Vous's table and exclaims, "Rassan, only son of Parthia's most beloved general, the noble Surena. Please stand and let me have a look at you."

The entire hall goes silent at the elevated voice of the emperor, and all eyes fall on him and Rassan as the young Magi apprentice stands and gives the emperor the proper court gesture and bow that Phraates V taught him to do when he petitioned the emperor for custody of the sacred star charts almost three years ago. Phraates IV does not hold him nearly as long this time and stands up, which brings everyone in the room to their feet. Then he walks around the table to Rassan. "Rise, Rassan," he says.

Rassan lifts his eyes, then straightens up. Then the emperor steps up and gives him a gentle pat on the shoulder. "My son made me promise that I would check in on you when we arrived in Babylon. He misses his friend and training partner very much. Tell me, how goes things for you, young man?"

"Very well, thank you, Emperor. I miss Phraates V as well, but please tell him that I am quite fulfilled in my studies at the Astronomical Temple and truly believe I have found my life's calling. If it pleases you and him, I do want to continue with Headmaster Daraya-Vous indefinitely, if possible."

The emperor smiles brightly and looks to Headmaster Daraya-Vous. "That is totally up to the headmaster, Rassan. As for us, we have already given you our leave to pursue this path."

Rassan matches the emperor's smile and bows his head. "Thank you, Emperor."

"Now, tell me, Rassan, what has happened to your betrothal to the papyrus merchant's niece?"

Though the room is silent, the silence only deepens when Phraates IV asks this question. The high priestess walks to a place in the back of the room where she can see the emperor and Rassan directly. That place also gives her a direct line of sight to both Dvandas and Mihri. As all three sets of eyes meet in silent acknowledgment, an unspoken threat is conveyed in the high priestess's stare that is completely understood by both Magi. Dvandas moves around his table toward the emperor.

As Rassan is about to answer, the emperor sees Dvandas and holds up a staying hand to Rassan. "Dvandas, Grand Master Artapan informed me that you and your man Mihri had a part in this debacle. Please join us as Rassan explains why his life has been so toyed with as of late." He then looks back to Rassan. "Please carry on, Rassan. You have your emperor's ear."

Fortunately, Daraya-Vous told Rassan that something like this might occur and coached him on how to handle it if it did. They both agreed that the debate was the most important thing for either of them to concentrate on, and that starting a political war with the Magi Magician Sect or the Temple of Zarpanuta was not in their best interests.

"Forgive me, Emperor. Though my education in court politics

and social protocols has been exemplarily conducted mainly by your own son, I fail at times to grasp the intricacies. Such is the case in my betrothal to Varaz, who is a priestess of the Temple of Zarpanuta. I thought at the time of our betrothal negotiations that she had already left the Temple and was no longer a priestess. So the day that I saw her here in her priestess's robes and accompanying the high priestess, I became shocked and confused. I knew a priestess could not be married and, therefore, suspected a deception of some sort. But later, after conferring with Headmaster Daraya-Vous, I was made to realize that leaving the Temple takes time and there are processes that cannot be ignored."

Astonished, the emperor steps in closer and puts a hand on Rassan's shoulder. "So, you do not need me to intercede on your behalf and see that this priestess, Varaz, is punished for her deception?"

Rassan sighs and says, "No, Emperor, I do not."

"Do you still wish to marry this girl, Rassan? We can make that happen immediately if you like."

"Thank you, Emperor, but no. Though she had no ill intent in her heart, she knew I was unaware that she had not fully left the Temple yet and let me believe she was free to be betrothed. Currently, I wish only to concentrate on my studies under Headmaster Daraya-Vous. Maybe later I will be ready to seek a wife, but for now, the Creator's message in the stars is the only passion I wish to pursue."

The emperor nods his head. "It is understandable that the girl did not want you to know of her status for fear of losing you. You are a fine candidate for a husband to any maid, priestess, princess, or noble. When it is time for you to marry, you will have my and my son's protection and blessings." He then turns and says to everyone present, "It is our judgment that the matter of Rassan's failed betrothal to the priestess, Varaz, is closed. No penalty or judgment will be levied against her or the Temple of Zarpanuta." He then turns back to Rassan. "As for your continuing with Headmaster Daraya-Vous, we wish you good fortune in the upcoming debate. I promised

Phraates V that I would attend." He holds up his finger and shakes it at Rassan in a feigned, chiding fashion. "But be warned, young apprentice. You will get no favoritism from us. If you win, it will be because you have earned it by proving your points to all concerned."

Rassan's smile beams with enthusiasm. "I would not have it any other way, Emperor. Thank you."

As Rassan makes his way back to his seat, Daraya-Vous greets him with a cheerful smile and mouths, "Well done."

Phraates IV looks over to Ambassador Samekh. "It is good to see you, my friend! I trust your pilgrimage here to confer with Headmaster Daraya-Vous has been everything you hoped it would be."

Samekh bows his head and gives the proper court gesture with his hand. "Indeed it has, Emperor. The time I have had with the Magi Astronomical Sect of the Parthian Empire has been one of the significant events of my life. I will always be in your debt for the opportunity." The emperor smiles and moves on to some others seated close to his table as he continues to catch up with some of the more important guests.

Meanwhile, at the rear of the room, the high priestess steps back to her table with a completely astonished look on her face. She totally expected to receive some sort of repercussions for the debacle of Varaz's betrothal and was even willing to sacrifice her favorite priestess to the emperor's punishment for the good of her order. But to have the Magi apprentice ask for clemency for all concerned was not something she would ever have expected.

That Evening, Temple of Zarpanuta

The emperor's arrival caused General Barach to recall the guards stationed by the garrison at the front of the Temple. In their place, however, are five heavily armed, elite empirical bodyguards with ten more stationed at key points in the Temple and one outside the high priestess's door. The door swings open and the bodyguard steps to the side to let Phraates IV step through, with the high priestess bow-ing almost to the floor as he leaves. As he steps through the threshold, she lifts her head just enough to see him and says, "May the blessing of Zarpanuta keep and elevate you, my Emperor."

Without turning, the emperor says with a smirk, "They have kept and blessed me well this evening, High Priestess. Good night to you." He looks at his bodyguard, nods, and allows him to escort him away.

Once the emperor is out of earshot, the high priestess looks to the end of the corridor where her personal bodyguard is standing and motions to him. He is a tall, ebony man from the African nation of Somalia, famed to spawn the fiercest of that continent's warriors. His usual place is just outside the high priestess's door, especially when the Temple is as busy as it is tonight. Practically the whole of the officer's corps from the emperor's party are there tonight, partaking in the Temple's rituals. He steps up and says, "High Priestess."

"I need to talk with Varaz. Once she is done with whatever offi-cers she is taking care of, have her come to my quarters."

"Varaz is not with any of the officers. She chose to work in the kitchens with the older priestesses," the bodyguard answers flatly.

The high priestess glares at him for a moment and then blurts out, "Who does that girl think she is?! The most important man in the empire is here in Babylon, and all of us need to be doing what-ever we can to procure his favor. She should not be wasting her time in the kitchen with the hags!"

"I agree, High Priestess, but it was you who elevated her to a position where she can decide such things for herself. You are the only one who could have ordered her to minister to the men, and you have been preoccupied in securing the emperor's favor all eve-ning."

Her cheeks flush red at the jibe from her bodyguard, but she refrains from rebuking him. Unlike others that serve her, honesty and frankness are at the core of what she needs from the man responsible for keeping her safe. She huffs and says, "Find her and bring her to my quarters. But be respectful. She is still quite important to me, especially after what I just learned from the emperor."

Half an hour later, she hears her bodyguard's knock on the door. "Come in."

The door opens, revealing Varaz standing next to the bodyguard, dressed in a simple smock and apron.

"You called, High Priestess?"

"Yes, come in, Varaz."

The two stand and stare at each other. The high priestess sighs. She knows that this scruffy-looking girl, who purposefully and ridiculously worked in the kitchens during the grandest night of her Temple's history, has all the makings of a high priestess and is still her preferred successor.

"Oh, Varaz, falling in love is an occupational hazard for women of our calling. The goddess Zarpanuta has oft been tempted to favor many of her lovers through the centuries but has always been loyal to her lord. What we offer men is a spiritual experience through erotic touch. Our worship services are a sacred duty to all priestesses of our order and are not to be neglected by any capable of performing them."

She waves a hand around the room. "For the very first time in my tenure as high priestess, the emperor himself has come here and partaken of our services. His men are also here and will carry tales back to the capital about how the priestesses of the Temple of Zarpanuta ministered to them. And yet you stubbornly withhold yourself from partaking in our greatest victory…for that boy!"

Varaz steels herself. "If not for that man, Rassan, I would now be dead by execution, and you would be exiled from being a high priestess of this Temple. I heard how he begged for clemency for us when the emperor showed him favor before everyone today."

Despite herself, the high priestess is not angered by her words. On the contrary, they only strengthen her desire to bring her to realize her full potential. She steps closer, and with almost motherly pride, replies. "Your words are true, Priestess. Rassan surprised everyone, including the emperor. He loves that boy. He sees him as his son's closest advisor someday."

She sees the look of confusion on Varaz's face at her sharing such details about the emperor's feelings about Rassan. "You know it is a man's nature to share such things with us when we minister our rituals to them. The emperor shared much with me tonight about your Rassan. Though he will never stop him from pursuing the path of a Magi, his hope is that Rassan will return to full military service and become a general like his father. To that end, he has a surprise for Rassan after the debate is concluded tomorrow."

"What surprise, High Priestess?"

"The emperor has sworn me to secrecy regarding that, and I am not so foolish as to think my revealing it would not somehow find its way back to his ears. Suffice it to say that once the Astronomical Sect of Magi loses the debate tomorrow and Headmaster Daraya-Vous loses stature and support in the empire, Rassan will have options."

"Why are you so positive they will lose, High Priestess? I have heard the best of their arguments and believe they have the truth concerning the purpose of the zodiac."

"Varaz, I know you are not so naïve as to believe that logic and intelligence are the only devices that count in such a hot political topic as will be debated tomorrow. Headmaster Dvandas has had plans in place for decades to prevent the Astronomical Sect from ever winning a contest such as this and especially before the emperor himself."

An icy chill goes up Varaz's spine as she realizes that all of Rassan's hard work will come to naught because of treachery and deceit. "High Priestess, you don't understand! Rassan is committed to his path. He will never swerve. Whether his sect wins the debate is of no consequence. His allegiance is to the Astronomical Sect, and he will rise or fall with them! Please, we must help him. He showed us mercy. We can't ignore him now!"

"Oh, Varaz, your mind is clouded with the illusions of love. I was going to invite you to join me tomorrow at the debate so you could witness the emperor's surprise for Rassan. Perhaps it is best if you stay here. You can sleep in the spare room in my suite. When I get back, we will discuss my plans for, in a fashion, reuniting you and Rassan. Now, cleanse yourself in my bath and throw those filthy kitchen rags away. I will have your priestess attire brought here. From now on, you will assume your rightful place as my second."

Varaz has no more words in her for her superior and readily consents to stay in her suite, but not for the same reasons the high priestess has. She bows and heads off to the bath.

Once Varaz is in the next room, the high priestess goes to the door and opens it to find her bodyguard at his place in front of it. She smiles affectionately at him. "Send for Varaz's belongings and have them brought here. Tomorrow she will assume her additional duties as my second." She then steps closer to him and places her hand on his massively muscular bare chest and whispers, "The emperor has invited me back to the capital with him to assume my duties as high priestess there. When that happens, you will join me, and we can continue as we have." She presses her cheek against his chest and continues, "Varaz will stay here to be my hand in this Temple. See that the rumors of this change circulate throughout the Temple tonight. I want all in agreement and ready for this change when it happens."

"Yes, Mistress." He releases himself from her embrace and walks down the hall to carry out her instructions.

She watches him leave, then closes the door and goes to the bath area on the balcony of her suite. She stands in the doorway as Varaz steps into the large pool of water and scrubs herself. It is quite apparent by her nude form why Varaz is the most popular of her priestesses with all the male patrons. "You will never marry Rassan, my child," she says to herself. "But when the Astronomical Sect is ruined and Daraya-Vous is disgraced, Rassan will find solace in you and in the emperor's gift. Someday he will be the commander of Babylon's garrison and you must care for him as high priestess of this Temple."

17

Day of the Debate

Since the emperor is attending the debate, it is being held in Grand Master Artapan's Temple of the Zoroastrian Magi Order, which has the largest auditorium. The back of the auditorium has a stage four steps in height. At the bottom of the steps there is a large platform where the debaters from both sides are seated at long tables and facing the emperor. Phraates IV is seated at the highest point of the auditorium. There are two bodyguards, one on either side, attending him. The Grand Master sits directly below the emperor by one step, with Daraya-Vous on his right and Dvandas on his left. Two steps below them are seated twelve members of the Astronomical Sect of Magi, who are set to judge the outcome of the debate. The table that sits directly in front of Headmaster Daraya-Vous is filled with Rassan, Kaufa, and Rita-Raina. To their right and seated directly in front of Headmaster Dvandas are Hymayeak, Whama, and an older Magi apprentice named Tamazia from a freshly graduated group. Stationed around the perimeter of the bottom floor of the auditorium are twelve more of the emperor's personal guards.

Rassan looks around the auditorium and sees that it is full. All the religious sect leaders are present, and he even recognizes the Magician Magi he encountered at the house in Babylon who had the familiar spirit. He is sitting to Rassan's right, with the other Magi from Dvandas's sect. He is a little wary of the man but feels he is in control of his emotions enough to handle his presence.

He recognizes the high priestess of the Temple of Zarpanuta seated close to the Magician Magi, along with some of her order. He is disappointed to not see Varaz with them. He quickly grabs his mind and looks down at the star charts and graphic depictions drawn of each constellation, along with notes and diagrams. He looks behind him to nod to Arsam, who drew them from his memory of the sacred star charts. Ambassador Samekh is seated next to Arsam, and Rassan smiles at him. The Nabataean Magi nods his head, letting Rassan know he is at peace with the present circumstances.

Rassan then turns to his companions to see how they are and finds Rita-Raina glaring at his father, who is seated just below the emperor. He knows that the headmaster of the Magician Sect has not even attempted to visit his son and now refuses to make eye contact with him. Rassan puts a hand on his shoulder. "I am sorry that you must do this in front of him, Rita-Raina. It must be very hard to come out publicly against your own father's beliefs like you are."

"Rassan, there is nothing I could want more than to make that man squirm in his seat up there while he has to control his ego and temper in the grand master's and emperor's presence."

Rassan shrugs and then turns to Kaufa. "Are you ready, my friend? You speak first. You know that your presentation is going to be the most controversial."

Kaufa laughs. "When I am done, they will have no choice but to acknowledge that truth and more. Don't worry."

Rassan turns in his chair. "Remember what Ambassador Samekh said. We don't fish with figs, and you don't catch a lion with a pomegranate. The empire has long suppressed the Hebrew doctrines and will not take it kindly if we appear to force their dominance over them. Your job is to simply show how they emulate what we have known for centuries about the Creator's true intent written in the heavens. Headmaster Daraya-Vous sent you to study at the Jewish settlement because he believes the Hebrew scrolls are the Creator's words, but to push that too heavily here will be counterproductive to our intent."

Kaufa stares blankly at Rassan for a moment, then places a reassuring hand on his shoulder. "You worry too much. I know what is expected of me and what needs to be said here, and I will do my part."

The auditorium is now filled and Grand Master Artapan stands, then Headmasters Daraya-Vous and Dvandas also stand. He looks out to the crowd, smiles, and then turns to the emperor. "Emperor Phraates IV, the entire Magi Order present in Babylon are deeply honored by your presence at this historic debate to clarify the true meaning of the zodiac and what is the divine message it conveys. As is our tradition, the debate will be conducted among our best students. As this question has arisen within the Astronomical Sect of the Magi, it is their apprentices who will debate this issue. They have been instructed and tutored by the most wise and knowledgeable of their masters in this area and are now ready to present their arguments before us all. With the emperor's permission, we will begin."

The emperor stands and holds out both hands to the auditorium. "You have our permission to begin, Grand Master." Then he sits down and catches Rassan's eye and gives him a subtle wink and smile. Grand Master Artapan nods to the emperor, then to the headmasters, and says, "Headmaster Daraya-Vous, you may begin your debate. Please call your first speaker."

Daraya-Vous stands and looks to Rassan's table. "Magi Apprentice Kaufa, please stand and give us your presentation on correlations between the message in the zodiac and the Hebrew scrolls."

There is a bit of rumbling in the crowd at the mention of the Hebrew doctrines being introduced in this debate, and Grand Master Artapan must raise a hand in a staying gesture to quiet it down. When the chamber finally settles, Kaufa stands and bows to the emperor, the two headmasters, and the Grand Master, and then to the Magi panel of judges seated below them.

"Emperor Phraates IV, Grand Master Artapan, honorable headmasters and judges, thank you for this opportunity." He pauses, holds both hands wide, and addresses the entire auditorium. "Esteemed members of the Magi Order, since the dawn of the very first day that man walked this earth, the heavens have had a story to tell us all. Though it is forbidden for me to quote direct passages from the ancient Hebrew scrolls, they perfectly collaborate this truth.

"The great King David, most notable of the Judean monarchs, discloses in his own writings that the Creator Himself, known to them as *Elohim,* gave the first man the names and the meanings of every star in the sky. He also said that the message of the coming redeemer of mankind is foretold in their meanings. And that message is available to all the earth. Moses himself, the greatest of the prophets, foretold of a coming one who would vanquish the serpent and restore mankind back to paradise. In the ancient manuscript about the man, Job, many of the stars we know and understand are mentioned and given their natures in the reading thereof."

Though never directly quoting any passage of the Hebrew scrolls, Kaufa paraphrases dozens of them with painstaking accuracy. He makes it emphatically clear that they are the ultimate authority. Half an hour later, Kaufa finishes his presentation. "So honorable members of the Magi Court of Judges, Grand Master and Headmasters, and most esteemed and sovereign Emperor Phraates IV, the sacred Hebrew scrolls testify, augment, and substantiate that the true nature of the zodiac is to declare the Creator's plan to redeem mankind by sending His champion to save us all!"

The entire room is frozen in bitter silence as each person processes what and how the Magi apprentice just presented his argument. Kaufa takes his seat and stares blankly into the air, not willing to make eye contact with anyone. Ambassador Samekh leans forward and whispers to the three apprentices: "No truer words could have been spoken. But to this audience and before the panel of judges, I fear this presentation may have killed any chance of us winning this debate."

Without turning his head, Kaufa simply replies, "I said what I needed to say. That is the end."

Headmaster Dvandas can't help but relish in the victory he now sees his side about to achieve. With the slightest of a twinkle in his hard, gray eyes, he makes eye contact with Kaufa and subtly nods. The gesture is returned in kind.

Same Time, Temple of Zarpanuta, High Priestess's Quarters

Varaz has had a very fitful night's sleep after her bath. The high priestess was up very early that morning preparing to go to the Magi debate at Grand Master Artapan's Temple. Varaz watched the high priestess's attendants from the guest bedroom as they helped her don her most prestigious high priestess robe and jewelry. After the emperor left the night before, the high priestess bombarded her with all the great things that were about to happen in their order, including that she was going to be living in the capital now and would become one of Phraates IV's new advisors. "Perhaps I can even replace Dvandas as first," she gloated.

When the high priestess finally leaves the Temple, Varaz gets up and dresses in her formal priestess gown and calls the attendants to the high priestess's rooms. Once there, she tells them of her impending promotion, which they have already heard about from the high priestess's bodyguard the previous evening. "I will attend the Magi debate this morning, but before I go, there are a few things I need you to do for me."

Before the high priestess left, she told the same attendants that Varaz would be permanently staying in her quarters and had full authority to attend to Temple business. They quickly set about fulfilling her wishes, wanting to make a good impression on their new mistress. One hour later, Varaz has a large box loaded into her carriage, then she climbs in and orders the driver to take her to Grand Master Artapan's Temple.

Back at the Debate

Rassan squirms in his seat as the second debater finishes his discourse. Whama has spent his entire time arguing that the Parthian Empire is not subject to the beliefs of the Hebrews and should not be swayed by anything that is contained in their scrolls. He argues that long before they were written, ancient Persian and Egyptian astrologers had accurately prognosticated the future events of kingdoms, cultures, and men. "The heavens are our window into the very heart and soul of the gods, and it is by them that they tell us their plans for us all." He bows to the emperor and others seated before him, then takes his seat. There is a clapping of hands that starts with Headmaster Dvandas and then is joined by many in the room.

Rita-Raina, the next speaker, steps to the center of the platform with a cold, steely look of determination in his eyes that does not go unnoticed, most especially by his father. He is not fazed by Whama's presentation or Kaufa's betrayal. All that is going through him is the happiness of knowing that what he is about to say is the truth, and it totally goes against everything his father stands for. He bows and formally gestures with his right hand to the emperor and says, "Emperor Phraates IV, Grand Master Artapan, Headmaster Daraya-Vous, headmaster and Magi judges, it is my honor to present to you the historical proof of Persian and Babylonian astronomers, who have for thousands of years shown that the real and exact meaning of the zodiac is to declare the Creator's purpose to once and for all conquer His archenemy, Cetus, by sending forth His champion to crush Cetus's head with his foot and restore man back to paradise. Proof that this proclamation begins with the constellation Virgo and ends with that of Leo. And proof that all of this was well known throughout the East until the armies of Alexander conquered our lands and forced their own interpretations of the zodiac on us.

"I will prove to you today that the lies they forced on us with these heretical interpretations are the very foundation of the arguments our opponents are postulating. I will show that when we look to the astronomers who lived before those times, the message of the stars is very clear and has nothing to do with the prognosticating of individual lives according to what time they were born; but the stars do reveal the Creator's plan to save us all from utter damnation. It is time that we throw off the nonsensical myths of the Greeks and return to our own heritage of understanding the zodiac."

When Rita-Raina finishes his opening statement, he pauses for a moment and looks to his father, whose name he purposely did not mention in his greeting. He can see that the jibe and his remarks have had the desired effect. Headmaster Dvandas is almost vibrating with rage while he glares at his son. Rita-Raina smiles and nods to him, then looks to the other faces before him. He can see that his words have had a profound impact on all. He knows it is his father who has started a new movement to return to the Persian and Babylonian roots of the empire. By popularizing throwing off the Greek and Roman influences, he is trying to make it look as if it is the family line of Phraates that is responsible. He is elated that he can use his father's duplicities against him and cash in on the movement's momentum to oppose him here. His desire is that the emperor will see this as an opportunity to show that he, too, wants to promote the movement's notions and dilute the blame on him and his family line. He smiles and holds out both hands speculatively and rhetorically says, "Shall we begin?"

Half an hour later, Rita-Raina is holding up a piece of parchment and pointing to it. "This documents that, during the reign of Hyksos of Egypt, the chief astronomer certified that the purpose of the ancient monument of the Sphinx is to show the beginning and end of the zodiac; starting with the head of a woman, depicting Virgo, and ending with the body of a lion, depicting Leo. This conforms with what I showed earlier from the Persian astronomer Khayyam and what he said about the ancient stories of the first Tower of Babel and the construction of its planisphere and how the signs were put in this order there. In conclusion, I have quoted four different Babylonian and Persian astronomers who lived hundreds of years before the Greek invasions and in different kingdoms of their respective empires, and they all concur that the true meaning of the zodiac is as we have affirmed here—the great plan of the Creator to vanquish His enemy and save mankind by sending His champion to accomplish that task."

Rita-Raina takes a bow and returns to his seat. The room is silent for a moment as people process what was just spoken. Some eyes are on Headmaster Dvandas and some on Headmaster Daraya-Vous. Contrary to Dvandas's actions earlier after Whama's presentation, Daraya-Vous refuses to show any favoritism while sitting in a seat of judgment. But then a clapping of hands from behind him touches his ears and all eyes in the room turn to see the emperor standing up and smiling as he bellows, "Well done, young man! A very thorough and thought-provoking presentation. I am pleased."

At seeing the emperor's enthusiasm for Rita-Raina's presentation, the rest of the people in the room begin to stand and clap as well. The only ones who remain seated are the Magi judges. However, Grand Master Artapan stands and so do the two headmasters seated next to him. The grand master looks up to the emperor, who nods as he takes his seat. Artapan then turns to the assembly and holds out his hand, indicating for everyone to take their seats as well. "It is pleasing to know that our emperor is enjoying the debate today. Headmaster Daraya-Vous, who is next?"

The headmaster stands and says, "Next is Hymayeak, who will argue why the constellations of the zodiac have a direct impact on all of us, but most especially those born during the time they are seen in our skies."

Hymayeak stands and walks to the center of the stage and takes a bow as he extends his right hand to the emperor and says, "Emperor Phraates IV, Grand Master Artapan, Headmasters Daraya-Vous and Dvandas, and esteemed judges, it is my honor to speak before you today." He then walks back to his table and retrieves a large drawing of the zodiac that has the corresponding months of the year to the time that a certain constellation is predominantly apparent elliptical of the night sky. He points to a certain section that is associated with the signs of Aries and Taurus. "Why do our farmers mainly plant their fields under these signs? Why is it that most of the beasts of the earth are born during these times? During the months that correspond to Leo and Virgo, we need to conserve our water and much of our agriculture depends on irrigation. Then, during Libra, we have our harvest. During Sagittarius, Capricorn, Aquarius, and Pisces, much of the land sleeps, and we bring our beasts from grazing in the mountains to our farms where we can shelter them.

"With every sign of the zodiac that is apparent in the night sky comes changes to the surrounding earth. The migration of birds and fish happen at set times and under set signs every year. All the kingdoms of plants and animals are ruled and orchestrated by the times of the year that are calculated by what sign is in the sky. Most species of animals and fish are only born during a certain time in the year that is set under a certain sign. From this relationship, we find order and explanations of what the gods wanted creation to do and be. But then we come to man. In some ways, it would seem that man breaks this mold; for men are born in every season and under every sign. Why? Because man is the image of the gods, and in us they made their own reflection. It is in this great order of things that the gods have set forth by having different creatures, weather, and conditions transpire under set signs in the zodiac that we see the accurate gauge by which we use to interpret man. Since man is the only creature in the world that breeds at every season and sign, it only makes sense that the sign in which he is born under governs his characteristics, nature, and destiny. Knowing this, how can one set a beginning and an end to the circle of life depicted in the stars of the zodiac? This circle is as endless and fathomless as time itself. Indeed, all reality and knowledge are contained therein, and the gods have gifted some among us with the ability to ferret it out and see its depth for each individual."

Hymayeak continues his discourse for another half hour as he draws comparisons between the signs of the zodiac and what is transpiring in the physical earth at each of the constellation's appearances in the sky.

He takes a deep breath and gives his closing statement. "I give it to you, Great Emperor, Grand Master and Headmasters, judges, and assembly. What more is there to say but perhaps, why is it that when the moon hangs full in the sky, do men seem more temperamental? Or, when the blankets of snow cover the earth, why do they hunker down and are more passive? If not for the truth that the universe and the earth all have a profound effect on us all, and the gods have given us a window into their purposes by telling us about the meaning in the stars and how to interpret them for every man." He bows and turns to take his seat.

Unlike Rita-Raina's presentation, there is no silent pause but a thunderous applause from a majority of the assembly. From his seated position, the emperor raises his hand to quiet the room down and says, "Quite a compelling discourse of logic, young man. You are a skilled debater and a charismatic speaker, though you could have given us a few more of your sources that you gleaned your powerful presentation from. Anyway, well done."

Hymayeak smiles, stands up and bows, and says, "Thank you, My Emperor." Then he sits and briefly makes eye contact with Dvandas. It would not have been appropriate for him to proclaim the source of most of his material, seeing as how it was subtly delivered to him by Mihri, and the source was Headmaster Dvandas's personal speculations of the matter.

Headmaster Daraya-Vous stands and looks to the emperor, who nods. He then turns to the assembly and points to Rassan. "Our next speaker is Magi Apprentice Rassan. He will give his discourse from knowledge he gained under Emperor Phraates IV's personal sanction in studying the sacred star charts that were handed down from the times of the first Grand Master of the Magi Order, Belteshazzar. Rassan's unique perspective will be argued from that vantage point."

Rassan stands and moves to the center and gives his courtly bow to the emperor, the headmasters, and the Magi judges. "Esteemed Emperor Phraates IV, Grand Master, Headmasters, and Magi assembly, in the first constellation of the zodiac, which is Virgo, the woman holds a branch in her right hand. In the center of that branch is the star, *Al Zimach*. The first Grand Master of the Magi Order, Belteshazzar himself, said that this star's meaning is branch, or offshoot of corn. We all know the significance of this to mean the prophecy of the coming champion, sent by the Creator and born of the woman, who will defeat all enemies and save the world from damnation. In this we learn that the entire zodiac is dedicated to the telling of the story of our great rescuer and savior, who will come and do all that is needed to bring man back to the Creator and destroy His archenemy. Each star's meaning that has been passed down from the ancients before the great flood is an integral part of the tapestry of this great tale. From Virgo to Leo, in every season of the year, the Creator of the entire universe has allowed us to study the path that this champion must take and the victories he will accomplish in the saving and redeeming of us all."

He walks over to the table and grabs the drawing of Virgo that Arsam did from his memory of the star charts and holds it up for the judges to see. There is a gasp from the entire room as everyone present knows the law concerning the charts and that the emperor himself is the only one who can allow a public display of their likeness. The emperor sees the astonishment and clears his throat to get everyone's attention and casually remarks, "Rassan, you may continue with this, as you have our permission to do so."

Rassan bows his head and says, "Thank you, Emperor." He then points to the arm of the depiction. "In the arm is the star called *Vindemiatrix* in the Chaldean tongue, which is a symbol of the branch or son who cometh. The beginning of his coming is foretold in the stars as the birth of an offspring from the Creator Himself." [20]

Rassan looks around the room and can see that everyone is hanging on every word he is now saying. He knows that what he is doing is unprecedented in the Magi Order in using drawings copied from the ancient sacred star charts. Headmaster Daraya-Vous instructed him that for a period after the times of Belteshazzar, the charts were freely available to any Magi to look at and study in the empire's library. But that as time went on, Magi separated themselves from the truths that the first Grand Master showed in the charts and embraced other interpretations and labels for each of the stars in the zodiac. Soon these Magi, who later came to be known as the Magician Sect, petitioned the empires of their days to isolate and limit the access to these charts. During the times of the first emperor of Parthia, they persuaded the ruler to sign a law that could not be altered that proclaimed only the headmaster who was entrusted with the sacred star charts could study them, and anyone else wishing to do so had to do it privately and in his presence. The only exception being when the emperor himself gave another the temporary stewardship of those charts, which happened when Rassan petitioned Phraates IV to bring them back to Babylon.

Rassan's mind goes back to his conversation with Headmaster Vinda-Farnah as he lay dying on the road those years ago. *"Why do you say 'we,' Master? I am not Magi and I know almost nothing of the meanings of the stars in the sky." Master Vinda-Farnah leans back and closes his eyes and with his last breath, he says, "Of course not. You first must become a Magi apprentice."*

"I am a Magi apprentice, and I will continue this watch," he whispers under his breath as he points to the drawing of the constellation Coma, just to the left of the depiction of Virgo. "This depiction of a mother and a son in her right hand shows the result of the star *Al Zimach's* meaning. This son is the desire of all nations, the long-awaited savior and champion of the Creator, who will right every wrong and bring justice, peace, prosperity, and reconciliation to the Creator's peoples."

For one hour Rassan continues his dissertation, touching on each of the constellations of the zodiac, showing how they tie into the subject of the coming champion and savior of mankind. When he comes to the last one, he looks up to Headmaster Daraya-Vous, who smiles at him with a pride that can only be associated with that of a father admiring a son who is proudly carrying on a family's cherished legacy.

Rassan pulls one more depiction from the table and continues. "Now we come to the end of the cycle. The constellation of Leo, the lion who will destroy the great enemy, Hydra, who deceived the first man and enslaves the world in his lies." He points to the shoulder of the depiction and to the star Regulus. "This is the King's Star, Regulus. It represents the champion of the Creator, who will take up the throne that the first man forsook, by putting down all the enemies that stood against him and casting down those that enslaved man with his corruption and deceitfulness. He will be the great and last King who will rule with justice and mercy forever!"

When he finishes his presentation, Rassan stands there for a moment looking to the judges, the Grand Master and headmasters, and the emperor, surprised that he is not hearing any of their responses but only cares that they see the truth in what he says, not for his sake but for theirs.

The entire auditorium is silent for a few moments; but one by one, people scattered throughout the audience and some not of the Astronomical Sect, clap. The judges remain silent, but it is apparent by the look on their faces that Rassan's logic has won most of them to his reasoning.

The emperor stands and holds up a hand to calm the applause, then looks to Rassan and says, "It is not an easy thing for a young man to stand before his emperor and tell him that a greater ruler than himself will rise one day to take his power. Suffice it to say that it is not a simple thing for a monarch to hear. But your words are compelling, and the passion and charisma with which you delivered them are beyond anything I have ever seen. If what you say has truly been written in the stars since the beginning, who am I to doubt it? Well done, young Rassan. Your father would have been proud of you this day."

Rassan bows and takes his seat between Kaufa and Rita-Raina. When he is seated, Ambassador Samekh leans forward and whispers in his ear. "We have a chance to win now. Well done, Apprentice."

Headmaster Daraya-Vous stands and extends his hand to the other table and says, "Magi Apprentice Tamazia, you may now give your presentation."

The young man stands. "Thank you, Headmaster Daraya-Vous." He then bows and gives the proper gesture with his right hand, honoring the emperor. "Emperor Phraates IV, Grand Master Artapan, headmasters, judges, and assembly, it is my privilege to make known to you the true meaning of the zodiac and to expose a millennial-aged conspiracy to subjugate the world to the doctrines of the Jewish kingdom. I must admit that after Apprentice Kaufa was finished with his presentation, I thought I had ample points to substantiate my premise. But after that very passionate and long presentation by Apprentice Rassan, I think only a few clarifying points are needed for me to present my case.

"Let's start with the Jewish Scriptures. Apprentice Kaufa did an excellent job of not directly quoting them but paraphrasing their interpretation of the meaning of the zodiac. One would find it interesting to learn that his own mother is of that bloodline and that her father is a Jewish rabbi. Kaufa spent a majority of his childhood growing up in that Jewish settlement and being educated by his maternal grandfather. His father was, indeed, a loyal soldier in the emperor's armies and worthy of all our gratitude. But because of his constantly being away on empire business and not having the support from his family to take care of his wife and child, he was forced to leave them with her family while away.

"But we are not here to find out why such a man is studying with the Astronomical Sect of the Magi, though it appears suspicious that one such as he should debate on the side of an interpretation of the zodiac that favors their own scriptural prophecies. In this instance, I believe it would be wise to seek the counsel of our forebearers, who thought it prudent to suppress the Hebrew infestation of doctrine into our empire and ban the reading of their Scriptures anywhere but in their own settlements in Parthia. You might find it interesting to know that Headmaster Daraya-Vous sent Kaufa to one such settlement months ago to read and study those Scriptures to prepare for this debate. His own background and heritage gave him access to such a place. Therefore, it is my opinion that any contributions by Kaufa to the discourse we are taking part in must be taken with the understanding that he is truly endeavoring to continue with the Hebrew infestation of beliefs into our societies. I, for one, find it a little disorienting and concerning that a headmaster of the Magi Order would sanction one such as him to debate on the platform, which he did."

All eyes from the assembly turn to Headmaster Daraya-Vous and there is a grumble of agreement to the apprentice's words. Grand Master Artapan stands and holds up a hand to stay the commotion as he says, "Magi Apprentice Tamazia, we are not here to debate Headmaster Daraya-Vous's choice of participants. Stick to the topic."

Tamazia bows his head. "Of course, Grand Master Artapan. So, let us move on to Magi Apprentice Rassan. The son of the hero of the empire, the great General Surena. Charged by the emperor himself to carry the sacred star charts from the capital to Babylon, because he says that is what Headmaster Vinda-Farnah told him to do. Then, on the three-month journey here by caravan, he took advantage of a privilege granted to him to safeguard—not study, to look at them every night and yes, indeed, study them with a foreigner who is a stable boy, no less. One that was hired to minister to Rassan's personal needs during the trip. And study them they did. The boy Arsam is gifted with a remarkable memory and now can recall in detail all those sacred charts by memory and duplicate them, as we have seen here. He has also recently been found to be of Nabataean descent and has been recruited by Ambassador Samekh to go home with him and apprentice in the Nabataean Magi Order. These charts that we call sacred because they were drawn by the first Grand Master of the Magi Order are now, for all practical purposes, being shared with our Nabataean neighbors. Now, is this something that should concern all of us?"

He looks around the room and sees that most are getting riled up by his words, and he gleefully continues. "Not if the sacred star charts do, indeed, contain the correct interpretation of the purpose of the zodiac, for if they do, who are we to suppress them?"

A shrill of astonishment is felt in the entire room, but he is ready for that and waves his hand and continues. "But if they are the undeniable truth about the messages in the heavens, why are they so guarded and, yes, indeed, suppressed? It is because they are lies, Jewish lies handed down to us from one of their own. We call him Belteshazzar because that is what the emperor Nebuchadnezzar named him when he brought him here to his palace to serve him. Through his subtlety and mischief, he deceived his way into that great emperor's good graces. But let us here speak his real name, his Jewish name, the same name that is ascribed to the Hebrew scroll he himself penned, *Daniel*, the Jewish prophet and writer of one of those forbidden scrolls that Kaufa went to study. Scrolls that no Parthian may read.

"Let us consider these people and their influence. They that perpetuate that their scrolls are, indeed, the very words of the Creator Himself and hold the same authority as the stars in the sky in declaring His will. Yet, how faithful have they themselves been to their dictates? In their own line of kings, very few actually believed and followed them. Mostly, they tried to lead their people back to worshipping our gods and practicing our beliefs. I am told that they constantly followed Baal, whom we know as Marduk, and more times than not were trying to model themselves after our religion and philosophies. Yet there always arose some radical prophet, priest, or even king who would persecute, annihilate, and destroy those who would seek our path. The infighting and lack of unity in their own ranks led to the utter destruction of their two kingdoms and the enslavement of their peoples. Was it not the clemency of the Persian Empire and her rulers that let some of them go back and resettle their ancestral lands? But never have they truly governed themselves.

"Even today, under the rulership of Herod the Great, Israel is still subject to the Roman emperor Augustus Caesar. For over four hundred years after their resettlement of their lands, they have been a thorn in the side of any who had ruled over them. Their own religious sects of Pharisees and Sadducees openly proclaim that the peoples of Israel are separate and above all the peoples of the earth. That the Creator chose them out from all of us to be His special ones. So, I ask, why is it that we of the Magi Order even look to these charts as sacred and hold them in such high esteem as the standard by which we should interpret the meaning of the zodiac? If, indeed, they are true, then I openly concede that everything Magi Apprentice Rassan perpetuated in his presentation is undeniably true. But are those star charts and the notes that Daniel the Jewish prophet wrote on them really the truth about the zodiac? What proof do we have that could substantiate such a theory?"

He stops and takes a breath, looks around the room, and briefly makes eye contact with Headmaster Dvandas, who subtly nods his approval to him. Tamazia waves his hand in the air in a nonchalant way and continues. "We are here to debate the true meaning of the zodiac, and the premise propounded by Rassan and his colleagues is that it begins with the constellation Virgo and ends with Leo. Quite an assertion, but if Daniel's star charts cannot be trusted, then what substantiated proof do we have to legitimize this claim?"

He then walks over to the other table and looks at Rita-Raina and asks, "May I see the papyrus you have there about the Egyptian monument, the Sphinx?" It was agreed before the debate that each team would have free access to the other team's material during their discourses if they wished to comment on them. Rita-Raina looks through his material and pulls out the papyrus, which signifies the authenticity of the Sphinx's true meaning, that being to show the beginning and the end of the zodiac. He hands it to Tamazia, who takes it and looks at it for a moment then holds it up and continues. "A rare artifact indeed. This dates back almost two thousand years to the time of the Hyksos of Egypt. In fact, this document was made while the Hebrew slave Joseph was promoted to chief steward of that nation under that pharaoh. Proving again that these pesky Hebrews have a proclivity for maneuvering themselves into positions of power and influence while being enslaved in a foreign nation."

A sarcastic laugh goes through the whole auditorium. Tamazia then holds up his hand and says, "Now, I am not detracting from the solid work that Rita-Raina put into his presentation. He has magnificently arranged his discourse and used solid research to prove his points. He proved himself a formidable debater here and has well represented the legacy of one of the oldest families in the Magi Order. But again, we have an assortment of ideas and proclamations that are founded in the Hebrew persuasion of thought."

His discourse lasts another half hour as he consistently refutes any reference that can be traced to Hebrew doctrines. At the conclusion, he stops, holds out both hands, and proclaims, "So, I leave you with this last thought. If the source of the assertion cannot be trusted, how can we trust the proclamation of doctrine taken from it to be true and accurate? Thank you." He bows his head and walks over to Rita-Raina and hands the papyrus back to him and takes a seat.

Before he sits, three-quarters of the room are on their feet, applauding his presentation. The applause lasts for a few moments and as it dies down, Grand Master Artapan stands.

"Well, that was quite a discourse, Apprentice Tamazia. Now we come to the vote. Are the judges ready?"

The twelve members of the panel all turn and nod their heads in the affirmative and the grand master says, "Then, let us begin…"

Before they can start, a female voice booms from the very back of the room. "The Temple of Zarpanuta has critical evidence pertaining to this debate that it would like to hand over to the Grand Master of the Order of the Magi."

All eyes turn to the back of the room, and standing in the entrance with several servants next to her who are holding a large crate, is the priestess of the Babylonian Temple of Zarpanuta, Varaz.

From her seat, the high priestess sees Varaz in the doorway. She is first astonished but then recognizes the crate, and it settles in her what Varaz is attempting to do. A hot flash of rage goes through her. She stands and bellows, "I did not allow any such thing. Grand Master Artapan, I demand that you arrest this girl and tell my servants to take my property back to the Temple."

Grand Master Artapan is astonished, but protocol dictates that he must recognize the authority of any head of a Temple in Babylon and he starts to give the order to arrest the girl. But before the words leave his mouth the emperor stands and says, "Who are you, girl, and what do you have that is so important that you risk your life to present it here?"

"I am Varaz, priestess of the Temple of Zarpanuta. I have evidence here from the priests of On in Alexandria of Egypt. It was purchased with Temple monies and brought to Babylon by the high priestess twelve years ago."

The high priestess jumps up. "Emperor, Varaz is one of my priestesses, but she never asked my permission to come here and offer the contents of this crate for evidence in this debate."

Emperor Phraates IV looks to Varaz. "Varaz, is it?" He looks at the high priestess and points to Varaz. "This is the one you told me last night would be your replacement as high priestess when you leave with my caravan tomorrow." He then looks down at Rassan and says, "This Varaz is also the one you were going to marry until her deceit was discovered, correct?"

Rassan had been sitting there in shock since Varaz appeared and spoke. He has not taken his eyes off her since she came in. "That is correct, Emperor. She is the one."

The emperor looks back at the high priestess. "You were not at the Temple, and she had full authority to act as she saw fit, being not only your second, but also your replacement. Let her come forward. I am curious to see how this plays out."

He looks up to Varaz. "Come closer, girl, and bring your evidence with you."

As Varaz makes her way to the front, the emperor steps forward a little and addresses the whole assembly. "I want to make this very clear to the entire Magi Order here today. I agreed to be here to listen to this debate as an observer. This discourse here today is to decide doctrinal standards for the Astronomical Sect of the Magi and nothing else. Some of these young apprentices have argued before us here like they were setting precedents for the empire. I assure you that is not the case. I understand that my presence would cause some to believe the latter is true. I also know that whatever happens here will have a far-reaching effect throughout the order, but the only official one will be with Headmaster Daraya-Vous's sect. Is that clear?"

Coming from the emperor and everyone seeing that he will tolerate nothing else, there is a unanimous affirmative consent from the assembly. He smiles and says, "Good. Now, Priestess Varaz, what do you have?"

As Varaz makes her way to the front, she passes Rassan. They both make eye contact, and he can see the trepidation in her face. To his amazement, he offers her a kind smile and silently thanks the Creator in his heart for protecting her.

She steps up and bows to those in front of her. "Emperor and members of the Magi Council, my mistress and I took our journey to the city of Alexandria of Egypt to procure what is contained in this crate. It concerns the monument of the Sphinx, and its intended meaning by those who built it. We had thought that once we got this hieroglyphic, we could tie the monument of the Sphinx to the goddess Zarpanuta. It would have been a significant find for our order if that were so. Unfortunately, this hieroglyphic shows no such correlation. In this box you will find the purchase order and certification from the priests of On as to its authenticity, along with the plaque itself."

Ever since Varaz entered, Headmaster Dvandas has been sitting in his chair, fuming. He cannot believe what is transpiring. To think that the debate was over and, after Tamazia's discourse, he was sure that his side would prevail. He knows that no matter what the emperor said, this debate *will* decide the policy of the empire. That is why he worked so hard to make sure the emperor was present so that at its conclusion he could use the result to insult Headmaster Daraya-Vous and begin his smear campaign to not only bring about his and the Astronomical Sect of the Magi Order's fall, but to finally get his hands on those treacherous star charts and bury them for good.

No longer able to contain his anger, he stands and blurts out, "This is preposterous! The debate is over, and the Grand Master has called for a vote. Why should we entertain this traitorous woman's actions here?"

Grand Master Artapan turns to Dvandas and smiles. "You are right, Headmaster. I called for a vote but as the emperor just pointed out, this is a debate that is taking place in the Astronomical Sect of the Magi, and it was not really my privilege to do so." He turns to

Daraya-Vous. "Forgive me, Headmaster. Do you wish to have a vote, or should we look at the evidence as the emperor wants?"

Headmaster Daraya-Vous chuckles and looks at Varaz, gesturing with his hand for her to continue, then he nods to the emperor and says, "I think that this young woman has placed much potential hazard on herself to come here. Let's do as the emperor suggests and hear her out before we take a vote."

"Your emperor appreciates that," Phraates IV remarks to Daraya-Vous. Then he turns to his head counselor. "Dvandas, see me after this is over. We need to have a talk."

Dvandas sits with a solemn look on his face. "Of course, Emperor."

Varaz directs her servants to open the crate, and she pulls out an old piece of parchment that has been waxed over for preservation. She looks up to the panel of judges and hands it to one of them and says, "This is the original document from the time of Hyksos that declares that the purpose of the Sphinx is to show that the beginning of the zodiac is Virgo, and the end is Leo. As you can see, it has a notation at the bottom that states it was written from information garnered from a plaque that was written in hieroglyphics from the time of Kufa Cleops, who reigned as king of Egypt a thousand years before the Hyksos dynasty pharaoh in the time of the Hebrew slave, Joseph."

As that is passed around, she pulls out a square stone plaque and hands it to the judges. "If you can read hieroglyphics, you will note that this says exactly what the parchment says. On the back of it you will find the date and inscription of the chief astronomer of the court of Kufa Cleops, who oversaw the making of the Sphinx."

She then pulls out a much newer papyrus and unrolls it, then shows it to the judges. "This is the certification of authenticity of the contents in this crate from the priests of the order of On in Alexandria, Egypt—dated, signed, and sealed by the high priest of that order. Attached is the price they exacted from us to purchase these things."

Several of the judges are quite fluent in several forms of hiero-glyphics and easily read the material. One by one, they all see that the evidence is overwhelmingly in favor of Rassan's group's position. When asked if he wanted to look at the items, Headmaster Dvandas gruffly refuses, but then turns to the emperor and says, "How do we know that these priests of On did not deceive the high priestess and her acolyte?"

The emperor rolls his eyes. "Dvandas, please, you know as well as I that these Egyptian priests of On are fanatics. To lie about some-thing like this would mean them taking their own lives in penance. They did the one logical thing they could do—they got these abom-inations to them out of their ancestral lands and thus, out of their existence. We all know how these harebrained priests reacted when Queen Cleopatra died and they had no pharaoh. So desperate were they to fill that most holy position in their religious hierarchy that they begged Augustus Caesar to be their pharaoh, a man with no Egyptian blood in him. They will do anything to keep their own sense of religious truth alive, including embracing falsity to do so. Once this hieroglyphic left their lands, they could act like it did not exist and move on with their self-imposed ignorance." He holds his hand out and says, "Let me have a look at that document of sale for the artifact and certification."

The judge who is looking at it stands and hands it to the emperor. He takes the document and looks at it closely and then turns to the high priestess. "This is quite a hefty sum you paid for this, High Priestess. Tell me, was this reported to Grand Master Artapan to record your use of religious tithes given to your order?"

All eyes turn to the high priestess, who has been sitting stone cold in her seat and glaring at Varaz with barely veiled rage. She takes a moment to compose herself, then she clears her throat and stands, turning to the emperor to address his question. "I was not high priestess at the time of the purchase. All accounting of our journey and expenses were delivered to my predecessor, as was my duty. What she did with them is unknown to me."

Phraates IV huffs and then laughs in a sarcastic tone. "Quite convenient for you, High Priestess. I think it best if you should stay in Babylon and get your house in order. It would seem that the order of priestesses in the Temple of Zarpanuta are not as ready for your absence as you had me believe."

Despite herself, the high priestess lets out an angry huff. She glares at Varaz and says, "As you wish, Emperor. I think I know exactly where I will start in order to get that accomplished."

Phraates IV sees the evil in her eyes intended for Varaz and then looks over to see the concern in Rassan's eyes. "Headmaster Daraya-Vous, before you call for a vote to conclude this fascinating debate, let me handle a little state business, please."

Daraya-Vous knows what the emperor is concerned about and stands and bows. "By all means, Emperor. We are here at your pleasure."

The emperor nods and looks down at Varaz. "Priestess Varaz, you have put yourself into quite a predicament here. I could order everyone to let you be, and that would protect you for a while. But subtleties and intrigues are the very nature of many in this auditorium, and I fear some of them want you to pay with your life for what you did here. I could also take you with me back to the capital, but …" he glances over to Dvandas and continues, "I think you would have even more potent enemies there. What you need is a powerful protector." He looks out to the assembly and says, "Does anyone here care to take this girl under their authority and keep her safe for your emperor?"

Without a moment of hesitation, Headmaster Daraya-Vous stands. "I will take her into my protection and service at the Astronomical Sect's Temple, Emperor."

The emperor is delighted. "What kind of service do you have in mind, Headmaster?"

Daraya-Vous looks over at Arsam, who is sitting next to Ambassador Samekh. He smiles brightly and answers, "Ambassador Samekh will leave our fair city soon, and he is taking with him one of the best servants our Temple has ever had. We need someone to take his place in the Temple, cleaning and working in our kitchens."

The emperor nods approvingly and looks to Varaz. "Is this agreeable to you, Priestess?"

Varaz's heart flutters and amazement courses through her being. She truly thought her life was over for doing what she just did. She takes a deep breath and turns her head to look at Rassan and can see the relief in his eyes. She then turns back to the emperor and says, "Yes, Emperor. I will renounce my priestess status and submit to Headmaster Daraya-Vous's order."

"Excellent. Now that we have settled this matter, let's get on with the vote. The anticipation is almost overwhelming."

"As you wish, Emperor. Judges, you may cast your votes," Headmaster Daraya-Vous says.

The vote takes only a few moments. Nine of the twelve judges vote in favor of Rassan's team, most notably because of the overwhelming persuasion brought on by the Egyptian hieroglyphics that Varaz offered as evidence. The other team, having predominantly argued from a position that Rassan's side based their hypotheses on Hebrew histories, doctrines, and beliefs, received only three votes.

Ambassador Samekh reaches forward and places his hands on Rassan's and Rita-Raina's shoulders and affectionately shakes them. "Daraya-Vous and I dared not hope for a victory of over seven to five. This is truly a miraculous outcome for sure!"

Kaufa has sat stone cold since his turn and refuses to look at or interact with any of his companions.

Headmaster Daraya-Vous begins to dismiss the assembly when he hears the emperor say, "There is one more piece of state business I would like to conduct at this assembly." He looks to the back of the room. "General Barach and General Bozan, please join me in the front of the room."

All eyes go to the rear as the two generals step in with a group of officers, including Commander Sasheen and Commander Dareh, accompanying them. The tension in the room goes very high, as some think they are coming for them.

Once they reach the center of the room just in front of the debater's tables, the emperor steps down and walks up to Rassan. "Magi Apprentice and Officer Rassan, son of General Surena, please stand and join me with your superiors."

Rassan is completely taken aback by this unexpected proceeding, but he makes his way over to stand between Commander Sasheen and Commander Dareh, where the emperor directs him.

The emperor smiles approvingly and holds his hands out to the assembly as he says, "Some of you might not know that Rassan here is in the first hundred in line of succession for the Parthian throne. His father was one of our greatest heroes, and Rassan graduated from the same imperial officer's academy that he did. Rassan has since chosen the path of a Magi, which is his right and that which I granted to him before he came here. But he has also maintained his officer's status, and I have received glowing reports from General Barach as to his conduct and training.

"It is my wish that Rassan have a clear path back into full military service and leadership available to him should he desire to do so. Although, after seeing his passionate presentation here, I believe that the call of a Magi is where his heart truly lives. Nevertheless, it is our intention that he will always have access to our service as a leader like his father. It is, therefore, our decision that he is now elevated to the rank of high commander in the Parthian military. With this promotion, he need only to answer to General Barach and General Bozan while in Babylon. Should he ever want to take up in his father's stead, be it known here and now that he has his emperor's love and support to do so."

The whole of the assembly is immediately on their feet and clapping. High commander is a rank rarely used in the Parthian military and has the status of that just under a general. Most of the time it is done as a field promotion to an exceptional commander who is too young to be a general but is needed to command like one during times of war.

While most are overjoyed at the emperor showing such favor to the young Magi, there are three in the room who simply stand at attention, stare at Rassan with lightly veiled jealousy, and hold themselves from applauding. The first is Rassan's friend, Commander Sasheen, who is astounded that in a flash Rassan is promoted over him and could now, if he chooses to, take everything away that he has been working so hard to achieve these last two years. The second is Commander Dareh, who now feels a wave of panic course through his soul as he contemplates what this boy could now do to him if his secrets were ever revealed about how Vinda-Farnah met his doom. The third is Kaufa who, for a reason only known to him, almost ruined his team's chances to win today's debate and has remained stoically silent since his presentation.

When the assembly is finally dissolved and sent away, all make their way out to privately sort through their thoughts.

18

Traitor's Reward

January 14, 3 BC, Astronomical Temple of the Magi

It has been one year and two months since the debate and the emperor's departure from Babylon. The Astronomical Sect of the Magi has experienced a long, drawn-out upheaval of departures and turmoil since. Hymayeak and Whama were the first to leave, followed by a third of the apprentices and Magi who lived at the Temple in Babylon. Rita-Raina was the biggest surprise of them all. He left, not to join the Magician Sect of his father, but to apprentice under Grand Master Artapan in the Zoroastrian Sect, stating that he felt his calling was to pursue a lifelong study of moral discipline in service to the Creator. It was later found that many of the rest who left were not truly Astronomical Sect Magi but spies loyal to Dvandas and the Magician Sect. Rassan had felt that this was all going to be turned for the good of the order, but he can't help but be infuriated by the out-and-out duplicity of many of them.

Varaz has settled into her duties in the kitchen and cleaning, and they have time to talk. Rassan has forgiven her in his heart and moved on. Sometimes he even entertains the notion of marrying her, but he knows the timing is not right to resume their betrothal. Nevertheless, he finds great solace in her nearness and looks forward to seeing her almost every day. He has spent the last year juggling his responsibilities with the garrison and the Astronomical Temple. He knows that his heart as a Magi will always belong to understanding and declaring the Creator's message in the stars, but he also knows that he is on a political tightrope since receiving his promotion from the emperor. Headmaster Daraya-Vous counseled him, telling him that the Creator called him to this station in life for a reason and He always makes those reasons clear when they need to be.

Rassan straps on his military boots and sword, ready to join Commander Sasheen in the courtyard for sword practice. General Barach had instructed him that with his new rank, he wanted Rassan to drill not only with Sasheen but also all the officers under his command. Of course, with his new rank of high commander, Rassan was now the one drilling the rest. Even though the debate is over and the remaining apprentices and Magi have less to do, there is still the nightly watch, research, and study that happens every day. He always has to contend with the feeling that every moment he is away, he might miss something new in the signs of the zodiac that could lead to further understanding of the coming of the Creator's champion.

He puts his officer's helmet on and steps into the corridor leading to the exit when he catches movement out of the corner of his eye near Kaufa's quarters. Since the debate, he and Headmaster Daraya-Vous expected Kaufa to leave with the rest and were perplexed when he continued his studies and looked to be content to stay. He had been aloof with everyone after that day, and after the headmaster had a counsel with him, he informed the rest to leave him be and let him sort out his thoughts. As he peers down the hall past Kaufa's quarters, he barely makes out his silhouette stealthily making his way to the Tapestry Observatory area of the Temple. He still has about two hours before he needs to be at the garrison, so he follows the apprentice to see why he is acting so stealthily. He can tell that Kaufa thinks he has gone unnoticed and lets him believe that until they get to where he is going.

When Rassan gets to the door, he quietly opens it and can see that Kaufa is creeping up from behind someone who is cleaning in the Tapestry Observatory, and then he sees it! Kaufa pulls a sword from his hip that was covered up by his long outer robe and raises it above the person who is cleaning and is about to strike them. Rassan hurries forward, already grasping his own sword from his hip.

Kaufa is attacking Varaz! Before Kaufa gets within striking distance of her, Rassan yells, "Kaufa, stop! What are you doing?!"

Varaz turns around and sees Kaufa approaching her with his blade, screams and throws the pail of dirty, sudsy cleaning water that she is carrying at him, and runs to Rassan.

Momentarily stunned, Kaufa uses his free hand to rub the suds out of his eyes and turns to see Varaz standing behind Rassan. He sneers at both. "Two for the price of one. I'll have to ask for a bonus on this one."

He then lunges at Rassan with his blade, aiming for his chest. Rassan parries the attack and brings his own blade up and arcs it past Kaufa's face in a perfect counterstrike. Rassan notices immediately that Kaufa's blade is six inches shorter than his and double-edged. He is astonished. He realizes he has seen that Roman sword before and has fought its wielder. He glares at Kaufa. "You! You were the man who attacked me in my tent and tried to kill me!"

Kaufa stands there and glares back at him. "I would have killed you just like I killed Vinda-Farnah if not for that little rat stable boy of yours, Arsam."

He steps to the side, ready for another attack. "Look at you, the great General Surena's pathetic little son, trying to play soldier again. Everyone at the capital garrison would always talk about how the prince himself chose you to train with. That you must be the greatest swordsman in the Parthian Army. Yet I had you on your knees and staring into the death of my blade with a few basic moves."

He looks at Varaz, who, being backed into a corner behind Rassan, has no clear path to flee. He then looks back at Rassan. "My orders were to kill that treacherous whore and then leave. But I am sure that my master will be doubly pleased to know that you met your death while trying to defend her."

He lunges once again, going high for Rassan's head. The move is quick and decisive, but Rassan tucks his chin into his chest and Kaufa's blade bounces harmlessly off his steel helmet.

As the blade bounces upward, Rassan uses his right foot and kicks Kaufa in the chest, sending him back several paces. But Kaufa recovers instantly and counters with several arcing swings of his double-edged sword to keep Rassan at bay.

But just as he is ready to press his next attack, Rassan uses his longer, single-edged Parthian blade to arc in and catch Kaufa's blade in the rain guard and ricasso area of his own. Rassan violently twists Kaufa's blade, causing him to lose his grip on it and send it spinning across the floor to the other side of the room. Kaufa goes for the dagger under his garments; but Rassan is ready and slashes his hand. Kaufa shrieks in pain and Rassan steps in once again and kicks him in the chest.

Rassan puts his blade to Kaufa's throat. "Roman swords can be quite effective when wielded by three or more men at a time who are fighting in unison. They can provide a nice offensive shield that will allow them to progress their attack to victory. But they are rarely effective in a single-combat situation when the opponent has a longer sword. You surprised me that night in the caravan, but the outcome would have been the same as it is here if Arsam had not saved you." He steps a little closer to Kaufa, maneuvering to thrust his blade into the man's throat. "So you are responsible for Headmaster Vinda-Farnah's death! Who gave you that order?"

The razor-sharp point of Rassan's blade is now touching Kaufa's Adam's apple in the middle of his throat and there is a trickle of blood sliding down his skin.

Before he can press him harder to answer, a loud voice booms from the rear of the room. "Rassan, calm yourself! Vengeance is not our way. It belongs to the Creator, and it is His to exact, not ours."

Everyone recognizes Headmaster Daraya-Vous's voice and turns to the entrance to see him walking quickly in their direction.

Rassan relaxes his press on the sword at Kaufa's throat and exhales deeply. "As always, you are right, Headma—"

In the middle of Rassan's response, Kaufa rolls to the side, grabs his dagger from under his garments and slashes out at Rassan's leg, causing a deep cut along his left calf. He then scurries across the floor to where his blade had landed. Rassan screams in pain and drops to his right knee but holds his sword out in a defensive posture.

Kaufa grabs his blade and steps toward Rassan, thinking to take advantage of his injury. Before he can get to him, several doors on the other side of the room open, and many Magi and apprentices burst in to see what all the commotion is about.

Kaufa, now surrounded, curses at Rassan, then turns and runs through the door behind him and out of the Temple.

Rassan endeavors to give chase despite his injury, but Daraya-Vous stays him with his hand. "As I was leaving the night watch platform on the east side, I had a very unsettling feeling about Kaufa. He has been aloof of late and has refused to meet with me. Before I went on watch last evening, I visited him in his quarters to discuss these things. When I entered, he was looking at his military uniform and sharpening a sword. I noticed that it was Roman and not Parthian. When I inquired about why he had such a weapon, he became very agitated and quickly put it away, stating that any soldier tries to collect memento military equipment from foreign lands for souvenirs. I told him that I found it odd for him to be keeping such things openly ready for use since he had resigned his status in the Parthian military to become an apprentice Magi. He rebuked me by citing that you keep your military things readily available."

Rassan becomes agitated. "Headmaster, he knew that the emperor himself expects me to maintain my rank and active status in the military here under General Barach! I am simply following orders."

Daraya-Vous's eyes take on a soft tone as he affectionately responds to Rassan's obvious disdain for his present circumstance. "Apprentice Rassan, we of the Astronomical Sect know fully that your heart truly belongs to the Creator's message in the stars and that is where a hundred percent of your efforts would be if allowed."

He then looks back to Varaz who is still standing behind Rassan. "Are you all right, my dear?"

Varaz begins helping Rassan with his injury and wrapping his calf. She tears off her sleeve and uses it as a bandage. "I am fine, Headmaster. Only because Rassan saved my life." She raises her eyes to meet his and stares deeply into them. "You defended me. After all I put you through, you risked your life for mine!"

Rassan self-consciously shrugs his shoulders and mumbles something about it being his duty as a Parthian officer and then gets a thought. "Wait a minute! Aren't you supposed to be working in the kitchens in the morning? Why were you cleaning out here?"

Varaz starts to respond, but Headmaster Daraya-Vous interjects. "I found of late that I missed my early morning astronomical discussion with young Arsam. About two weeks ago, I was discussing with Varaz here about the rather lengthy conversations you both had in the market when you were preparing for the debate. She told me that she used everything she knew about the zodiac to convince you that you were wrong. But you won her over to your way of thinking. I was so intrigued by this that I invited her to meet me here every morning after my night watch, where we could discuss more about what she learned from you. Therefore, I had her reassigned to Arsam's old duties to clean here and we've met every morning since. It has been a delight to watch her put all your lessons together for me by describing them with the use of the tapestry's depictions."

The headmaster smiles. "If you care to continue that arrangement with us, I would be more than pleased to have you." He then winks at Varaz. "I am sure you would not object to his addition to our group. Would you, dear?"

Varaz takes a nervous but excited gulp and replies, "Uh, of course not, Headmaster. That would be fantastic."

Rassan considers how wonderful it would be to discuss the stars and their meaning with Varaz again. But he gets control of his emotions and calmly says, "I think that occasionally that is something I could see myself taking advantage of, Headmaster. But now I need to go. I am expected at the garrison, and I must check on those men you sent for and see if they apprehended Kaufa yet."

Daraya-Vous looks to Varaz to confirm that Rassan is OK to leave. She nods her head and says, "They have healers at the garrison who can take care of this much better than I. The bleeding has stopped, so he should be OK."

"Good, then I am on my way." Rassan bows to them and heads for the door.

Rassan finds the men from the garrison, and they report that they spotted Kaufa exiting the Temple. They gave chase, which took them into the main market in the center of the city where he eluded them and disappeared into the crowd.

They continued to search for days, but to no avail. Kaufa was never heard from or seen again. In the weeks and months to follow, Rassan made it to almost every early morning discussion with Headmaster Daraya-Vous and Varaz.

August 12, 3 BC, Venus and Jupiter in Conjunction in the Constellation Leo, First Sighting!

19

Purpose of the Ages

**August 12, 3 BC, Jupiter and Venus in Leo, First sighting
Astronomical Temple Tapestry Observatory, 6 a.m.**

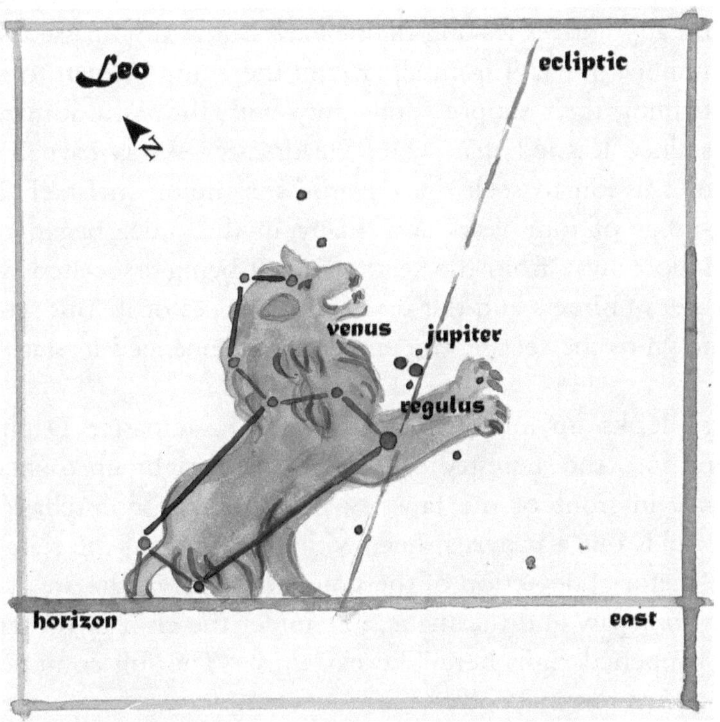

Varaz is just finishing her assigned cleaning duties in the Tapestry Observatory and is eagerly anticipating her conversation with Headmaster Daraya-Vous and Rassan. For the last ten days, there has been an electricity in the Temple at what has been occurring in the constellation Leo. Varaz swears that the excitement she feels vibrating from the Magi, the apprentices, and the staff is beyond anything she has ever experienced at even the most prestigious of festivals she partook of in her old order of Zarpanuta. Since coming under Headmaster Daraya-Vous's protection at the "Great Debate," as it is now called, Varaz has seen huge changes in not only the Astronomical Sect of Magi but also in the whole religious community. With the personal presence of the emperor, the grand master could immediately ratify the outcome of the debate as an official imperial doctrine for the Astronomical Sect.

At first, the Astronomical Sect experienced a great upheaval of Magi and apprentices leaving their ranks. But as time passed, a much larger number of Magi from all around the empire began to respond by reaffirming their support and unity with the Astronomical Sect. She has since learned that when Headmaster Vinda-Farnah left on his rogue mission to seek the Creator's champion in Israel after the star sightings of four years ago, many in the order began to draw their support away from the sect, afraid of being associated with the headmaster's rashness and the dire consequences of it. But seeing the favor shown to the sect by the emperor has enhanced its status in the empire.

Varaz looks up and sees Rassan and Headmaster Daraya-Vous scurrying into the Tapestry Observatory and right up to her while she stands in front of the tapestry depicting the constellation Leo. Rassan holds out a papyrus sheet with a drawing of the stars in Leo and the pictorial depiction of the lion and points to the area between the left front paw and the mane, just under the chin of the lion.

"It happened right here!" he exclaims. "The full conjunction of Jupiter and Venus in Leo!"

Varaz realizes that Headmaster Daraya-Vous allowed Rassan to make the drawing of last night's stars in the eastern sky that will be used in the training of the first-year apprentices, a privilege usually left to a full Magi. She steps in close and looks at the depiction of the conjunction and comments on how well he drew the scene. Of course, she was up very early this morning before she needed to be at her work location and saw the same conjunction for herself and was keen to talk to them about it. Knowing full well that a conjunction of Jupiter—the "King's star," depicting royalty and majesty and often associated with the birth or reign of a king—with Venus—the star long associated with the coming of the Messiah and termed "The Bright and Morning Star—happening in the constellation of Leo could mean everything the Magi of the Astronomical Sect have been looking for for centuries.[21]

She looks at the headmaster. "Does this mean that the Creator's champion is here?!"

Daraya-Vous walks to the tapestry of Leo and puts his hand to his chin. "It very well could show that the Creator is about to or already has sent him. But if Headmaster Vinda-Farnah's fate has taught me anything, it is to be cautious. No, we must wait. If this is truly the time for all ages, then I am confident that the Creator of the universe will give us more in the heavens to substantiate that He has now fulfilled His greatest promise." He looks over to Rassan. "What are your thoughts, Apprentice? After all, you were sent here by Headmaster Vinda-Farnah, who learned your name and calling from a messenger sent by the Creator Himself."

Rassan gulps. "Headmaster, if this is, indeed, the sign we have waited for, then the one we seek will be or has already been born in Israel. We are Parthian, and Israel now belongs to Rome. To go there, we must first get the emperor's leave and safe passage. Even that will not be enough. Somehow, the emperor will have to convince the Romans that we are there on a peaceful mission to find and pay homage to the Creator's champion, who is also prophesied to be the true king of Israel. Not the news a man like Herod the Great will welcome. Then there is the resistance we would receive right here in the empire from people like Dvandas to even take on such a pilgrimage. Just gaining permission to go to the capital and entreat Phraates IV for such a thing will be difficult. So, no matter when we decide to act, it will take a lot of time and effort to plan and execute any kind of response to what we have seen tonight."

Daraya-Vous proudly holds Rassan in his gaze as the impact of the apprentice's words clear his vision. He shakes his head and, with a paternal smile, answers. "Then I perceive it has been quite fortuitous that we have a high commander and member of the first hundred to imperial succession in our ranks. Though I am not ready to act on what we have seen, I believe it would be prudent for you to inquire with General Barach and the city's chief magistrate about how we in the Astronomical Sect could gain safe conduct and permission to caravan to the capital and entreat Phraates IV about visiting Israel."

Rassan almost balks, but then he sees the wisdom in the headmaster's words. "How big of a caravan do you think we would need, Headmaster?"

Daraya-Vous walks up to Rassan and puts his hand on his shoulder and laughs. "Magi Apprentice, Babylon is merely the home to our main observation and education facility. There are members of the Astronomical Sect of the Magi in every major city in the empire and that is not even counting our brothers in the kingdoms of Nabataea, Egypt, and the Arabian tribes. I am sure that we will receive reports of tonight's sighting from all of them. To answer your question, thousands of our order will want to take part when we go. I have been sending dispatches to Ambassador Samekh daily since Jupiter and Venus started approaching one another. I am positive that his order will be a great help and ally in the days to come. This will not be a small caravan, by any stretch of the imagination."

September 1, 3 BC, Tapestry Observatory, Magi Astronomical Temple

Rassan and Varaz stand in the observatory and look at Leo together. Headmaster Daraya-Vous had left them about half an hour ago to go to his morning lecture with the new apprentices. Ever since the debate of almost a year and a half ago, the ranks of the Astronomical Temple have swelled. Along with more enthusiasts to study the Creator's message in the stars, more apprentices bring more wealth to the Temple. Their families pay a generous sum for tuition, and the city magistrates allow them to keep a greater portion of the religious tithes collected each month.

Varaz points to the area that Jupiter was spotted in last night and traces a path in the air to where the star Regulus is. "Do you think Jupiter will go into conjunction with Regulus soon, Rassan?"

Rassan feels her excitement. "It's on the right path and should be there within two weeks. But look at this." He walks over to the planisphere depiction of the zodiac in the middle of the room and points to Leo, putting his hand above the area and cutting off all of Leo and half of Virgo. He says, "Right now, half of Virgo and all of Leo are hidden beneath the western horizon, but if our calculations are correct, then sometime today Mercury and Venus will be in conjunction in Leo. That's the messenger aligned with the son and the morning star. Though the king planet is not involved, the headmaster believes it is significant as well."[22]

Varaz steps very close to Rassan to look directly at the area he is talking about and imagines in her mind those two planets in conjunction with Leo and she shakes her head. "I agree! This is significant. It is like the Creator is announcing through Mercury that the morning star is coming soon!"

Rassan can feel her breath on his neck as she talks and for a moment her shoulder rubs up against his. The sensation of her closeness almost overpowers him, and he has to force himself not to embrace her. There is something he has been wanting to talk with her about for a while now, and he sees that it is past time he did. He lets out a puff of air and steps away and turns to her. "Varaz, I have really enjoyed my time with you and Headmaster Daraya-Vous each morning, discussing the signs in the zodiac. It reminds me of those times we talked in the market at your uncle's papyrus stand. But like then, it's probably not appropriate that you and I should be alone together."

A wave of emotions passes through Varaz as she considers that Rassan does not want her company anymore, and the panic she feels makes it hard for her to breathe. "Rassan, I am sorry for how I hurt you. I love your company, and your enthusiasm for the messages from the Creator in the zodiac is the most thrilling thing I have ever experienced. I only wanted to be around you to share it with you. Please don't say that we cannot be friends and enjoy this together!"

Rassan gulps as he absorbs the pleading in her voice and the anguish in her eyes. "Varaz, we can't just go on as friends after all that has happened."

"But you said you forgave me, Rassan. Please!"

Rassan takes a step forward and looks deeply into her eyes. "Varaz, I don't just want to be your friend, I want to be your husband."

Varaz gasps. "Rassan, are you sure?"

He holds out both hands in a calming fashion and continues. "I talked this over with the headmaster since he is now your guardian. He says that if you agree, we may proceed with our betrothal. But that also means that when we become betrothed, we cannot be alone together until we are wed."

Rassan's words astonish her. Since she has come to this Magi Temple, with her whole heart she has longed to hear him utter those words, but dared not believe it would ever be possible. Tears start running down her face as she exclaims, "Of course I agree, Rassan. I love you and want no other!"

"Good, then it is settled. I have already reached out to your cousin, General Bozan, and we have both signed the betrothal agreement." A voice says from behind them.

Rassan and Varaz turn to the back of the room and see Headmaster Daraya-Vous standing in the entrance, grinning from ear to ear. He holds out his hand to Varaz and says, "Rassan is right. It is not proper that you should be together unchaperoned. Come with me, my dear. We will work out suitable times for you two to visit and make plans. Although I believe that every morning after Rassan and I finish our night study of the stars, meeting you in here would be an excellent choice. What do you both think?"

Rassan and Varaz slyly gaze at each other for a moment, both trying to hold their composure. Rassan's lips curl into a smile, and both burst out laughing.

Nabataean Capital City, September 14, 3 BC, second sighting, conjunction of Regulus and Jupiter in Leo, Pre-dawn

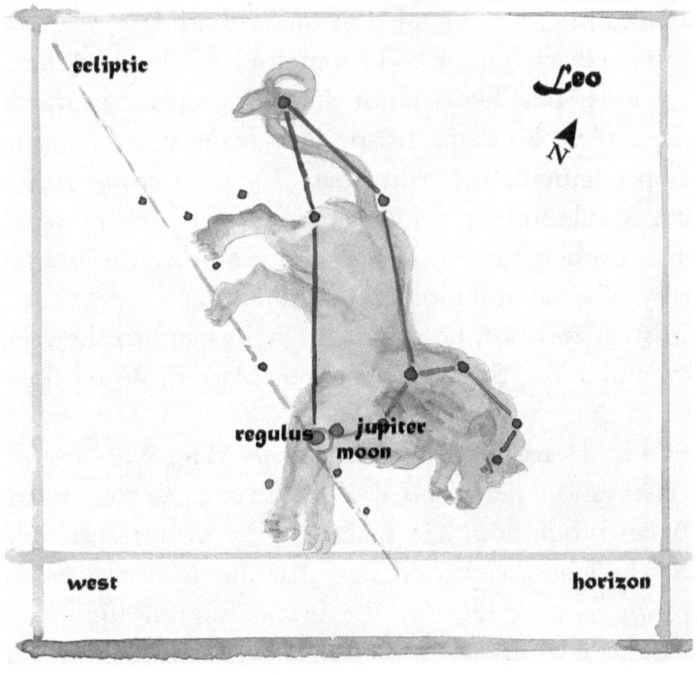

Arsam and Magi Master Samekh gaze at the eastern sky with several other Nabataean Magi, beholding this second wonder that has transpired in the constellation of Leo within the last month. Jupiter was in conjunction with Venus in Leo just a month ago and now is in conjunction with the star Regulus of Leo. Arsam thinks back to his days studying the sacred star charts with Rassan on their way to Babylon and all they learned and can't help but marvel that he gets to see and understand this with the wisest men of his native country of Nabataea. He looks to Samekh and says, "In the sacred star charts, Belteshazzar said Regulus stands for the champion rending underfoot the great serpent once and for all time, destroying him and freeing all people from his tyranny.[23] It is the very heart of the lion. To be in conjunction with the king planet of Jupiter must have fantastic meaning, Master."

Samekh puts his hand behind the boy's head. "Precious knowledge to impart, Apprentice. Jupiter is one of the five wandering stars; and by its meaning, we are aided in understanding much of the Creator's plan for His champion to become our everlasting king. Regulus does not wander but, like a sentinel, holds its place in the constellation of Leo and is also a star that projects majesty and kingship.[24] This conjunction augments the truth that *'The Lion of the Tribe of Judah'* shall someday rule forever as king of kings. But coming together with first Venus, another wandering star, and now Regulus is a phenomenon worthy of great attention and meditation."

Arsam steps forward, holds out his right hand to the conjunction in the sky, and asks, "So has he arrived, Master? When do we go to Israel?"

Samekh looks to the other Nabataean Magi who are with them on the observation deck and can see that they, too, want him to answer Arsam's question. He takes a deep breath and sighs. "This could very well be the second sign that our Messiah has come, but we need more. I have received the first communication from Headmaster Daraya–Vous in Babylon by messenger since these signs began to unfold. We agree that caution must still prevail, but that we also need to begin our efforts to seek safe passage to Jerusalem and seek an audience with King Herod to inquire where Israel's promised savior would be born. To do this, we will need much help.

"Daraya-Vous has Rassan working to get Emperor Phraates IV to give them leave to travel to their capital and seek safe passage into Israel. I have already talked with our king, and he wants me to seek the help of the Roman governor of Syria, Tertullian. He alone has the power that could assuage King Herod to let us come in and find the child, should he already have been born. I have also sent letters to Cyrenius, the proconsul who is overseeing the empire-wide registration of Roman citizens and client kingdoms,[25] to help us in this matter. I have met and done negotiations with both and find them to be reasonable and honorable men. If they give us Rome's permission to visit Israel, none will stand in our way, not even Herod the Great."

"What do we do now, Master?" Arsam asks, a hint of disappointment in his tone.

Samekh has great empathy for the boy because he, too, finds it hard not to act on what is transpiring in the zodiac. But many years of negotiating with emperors, senators, and kings has taught him not to let his emotions get the best of him. He points to the conjunction in Leo and says, "We wait and watch for more phenomenon like this, and we pray that the Creator will grant us wisdom on how and when to act on what we see."

January 21, 2 BC, Capital of Parthia, Royal Court of Phraates IV

Phraates IV sits on his throne and listens to the endless barrage of petitions, reports, and briefings that he now finds so tiresome. When he first usurped this throne from his father almost thirty-five years ago, he loved the intrigue and complexities of court life. Having the final word of life and death for all his subjects was both intoxicating and invigorating. Now all he can think about is securing power so that his son can have an easy ascension to the throne when he is gone. He can feel that his body is shutting down, and that he does not have much time left to protect his son and the empire he wants him to rule. There are enemies everywhere, and many in his own court would be very pleased to wrest power from him and his line. Some he knows, others he suspects, but it is those he is not aware of that scare him the most.

These days, the Romans are the least of his worries. Ever since Augustus sent him Musa as a gift and he took her to wife and she bare him Phraates V, he and Rome have had relative peace. But this latest movement in the empire to seek their Persian roots and isolate themselves from the western world has him concerned. True, it was that very movement that prompted him to support the Astronomical Sect of Magi in their interpretation of the zodiac during the debate in Babylon a year and a half ago, but now some try to use it against him because he chose Musa's son as his heir. He knows he must get on top of this latest potential political disaster before it threatens both their lives.

The next one to enter his court is an old and familiar friend. Ambassador Samekh has not been to his court for some time, and he has heard rumors that he will soon retire from political life to devote himself as head of the Nabataean Magi Order. "Ambassador Samekh, it has been too long since we have had you in our court. How is King Philopatris?"

Samekh makes his courtly bow of respect and steps forward. "He is in good health and his reign is prosperous, Emperor."

"That is good to hear, Ambassador. Although I am saddened to understand that he has lost favor with Rome and Emperor Augustus of late."

"Precisely the reason for my visit, Emperor. As you know, politics between kingdoms and empires can be fickle. We are grateful for the peace and prosperity Nabataea enjoys with Parthia and we wish to offer you an opportunity in our dealings with Rome and Israel."

Dvandas has been standing idly by, listening to the ambassador. Since the debate in Babylon, his lofty position in court has been diminished somewhat, but he still holds a place as chief counselor to the emperor. He finds that if Phraates V is not in court he has more access to speak. Consequently, he feels more at ease to manipulate and nullify anything the Nabataean ambassador may try to instigate.

He does not like Samekh for obvious reasons and has been glad as of late to see the man's sovereign lose status and wealth by angering the Roman emperor. He has tried to think of ways to advise Phraates IV to capitalize on the circumstance but has so far come up with nothing worth mentioning. But he knows he has to say something soon, or this Nabataean Magi will probably end up gaining more favors for his enemy, Daraya-Vous. He raises his hand, asking for permission to speak.

Phraates IV waves him forward.

"If Ambassador Samekh is here to petition Parthia to make up for his country's loss of commerce with Rome by dangling Israel as a prize, I counsel that we proceed with extreme caution. Our last conflict with Rome over that country was costly and unproductive, to say the least. When Mark Anthony committed his troops to Herod the Great, we were beaten out of Jerusalem, and I think it would be very unwise for us to now anger Augustus Caesar and make a play for that country."

Ambassador Samekh ignores Dvandas and says to the emperor: "But isn't it the instability of that country that is the problem? Honestly, Emperor, their king is one of the most ruthless men in the world and his people hate him. We have it on good authority that he is about to have another son executed. No proconsul of Rome wants the job of governing Israel, and Augustus tolerates Herod for that reason alone."

Dvandas steps forward. "What are you proposing here, Ambassador? That we offer to take the burden of Israel from Rome for some kind of price? Preposterous!"

"Of course not, Headmaster Dvandas. Rome would never agree to that for any payment short of half the Parthian empire. The strategic value of Israel alone makes it too valuable to them. What I am suggesting is that if the Parthian Empire and the Nabataean Kingdom could offer a more stable solution to Israel's obvious rulership problems, both our nations would have Augustus's gratitude and that could prove quite profitable for all concerned."

"That is absurd, Ambassador. Rome is our foremost enemy. There can be no real peace between the two largest empires in the world. Eventually, one will have to dominate the other," Dvandas blurts out.

Phraates IV grabs his chest and starts to hack and cough. He waves his hand at everyone in court, telling them to hold until his cough subsides.

"I thought I told you not to upset the emperor anymore, Dvandas. Do I have to have you removed from court altogether?"

All eyes look to the side as Phraates V quickly steps onto the throne platform with a goblet of water and a towel for his father. He hands him the towel and waits as the emperor's coughs and gags begin to subside and he uses the towel to clean his face. Phraates V then hands him the water and turns to Ambassador Samekh. "Interesting line of reasoning you are presenting, Ambassador. But I cannot see what either of our nations could come up with that would please the Roman emperor."

Samekh, relieved by the appearance of the prince, replies. "Under normal circumstances I would concede that as true. But what if we could offer Augustus a stable monarchy of true Israeli descent with a legitimate claim to their ancient throne?"

This time, Phraates IV manages to stand and speak without an outburst of coughing and gagging. "You speak of an heir to their King David?"

"Yes, I do, Emperor, but not just any heir. The heir of prophecy."

Dvandas starts to object, but the prince holds up his hand. "One more word out of you, and you will never enter this court again!"

Phraates IV waves his hand to his son. "Though he can annoy, my son, he is the headmaster of the Magician Sect of Magi and, therefore, a member of the electorate body that put me in power. Even I do not have the authority to permanently banish him from court." He then looks to Dvandas. "Give us your thoughts, Headmaster."

Dvandas tries to collect his thoughts and arrange a logical response. He knows where Samekh is going with all of this. He, too, has seen the signs in Leo and knows that the entire body of the Astronomical Sect of Magi is ablaze over the phenomena. Before the debate he could simply dismiss it as Jewish nonsense, but now that this whole idea of a messiah coming out of Israel had been given some serious empire-wide credence, he has to tread lightly.

"Emperor, Ambassador Samekh and his colleagues in Nabataea have obviously seen the important conjunctions that have occurred in the constellation of Leo as of late and would seem to interpret them as the coming of the long-awaited Creator's champion, and the ultimate ruler of Israel and then the world. But what I cannot grasp is how presenting Augustus Caesar with a proposition of setting someone like that on the throne could earn his gratitude. It is more likely that he will see it as an attempt to usurp his own throne and go to all-out war with both our nations."

Phraates IV sits back down on his throne. "I am better now. I will be fine." Then he looks back to Dvandas. "This is the counsel I need from you, Headmaster." He then gestures with his hand to Ambassador Samekh and says, "Dvandas makes a good point, Ambassador. After Rassan brilliantly made his case about the Creator's champion coming as 'The Lion of the Tribe of Judah,' I have made peace with the prophecy in the stars of that man ruling us all. But how, pray tell, do we convince a man like Augustus that this is beneficial to him as well?"

"We don't have to, Emperor. You see, all Augustus will need to be convinced of is that this new heir will bring stability and peace to that region of his empire. We simply show him that by installing this royal heir to the throne of David, the nation will be appeased and even grateful to the Roman emperor's benevolence toward them for doing so."

"But how do you really know the child has been born, Samekh? Has anyone seen this so-called wonder from the heavens in the flesh?" Dvandas asks.

"No, we have not seen him or verified his having been born yet," Samekh answers. "But the signs are pointing in its favor. But to be sure, we would have to journey to Israel and see for ourselves."

"Like Headmaster Vinda-Farnah did almost four years ago and got himself killed, and almost Rassan as well?" Phraates V responds.

Samekh holds up a hand in a calming gesture. "No, not like that. But with proper papers of safe passage from Emperor Phraates IV, coupled with the two Roman proconsuls in the area—Cyrenius, the governor of the empire-wide registration and Saturninus, the governor of Syria—it would be workable to accomplish. I have already gotten assurances from those two that, should we decide to pursue this matter, they would back our efforts and force Herod to receive us. So, with their and your leave, Emperor, our caravan of Magi to Jerusalem would be untouchable by any, even a madman like Herod."

"What does Headmaster Daraya-Vous have to say about all of this?" Dvandas asks, still grasping at straws to stay ahead of this potentially disastrous turn of events.

"He counsels caution in acting, but is optimistic that the heavens are not yet done with their celestial announcement of the fulfilling of the prophecy. He is, however, preparing to procure safe passage to come here and petition the emperor for the time when he feels there is enough celestial evidence to go to Israel and seek the newly born king of the Judeans."

"Who does he have making these inquiries for him, Ambassador Samekh?" Dvandas asks, already sure he knows the answer.

"Magi Apprentice/High Commander Rassan is handling that for him, with Babylon's chief magistrate and General Barach."

Before Dvandas can reply, Phraates V says, "That is good news. Rassan needs to learn how to navigate empire politics for when he serves in my court someday. Don't you agree, Father?"

"Yes, Son, and that day may come sooner than we all want it to," he answers as he grabs the goblet of water and takes another long drink from it. Then he looks to Dvandas and says, "You have our leave to probe into this matter deeper and give us counsel on what you find." Then he turns to Ambassador Samekh. "I am intrigued by your requests and reason. You may have presented us with a very profitable and mutually beneficial idea. But we must give it some more thought and will have to give you our answer at a later time."

Samekh is not pleased that Dvandas was just asked to actively take part, but he believes the emperor will grant them safe passage when he and Daraya-Vous need it. As for the rest, who can tell how the Creator will raise His champion up and set him on his throne? In the grand scheme of things, he believes that anything that temporary rulers do or don't do to aid the Messiah will have little effect on the true outcome. His sole purpose here is to secure safe passage to Jerusalem for the Astronomical Sect of Magi who want to pay their respects to the child. He makes his courtly bow. "Then by your leave, Emperor, I will depart and await word from your court on this matter."

Phraates IV waves his hand in response and immediately begins another round of coughing and gagging. His son calls for attendants to help his father to his private quarters. When they are leaving, he tells them to call for Queen Musa to aid her husband, and then he takes his father's seat on the throne and finishes handling court business for the day.

Later that evening, Prince Phraates V makes his way to the courtyard, where he and Rassan used to practice their sword fighting. He knows his father is very sick and could die. He feels he is ready to rule, but he is not ready to lose his father. Unlike the relationship that Phraates IV has with his other sons, theirs has always been close. Mostly because his mother, Queen Musa, truly holds the emperor's heart. Musing about these things, he turns the corner to the path that leads to the private quarters of the royal family and almost bumps into Dvandas before he notices his presence.

"Headmaster Dvandas, I thought you would be off scheming how to foil Ambassador Samekh and Headmaster Daraya-Vous's plans by now."

Dvandas ignores the jibe. "On the contrary, My Prince. I find Samekh and Daraya-Vous's interpretation of the astronomical sightings in Leo to have some credence. I have my doubts about sending a delegation to Jerusalem but have not ruled it out. The ambassador's idea of replacing Herod with an authentic heir to the ancient Hebrew throne could have value if this man could, indeed, calm his people down and keep them in line."

"You surprise me, Headmaster. Isn't any kind of win for Daraya-Vous a loss for you?"

"Not necessarily, My Prince. We all are subjects of your father, and the good of the empire must always be our priority."

"So, if this savior of the world is born, do we send a delegation to Jerusalem to honor him?"

"Perhaps, My Prince. I know that Ambassador Samekh is a clever statesman and diplomat. His idea of us and the Nabataeans helping Augustus Caesar stabilize the country of Israel could bring many diplomatic benefits to the empire."

Phraates V stares into Dvandas's hawkish eyes. "Then what will be your counsel to my father?"

Dvandas has been playing court politics long enough to know when he has a ruler ready to see things his way. "My Prince, you and I have rarely seen eye to eye on any matter. But I think you know that dealing with politics between empires is not something Daraya-Vous of the Astronomical Sect is even remotely qualified to do. My counsel will be that you should lead the delegation to Jerusalem in your father's name, and that I should be appointed as chief Magi for the Parthian contingent of the group."

"What will Headmaster Daraya-Vous do then?"

"Oh, he will need to come along, if not for anything else but to appease Ambassador Samekh."

The prince holds Dvandas's gaze for a moment and sighs. "Unbelievable, but I agree with you. Proceed according to this logic and keep me posted on anything you find out about this prophecy and how the stars are telling of its fulfillment."

"By your leave, My Prince."

Dvandas quickly leaves the area and heads back to his Temple, where he finds Mihri in his private offices. Since coming back from Babylon, he has had Mihri on a new mission. He is eager to talk with him about it now. "The doses of poison you have been sneaking into the emperor's drink are too strong. I told you that we need to win the prince over to us before his father dies."

Mihri walks over to a table of jars full of different powders and picks one up and shows it to Dvandas. "As you can see, I have significantly cut down on the dosages since the last time we talked about it. I fear the emperor is developing other problems in his body that are increasing in intensity on their own."

Dvandas looks at the bottle and then back at Mihri and shakes his head. "It is fortuitous that I had a breakthrough with the prince today."

"Really, Master, what happened?"

"You know that all the Astronomical Sect of the Magi are up in arms about these conjunctions in Leo as of late. Well, as we thought, Samekh's visit was to see if the emperor would help him and Daraya-Vous go to Jerusalem to seek the champion they are all looking for. What is interesting is that he gave Phraates IV an idea I had not thought of before—to procure favor from Augustus Caesar. He suggested that we use a newly born heir of Israel's King David to depose Herod the Great and set up a more stable and manageable monarchy in that troublesome country."

"But how does that win the prince over to supporting us, Master?"

"It did not until I realized it is a perfect opportunity to get rid of him after his father dies. You see, I got him thinking that he should lead the expedition to Jerusalem with me as the leader of the Magi."

"That is brilliant, Master. Once there, you could entice Herod the Great and the Roman officials to kidnap and hold Phraates V for ransom and then come back here and depose him. With the isolation movement we have been fostering in the empire, it will be easy to convince the electorate to abandon him and set up a new monarchy here."

"Exactly. This is our destiny and the stars are directing us to achieve it."

February 17, 2 BC, Headmaster Daraya-Vous's Private Study, third sighting Jupitar and Regulas in Leo

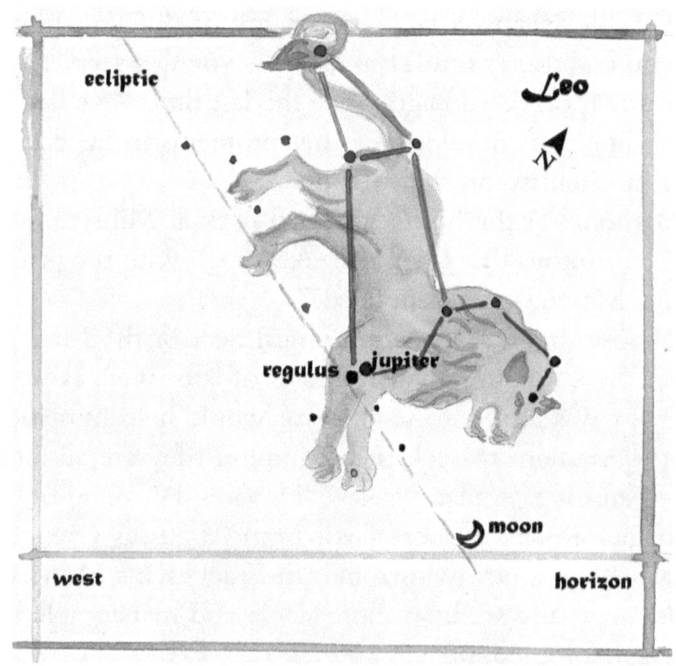

Headmaster Daraya-Vous has the drawing of the conjunction of Jupiter and Regulas in Leo that Rassan did last evening laying before him on top of the sacred star charts that are laid out on his table. He closes his eyes as a tear runs down his cheek. He finds it difficult to control the wave of emotions that is flooding his soul. Three sightings that all point to the coming of the long-foretold messiah. "Can this really be the fulfillment of our purpose? Has it truly happened?" He mutters. Rassan and Varaz are beside themselves with eager anticipation. He felt awful having to once again counsel caution and patience. With his whole heart he wants nothing less than to leave for the Capital tomorrow to petition to go to Israel and seek the one he has waited for his whole life. A gentle cool breeze from the brisk morning air touches his face and a small still voice echoes in his heart. "Patience my servant, soon, but not yet."

May 8, 2 BC, Babylonian Garrison Command, Fourth Sighting, Jupiter and Regulus in Conjunction in Leo

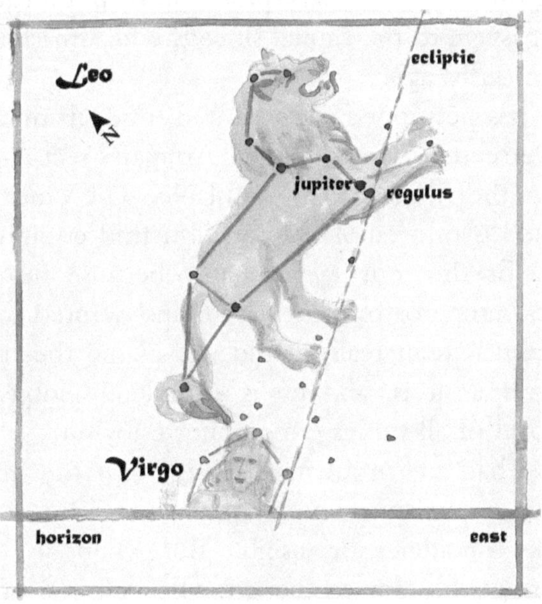

Rassan walks into the command center of the Babylonian garrison with an enthusiastic pep in his step that the previous two hours of military drilling he just conducted with the men should have kept him from having. Usually, after drills, he would rush back to the Temple and get some needed rest from having stayed up half the night with Headmaster Daraya-Vous and then coming here. But today was different. He can hardly fathom the magnificent and profound majesty of what he and others witnessed just before midnight last night. They have all seen for months that it could happen, but to think that Jupiter for the third time in less than a year came into conjunction with Regulus in Leo[26] has him reeling with excitement.

Even so, last night Daraya-Vous again cautioned everyone to be patient and keep looking for more proof that the Creator's champion, the true king of Israel, has been born. But this morning, at the end of their meeting with Varaz in the Tapestry Observatory, he tells Rassan to speak with General Barach about securing a military escort for their upcoming caravan to the capital and then to Jerusalem. He has been working on the preliminary protocols to put a caravan together and gain safe passage to the capital since the headmaster asked him to do so several months ago.

So far, he has petitioned for allocated funds from the Magi treasury that is overseen by Grand Master Artapan's sect and has received assurances that the funds will be available. The chief magistrate of Babylon seemed overjoyed at helping him find equipment and livestock sources for the journey, probably because he witnessed the fondness of the emperor toward Rassan and wanted to benefit from that relationship. Rassan really could not blame the man. He really had little power as it is, and he is completely subject to General Barach's approval of all things concerning Babylon.

Rassan has had no problems dealing with the general. What's there to deal with, anyway? The man's a general, he gives orders, and sometimes asks for advice or insight. But when his word is given, that's it. He makes his way to the general's personal offices, steps up to his desk, comes to attention and throws a salute. "General, may I have a word?"

Barach looks up from the city charts on his desk and tries to hide the smile he gets whenever he deals with Rassan. He really can't help but like the young man. He is humble, driven, talented, and capable. A good officer. "Have a seat, High Commander. How went drills this morning? And how is my new son-in-law handling being your aide during them?"

"The drills are going very well, sir. I believe that our response time to the wall for perimeter defense is at an all-time best. Commander Sasheen has been quite helpful in this. He has figured out faster ways for the men to get their equipment in place without having to run up and down the access stairwells several times. He uses planks and pulleys to bring them up once we are there. It saves the equipment from staying up there all the time and being ruined in the rainy season or stolen by thieves."

General Barach sits up and smiles. "That is good to hear. You know I was worried that Sasheen could not handle you being promoted above him, and at first it seemed he did not. But after the traitor Kaufa tried to kill you and that girl from the Temple of Zarpanuta, he has seemed to grow up a little. That, coupled with the good reports I have heard, has now caused me to think that he can handle my job someday. What do you think?"

"I think you are correct, General. Commander Sasheen has made significant progress in the last year and is becoming the friend I knew back in the academy."

"That's good to hear. Now, what is it that you wish to discuss?"

"Well, sir, you know that the Astronomical Sect of the Magi has been exploring the possibility of caravanning to the capital and petitioning the emperor for safe passage to go to Jerusalem, considering significant astronomical conjunctions in Leo as of late."

Barach leans back in his chair and rubs his eyes. "Yes, the prophecies of the newborn king in Israel. I have heard. But did you know the Romans don't interpret those signs the same way you do? This year marks Caesar Augustus's twenty-fifth anniversary as emperor of Rome, and they see these astronomical phenomena as the heavenly attestation that he is the one true ruler of the world."

Rassan is taken aback. "No, sir, I did not know that!"

"Well, it is something that a good officer needs to know about a potential enemy. If you show up in Jerusalem with an entourage of Magi and other Parthian officials proclaiming that you are there to honor a king who will rule the world, it could be disastrous."

Rassan slumps back in his chair and sighs. "Well then, maybe I should rethink asking you for a military escort for our caravan to the capital, should we decide to go."

Barach shakes his head and laughs. "You don't have to. It has already been granted to you by my superior." He grabs a parchment off his desk that has the Parthian empirical seal and reads it to Rassan.

> *"General Barach, the Magi of the Astronomical Sect wish to come to the capital and petition my father to gain safe conduct to Jerusalem to pay homage to a newly born heir to the ancient throne of King David. They believe that the recent sightings in the heavens declare that this phenomenal birth has occurred. It is our will that you grant any and every aid to them to make their journey here. Signed by the prince and heir apparent, Phraates V."*

Barach puts the parchment down and looks Rassan in the eye. "If it is in my power to do, you will have it. But it will not be my son-in-law who commands that escort, High Commander. It will be you."

June 17, 2 BC, Fifth Sighting, Jupiter and Venus in Conjunction in Leo

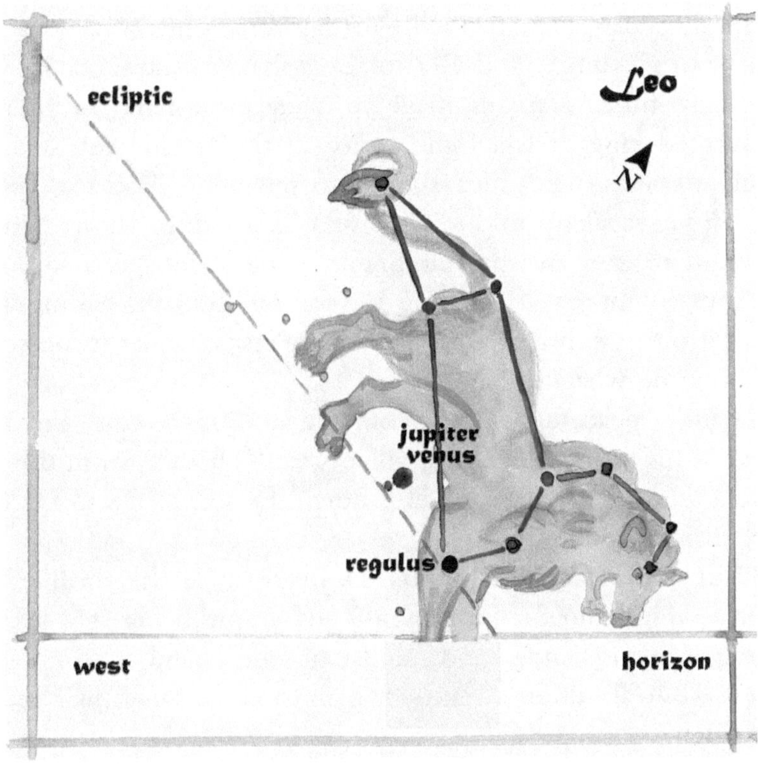

After last night's sighting of Jupiter and Venus being in conjunction with Leo for the second time in less than a year, coupled with the three conjunctions of Regulus and Jupiter during that same period,[27] Headmaster Daraya-Vous had to excuse himself from the night watch. He headed straight for the prayer-meditation chamber where he has been for the last twelve hours. He sits on a little stool holding a piece of parchment, where he drew each conjunction from memory and marvels at how significant these phenomena are. He has been searching all the ancient records of star charts, including the sacred ones by Belteshazzar that only he has free access to, and has found no time in history where something like this has occurred in a year's time in the constellation of Leo.

He closes his eyes and puts the parchment on a little table in front of him, then clasps his hands in his lap, bows his head, and prays. "Creator of all things, and God of Belteshazzar, show me if it truly is the right time to pay homage to Your promised champion, the long-awaited king of Israel and savior of the world. You sent Your messenger to instruct Vinda-Farnah to tell us to look to '*The Lion of the Tribe of Judah*' to find our answers. With all my heart, I believe these signs in Leo are the fulfillment of that message. I know that with Your mighty hand guiding us, we can find the promised one and fulfill our watch that your servant Belteshazzar set us on so long ago. Show me what to do."

A gentle, peaceful serenity comes over Daraya-Vous and in the stillness of his heart a small still voice says, "These signs in the heavens are Mine. The king of Israel is born, the son of David has come. Go, pay him homage."

Headmaster Daraya-Vous lifts his head up as the thrill of what the Creator just did for him engulfs his whole being. He takes the parchment in his hand, stands, and exits the chamber to go discuss with everyone about enacting their plan to go to the capital and then to Jerusalem.

Same Time, Nabataean Capital City, Magi Temple

Samekh and Arsam are standing in the courtyard talking with a group of Magi from neighboring kingdoms who have been arriving for the last week. Most are from eastern Arabian tribes, but a few have journeyed all the way from India. They are all there because of the sightings in Leo showing the birth of the new Jewish king.

Samekh holds up his hand to get everyone's attention. "After what just happened last night, I know that the prophecy has been fulfilled. I am sending a dispatch to Headmaster Daraya-Vous in Babylon informing him that we will depart soon for the Parthian capital and await his arrival."

One of the Arabic Magi steps forward. "We have heard that the Romans boast that these signs in Leo declare that their emperor is destined to rule the entire world. How will we enter a client kingdom of Rome, such as Israel, and deal with a man like Herod the Great under these circumstances?"

"I have been working on that with the Parthian emperor Phraates IV and the two highest ranking proconsuls in this part of the world. We believe that when we enter Israel, our path will be clear because it will be in Rome's best interest that we are there."

"Impressive news if it can be done, Samekh. But how did you accomplish that?"

"Diplomacy is nothing more than showing one party how they will benefit by giving them what they want. Phraates IV wants better and more profitable relations with Rome. Rome wants a more stable and less volatile client kingdom in Israel. I merely convinced both parties that by finding and supporting the newborn heir of King David of Israel, both can have what they want."

As he finishes speaking, a messenger from the royal court runs into the courtyard and up to Samekh. "Ambassador, Emperor Phraates IV of Parthia has died. King Philopatris summons you to his chamber immediately."

Disappointed but not surprised, Samekh nods his head. "Tell His Majesty that I am on my way."

The messenger bows, turns and runs off. Once he is gone, Samekh looks to the others and says, "This has been unavoidable for months. I had hoped that he could have lasted until we all left for Jerusalem, but I have assurances from Prince Phraates V that every promise his father gave to me will be carried out. But this will mean that I must leave for the Parthian capital immediately. My liege will want me to be there as a representative to witness the transition of Phraates V to emperor of Parthia."

He then looks at Arsam. "I think it best if you stay behind and accompany these Magi and the rest of our order to the Parthian capital. You can show them some of what we know from the Belteshazzar star charts. Also, I need you to draft a letter in my name informing Headmaster Daraya-Vous of what has transpired and that he should make all haste to the capital. Tell him that Dvandas will no doubt make a play for power because of this, and we need to be ahead of it at all costs."

Arsam sees the urgency in his master's demeanor and runs off to perform his assigned tasks. Ambassador Samekh bids his farewell to the Magi in the courtyard and turns to make his way to discuss the situation of Phraates IV's death with his king. Once out of eyeshot he stops, bows his head, and prays. "Creator and God of Israel, He who shows mercy and wonders with His right arm, and strength and power with the breadth of His nostrils, guide us to do Thy bidding and keep safe all who seek to pay homage to Your newborn Messiah, the promised seed of the woman."

20

The Journey Begins

July 30, 2 BC, Babylonian Garrison Courtyard

Rassan and Varaz stand in the garrison courtyard, saying their good-byes as Rassan readies to take command of one of the largest caravans to the capital from Babylon in recent history. Daraya-Vous stands back and away, trying to give them a modicum of privacy. He is accompanied by General Bozan and his wife, Mahre, who have agreed to take Varaz to their home for the duration of Rassan's absence. There have been no active threats against Varaz's life since the attack by Kaufa, but there is still the high priestess of Zarpanuta to consider, and she has shown no signs of forgiving or forgetting Varaz's betrayal of her at the debate. Oddly enough, it has been Commander Sasheen who has kept Rassan informed about any rumors of threats against him and his betrothed.

Since stepping up to help General Barach at the garrison, Bozan has been assigned a military detachment of a hundred men in his home village to deploy as needed. Rassan felt Varaz would be safest there and insisted on it with her and Headmaster Daraya-Vous. Before coming here, he asked and received permission to hold Varaz's hand when he said goodbye to her. He reaches out and takes both her hands in his and bows his head down and lightly touches them with his forehead. When he looks up, he sees her beaming with joy and the beginning of a tear rolling down her left cheek. He moves both their hands over and wipes it away. "When I return, the headmaster says we can be wed and that he will perform the ceremony."

"Then every moment you are away will be filled with my longing to have you back. But I will also have great gladness in knowing that you are on the greatest adventure of your life. The Creator has called you to do this, and I rejoice that you have finally come to realize the path that Vinda-Farnah set you on. When you return, I will want to know every detail of what you have done and seen."

Rassan laughs. "I think, that once I have returned and you and I start our lives together, that I will spend the rest of that life telling and retelling you this tale." Rassan lets go of her hands. "Goodbye, my love. I will be back. I promise."

"And I will be here when you come back. I promise."

Rassan sees officers and soldiers in his caravan escort unit standing at attention and waiting for his orders. He steps up to them, then looks at them and their mounts. There are seventy men standing there, almost twice the force that escorted his caravan when he came to Babylon all those years ago as the emissary for Emperor Phraates IV. But the caravan he is leading is almost twice the size as well. When the emperor died a month ago, it caused General Barach to leave immediately, leaving Rassan's cousin Bozan in charge of the garrison. He officially was Barach's second, but because of his many other responsibilities, including putting together this caravan, Commander Sasheen took a more active role in that responsibility.

Many more officials in and around the city of Babylon wanted to make the trip to the capital and pay their respects for the old emperor and show allegiance to the new one. So, the number of members of the caravan has swelled with their addition. He draws a breath and loudly says, "You all know your positions and responsibilities. Get into position." Rassan finds his mount and makes his way to Daraya-

Vous's camel. "Everything is ready, Headmaster. We will move on your order."

Daraya-Vous smiles and nods his head. Rassan holds up his hand and yells, "Move out!"

The caravan takes an hour to get out of the city.

August 27, 2 BC, sixth sighting, Massing of Planets: Jupiter, Mars, Mercury, and Venus in Leo. Jupiter and Mars in Conjunction.

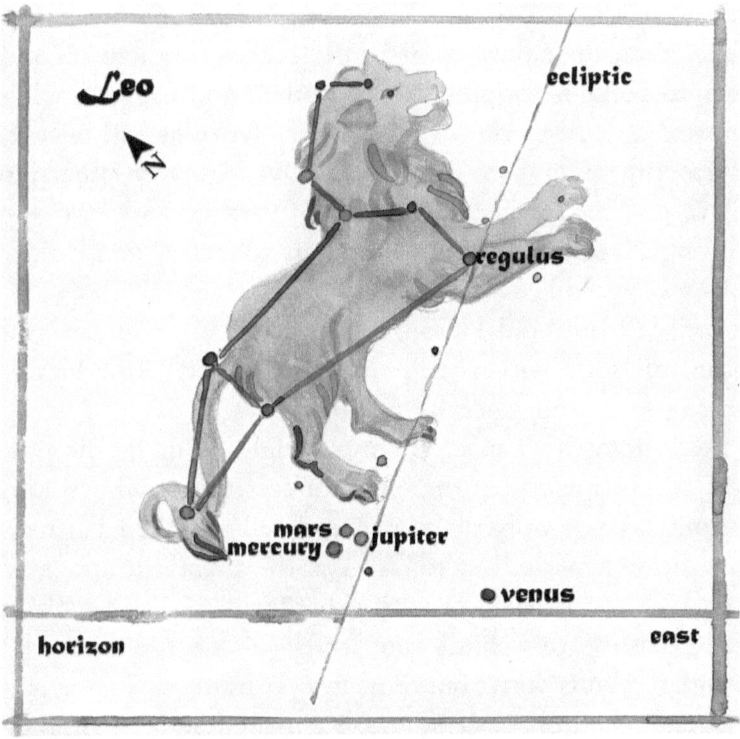

Ambassador Samekh and Dvandas stand before Phraates V as he mulls over what both are saying. The underlying animosity between the two men is palpable, and if this was even six months ago, the new emperor would have sided with Samekh in a heartbeat. Dvandas is insisting that only Parthian Magi, except for Samekh and his countrymen, should be allowed to go to Jerusalem once Daraya-Vous and his contingent shows up. Dvandas says it is because he is concerned for the emperor's safety and feels he could not be properly protected with so many unknown foreigners in the company. Phraates V knows that Dvandas's main motivation is that the Magi from other lands do not hold him in the esteem he enjoys in the Parthian Empire as headmaster of the Magician Sect, and, therefore, he could not count on their obedience to his leadership of the group. Ambassador Samekh insists that the more foreign Magi who show up in Israel will only strengthen their position with the Roman proconsuls and allow the party to make it to Jerusalem unscathed and unhindered.

Phraates V focuses on Dvandas first. "Do you still believe that I should accompany you in this caravan, Dvandas? My father just died, and I have just been declared emperor of Parthia. I am not convinced that visiting Herod the Great's kingdom is such a good idea. What kind of message will that send to Augustus Caesar?"

"It will tell him and Herod that you will authenticate this newborn king of Israel with your personal presence. How better a way for you to prove your sincerity in this matter?"

Samekh holds his hands out imploringly. "But Rome could also interpret this to mean that the emperor sees this newborn king as an opportunity to not only depose Herod, who kicked Parthia out of Israel in the first place, but to also use the great entourage of Magi from our two countries to proclaim that his is the empire that should foster and develop this child's rule."

Dvandas rebuffs him, but Phraates V holds up a staying hand. "That is enough from both of you. I am tired and my mother is still grieving and wishes me to be with her. Ambassador Samekh, when is Headmaster Daraya-Vous's and Rassan's caravan due to arrive?"

"If all goes well, in two months, Emperor."

"Good. Then after I confer with Rassan upon their arrival, I will give you my decisions. In the meantime, I want you both to concentrate on educating me in your interpretations of what all these star conjunctions mean to my rule and this empire. Especially this last one. What did you call it, a massing of planets that happened this morning?"

Samekh is faster to respond. "Yes, Emperor, this sixth occurrence that happened in Leo last night with Jupiter, Mars, Mercury, and Venus all massing in Leo, with Jupiter and Mars in close conjunction,[28] has convinced all of us in the Astronomical Sect of Magi that the prophecy has been fulfilled and the Messiah has been born."

Phraates V exhales loudly. "I swear, none of this stuff ever made sense to me when my tutors tried to explain it. Now, like my father before me, you Magi are counseling me to rule my empire according to their dictates. I am very curious to hear how High Commander Rassan will explain these things to me. He is a soldier and knows how to speak to me on my terms."

Dvandas glares at Ambassador Samekh with unveiled contempt, then bows and takes his leave from the throne. Ambassador Samekh leaves soon after.

Arsam is waiting outside the palace for the ambassador and steps up to him. "Master, are you faring any better against Dvandas today?"

"No, Apprentice. We are still at a stalemate before Phraates V. I fear his grief over losing his father is clouding his judgment. I think the only one who can bring him back in balance is his friend Rassan. Let us pray the caravan moves quickly. Come, let's go discuss this morning's massing of planets with the rest of the Magi. That should be quite enjoyable."

October 30, 2 BC, Parthian Capital

Rassan sits high on his mount as he leads the procession of Magi and nobles from the eastern part of the empire into the capital. He can hardly believe that it has been over four years since he has been here and finds himself eager to see old friends, most especially Phraates V. The caravan encountered no difficulty on the way, and he and Headmaster Daraya-Vous enjoyed many long nights studying the constellations and discussing their meanings, most especially the massing of planets in Leo that happened one month after they left Babylon.

As he comes to the stable area where he first left the capital from four years ago, he sees a very welcome sight. Standing in the area where the caravan is designated to set up their camp is Magi Master Samekh and his apprentice, Arsam. He looks behind him to the first carriage and sees that Daraya-Vous also sees the Nabataeans and is waving to them. Rassan waves the headmaster's carriage in Samekh and Arsam's direction and leads the rest to the designated camp area.

Three hours later, Rassan walks into the garrison command headquarters, where he is greeted by a most unpleasant sight. Seated at the desk designated for the general in charge of the capital's garrison is the one man he hoped to avoid while in the capital—Commander Dareh, only now he is General Dareh. He sucks air through his teeth and steps up to him and gives a smart salute. "General Dareh, High Commander Rassan reporting in from the Babylonian caravan. We have settled in and the leadership of both the Magi and the nobles request an audience with Emperor Phraates V."

A sneer crosses Dareh's face as he holds Rassan in his gaze. "By order of Emperor Musa, the nobles may meet with her and her son immediately, but the Magi will have to wait until there is a convenient time."

Rassan is shocked and bewildered. "*Emperor* Musa?! I don't understand, General. We were told that Phraates V was confirmed as emperor before we left Babylon."

"Indeed, he was. It was his mother who made sure the electorate did so as soon as possible. But after her grieving period for her husband was complete, they both revealed that she would reign with her son as coemperor. So, High Commander, a lot has changed in the capital since you left as a lowly junior officer going off to be a stargazer."

Rassan retains his composure. "I imagine it was Musa that promoted you, too, General. Knowing my friend Phraates V's opinion of you and your military abilities, I cannot imagine he is the one who did it."

Dareh jumps out of his seat and yells, "You watch your tongue, Commander! I am a superior officer and will be treated as such."

Rassan stares at the man for a moment, unfazed by his rebuke. "That is High Commander, General. On the field, a high commander holds the same status as a general. My caravan's commissioning from Phraates IV is all the way to Jerusalem. Therefore, our statuses are equal, and I will not be treated in any lesser degree by you or anyone else until so ordered by the emperor."

He turns and begins to walk out the door but stops and holds up a hand, pointing his index finger upward, emphasizing that he has another point to make. "As son of General Surena, I believe that my status as first hundred in the empirical line has been elevated to first fifty since Phraates V became 'coemperor.' This makes it available for me to be one of his close advisors, a topic he and I discussed before I left for Babylon. Therefore, it is my right to order you to tell him personally that I would like to have an audience with him as soon as possible."

General Dareh glares at Rassan for a few moments, desperately trying to find some way to rebuff the order but can find none. He slinks down in his chair and concedes. "Yes, High Commander. It will be done."

Rassan makes his way back to the caravan encampment where he can talk with Daraya-Vous, Samekh, and others about this upsetting turn of events. Once in the stable area, he sees where the headmaster had his carriage parked and tent erected and he heads there. Daraya-Vous and Samekh are seated around a newly made fire pit, drinking some tea when Rassan walks up to them.

Both Magi masters stand to greet Rassan, and Daraya-Vous puts a hand to his shoulder. "You obviously have heard the news and have encountered your own set of difficulties, haven't you, Apprentice?"

Rassan's shoulders slouch a bit. "Yes, Headmaster, and it is quite disturbing. I used my status here to order the commanding general to tell Phraates V that I wish to speak with him. It is my right, and he has to comply. Maybe once I get in front of him, we can get everything sorted out and be on our way."

"That might not be so easy, Rassan. Dvandas has been pushing Phraates V himself to join our caravan and make Dvandas chief Magi of the entourage to Herod the Great's court," Samekh says.

"But why is he listening to him? When I left, the prince despised Dvandas and sought to replace him the moment he assumed the throne."

"The only reason I can come up with is that his mother, Musa, has aligned herself with Dvandas. For what reasons I can only imagine. Believe me, Rassan, Phraates V's decision to allow his mother to be coemperor with him has all of us perplexed."

"Politics and court scheming are not hindrances to the Creator of all things. We have come this far, and I do not believe that any force on this earth can stop us from finding the promised champion and paying him the homage he deserves," Daraya-Vous says. He takes a seat and points to one for Rassan to take as well.

As the men are sitting, a voice booms from behind the wagon. "It is like when Rassan and I were standing in front of the constellation Cetus and discussing how big and formidable the Creator's enemy is. You both showed us in the stars how the Creator has Cetus surrounded with champions that will always be one step ahead of him. Do you remember, Masters?"

All eyes turn in the direction of the voice. Rassan jumps out of his seat, almost spilling the hot tea that the headmaster had just handed him. He rushes to Arsam and gives him a huge hug. "My friend! It has been too long. I have sorely missed your company."

Daraya-Vous looks to Samekh and smiles. "Out of the mouth of our own apprentices, we are educated." He steps up to the two. "I remember that time very well, Apprentice Arsam. You are correct. No matter how formidable the enemy is, the Creator always has an answer of victory in store for His own."

Over the next couple of weeks, Rassan and his company are met with one delay after another regarding their admittance to Phraates V and his mother Musa's court. Rassan walks out to the caravan encampment and sees Headmaster Dvandas with General Dareh, talking with his officers. He steps up to them and directs his question to Dareh. "What's going on here, General? Shouldn't questions you have for my men be directed to me first?"

Dvandas replies, menace in his tone. "These are no longer your officers, and this is not your command anymore, High Commander. By order of Emperor Musa, you have been relieved and General Dareh has been put in your place."

Rassan ignores Dvandas and steps up closer to General Dareh. "And what of my request to see Phraates V? Have you asked as I requested?"

Again, Dvandas does not give Dareh a chance to speak. "General Dareh brought your request before Emperor Musa, who said to tell you that it is denied and that any request to her son is to her. You are now under the direct command of General Dareh and will take command of the rear guard as he escorts Phraates V, myself, and the caravan to the court of Herod the Great."

Rassan is beyond exasperated as he stares into those evil eyes that he has come to so despise. He gets a hold of his faculties and steps back and salutes General Dareh and says, "With your permission, I will attend to my duties, General."

"Permission granted. Report to me when you are ready, High Commander."

"I will, sir." Rassan steps back one pace and smartly turns and heads toward the stables where his mount is kept.

Once out of eyeshot, Dvandas turns to Dareh. "You see, once a soldier, always a soldier. He will follow orders, or he will be executed for treason."

Rassan gets to the stables and finds his mount and begins to put on its saddle when a wave of emotion hits him. He drops the saddle back on its pole and sits down and cries. In his anguished frustration, he pours his heart out to the Creator of all things. "I know You set us on this path, and that there is nothing You can't do and no obstacle You can't overcome. Please, show me what to do!"

When he finishes his supplication, he finds that his hand is in the breast pocket of his jacket, fiddling with something he has kept on his person for a long time. He thinks back to what they were discussing at camp when he first arrived, and how Arsam recalled the lesson about Cetus and how the Creator always has him surrounded by champions ready to vanquish him. Orion with his club, Perseus with his sword, and the raging bull Taurus ready to trample. He clutches the item tightly in his fist and says out loud, "There is no course for the enemy to win. He is outflanked on every side."

He stands and heads immediately to Headmaster Daraya-Vous to share with him his plan.

One hour later, Rassan, Headmaster Daraya-Vous, and Ambassador Samekh, along with several high-ranking Parthian nobles, are making their way through the royal courtyard, where Rassan and Phraates V used to spar, to the entrance to the royal court. Before getting to the door, Headmaster Daraya-Vous stops and puts a hand on Rassan's shoulder. "Are you sure you want to do this, Apprentice? It could mean that you cannot go with us to Israel and more than likely never return to Babylon with us when we are done."

Rassan lets out a heavy breath. "I know, Headmaster, but what choice do we have? Just promise me that if I can't return, you will send Varaz to me as soon as possible."

"That goes without saying, my friend. But I refuse to believe that you will miss out on seeing the purpose of our order in the flesh. The Creator will provide a way. I am sure of it."

Rassan is in his full-dress uniform, sporting his very rare and significant emblems of High Commander rank. Daraya-Vous is wearing his ceremonial headmaster robes and Samekh is in his most stately ambassador attire. The sight of them with an entourage of the capital's most powerful nobles has the front guardsman at the door shaking in his boots as he holds up his hand to stay their entrance. "By order of the emperor, no one is to enter these doors without prior permission from the emperor."

Rassan reaches in his pocket to pull something out, but Daraya-Vous stays his hand with his own and quietly says, "Not yet, Apprentice. Let the nobles handle this one."

As if on cue, an elderly man steps forward and sneers at the guard. "Do you really think that you can keep me from entering through this door? If so, then you can go in there and tell Emperors Phraates V and Musa that you are holding the chief magistrate of the imperial electorate hostage from entering a chamber that is his birthright to do so."

The guardsman hastily opens the door for the man as he walks in.

Once inside, they see that Dvandas is standing next to Emperor Musa's chair, talking to a member of the Magi delegation from the Arabic regions. He is informing the Magi that he cannot accompany the caravan to Jerusalem, and that if he wants to leave his gift of frankincense with them, they will deliver it to the new heir to the throne of David for him. Before the man can answer, the same magistrate who dealt with the door guardsman steps up to the throne, makes a courtly bow, and bellows, "Emperors Phraates V and Musa, I have urgent state business that cannot wait. May I have your attention, please?"

Dvandas is shocked and appalled by the interruption until he sees who made it. Then he looks behind the man, and rage fills his being as he points to Rassan and his companions and says, "They are not allowed in here. Emperor Musa forbids it!"

Until the entrance of the chief magistrate of the electorate, Phraates V had been sitting quietly, lost in his own thoughts. But hearing him make his announcement and then Dvandas's rebuttal immediately shakes him from the daze brought on by boredom. He looks up with a huge grin, springs out of his seat and bellows, "Rassan, where in the name of all that is holy have you been?! Every time I ask for you to come, they tell me you were sent away on urgent state business."

Rassan begins to answer. "I am sorry…"

"Remove these persons at once from my throne or I will have you all executed!"

Everyone turns to Emperor Musa and sees that she, too, is out of her chair and vehemently glaring at Rassan, Daraya-Vous, and Ambassador Samekh.

The magistrate steps forward. "These men are here under the authority of our late emperor, and High Commander Rassan has an imperial duty to perform in this court that even you as emperor have no power to stop." The magistrate and Musa glare at one another for a moment and he then says, "Don't forget who put you on that throne, Musa. You will regret it if you do."

She holds his stare for a few moments longer, then her face turns ashen and she takes her seat. Dvandas, on the contrary, steps forward and shakes his fist. "This is preposterous! I insist you—"

"Dvandas, take a seat or I will have you removed from these chambers," Phraates V says with an icy sharpness to his tone. He looks over to his mother, and he can tell that she has gone into one of her stubborn, silent modes, so he turns to Rassan. "What is it that you have come to do, High Commander?"

Rassan steps forward. Once in front of both thrones, he reaches in his breast pocket and retrieves the coin of commissioning that Phraates IV gave him four years ago. He then holds it out to the emperors. "I have fulfilled my commission to bring the sacred star charts to Headmaster Daraya-Vous and then apprentice at the Magi

Astronomical Temple. Headmaster Daraya-Vous has released me from my apprenticeship and has sent me back to service the emperor and the Parthian Empire."

The room is completely silent as everyone grasps the importance of what Rassan just did. The magistrate steps up next to him and looks directly at Emperor Musa. "Now do you see why we brought him here? Anyone, emperor included, who hinders the quest of the bearer of one of these coins commissioned by a Parthian emperor shall be put to death without question."

Phraates V receives the coin, then looks to his mother and starts to say, "Do you know..."

Before he can finish, Musa jumps out of her seat and points a trembling finger at Dvandas and screams, "You treasonous pig! You did not tell me he was here to deliver his coin and come back into my son's service!"

Dvandas's eyes dart back and forth between Rassan and Phraates V. He can barely speak when he mutters, "I did not know that is why he was here."

Phraates V then asks Rassan, "Where have you been, Rassan? Dvandas and General Dareh told me they sent you away to handle a border nest of bandits that could have impeded your caravan to Jerusalem."

Rassan shakes his head dismissively. "I have been here since we arrived two weeks ago. Every time we tried to gain entry we were denied. I even used my birthright privilege to order Dareh to ask you for an audience. He said that Emperor Musa denied it."

"I denied it because this pig said that you would counsel my son against me."

Ambassador Samekh, who has been silent until now, steps forward. "Emperor Phraates V and Emperor Musa, may I speak?"

"Yes, Ambassador, I would welcome your counsel," Phraates V says. "And so would my mother."

"I believe the truth of which I have been speaking to you about all along is becoming manifest. Dvandas wanted your father out of the way because of his loss of favor with him, and he has been working against him for some time by fostering the 'back to Persian ways' mind-set generating throughout the empire. It is the sentiments from that very movement that he will use when his plans come to fruition, and you are taken for ransom by King Herod in the name of the Roman emperor. It's not the first time that Octavian has done that with a member of your family, as you are aware. Then, when he returns after leading the caravan, he will use what has happened to depose your mother and push to insert himself onto your thrones. That is my humble opinion."

All eyes are now trained on Headmaster Dvandas, who is so petrified with fear that he can't even speak. Phraates V waves his hand to the guards in the chamber, and they quickly bind and gag Dvandas and then cover his head with a cloth and drag him out of the throne room.

Phraates V watches them take Dvandas out, knowing that he will be deposited in the dungeons until his trial for treason takes place. He looks over to his mother, who is blankly staring into space. "Emperor Musa, please retire to our family quarters. I will join you after I have finished with Rassan and the Magi."

All the fire has gone out of her, and she simply nods her head and exits to the rear of the thrones.

"My mother is still not herself from the shock of my father's death. But she thought it necessary to take a more active role in ruling the empire to safeguard my ascension. Now, I believe I will not be joining the caravan to Jerusalem, and Dvandas will obviously not be going either. Why my mother ever promoted that fool Dareh to general is beyond my comprehension. So, he will not be joining you either Rassan."

"Yes, Emperor."

"Explain to me in your own words what all this stargazing prophecy of a savior means. And why these latest conjunctions have prompted your Astronomical Sect of the Magi to put so much expense and effort into this quest of yours."

A surge of joy erupts in Rassan's soul as he feels a huge barrier has been broken down and the Creator has once again shown him a clear path to victory. He smiles brightly and begins. "Of course, Emperor. The very first constellation in the zodiac is Virgo, and it depicts the woman who will bear the promised champion of the Creator who will destroy the ancient enemy and save mankind from evil …"

For the next two hours, Rassan meticulously, in terms he knows his friend the emperor can understand, goes through the speech he made at the debate in Babylon, elaborating on salient points in a militaristic fashion to keep Phraates V engaged and tracking. As he finishes, not only is Phraates V intoxicated with his words but also the whole room is as well.

"So, Emperor, Leo depicts the Creator's champion in his regal position as the conqueror and spoiler of the great enemy. When done and all enemies have been vanquished, then shall mankind live in peace with the everlasting monarch sent by the Creator of all things to rule, protect, and bring us all to know the One Who sent him forever."

Phraates V sits there and marvels at his friend's words. Never has he heard it declared with such boldness and clarity. He sighs and shakes his head and points his hand at Rassan. "You are a better philosopher and orator than you are a swordsman, and that speaks volumes." He stands up from his throne and walks down to Rassan, puts both hands on his shoulders, and shakes him affectionately. "When my father returned from Babylon, he told me about the debate and how your words struck him with awe. He said he gave you that promotion but never expected you to take advantage of it because he saw that the true calling of your heart is with Daraya-Vous's Astronomical Sect of the Magi Order. I can only imagine how much it hurt you to give up your chance to go with him and see for yourself this prophecy in the stars come true. I see now that you made this sacrifice so that you could get past Dvandas's veil of lies and see me personally, didn't you?"

Rassan sighs. "I did, my friend. It was the only way that I could ensure our quest would not be stopped. To me, it is a fair sacrifice."

"Sacrifice, huh? Well, far be it from me to hinder one of my true friends from achieving his most important dream. You are free to go with Headmaster Daraya-Vous and finish the quest you have started. If you come back and you wish to stay in the Magi Order with him, I will not stand in your way." He then looks to Ambassador Samekh and the magistrate who spoke earlier and says, "Have you gained the proper safe passages from the Roman proconsuls of the area, ensuring that the caravan will have full access to King Herod's court with no fear of repercussions?"

The magistrate steps forward. "Yes, we have, Emperor. All is in order. They only ask that this be a caravan of Magi and not military or diplomats. They are allowed a guard, of course, but nothing more."

Phraates V looks to Rassan. "Since your commission in my army is still active, I will appoint you as commander of that guard, and Headmaster Daraya-Vous will oversee all the Magi. Take care, my friend. Leave with your caravan when you are ready. Oh, one last thing, High Commander."

"Yes, Emperor?"

"Meet me in the outer courtyard at dawn tomorrow for a sparring session."

Rassan shakes his head and laughs. "Of course, Emperor, I look forward to it."

"As do I," Phraates V says as he waves his hand and dismisses the royal court for the day.

21

The Desire of our Hearts

December 24, 2 BC, Jerusalem

All day long, the city has been ablaze with the news of a large entourage of Eastern Magi entering the gates. Herod the Great sits on his throne and stares at the papers he is holding in his hand. In his almost forty years as sovereign ruler of the Roman client kingdom of Israel, he has never seen so many documents like these in one place that are basically asking the same thing. One is an official request from the newly appointed coemperor of Parthia asking him to accept and aid the Magi. Another comes from his cousin, king of the Nabateans, telling him that they represent him and asking to aid them in any way he can. And there are similar letters from monarchs as far east as India, and from the southern kingdoms of Arabia. All officially stamped and sealed, undeniably authentic.

But the most impressive and alarming are the ones that are from the three most powerful proconsuls of Rome in that part of the world, instructing him to receive and aid them in any way he can. To ignore their requests would be suicide, politically and literally. He was told by his advisors that they came for spiritual reasons, not political, and they needed the aid of his best rabbis and priests to answer their questions. When he was told that the delegation of Magi from the caravan would be at his court within the hour, he gathered the high priest and his aides along with the most knowledgeable rabbis in Jerusalem, and they are standing up next to his throne when the doors open and the Eastern Magi step in.

Matthew 2:1-8:
Now when Jesus was born in Bethlehem of Judaea in the days of Herod the king, behold, there came wise men from the east to Jerusalem,

Saying, Where is he that is born King of the Jews? for we have seen his star in the east, and are come to worship him.

When Herod the king had heard these things, he was troubled, and all Jerusalem with him.

And when he had gathered all the chief priests and scribes of the people together, he demanded of them where Christ should be born.

And they said unto him, In Bethlehem of Judaea: for thus it is written by the prophet,

And thou Bethlehem, in the land of Juda, art not the least among the princes of Juda: for out of thee shall come a Governor, that shall rule my people Israel.

Then Herod, when he had privily called the wise men, enquired of them diligently what time the star appeared.

And he sent them to Bethlehem, and said, Go and search diligently for the young child; and when ye have found him, bring me word again, that I may come and worship him also.

When they left the court of Herod the Great, everyone was ecstatic that it would only take a few hours to get to the home of the promised one. Riders were sent ahead to warn the chiefs of Bethlehem that a great caravan was coming their way. When they finally got out of the city in the late hours of the night, Rassan points to the heavens and says, "Jupiter is in its heliacal rising and it now goes before us to our destination, Headmaster."[29]

Matthew 2:9 and 10:
When they had heard the king, they departed; and, lo, the star, which they saw in the east, went before them, till it came and stood over where the young child was.
When they saw the star, they rejoiced with exceeding great joy.

Three hours later, the head of the caravan reaches the crest of a hill where they have a clear view of the village of Bethlehem, and Daraya-Vous solemnly looks over to Rassan, who is seated on his mount and inquires, "How do you feel, Rassan, now that our quest is about to be complete?"

Rassan looks up to the wandering star, Jupiter, that now appears to stand right over the village, then takes a deep breath and says, "How do I feel, Headmaster? Words cannot convey what my heart wants me to shout. I go to see the promised champion of the Creator, the Messiah, the prophesied king of Israel, the Lion of the Tribe of Judah. He who will vanquish all enemies and save the world. It is beyond my ability to describe."

Headmaster Daraya-Vous takes his reins and shakes them, exciting his team forward as he says, "Then let us go see this wonder of the ages together, young Magi."

Rassan kicks his heels into his own mount and follows. Not lost on him is that the headmaster did not call him *apprentice.*

Matthew 2:11 and 12:
And when they were come into the house, they saw the young child with Mary his mother, and fell down, and worshipped him: and when they had opened their treasures, they presented unto him gifts; gold, and frankincense, and myrrh.

And being warned of God in a dream that they should not return to Herod, they departed into their own country another way.

22

Afterward

After leaving the young child and receiving instruction from the Creator, the Magi went south into the kingdom of Nabataea and from there separated to go to their homes. Daraya-Vous and Ambassador Samekh were sickened to find out the treachery of Herod the Great and his slaughter of the male children two years and under in the Bethlehem area. But they learned that the family of the child got him out and fled to an undisclosed land. Samekh said that with the abundance of gold, frankincense, and myrrh that all the Magi presented to honor the child, the family would have no problem gaining passage to and living in a foreign land.

Oddly enough, the slaughter of the children took all ambition away from any foreign government that might try to find the child and use him for political gain. A similar execution had been done in Rome sixty-three years ago when they feared that the stars predicted the birth of a Roman king. Rome, being a republic, had gotten rid of its last king centuries earlier. Because of this, many Roman senators had voted for the slaughter. Herod probably knew of this and capitalized on its stigma to justify his own actions with the Romans.

Of course, within a few months, he died a horrible death and his family influence and power began to decline from that time on.

Ambassador Samekh retired from his courtly duties and devoted himself to his Magi responsibilities for the rest of his days. Arsam stayed for many years and eventually earned the title of Magi Master. Later in life, he traveled back to Babylon to be with his friend, Rassan.

Rassan and Headmaster Daraya-Vous made a quick stop in the Parthian capital, where Rassan said his goodbyes to his friend, Emperor Phraates V. Later it was discovered that Musa had been in league with Dvandas all along and they had Mihri subtly poison Phraates IV until he died. When the electorate nobles discovered this, both she and Phraates V were ousted and executed. Rassan grieved for many days upon hearing this about his friend.

Rassan made it back to Babylon, finding Varaz waiting at the gates for him. They married almost immediately and spent their entire lives in Babylon, serving at the Astronomical Temple. True to his word, Rassan spent almost all his time with Varaz discussing every minute detail about his epic quest with Headmaster Daraya-Vous, Magi Master Samekh, and Arsam to see the purpose of the ages, the Lion of the Tribe of Judah, heir to the throne of David, and the savior of the world, a young child whom his mother Mary told them was named Jesus.

Epilogue

58 A.D., Babylon, Astronomical Temple of the Magi

Headmaster Rassan sits in the Tapestry Observatory and stares at the planisphere in the middle of the room, thinking over his long life and all the things that God has allowed him to see and understand over the years. When they first returned home from Jerusalem almost sixty years ago, he was barely twenty-five years of age; and now at the ancient age of eighty-five he still feels the amazing thrill he felt the first time he laid eyes on Jesus the Christ, whom he now understands is the only begotten Son of God Almighty. He and Daraya-Vous did their best to listen attentively to any news coming from Israel about the child but heard none until almost thirty years after their return. Reports came of a preacher who became famous teaching baptism and repentance to the citizens of Israel.

At first, they thought it might be the grown boy that they visited in Bethlehem, but later heard that the man was executed by Herod the Great's son, King Herod Antipas. He knew in his heart that this man, who they later learned was John the Baptist, was a great prophet and integral part of God's plan, but that he was not the Messiah. Then rumors, stories, and even eyewitness accounts started flooding out of Israel about a "Jesus of Nazareth" traveling the land, preaching and showing forth incredible signs and wonders openly before all, and he knew it was him.

It deeply distressed him when news came that the man had been betrayed and turned over to the Romans to be crucified. But then the news came that he had risen from the dead and eventually was taken up into the heavens. He knew the zodiac foretold a lot of this, but what happened on the Jewish celebration of Pentecost baffled him and the rest of the Magi for many years.

They heard stories of thousands of Jesus of Nazareth's disciples spreading out all over the world and telling people of this new experience of Pentecost, but it was not until the Apostle Thomas had passed through Babylon on his way to India that anyone shared with him the true meaning of what happened. Thomas led Rassan, Varaz, Arsam, and many others into the new birth and the experience of speaking in the tongues of men and angels. He stayed long enough to give them the basic doctrine they needed to understand and live the life that Jesus the Christ made available.

Since that time, Rassan has been leading small, organized fellowship groups every week in the Magi Temple. They make it available for anyone to join and are eager to share their knowledge with anyone.

As he sits and thinks on these things, his wife, Varaz, and Arsam come into the chamber with a man who is at least twenty years his junior. He has a presence and dynamic to his countenance that reminds him of Headmaster Daraya-Vous. His wife and friend seem to be overjoyed with the man's presence, and he can feel the electric excitement in both their demeanors. As they approach, Rassan stands and looks to his wife and says, "Do we have a guest, my dear? Who might this be?"

Varaz just smiles brightly and looks to the man and nods her head as if to say, *he will tell you.*

The man smiles, steps forward, and reaches out his hand and clasps Rassan's with such robust intensity that Rassan knows he has wanted to meet him very much. The man takes in a deep breath and says, "I am Peter, apostle of the Lord Jesus Christ." He removes his hands from Rassan's and wipes the beginning of a tear from his eyes and continues. "It has been a long-time prayer of mine that I would meet at least one of the Eastern Magi who visited my master in his youth." He looks back at Arsam. "Today, I have met two. This is a gift of God to my life."

Rassan's knees buckle as he realizes who stands before him. With an emotional quiver in his voice, he barely utters, "Peter, the leader of the twelve!"

Peter steps forward and helps Rassan take his seat under the planisphere and sits down next to him and says, "God told me to come to Babylon and so here I am. Tell me, Headmaster Rassan of the Magi Astronomical Temple, what great secrets are you contemplating here today?"

A thrill goes through Arsam's heart as he looks up to the planisphere and points to a blank space in the northern section and says, "I have studied God's message in the zodiac all my life and have learned so many things about His plan. But I could never surmise why this space exists. I feel in my heart that it has great significance, but of what I cannot tell."

A huge smile crosses the Apostle Peter's face as he stands and points to the empty space. "It was to our brother, the Apostle Paul, that the secret behind this empty space in the heavens was revealed. It represents the Great Mystery of the Body of Christ, the church that you and I are a part of today." He then takes a seat and invites Varaz and Arsam to sit and looks back to Rassan. "Let me explain it to you."

I Peter 5:13 and 14:
The church that is at Babylon, elected together with you, saluteth you; and so doth Marcus my son.

Greet ye one another with a kiss of charity. Peace be with you all that are in Christ Jesus. Amen.

THE END

Endnotes

1   Wierwille, Victor Paul, *Jesus Christ Our Promised Seed*, (New Knoxville, Ohio: American Christian Press, 1982), pp. 57-58

2   Wierwille, Victor Paul, *Jesus Christ Our Promised Seed*, (New Knoxville, Ohio: American Christian Press, 1982), pg. 38

3   Bullinger, E. W., *The Witness of the Stars*, (1967; repr., Grand Rapids, Michigan: Kregel Publications, 1995), pg. 89

4   Wierwille, Victor Paul, *Jesus Christ Our Promised Seed*, (New Knoxville, Ohio: American Christian Press, 1982), pg. 32,

5   Matthew 8:11: And I say unto you, That many shall come from the east and west, and shall sit down with Abraham, and Isaac, and Jacob, in the kingdom of heaven.

6   Waterhouse, John W., *Zoroastrianism*, (The Book Tree, 2006), pg. 61

7   Wierwille, Victor Paul, *Jesus Christ our Promised Seed*, (New Knoxville, Ohio: American Christian Press, 1982), pp. 7-8, 85-88

8   Wierwille, Victor Paul, *Jesus Christ Our Promised Seed*, (New Knoxville, Ohio: American Christian Press, 1982), pp. xii, 5-6 (referencing Genesis 1:14)

9   Bullinger, E. W., *The Witness of the Stars*, (1967; repr., Grand Rapids, Michigan: Kregel Publications, 1995), pg. 114

10   Koutoupis, Petros, "The Babylonian Orion and Cetus," Copyright 2007

11   Bullinger, E. W., *The Witness of the Stars,* (1967; repr., Grand Rapids, Michigan: Kregel Publications, 1995), pg. 93

12   Bible King James Version Revelation 5:5, Genesis 49:9-10

13   Bible King James Version Genesis 3:15

14   Bullinger, E. W., *The Witness of the Stars,* (1967; repr., Grand Rapids, Michigan: Kregel Publications, 1995), pg. 29

15   Wierwille, Victor Paul, *Jesus Christ Our Promised Seed,* (New Knoxville, Ohio: American Christian Press, 1982), Chapter 9, Prophecies about the Promised Seed, pp. 103-110 (referencing "the Branch") Bullinger, E. W., *The Witness of the Stars,* (1967; repr., Grand Rapids, Michigan: Kregel Publications, 1995), pp. 32-33

16   Bullinger, E. W., *The Witness of the Stars,* (1967; repr., Grand Rapids, Michigan: Kregel Publications, 1995), pp. 34-35

17   Seiss, Joseph A., *The Gospel in The Stars,* (1982, Pantianos Classics), pg. 114

18   Bullinger, E. W., *The Witness of the Stars,* (1967; repr., Grand Rapids, Michigan: Kregel Publications, 1995), pg. 121

19   Bullinger, E. W., *The Witness of the Stars,* (1967; repr., Grand Rapids, Michigan: Kregel Publications, 1995), pg. 113

20   Bullinger, E.W., *The Witness of the Stars,* (1967; repr., Grand Rapids, Michigan: Kregel Publications, 1995), pg. 33

21   Wierwille, Victor Paul, *Jesus Christ Our Promised Seed,* (New Knoxville, Ohio: American Christian Press, 1982), Chapter 4, Astronomical Candidates for "His Star," pg. 32

22   Wierwille, Victor Paul, *Jesus Christ Our Promised Seed,* (New Knoxville, Ohio: American Christian Press, 1982), Chapter 4, Astronomical Candidates for "His Star," pg. 47

23 Bullinger, E. W., *The Witness of the Stars,* (1967; repr., Grand Rapids, Michigan: Kregel Publications, 1995), pg. 164

24 Wierwille, Victor Paul, *Jesus Christ Our Promised Seed,* (New Knoxville, Ohio: American Christian Press, 1982), Chapter 4, Astronomical Candidates for "His Star," pg. 47

25 Wierwille, Victor Paul, *Jesus Christ Our Promised Seed,* (New Knoxville, Ohio: American Christian Press, 1982), Chapter 16, The Birth of Jesus Christ, pg. 202

26 Wierwille, Victor Paul, *Jesus Christ Our Promised Seed,* (New Knoxville, Ohio: American Christian Press, 1982), Chapter 4, Astronomical Candidates for "His Star," pp. 45-51

27 Wierwille, Victor Paul, *Jesus Christ Our Promised Seed,* (New Knoxville, Ohio: American Christian Press, 1982), Chapter 4, Astronomical Candidates for "His Star," pp .43-53

28 Wierwille, Victor Paul, *Jesus Christ Our Promised Seed,* (New Knoxville, Ohio: American Christian Press, 1982), Chapter 4, Astronomical Candidates for "His Star," pg. 55

29 Wierwille, Victor Paul, *Jesus Christ Our Promised Seed,* (New Knoxville, Ohio: American Christian Press, 1982), Chapter 4, Astronomical Candidates for "His Star," pp. 63-65

Authors Note

I have included end noting to acknowledge sources astronomical, biblical, religious, and historical information was used to put this story together. Below is a list of the major sources I used.

Bibliography

Jesus Christ Our Promised Seed, Wierwille, Victor Paul, (Copyright 1982, New Knoxville Ohio: American Christian Press,)

The Witness of the Stars, Bullinger E. W. (Copyright 1967; repr., Grand Rapids Michigan: Kregel Publications, 1995)

King James Version, Holy Bible

The Gospel in The Stars, Seiss, Joseph A. (Copyright 1982 Pantianos Classics)

The Babylonian Orion and Cetus, Kouto, Petros, (Copyright 2007)

The Antiquities of the Jews, Falvius Josephesus (Printed in United States)

Mystery of the Magi, Longenecker, Dwight, (Copyright 2019 by Dwight Longenecker, Regnery History: Salem Communication Holding Corporation. Washington DC)

Babylonian Mystery Religion, Woodrow, Ralph (Copyright 1966, 1982 edition, Ralph Woodrow Evangelistic Association, Inc.)

Zoroastrianinism, Waterhouse, John. W (Copyright 2006 The Book Tree, Original printing 1934 by Epworth Press London, England)

The Challenging Counterfeit, Gasson, Raphael (Copyright 1966 Logos International, 16[Th] printing 1979)